BROKEN SUMMIT

BROKEN SUMMIT

A Novel

LEXIE SLOANE

Sarah,
I hope you enjoy reading
this as much as I enjoyed
writing it. (PS ch 23)
xoxo
Lexie Sloane

Little Light

Cover photo credit: Andrii Medvediuk
Book design by Lexie Sloane

First Printing, 2022
ISBN 978-1-0880-2399-0

www.lexiesloane.com

To my husband, for sticking it out despite my
hyper-focus-mode and newly developed writer quirks.

Chapter One

Cold Calls

Erin

She couldn't remember anything ever being this quiet and still, certainly never in the city. Tipping her head back, Erin marveled at the millions of stars that shone in a clear, dark sky.

"Wow," she whispered, her breath puffing overhead.

Closing her eyes, she soaked it all in—the quiet, the snow, and a familiar scent which made her smile. A wood burning fire. That smokey sting mixed with the crispness of a cold night.

A memory surfaced—vague images of family trips to the snow, camping, nature, and contentment...With another breath came giddiness and a whisper of childhood joy. *This was a good idea,* she finally acknowledged.

"*¡Chingada!*"

"Mari!" Erin whipped her head to the flashing red light on the door, then to the dark, quiet, snowy street. "You'll wake up the whole neighborhood."

With an annoyed look, Mari dug her cell out of her coat pocket. "I'm calling Shauna." She put it to her ear, waited, then held it out in front of her, narrowed eyes to the screen. "Ugh!" Lifting it over her head, she crunched around the white covered deck. At the edge closest to the street, she set it back to her ear.

Erin stood silently with arms tucked tightly across her chest, feet numbing inside snow covered sneakers. Her fleece jacket was not going to be warm enough, and every shake and shiver acted as a reminder that she should have tried the bathroom at the last rest stop. Though she'd had no idea they'd be locked out of the cabin.

"Figures," Mari grumbled, tapping out a text. She stalked back to where the welcome mat probably sat under all the accumulated precipitation. "Here, hold this for me." She shoved the phone at Erin.

"Why?"

"I can't think when I have to pee!"

Stomping down a set of steps on the other side of the deck, Mari rounded the cabin and disappeared. "If it rings," she called from out of sight, "answer it!"

Erin shot her gaze out again to the eight or so tree shrouded cabins that stretched along the quarter mile of the neighborhood. Fortunately, she saw no signs of angry neighbors.

Her eyes lingered on the welcome glow of the cabin directly across the street. If she squinted, she could see a puff at the peak of the chimney. Sighing, she reassured herself that their cabin would be just as inviting once they were settled in.

Mari came bouncing back around the cabin, her long, bleached curls dancing around her head like a halo. "Ah, so much better," she sighed. She held her hand out and Erin returned the cell with partially frozen fingers.

"Anything?" Mari asked, dipping her head to check the phone.

"No."

"You need to go?"

"Ha!" Erin choked. "You're funny."

Mari knew her little secret. Plus, the thought of her naked backside out in the open in this weather...well, she didn't have to go *that* bad.

"You won't pee on your shoe. I keep telling you—"

"Nope. I'm good," Erin insisted, looking down at her black sneakers. "I can wait."

"Okay...You'd feel better, but whatever."

Mari moved back to the edge of the deck and tried calling Shauna again. "Hey *puta*, pick up your phone! You gave me the wrong code!" She hung up and tapped out another text.

"I thought you s-said you were friends," Erin observed, shifting in place from foot to foot. It didn't help. Her toes were still frozen.

"We are." Mari shook her head as she concentrated on the small screen, "But she drives me crazy sometimes! So unreliable."

"Huh." Erin chewed on the inside of her cheek as she joined her friend at the edge of the deck.

"*No preocupes,* she doesn't have to be here to let us in," Mari reassured her. "She just has to answer her phone!"

"M-maybe, we should make a b-back-up plan," Erin suggested over chattering teeth. "Like a hotel?" Not that she wanted to spend the extra money, but a hot shower sounded like a cure to all her problems.

"You know, that's a good idea!" Mari grinned. Her eyes met Erin's, then cut a line across the street to the glowing cabin.

"Why are you smiling like that?"

"Two birds, as you call it." Mari flitted across the deck and down the front steps towards their car.

Erin did her best to follow, though not as gracefully. She caught herself on the railing as she descended the icy stairs, narrowly avoiding a fall. Sneakers may not have been the best choice. "Hello? Mari, what are you doing?"

"Going to ask a neighbor for help."

"What? No! It's the middle of the night!"

"The lights are on." Mari paused by the car, fluffed her hair and adjusted her leggings. "Besides, what's the worst that could happen? They say no? They don't answer the door?"

"They call the police," Erin deadpanned, coming up to the car. "Let's just drive back down into town."

"*En serio,* look at us. They're not going to call the police." Mari tossed Erin the car keys. They hit her chest and slid down into the snow. "You were supposed to catch that," she sighed. "If you're so worried, grab a bottle of wine! It can be a peace offering." With a wink, her friend strutted across the snow-dusted street as if fearlessly leading as exploration party across the Mississippi.

Erin groaned as she bent from the knees to reclaim the keys. "Mari!" She lingered by the car in indecision. On the one hand, a bathroom would be really nice. On the other...this went against everything she'd been raised by. "Oh man..."

Opening the trunk, Erin pulled a beanie from her bag and shoved it over messy, ash blonde hair. Her scarf she wound until it sat like a coiled snake around her neck. Then, she selected a very "drinkable" cabernet sauvignon, but after slamming the trunk, she hesitated.

From the neighbor's porch, Mari turned back and stabbed a finger down at her feet. Erin swore she heard her hiss, "Get your ass over here."

"Bossy," Erin muttered.

Forcing her legs forward, she wondered, *Why do I let her talk me into these things?* She picked her way across the street and up the steps to her waiting compadre in crime. Looking around, a new wave of foreboding struck her and so did the added urgency from her bladder.

"What if an axe murderer lives here?" she voiced quietly. Mari scoffed. "No, really. I don't think this is a good idea. Let's just go back to town."

"Suck it up, *chica*. You got the wine?"

Before Erin could answer, Mari's knuckles rapped on the solid, wood door. A gruff bark came from deep within the cabin. Mari stood, unfazed, so Erin edged closer, hoping to absorb some of her confidence. She tucked the wine bottle under her arm and fidgeted with her hat and scarf until they mimicked a ski mask. Warm breath circled back at her, making her sniffle.

Erin thought she heard movement, then two, heavy thumps met them at eye level, rattling the door in its frame. A menacing growl permeated the wooden barrier.

"Seriously, Mari, I don't think—"

Mari brought her fist up to knock again, but Erin grabbed at her sleeve. "What?"

"Big, angry dog on the other side."

"So?"

Erin wasn't afraid of dogs per se, but now that they were at the door, the cabin seemed to loom over them as if taunting them with its glowing interior. It reminded her of Hansel and Gretel. She stole a glance over her shoulder at the rental. "Don't you think if someone were home and wanted to answer the door, they'd know we were here?"

Mari yanked her arm free and knocked again. In the dark of the small porch, a stinging chill sank through Erin's flimsy fleece and stretchy yoga pants. She tucked her arms tight around her chest—the wine bottle jutting out behind her—thinking that a week of freezing her butt off suddenly didn't sound so appealing.

Mari grumbled something in Spanish, checked her phone, then leaned in and pounded on the door.

Erin grimaced. "M-Maybe no one's home."

No sooner had the words left her mouth, there was a scraping like nails down a wall. Then she heard a new noise, the thunk of a deadbolt. Erin held her breath as the door swung in a foot.

A sudden, sinking feeling filled her gut. She'd read enough crime novels to know how this could play out—women lost and alone in the woods, a cliché but a common setup. Add to that, a lone stranger with a shotgun, a really big dog, and an opportunity. This was how people went missing.

And if the dog was as big as he sounded, there wouldn't even be any evidence left to find. Erin really didn't like the idea of being shot, then eaten by a dog. And no way was she going to pee her pants on a strangers stoop in the middle of the night. She squeezed her inner thigh muscles together. There were some things a girl just couldn't come back from. That is, if she wasn't abducted first.

"I think we should go," she whispered in Mari's ear.

Mari either didn't hear, or ignored her, eyes fixed straight ahead.

A massive silhouette filled the narrow opening of the door. Aggression seemed to roll out like heat from an oven. Erin had to tip her head up to see the foreboding frame of half a man. A large, very solid man. A large, solid, seemingly hostile man.

She shrunk back, dipping her face deeper into her scarf. The stranger's rigid outline faced them as his arm reached for something just past the doorframe, something waist height, something he only needed one hand for. *Oh my God! A shotgun!*

Panic seized her. Erin dropped their peace offering, the bottle thudding dully into the snow. She debated whether to retrieve it or make a run for it. Eyes darting around, she realized there was no immediate cover. She'd have to get to the trees at the edge of the property. What were her chances of crossing that distance before he lined her up with his scope? Did shotguns have scopes? The dark around them felt suddenly, sinister as if it purposefully offered no place to hide.

She looked to Mari. She couldn't ditch her friend. Pushing down what she hoped was an overreaction, she crouched to retrieve the bottle, nearly grunting with effort needed to keep her bodily fluids in. She almost lost it. In light of things, peeing her pants now seemed like the lesser of evils.

Her fingers clenched around the bottle's neck, ready to use the heavy glass as a weapon if necessary. As she rose, a rusty porch light flickered to life and the man's hand came back into view...empty.

Mari's posture changed—hips jutting to the side, she pulled her shoulders back, pushing out her chest. Erin knew that stance. To finish the look, Mari elongated her neck, then flipped her head, sending curls out in a playful wave. *Le femme.* Erin's eyes moved in the direction of Mari's gaze and her jaw dropped under the cover of her scarf.

The man folded his arms across his broad chest, drawing Erin's eyes to a flexed bicep which fought the confines of his short sleeve. The traces of a tattoo peeked out from under the stretched fabric and she found herself too distracted to realize he'd spoken. "You gotta be kidding me."

Mari cleared her throat. Erin's guilty gaze shot up to meet steel, grey eyes. It felt eternity before he sliced his glare to her friend. When he did, his mouth tightened into a firm line, his stubble doing nothing to cover the hardened planes of his face. Hiding the bottle of wine under her scarf, Erin was certain of one thing. Axe murderer or not, he did not look like the type who enjoyed a "drinkable" cab.

"Hi!" Mari chirped. "Listen, I know we're total strangers, but we need some help and we saw your light on. Can we come in for a minute?"

The man didn't respond except to perhaps expand in the doorway. Erin squirmed, and tried crossing her legs discreetly.

"Oh, right! Don't let strangers in..." chuckling, she continued. "I'm Marisol—Mari for short. This is Erin." She paused long enough for him to offer his name. He didn't. "Okay. Anyways, we're renting the cabin across the street, but Shauna gave us the wrong door code. Sooo Shauna, right?"

A whine streamed out from behind the door. *The woman-eating dog,* Erin concluded, still not convinced the man was truly innocuous. He had the perfect cover though. *Nobody would suspect someone so good looking, right?* Although, she'd read enough thriller novels to know it usually was the charming one...

He glared behind the door and the firmness along his jaw made her gulp. Mari shot her a silent, wide-eyed *Wow!* Erin wasn't usually attracted to the rougher, potentially danger-ous look, but even she couldn't deny it, the man *embodied* masculinity.

"Enough," he bit out, and the whining stopped.

Scratching his chin, he turned back to the doorstep. "Wrong door code? That's between you and the owner." The words tumbled out like water over river rocks, smooth, low and compelling.

"Of course," Erin pouted under her breath. He wasn't 'thriller novel material.' No, he was 'cheesy-romance ma-terial,' or so she guessed without having really read any.

His eyes cut to her and his face turned glacial. Erin shifted under all her layers, clenching, shivering and teeth chattering. And seriously regretting skipping that last pit stop.

"I think we got off on the wrong foot," Mari interjected. "I know how rude this seems. Erin tried to talk me out of it."

Erin sunk deeper into her pile of scarf, wishing he'd stop staring at her.

"We wouldn't ask, only us city girls aren't used to this kind of cold and Shauna isn't picking up her phone."

"Sorry, you're on your own," he replied, eyes still locked with Erin's. His brow creased and the corners of his mouth tipped down.

Something about that ticked her off. "Can I help you?" It came out snarky. She didn't care, feeling self-conscious enough without all the moody furrows and frowns.

For a moment, his expression lifted, the harsh planes smoothing in surprise. And even Mari turned back to look at her. But then he shook his head, stepped back into the house and uttered a "good luck," though his tone didn't sound overly sincere. Erin didn't mind. She decided she rather let her backside hang out in the cold and she didn't even care if it got on her shoe.

"Wait!" Mari interjected.

"Mari, let it go."

"My friend here really has to pee!"

"Mari!" Erin hissed.

At that, he paused, hand clenched around the edge of the door which now only revealed an arm, a shoulder and his profile—still plenty to make a person stop and stare.

Mari took advantage of his hesitation. "What's your name?"

Erin scrunched her face. "Oh my God..." *Walk away,* she projected to the head of bouncy, blonde curls. *Just walk. Away.*

"Jude."

"Juuude," Mari gushed, nodding, "we would be forever grateful if we could come in for a few minutes, so Erin can use the bathroom and I can call for a hotel."

Erin held in a groan, shooting daggers at the back of Mari's head. As the seconds stretched, it appeared her embarrassment was in vain. Her only concession, those unrelenting eyes focused on Mari now, no doubt questioning just how persistent the woman might be.

Very persistent, she cringed.

"A few minutes," Mari insisted. "Erin pees, I find a hotel, then we're gone." Erin really wished Mari would stop talking about her physiological needs. "It's a win-win. You won't regret turning us away in the middle of the night and we'll have somewhere safe to go."

Jude's stare cut back to Erin and did a top-to-toe. His eyes narrowed, almost like a wince. She was going to kill Mari. Just as soon as she peed. His eyes drifted over their heads to the dark cabin across the street and Erin waited, hoped, almost, he'd just slam the door in their faces and get it over with.

Chapter Two

Lost and Found

Erin

As she stood there in agonizing anticipation, it occurred to her that he was probably *not* an axe murderer. *An axe murderer would have let us in.* Not that she could blame him. Though the contemptuous looks he shot them felt a little over the top. *Maybe he has a really possessive girlfriend.*

Whatever his reasons, she'd just gathered enough courage to end the debate when Jude pulled the door open wide and shifted, fitting his back against the side of the threshold. He crossed his arms again, stretching navy blue fabric across his chest, not quite welcoming and definitely intimidating.

Erin cowered into her layers, hoping like hell she could hold herself together and walk at the same time. Mari on the other hand, strutted in with an approving "thank you," brushing against him as she passed, and totally oblivious to the scowl he directed at her.

"You comin' in?" he bit out.

Erin realized she'd just been standing there, staring...shaking like a chihuahua. She sighed, not a fan of being used as the pitiable sidekick. But, the damage had been done. It would look more stupid if she *didn't* go in. She and Mari would definitely have words later. Body functions were a private thing; that was an unspoken rule.

She eased towards the threshold with small, smooth movements, glad her face was covered. Jude's body took up so much space she had to hug the open edge of the doorway, pivoting sideways to fit. Unlike Mari, Erin resolved not to touch him. Her eyes swept over taut muscles, just inches from her nose, when a sudden blur of movement stopped her.

"Etta, stay!" he ordered.

Erin froze, shooting wide eyes up. Jude's turbulent, gray ones pierced straight into her. She shivered again, but this time not from the cold.

"The dog," he clarified in a low rumble that matched the storm in his gaze. She felt the timber of his voice all the way down to her frozen toes. When she didn't move, he lifted his brow. "You're letting all the cold air in."

"Right," she whispered. "Sorry."

After a single step, she stopped again. There, in the middle of the entry sat a huge, shaggy, grey dog. *Huge.* Sharp, black eyes zeroed in on her. *Holy shi...*

Jude cleared his throat. Fingers choking the wine bottle again, Erin forced herself in, side-stepping a wide berth to the right around the entry. The dog tracked her movements. She met Mari next to an oversized armchair that faced a rustic stone hearth and blazing fire.

"Bathroom's at the back. Right side," he stated, swinging the door shut.

Erin eyed the dog. Even sitting, the animal reached her chest. She looked back to Jude.

He crossed his arms again. "You planning to go on the floor?"

Her cheeks grew hot. "No."

Under other circumstances, she liked to think she'd have had a better retort. Instead, shuffling to the back of the cabin, eyes on the dog, Erin muttered her thanks. She closed herself in the little room and stowed the wine bottle on the floor in the corner, out of the way.

Blessed relief swarmed her and she could think again, move freely again. So naturally, the mortification of her situation settled in. She considered the bottle. If she'd had the means to open it, she'd have been tempted to stay in there and drink it, regardless of how weird that would seem. *It can't get any worse.*

Lingering a few extra minutes at the sink, Erin let the warm water defrost her hands. Her scarf hung open, down to her knees and her nose glowed red. Spikes of unruly, pale hair stuck out from under her beanie. She looked a mess. *Lovely.* Surveying the space, she pondered the possibility of staying in the bathroom indefinitely. It looked clean enough, there were no obvious stains or unpleasant odors.

Why couldn't he be homely, or elderly, or even just averagely good looking? A man like that, he'd pass her over without a second glance. Her eyes focused on the reddest part of her nose. Add to that the suffocating intensity he gave off, she didn't want to go back out there. The reluctance weighed like an anchor in her stomach.

But she couldn't stay in the bathroom.

Just get it over with.

She considered the faded, frayed bath towel hanging on a bar opposite the sink. An unsolicited image struck her, one of muscles and skin, and not much else. *Nope.* She shook the excess water off, wiped her hands on her pants, then exited the small, unconventional haven.

"What kind of dog is Etta?" Mari asked as Erin emerged from the bathroom.

"Irish wolfhound."

Jude occupied the kitchen, his butt settled into the counter, arms and ankles crossed. He seemed to do that a lot, cross his arms. Erin kept her gaze down, moving to the breakfast bar that separated the kitchen from the living space. There, Mari stood with her phone to her ear.

As she rounded the counter, she spied Jude's companion sprawled over a tiny woven rug in front of the flickering flames. The dog perked up its furry head, its body tensing, but that didn't phase Erin. No, her eyes were focused on the shotgun she'd just noticed, mounted over the mantle.

"Settle." Jude's voice traveled across the space as if he stood next to her. Erin swallowed down her anxiety. *If he wanted to use it, it wouldn't be way up there*, she reasoned. Besides, the place didn't feel creepy—in fact, just the opposite.

Mari's voice eased the awkward tension. "Hi!" she chirped into the phone. "I'm looking for a room for tonight. Two adults."

Erin moved in beside her.

"Double room, if you have one." A pause. "Oh. Okay, a single's fine too. Yes, I'll hold." She covered her hand over the phone and addressed Erin. "But you better behave." She winked.

"Stop making me look bad," Erin scolded under her breath.

"I'm not."

"You are!"

Mari grinned. "He's probably thinking about us in bed."

"I highly doubt that," Erin grumbled, her cheeks burning as hot as the fire behind her.

"*Mira*, he's watching us. It's a start."

"I hate you," she muttered through a tight jaw, peeking up to see that Jude was in fact staring at them. She averted her eyes, searching for anything else to look at while casually skimming the inside of his cabin.

It was sparse but neat, with minimal furniture. The front spread wide and open with a staircase leading to the upper level opposite the front door. The space lacked knick-knacks, pictures, or really any kind of decorations. It should have struck her as impersonal, but it didn't—it felt oddly homey.

Erin's eyes rested on a plaid blanket draped over the arm of a well-worn, brown couch. The sofa barely fit in the corner under the front window. A puckered cushion at one end sent her mind wandering. *Is that his favorite spot?* She pictured him sitting there, boots up on the worn, wooden coffee table, having some masculine drink like a cheap beer right out of the bottle.

Palling at how the image appealed to her, Erin forced her attention to something else. The single set of boots by the door. The tan armchair covered in dog fur. She leaved a hand into the light brown fabric and stared into the fire. The place didn't show any evidence of a spouse or a girlfriend. Just his huge, scruffy dog.

The canine pushed up into sitting, a cumbersome-looking task. Her tail swatted the wood floor as she craned her neck forward, nostrils expanding, and eyes wide and curious. *Definitely not a woman-eater.*

Erin held her palm out. The dog stood and lumbered over, sticking her nose past the offered hand and into the low hanging fringe of the scarf.

"Oh!" Erin jumped at the sudden pressure against her inner thigh.

"Etta," came a low warning from the kitchen, reminding her of the dogs name.

"It's fine," Erin defended, stepping back and dislodging the damp nose from her more private areas. Daring a peek over her shoulder, she saw Jude staring at her...no, more like studying her. She wouldn't have minded if he didn't look so displeased.

She tried again. "Really. She's fine."

Etta dug her head under Erin's palm, directing fingers to the back of one heavy ear, and then the other.

"Aren't you sweet," Erin cooed, leaning down the few inches to Etta's face. "I'm sorry for earlier, you just took me by surprise." The hairy, whiplike, grey tail swung back and forth and Etta deposited a sloppy, wet kiss right up the front of Erin's face.

"I had that coming," she laughed as she straightened, swiping a sleeve across her mouth and nose.

Jude's command rang out over her words. "Etta, come."

Dark, pouty eyes pointed over the kitchen counter at her owner. Erin didn't know a lot about dogs, but it reminded her of a standoff.

"Etta, come here," Jude ordered again, his tone lined with irritation. Head dipping low and tail sagging, she crept towards him.

"I really don't mind. You don't have to—" Erin halted at Jude's stoney look. Mouthing a 'sorry,' she turned her focus back to her friend, hoping they could wrap this up and head to a hotel.

"On hold," Mari informed her, rolling her eyes, then she perked up. "Hi. Hello? Yes. I was holding for a room. Oh." Her face scrunched and Erin's heart sank. "What about the other location?" Mari pressed, frowning at the response. Her phone dinged and she pulled it away to check the screen. "Finally!" Putting it back to her ear, "Okay. Thanks for checking. Bye."

She hung up then made a new call.

"Giiiiiiirl!" The single syllable blended irritation with humor, and Erin guessed Shauna had finally responded. "Yeah, I bet you are! *¿Estas a casa?*" Mari seemed to forget that it was late and they were in a stranger's house. "*Sí*, about thirty minutes ago," she continued. "No. That's the same one. It flashed all red and angry." Leaning elbows deep into the breakfast counter, she jutted her butt out behind her.

Erin stole a glance at Jude. He'd directed his attention down to Etta, who'd flopped to the floor next to him, looking forlorn.

"No, we're at your neighbor's cabin," Mari went on. "Mmmhmm," she added, not so subtly. "That's the one."

Erin shot her a look and Mari flashed a devious smile back.

Almost feeling bad for the guy, Erin thought, *he's gotta know they're gossiping about him.* She would have been more sympathetic if he'd been a little less prickly.

"*Mira, no problema.* Just get me the new code," Mari said, getting down to business. "*Sí, digame.*" She tapped Erin's arm. "Help me remember this."

Erin went to get her phone out of her pocket and remembered that after her battery had died, she'd tossed it in her bag, which was still in the car.

"Eighty-three, seventy-two," Mari called out.

Erin repeated the code aloud, then again, continuously under her breath, staring at the countertop and visualizing the numbers on the white tile.

"*Sí.* Erin's got it. She's good with numbers."

Muttering the combination, Erin felt Mari's praise a little too generous, all things considered. She ignored the conversation next to her, trying not to disappoint. A sheet of paper and a pen slid into view. Her head shot up and Jude stood opposite her at the counter.

"Thanks," she mumbled, then scrawled out the numbers on the paper.

She started to return the pen, but changed her mind, writing it again so she could keep a copy in her wallet, just in case. Then, as an afterthought, she scribbled it several more times to commit it to memory.

"Once wasn't good enough?" Jude's voice sounded different, less harsh, almost teasing.

Erin wrenched her head up again, heat rising to her face. He leaned over the counter toward her, his hair falling over his forehead, and that defined jaw taunting her. She wondered if he knew how sexy he looked when he wasn't scowling.

Flustered, she tried to explain herself. "I'm just writing it so I'll remember. They say that if you write something three times, it's, um, supposed to help you commit it, you know, to memory. But I figure, more times can't hurt and so...yeah." The more she spoke, the more she wished she hadn't.

Erin cleared her throat and finished her fifth repetition on the paper. She would have kept going, making sure it really stuck, but she could feel his eyes on her. Setting the pen down, she folded the page and tucked it into her jacket pocket. She forced an awkward smile as she met his gaze. His return look felt expectant and Erin worried there was something else she was supposed to do.

"Yup. All good," Mari sang into the phone. "Go back to drinking, you lush! Okay, bye." Jude straightened away from the counter as Mari tucked her cell into her coat pocket. She turned to Erin. "Door code?"

Erin repeated the four digit code from memory.

"Okay! *¡Vamos!*" Mari zipped her jacket and beamed at Jude. "Thank you so much! Good timing, huh?"

His face settled back into the stony, agitated expression from before. Mari seemed unperturbed, as only Mari would. Erin wrapped the ends of her scarf around her neck as they moved to the front door. At the commotion, Etta jumped up and hustled out of the kitchen toward them.

"Etta, bed," Jude ordered as he followed the procession. She paused, tossing a look back at him, then continued on as if he hadn't spoken. Erin hid a smile behind her scarf.

"Etta," Jude rumbled low in warning, and this time, even Erin hesitated.

The dog's tail sagged between her legs. Giving Erin a pitiful look, she lumbered over to a large cushy pad nestled under the staircase and plopped her butt down with an un-happy groan. Erin's smile grew. She liked Etta.

"It was nice to meet you, Jude," Mari sang. "Thanks again for your hospitality." Erin marveled how her friend could make anything sound sincere. *I'd call it more hostile than hospitable.*

Jude paused by Etta's little niche and gave her a scratch behind the ear. "Stay," he said, his voice uncharacteristically soft and sweet. "Good girl."

Pacified, she stretched out on her pillow with a yawn. Erin watched with awe and a little envy. *Etta is definitely his girl.*

Mari hooked an arm in her's and propelled them around to the door. "Nice to meet you, Etta," she called back.

Etta popped up again, ears perked. Grumbling something, Jude closed the distance between them and reached past the women to open the door. This time, he stood back, well into the cabin, giving them plenty of space to exit.

"Thanks," Erin muttered under his focused stare.

They moved from the toasty cabin into the cold, crisp night. Mari gave a wave. "See you around, neighbor!"

"Yeah."

To Erin, his reply sounded somewhat regretful. The door swung shut behind them and the icy chill swelled in around her. She hunched forward, a natural response, even though it didn't seem to help. Mari snickered and dragged her, arm and arm, down the steps and into the street.

Erin huffed half-heartedly. "I hate you."

"You love me," Mari countered, leaning into her shoulder with a hearty chuckle.

"'My friend has to pee?' Really?"

"Everyone pees!"

"That's not the point!" Erin whined.

"It was pretty obvious anyway."

"Was not!"

Mari laughed. "*Sí*, it definitely was!"

"I can only imagine what—Oh shit!" Erin halted on the porch of the rental.

Mari's smile dropped. "What? What's wrong?"

"I left the wine in his bathroom!"

Her friend burst out laughing, loud enough that Jude would certainly hear it across the street and through the door. And Erin couldn't help it, she joined in too, letting herself get swept up in the bizarre circumstances of the evening. What else could she do?

They shuffled like a pair of snickering drunks across the deck, halting at the door and staring down the keypad like an old archnemsis.

"*Digame*, the Code?"

"Eight-three-seven-two," Erin recited, wiping a jovial tear.

A green light shone, and Mari hooted a victory call before swinging the door open. Erin took one last glance over her shoulder before stepping inside the rental and officially starting their vacation.

Jude

Laughter filtered through the windows. Jude tugged back the corner of the curtain and watched as the taller woman keeled over into Erin, walking like she was drunk. He could hear their voices but he couldn't make out the words. A part of him, a cringeworthy part still hanging on from youth that refused to learn, wondered if they were talking about him.

He clenched his jaw and watched as they staggered arm and arm across the street and up the porch steps to the rental. Shauna hadn't mentioned renters this weekend, not that he made it a habit to check in with her. Only, usually she'd contact him to give him warning in case something came up.

Figures. The one time it slipped her mind and something did come up. But he wasn't her damn rental manager.

Outside, the women stopped at the top of the steps. Then suddenly, they burst into laughter, carrying on like it wasn't midnight nor twenty degrees outside. When they finally made it to the door, Erin didn't have to pull out her little paper for the code. His lip twitched. *Guess her trick worked.*

She was cute. Really fucking cute. *And those eyes!*

Jude muttered a curse under his breath.

He wasn't going there. She was trouble. All women were, as far as he was concerned. Renters especially. Something about the snow and the mountains put all kinds of ideas in their heads.

He stood at the window, waiting until they'd turned on all the lights, then he let the curtain fall back in place. Shaking his head, he rubbed his jaw. *Shauna's friends. Great...* He hissed out a breath.

He walked over to Etta's bed, squatted down and gave her a good scratch on the belly. Her tail thwacked the wall under the stairs. She'd taken an odd interest in Erin. Normally, she was his partner in crime—must've been what threw him.

"You're a good girl," he cooed.

She yawned and stretched her long, scruffy body out past her extra large dog bed. "We're gonna lay low this weekend," he murmured as he rose. "Calling it a night. Early morning tomorrow."

Jude went around, turning off all the lights and closing down the place. He stopped by the front window again, taking another gander across the street. The rental door was propped open and the friends were unloading the car. Normal renter stuff. Wouldn't have mattered what they were doing. He wasn't even sure why he'd checked. But he had, they were fine, and he'd done what he did and hopefully that would be the end of it. He let the curtain drop again.

He hit the light on his way into the bathroom. Pulling his toothbrush out of the medicine cabinet, he smeared paste on the bristles, thinking about the way Erin wrote her numbers with a slight, feminine slant. *Stop it.*

With a huff, he shoved the brush in his mouth, giving extra focus to the circular motions on each tooth. He'd just finished the bottom row when something in the mirror caught his eye. Squinting, and trying to make sense of it, he turned and cocked his head at the wine bottle sitting on the floor. He stopped brushing.

What the...?

Red nose, hair sticking out every which way and shit, he couldn't stop staring at her. He could return the bottle.

Don't be stupid.

Maybe he just needed to get laid. And soon enough they'd be gone and he could have his peace and quiet back.

Chapter Three

Vacation Mode

Erin

Ugh. Erin felt as though she'd only just fallen back asleep. Blind, white sunshine assaulted the room in an overly cheerful, fresh-fallen snow kind of way. She forced a heavy eye open, then winced. *This bedroom needs a curtain.*

"Erin!" Mari's voice came from the other side of her door—possibly for the second time, the first being what woke her.

"I'm up!" she croaked back. "Sort of..."

Grabbing her phone from the nightstand, she blinked until the numbers came into focus. *Seven fifteen?* Staring at her cell, she willed for a snooze button to Mari's wake-up call. There wasn't one, of course, so she clunked it back on the bedside table.

It wouldn't have been so bad if she'd actually slept. But that stupid dream! Thinking about it set her heart racing all over again and Vic's face surfaced behind closed lids. She dragged her hands down her face, yawned, then tugged the edge of the lush duvet over her head.

Clattering came from the kitchen, just on the other side of her wall. Erin hadn't thought of the noise when she'd picked this room. Her eyes sunk and her body relaxed into the heat and comfort of her cocoon.

"ER-IN!" Her bedroom door creaked, followed by a set of powerful stomps. "Get your lazy *nalgas* out of this bed!"

"It's Saturday," she mumbled from under her blanket.

"And I've been up for an hour. I'm bored! Let's go for a hike!"

Erin could feel the pull at the bottom of her blanket and held fast just as Mari yanked.

"Ah! You're such a brat! I'm doing this for you, you know!"

"Okay...fine." She pushed up, letting the duvet fall around her. "But I need some coffee," she vocalized around another yawn.

"You need some exercise."

"Are you calling me fat?"

With an exasperated huff, Mari rolled her eyes and stalked out. Erin grinned. Her friend hated when people asked that. 'Everyone is always so focused on fat, fat, fat! What about the rest of the body?' she'd complain. It was easy for Mari to say that. She had no fat.

Back arching, Erin twisted side to side in a full body stretch. Her limbs tingled with energy and despite her grogginess, it felt good. She never stretched in the mornings —it was always get-up-and-go. *Mental note*, she thought, *stretch more.*

In the spirit of vacation mode, she shuffled over to the single-pane window. *Wow.* The sunny, sparkling, winter wonderland was enough to chase away even the darkest nightmare.

Fluffy snow piled on branches. Pristine white carpeted the roofs of the neighboring cabins and sheds. Icicles hung from eaves, glinting in the sunlight. Their rental sat, nestled in frosted, untouched perfection. And this was her world for the next week!

Despite her rough night, something deep within her released and for the first time in months, Erin felt at ease.

"You want oatmeal?" Mari shouted from the kitchen.

"Sure!" she hollered back.

Leaving the view, Erin hoisted her duffle onto the bed, and dug through the rushed packing job. Her brow sunk. "Wha...?"

She flipped her bag and watched the shower of tanks, dinky long sleeves, and leggings pile atop the duvet. Last came a book she'd never seen before and her ease waned. Grabbing the novel, she stormed out into the kitchen.

"Mari!"

"*Sí?*"

"What the heck?" Erin held up the book.

"I packed you a book? It's a romance, but you'll like it." Mari winked from her spot at the stove.

"No. I mean, not just the book. Everything! The clothes!"

"What about them?" she asked, stirring oatmeal into the pot.

"Tank tops? You couldn't have packed me a sweater? Or a long-sleeve shirt?"

Her friends brow furrowed. "I packed you long sleeves."

"Yeah, and they're practically see through." Erin flung an arm at the window over the kitchen sink. "It's like, thirty degrees here!"

Mari set the wooden spoon on the stove and turned to face her, looking uncertain. Erin faltered. Mari never looked uncertain. "Okay, m*ira*. At the gym, I'm use to pushing people past their comfort zones. This whole thing with Vic...you needed a push. I didn't want his dumb ass mistake to make you feel unsexy."

Well, it did, Erin reflected. *Among other things...*

"Maybe I got *un poquito* carried away?" Mari pinched the air with her thumb and index finger, scrunching her face. "But that see-through sweater makes your boobs look awesome."

"Mari, who cares about my boobs?" she huffed, the anger ebbing.

"Are you kidding? Your boobs are amazing! I'd kill for bigger boobs!"

There were a lot of things Erin would like too, but she didn't go around vicariously imposing her style on others. Mari didn't get it—she'd always been a flaunter. Erin was not. Next trip, she'd find the time to pack her own bag.

Nothing I can do about it now. She shook her head, wondering if one could in fact freeze their ass off, as she wandered back to her room. Mari's voice trailed behind her as the door swung shut. "*¡Chica!* I'm sorry. I thought you had a ski jacket!"

Dressed in layers that snugged her curves, and straight hair thrown up in a ponytail, Erin unplugged her phone and shuffled into the main part of the cabin. The layout of the rental was much the same as Jude's—except, where he had empty space and an armchair by the fireplace, the rental boasted a heavy wooden dining set with six chairs. And the kitchen looked much more dated with its yellowed formica countertops and dull, worn, wood cabinets. It felt a little like *deja vu*, coming out from the back to see Mari perched at the breakfast bar, reading a magazine.

"Oye, chica...Can I make a suggestion about that top?"

She glanced down at her bumpy layers. "No."

"Fair enough."

Erin pulled her fresh grounds from the fridge, moving past the line up of wines and tequila they'd arranged on the back counter. The Walmart special sat tucked in the corner under the cabinets—a no-frills, 12 cup coffeemaker. The extra paper filters were sealed in a ziplock and shoved in the water tank. Erin would soon discover that it either made 12 cups of mediocre coffee, or disappointed even the most non-discerning drinker with one single, crappy cup.

Arranging the filter, she measured the grounds, and added what she hoped was twelve ounces of water. The measure lines had worn off and the numbers were barely legible. Flipping the switch, she waited for the gurgling, hissing sounds to indicate the thing actually worked.

Behind her, Mari cleared her throat. "So."

"So," Erin parroted, turning to see her friend set her chin on a propped hand and grin.

"That *man*." Mari's eyes grew wide and her whole forehead lifted as she mouthed a dramatic 'WOW.'

Erin laughed. "Which man are you referring to?"

"Oh please. You noticed. I totally saw you notice."

"Fine, I noticed," Erin admitted, picking up her cell. She held it up over her head to try to find some signal. Nothing.

"Way hotter than Vic."

"I guess so," Erin muttered, eyes to the screen, searching for WIFI.

Mari hopped off the stool and strutted into the kitchen. "Hey, can I see that for a second?"

"Sure." Erin handed her the phone.

Mari tucked it in the hip pocket of her leggings, then strode back to her spot at the counter.

"Uh. Are you going to give that back?"

"No," her friend replied, hopping up on her stool.

"What? Why?"

"Because! I don't want you talking with that *cabrón*." She flung her arm out like disposing of yesterday's trash.

"Who? Vic? What makes you think that's—"

Mari shot a knowing look that had Erin eating her words.

"Mari, I'm a big girl. You don't have to micromanage me."

"Apparently I do. And you wouldn't have had anything to do with him if it wasn't for me." Erin couldn't argue with that, but that didn't make it Mari's fault or her responsibility. "Besides, it won't do you any good," she advised, eyes back to her magazine, "There's no service in the cabin." Erin crossed her arms with a huff but her display of discontent went unnoticed, or more likely, ignored. "Hey, give the oatmeal a stir, will you?"

"You can't just take my phone for a whole week."

"You gave it to me," Mari argued without looking up.

"I thought you were going to enter the WIFI password or something."

Her friend looked up, crossing arms over the magazine. "Where you looking for messages from Vic?"

Erin pursed her lips and looked away.

"That's what I thought," then tilting her head to the stove, "Oatmeal, please."

With a grumble, Erin moved to the stove and lifted the lid on the pot. She mixed around the slosh of bubbling milk and oats, then replaced the cover. "You do plan on sharing that at some point, right?"

Mari looked up. "What?"

"The WIFI password."

"Oh." Mari's lips lingered in an 'O' shape and Erin got a sinking feeling. "No WIFI either."

"What?" She felt sure all the blood drained from her face.

"Kind of nice, right?"

"No! Not nice! Mari, you didn't tell me this!" She paced the kitchen, anxiety rushing in and vacation ease destroyed. "No WIFI? Who doesn't have WIFI?"

"Someone who doesn't live here?"

"But it's a rental." *This is bad.*

Mari shrugged, but Erin couldn't brush it off so easily. Maybe there was some validity to Mari's concerns that she might backtrack with Vic. The way she'd ended things with him left a lingering nausea in her gut that fed her doubt and left her second guessing everything. But her concerns went beyond Vic, and she realized, she should have been more upfront with Mari the night before they left.

"They don't have a wired connection?" she tried again. "Anything?"

"Nothing," Mari replied, her eyes narrowing. "What's up with you?"

Erin sighed, leaning hands into the counter, her appetite gone. This trip was meant to give her time away from Vic, to get her head on straight, which she'd been skeptical about. But she'd also justified it by convincing her boss she could actually get things done without all the interruptions at the office. With a huge deadline looming, her boss never would have given her the time off.

"*Chica.*"

Erin scrunched her face. "I told Paul I'd work remotely."

"*¡Chica!* You said you got the time off!"

"I got some of it off..."

"But you worked all night before we left!" Mari flipped her magazine closed and popped off her stool. "That's why I packed for you!" Her arms flung out then landed on her hips, and she shook her head, sending curls flying, less like a halo, and more like a firestorm.

Sullen, Erin nodded. "I know."

"This is supposed to be a vacation. As in a break. From everything!" Mari's face reflected disappointment and brooding anger. "*Mira,* how am I supposed to help you when you won't even help yourself?" She pulled her voluminous hair back into a ponytail with the hair-tie she always kept on her wrist. "You're worse than my rehab clients!"

"I'm rehabilitating, too! It might not be from a broken bone but..." Erin folded her arms over her chest, frowning at the corner of red couches snugged under the front window. Normally she'd find them inviting. They'd presented the perfect remote office space for the coming days. Great view, comfortable seating...Now, she'd have to borrow the car and trek out in the snow to find internet connection. With, or without her friend's support.

Mari strode into the kitchen and turned off the burner. She gave the oatmeal a hearty stir, sending flecks of oats out onto the stovetop. "It's ready."

Erin wasn't hungry. Her stomach felt full of rocks. She didn't like having so many unknowns floating around in her head. Pursing her lips, she asked, "Can I have my phone back, please?"

"No." Mari moved to the fridge , extracted a crate of blueberries, and crossed to the sink.

"'No' Because you're mad at me?"

"Because you said it yourself. You're rehabilitating, and I want what's best for you. And what's best is to stay away from that man."

"I won't call him."

"So you say."

"Please?"

"Why do you need it? It's Saturday." Opening the crate, Mari rinsed the pack under the tap, muttering. "...not even twenty-four hours."

"Fine," Erin sighed, turning to check her coffee. Evidently, Mari felt compelled to save her from herself. The machine gurgled and dripped, only halfway done, and Erin longed for her shiny, updated coffee pot back home. "How long has Shauna had this place?"

From all she'd heard about Mari's friend, Erin had expected everything in the cabin to be top of the line. Not that she minded—the place reminded her of going to Grandma's house. All it lacked was the crystal candy bowl.

"She bought it last year," Mari answered, her tone softening as she shook the extra water from the carton. "Foreclosure. But they spend all their time at the Chalet." She held out the crate, now glistening with water droplets. "You want some?"

Erin picked a few off the top and tossed them into her mouth, hoping to call a truce. "I'm sorry. I should have told you sooner about work."

Mari sniffed and shrugged. "It's fine. I'm over it."

Eyes narrowed, Erin watched her friend pop a berry into her mouth. *She's up to something.*

"I have an idea. Let's invite hunky neighbor over for dinner."

There it is. "No, thanks." Erin busied herself, opening up the cabinets, looking for bowls.

"Oh, come on! It's the polite thing to do."

"No, I know where this is going and I'm not sure even your cooking could seduce a man like that. Did you see him last night?" She found the mugs and selected a hand-glazed, brown one. The bowls lived two cabinets over. She pulled one down. "He seems like he just wants to be left alone."

"Oh, I disagree." Mari's mouth lifted into a sly grin.

"Can't you just make him some cookies and leave them at his door?" She hand Mari the bowl.

"Who says this is for me?"

"Mari."

"I guess I could say they were from you..." She took the offered bowl. When she rounded back to the breakfast bar with her blueberry topped oatmeal, she just had to add, "Men are suckers for good cooking. One of these days I'm going to teach you."

*Not just men...*Erin grouched, turning her attention to the coffee pot. Being such a miserable cook, she was a sucker for good cooking, too. Her lack of culinary sufficiency high-lighted just one of her many flaws.

Mari sighed dramatically behind her. "Okay, fine. I'll get *him* to invite us to dinner."

The drip finally finished and Erin grabbed the carafe. *Saved by the coffee.*

"When he does," she continued, "you should wear that scoop neck thingy. Or the sweater."

"The white one?"

"*Sí!*"

"No." Erin poured pathetically light, brown liquid into her dark mug, hoping it tasted better than it looked.

"*¿Por qué no?*" Mari pouted.

"Because, it's see-through!" She lifted the cup to her lips and let the steam warm her face. "I don't even know why I'm arguing. He's not going to invite us over." She took a tentative first sip, cheeks puckering and eyes squinting. "Blech!"

As she scraped the sides of her bowl with her spoon, Mari *tsked*, then sighed, "I'm going to have to get you drunk again."

Brainstorming how to make her coffee drinkable helped cover the sting from Mari's comment. *Double the grounds? Soak the filter first?*

"Don't you want to live a little?"

"I do live." Erin poured the coffee from her mug back over the filter of soggy grounds, hoping for the best. The hot plate sizzled as some of it spilled down the sides.

"No, like at the pub. Girl, I have never seen you take life by the balls like that!"

"Mari."

"I mean, the way you told Vic off! I've never been more proud! And the look on his date's face!"

"I actually feel kind of bad about that..."

"You shouldn't. She was way too smug. And too young. If anything, you did her a favor."

Erin leveled her eyes to the percolating machine as slightly darker liquid dribbled back into the carafe. "So, where are we taking this hike?"

Mari groaned but went along with the change of subject. "Not sure yet."

Erin pulled the carafe out and the drip paused. She poured just enough in her cup for a taste—one face-puckering sip. "Yuck. That's even worse. I can't drink this."

"I bet the locals would have some good suggestions."

Erin turned off the machine and dumped the sad excuse for coffee into the sink. "That's a good idea. How about someone at the nearest cafe?"

"I was thinking *more* local." Mari's voice lifted an octave.

Erin glanced over to catch her friend staring out the window and across the street. "Un—believable."

"*¿Qué?*"

"One track mind."

"Er-in," Mari whined like a girl with a school crush, her bottom lip jutting up and out.

"Don't." She returned her unused bowl to the cabinet. "I'm going to stop you right there."

"You're no fun. You're not going to eat?"

"I'm not hungry. Mari, I'm not up for drama. I'm here to clear my head about Vic, remember?"

"Yes! And the best way to get over someone is to get—"

Erin threw her hand up. "Nope. Please don't finish that."

"Well, it's true," Mari moped, but she didn't push it.

"*Well,*" Erin huffed, "it wouldn't matter. A man like that does not go for a girl like me." She realized she'd said the wrong thing when the air around Mari quivered.

"A girl like you? You mean like, hardworking?"

"Mari—"

"Smart. Funny. Loyal."

"Stop."

"Modest? *Dios mio*, you can't even take a compliment!" Erin had enough sense to keep her mouth shut. "Honest and giving," Mari continued.

"Alright. I get it. You've made your point."

"Understated natural beauty—"

"Mari. I got it."

"I hope so. I'll hear none of that!"

"He'd be lucky to have me," Erin conceded, though somewhat sarcastically.

"¡Claro!"

"Even if just for the weekend," she egged. Sometimes Mari got so ahead of herself she forgot that Erin wasn't the kind of girl who had one night stands.

"Giiirl!"

"But he won't." Erin ended it. "Because he's not my type."

"Whaaat?" Mari deflated. "Not your type? Honey," she argued, her tone patronizing, "I think he's everyone's type."

"He's intimidating and intense."

"You only think that because you want him."

"No. I'd say it's because of his words, tone and general body language," Erin counted out on her thumb and two fingers.

"His biceps are intense." Mari chuckled. Erin shrugged. "Girl, don't even. I saw you looking."

"Fine. Yes, he has nice arms!"

"And pecs," Mari added, her voice dreamy.

"Which makes him all the more off limits and more intimidating. Big muscles aren't really my thing."

"That's a load of crap!"

"I'm not into rough and rugged."

Mari snorted, clearly enjoying herself. "Oh honey, you have no idea. Besides, you don't know he'd do it rough." The way Mari said it, it sounded like she hoped he did.

"Ok. Whatever. You have at him," Erin offered halfheartedly. "But don't drag me into it."

"Just for that," Mari started, hopping off her stool and bringing her empty bowl to the sink, "I'm taking you up a big hill!"

Chapter Four

Cell Service and Self Worth

Erin

She wanted to marvel at the snow-capped beauty around her, but necessity had Erin focused on her footing. "Mari, slow down!"

Cold air burned her tired lungs. It hadn't taken long to remember how unwise it was to challenge Mari. The hike up had been intense, but the descent felt dire. Her cold, soggy sneakers slipped over the tamped snow as they wove back down the steep mountain path. A strange familiarity struck her as she glanced up ahead to where her overenthusiastic friend had stopped to wait. *Thank God.*

"Can I have my phone?" Erin puffed as she drew near, "For a picture."

Mari dug the cell from her pocket and held it out, but when Erin went to take it, her grip tightened. Cocking her head to the side, with a scolding look she warned, "Just for photos."

"Just for photos."

The screen boasted full bars and a long list of notifications. Erin ignored them, mostly, as she said she would, to capture the landscape in panorama. Mari shoved her palm out again. Erin stalled. "I won't call him." Her friend raised an eyebrow. "Or text."

"That's what you said before."

"Yeah, and then you had to go and make that comment about my dream. Now every time I have it, it's him, and it gives me the creeps. I won't call him."

Mari shook her head, lips pursed. "It was always him."

"Maybe..."

"You should've just blocked his number."

"If I do, can I keep my phone?"

Mari's hand dropped. "Fine."

With frozen fingers, Erin pulled up "Victor Fuerra" in her contacts. She hesitated. The long stream of texts had been from him. What if she was making a mistake? Mari lunged in for the phone. Erin whipped her arm back, inadvertently tapping "block this caller."

"See? That wasn't hard?"

Erin didn't reply. *I can always unblock him later,* she assured the lead in her chest. Blinking back the sting, she scanned the mountainside, again, getting that sense of intimate recognition.

Mari took a wide stance and squatted, stretching. "You didn't sleep?"

"Huh?" Erin realized Mari studied her.

"You look tired. Your eyes are all puffy. The dream?" Erin shrugged and Mari *tsked.* "I thought it would go away when we left the city."

Rubbing her eyes, Erin nodded and that's when it clicked —the familiarity of her surroundings. "It was different this time, though."

"Yeah?"

"There was snow, for one." Erin brought her hands to her mouth to breathe warm air on numb fingertips. "And this time I had a way out."

Mari tilted her head. "Interesting. So he didn't catch you? Or, like..." she brought her arms out in front of her, forming a circle with her hands and pulsing them in to constrict the empty space.

Erin grimaced. "No. He still caught me. But right before he did, I saw this *bridge*."

"A bridge? Did it have a gate or a guard or something?"

"No. No, nothing like that. Just an old wooden bridge, half-buried in the snow. It was just...in my dream, I knew if I could make it onto the bridge, I'd be safe."

Mari's brow scrunched as she leaned a hand in her thigh and sunk deeper into the stance. "Okay...But you didn't? Make it?"

"No," Erin sighed, adjusting her beanie so it covered her ears. "I was running as fast as I could, but it was always *just* out of reach."

"Huh."

"I mean, that's my life, right? Everything's always just out of reach." She scanned the mountain again, half expecting to see the splintered handrail poking out of the snow. Dreaming of a white, tree dotted hillside wasn't totally unexpected, given where they were. Still, the likeness felt eerie.

The sudden, musical tone of Erin's phone sent her heart into her throat. Mari jumped up and snatched it before Erin could see the called ID, let alone answer it. "Oh. It's your mom." She handed it back.

"Helen Simms" flashed on the screen. Erin reclaimed the cell with a creased brow. "Hi mom. What's going on?"

Her mother almost never called her. As the head buyer for a major, upscale department store, Helen vacillated between working, schmoozing or getting her beauty rest. They seldom had time for chit chat. Thus, she cut straight to the chase.

"Erin, honey, are you okay?"

"Yes. Why...why wouldn't I be okay?" She looked over at Mari. Mari shrugged.

"Victor called me. He said you were totally inebriated at a *bar* on Tuesday night!" She said "bar" like a dirty word.

Erin listed her head to the side even though her mother couldn't see. There were three things wrong with that statement. "Actually, it was a pub."

"Is there a difference?"

"Yes." Erin's jaw tightened. "A pub has a full menu. It's more like a restaurant." It bothered her that she felt the need to defend herself.

"If you say so."

Pushing down the urge to argue further, Erin moved on to her second qualm. "When did you talk to Vic?"

"Oh...well, let me see," her mother wondered aloud. "He called early Wednesday morning. I remember, because I assumed you would be sleeping off your hangover. I didn't want to bother you."

"How thoughtful. Well, it's Saturday now." *Plenty of days to get over a hangover, and take a call from a worried mother.*

"You have plans?"

"Never mind," Erin sighed, bending down to brush some snow off her sneaker. "I'm fine mom. Tuesday was rough, but it's over."

"I'm sorry, honey. I wish I could have helped. It has just been so busy here! Would you believe it, I'm at the office? We have a new fragrance launch going on so there is this big gala...you know how it goes."

"Yes. I do."

The galas were always a big deal and way over the top. She'd taken Vic to one once. That's where he'd met Lisa, his current girlfriend, and the woman he'd ultimately hooked up with not twenty-four hours after dumping Erin. Lisa had to have known they'd been an item, which was why Erin had little sympathy for her when she'd seen Vic at the pub on Tuesday with yet another woman she'd drunkenly dubbed 'Candy-Lips.' *Once a cheater...*

"Anyway," her mother continued, "Victor said Marisol was with you so I knew you were in good hands."

"Hi, Ms. Simms!" Mari shouted at the phone when she heard her name. Erin shot an annoyed look her way and Mari stuck out her tongue.

"Is that Marisol?"

Erin sighed. "Yes."

"Hello, Marisol! Tell her I say hello."

"I think she heard you."

Next to her, Mari snickered and pulled a leg back into a balancing stretch. It made Erin nervous just watching her. One tilt in the wrong direction and...

"Victor sounds well," her mother gossiped.

And that was the final thing. "Speaking of, *why* is Vic calling you?"

"Oh, don't be like that. He was worried about you honey."

Erin scoffed, but a sad little part of her liked hearing it. "You do know *he* broke up with me, right?"

"And he's miserable about that! I told him not to be so hard on himself, but men and their honor...you know."

"What? Mom! You're not supposed to support *him*!" Erin pivoted, needing somewhere to pace on the narrow path.

This sounded a lot like what her mother used to say right after her parent's divorce. Was her father still 'a good man' who 'shouldn't be so hard on himself,' after canceling his weekends, missing child support payments, then moving to Texas with his new wife and hardly a goodbye?

Erin took a deep, icy breath. "I'd rather you didn't stay in touch with Vic, mom." And she should've left it at that. "What do you even talk about?"

Mari shook her head and Erin had to agree. As soon as the words were out, she knew she shouldn't have gone there.

"Honey, a man like that, building his career? There's little time left to dedicate to a woman like she deserves."

Erin felt betrayal twist into indignation. "He told you he was too *busy* for me?"

"He's busy, alright," Mari muttered.

"I am just impressed he could recognize that. Maybe once he's more settled things between you two will work out."

Erin shut her eyes and tucked her lips in until she had the control to say something constructive. "Mom, there's things you don't understand. And I'd really appreciate it if you didn't talk to my ex."

"That is just unreasonable. Victor is my friend, too."

"What?"

"What is all this? Are you dating someone new?" Before Erin could respond, she added a heartfelt, "Oh, poor Victor!"

"Oh my God, Mother! Whose side are you on?"

"This isn't about sides, young lady. If you refuse to share what is going on with you, then you cannot expect me to drop everything and agree to silly little school games and silent treatments. *You* are the one getting drunk on a week-night and making a damn scene!"

Erin disengaged the call.

Mari stared, mouth agape. "Did she really just—"

"Yup."

"And you just—"

"Yup." Erin had never hung up on her mother before. And even in her anger, remorse set in.

"Your mom has always been a little..."

"Superficial? Self-serving? Self-centered?" Erin listed, dragging her gaze from the tree line to her friend.

Mari studied her, frowning. "I was going to say 'clueless.'"

"Well, she's that too."

"I can't believe she defended that *culo*."

"It's like dad, all over aga—"

Erin's cell sang out again.

With a sigh, she blindly brought it to her ear. "Mother, I'm sorry if I'm out of line, but I cannot talk about this right now. I'll call you later, okay?"

A deep, masculine vocal caress streamed out from the small communication device and wrapped around her like a warm blanket. "*¿Cariña?*"

Her chest tightened, heart filling up her throat, and she stood there, frozen, stuck between hope and disbelief.

Mari straightened. "What? What's wrong?"

There were no words. Erin's logic fought to surface past emotion, like a blade of grass struggling through a thick blanket of spring snow. *He called.* She'd told him not to, but he did anyway. *That has to mean something, right?*

That's when Mari understood. "No! Oh no. Hang up!"

Erin shook her head, mouthing, "I can't."

"You can and you should."

"Mari," she pleaded, lurching back, and blocking Mari's reach with her arm. "No!"

"Hello?" came the disembodied voice.

"You promised!" Mari hissed. "Hang up. When you say it's over, you do *not* take his calls! Hang up the phone."

"I...I have to...let me do this," she stuttered.

In the quiet of the mountainside, Vic's voice drifted up as if he were standing next to her. "*Cariña,* are you there? Talk to me."

Erin cleared her throat. "Yeah. Hi. I'm here." She eyed Mari's fuming expression, expecting her friend to wrestle the phone away.

"*¡Estupida!*" Mari muttered, shaking her head. "I cannot believe you."

"There you are," Vic purred, melting away some of her anger.

Mari pointed a finger at her and grumbled, "This is on you." Erin looked away and gave her focus to the man on the phone.

"I know you told me not to call," he continued, "but, *Cariña,* I can't stop thinking about you."

"Can you not do that, please?"

"Think about you?" He chuckled.

"No. Stop calling me *Cariña.*"

"I thought you liked it."

She kicked at a pile of snow with her sneaker, uncovering a large rock. "I did when it meant something." Just saying it out loud, even under her breath, felt like discovering the lie all over again. It hollowed out her insides and left her there, a frozen shell.

He whistled through his teeth. "You wound me."

"Is there something you wanted?"

"It's Saturday," he said as if that explained everything.

Erin shot a glance over her shoulder. Mari'd apparently given up on her and gone back to stretching. "Yeah. So?"

"So, what are you doing?"

"What am I doing? Vic, I don't—"

"I'd like to take you out tonight." He paused, but not long enough to let her respond. "Anywhere," he added. "Wherever you want."

Does that mean you're single? she wanted to ask. *Does that mean you finally choose me?* Irritated at her own stupid hope—that he kept doing this to her, that she let him—she closed her eyes and took a breath. "Were you there? In the bar?"

"You mean the pub?"

"Whatever!"

"Of course I was there, baby. You were drunk. But I forgive you. We both know you say silly things when you drink."

She gnashed her teeth.

"What? You're still mad? I bet you don't even remember what set you off," he teased, all flirt and charm.

Her silence stretched, and he laughed. The sound should have been warm and seductive but instead felt abrasive. Had it always been like that and she'd just been too caught up to notice?

He finally seemed to pick up on her mood. "Baby...I'm sorry. Tell me how to make it up to you."

Erin wished she could see his face to validate his words. Doubt and indecision swarmed her. What if he meant it this time? They'd been happy together, once. It didn't seem an impossible notion that they could get that back. Then again, what if it was all bullshit? The same lies on a different day? She grew tired of always making excuses for him.

Mari loped around into her field of vision and waved a hand in front of Erin's face. "Hello?" she scolded. "You're in charge here. Either rip him a new one or hang up the phone!"

Erin blinked at the well-meant pep talk, thinking about all those text messages he'd sent, and calls he'd made. *Mari's right.* She was the one screening calls, not him. *She* was the one blocking *his* number. On that thought, she looked at the caller ID.

"Where are you calling from?"

"What?"

"This number you called me on," she reiterated, "Is this a new line?"

"Baby."

Vic, always so confident. "No. Don't baby me. Are you calling from another woman's house?" When he didn't respond, a wave of hurt rushed through her. "This is exactly why I said whatever I said at the pub. And there is nothing you can do to fix it because you completely missed the point!"

Mari fist pumped the air and Erin appreciated her enthusiasm because her words felt self-destructive. She'd been pining for him to want her back, even hoped—though she'd never admit it to Mari—that breaking it off would force his cards. She'd put in the time and the tears for this. So what the heck was she doing?

"I didn't miss it. You just caught me at a bad time. Tell me now. You have my undivided attention."

He always did this. And she always gave in, always dropped everything for him. Focusing on Mari's vibes and not the chasm forming in her chest, she held her ground. "My feelings aren't 'silly,' Victor. Drunk or otherwise. And I shouldn't have to screen your calls just to get your *undivided attention!*"

"Okay. Okay. You're right," he rushed out, overly agreeable and eager. "I'm learning. Give me a second chance. Teach me how to be better." His smooth, controlled tone felt at odds with his words. But then, he always seemed in control.

In contrast, Erin felt totally out of control. Her emotions were everywhere. Was she just being overly suspicious? Could he mean what he said? This is what she'd wanted all along, for him to go the extra mile for her. How could she turn that down? A date, just the two of them, on a Saturday? What a huge step up from their discreet, lunchtime rendezvous! She wanted to believe she'd made her point and he'd finally recognized what he'd lost.

She looked down at the unfamiliar number on the phone. Erin felt she couldn't trust her own instincts anymore and panic rose at the urgency and importance of her response. *Hang up.* She knew she should but her body wouldn't cooperate. Fear dictated this might be her last chance with him, yet if that were the case, his promises meant nothing anyway. If he really cared for her, he'd give her time, prove his intentions and rebuild the trust. Realizing that, Erin found her backbone.

"I don't want this, Vic."

The words stabbed into her chest. Deep down, she knew this was it. He'd just go back to easy, agreeable, younger women. Women who'd fall for his charm—like she'd done for the past year. *I'm so stupid.*

Erin sniffed as a chill shook her and Mari moved in, offering a sideways hug. "You got this, girl," her friend whispered it her ear.

"*Mi Cariña.*"

He wasn't making this easy. "Victor," she forced out in warning.

Silence hung on the line for a moment and she wondered if he finally understood. But when he spoke, his voice darkened. "Is there another man?"

She scoffed. "If there was?" The words came out before she could stop them. *He has no right to talk to me about monogamy.*

That gave him pause. When he spoke again, he'd switched back to charming and flirty. "Let me take you out tonight."

"Sorry. I'm busy."

"I'll give you more," he urged.

"More what?"

"More than him. More than before."

Pressure clawed up her throat, a building eruption of exasperation and bitter tears. "Why?" she cried. "Because you don't like the idea of me with someone else? Because you think I *enjoy* having sex in your car on my lunch break? Because you assume I'm fine hanging around as your side piece?"

"Say it girl!" Mari chimed in, throwing her arms up. "She doesn't, *cabrón!*"

"Why, Victor?" Erin pressed.

"Because, I love you."

Standing there, a tiny dot on the side of the massive, tree covered mountain, Erin realized he couldn't possibly know what those words meant. Not in the way she did. Not now, not ever. Otherwise, they wouldn't be there, having this conversation. It hit her harder than everything else. Her gusto deflated, leaving her feeling smaller than a speck on the mountain.

"*Te quiero, Cariña.*"

Erin blinked and a hot tear escaped down her check.

"Hang up the phone," Mari insisted, reaching for it. Erin made a halting sound in her throat and swatted at Mari's hand. It might make her a masochist, but she wasn't done. Somehow, he'd understand. Somehow, she'd get through to him.

"This is not how you treat people you love."

"Where are you? I need to see you."

Her voice wobbled. "I'm on a trip."

"Erin!" Mari groaned.

"Where? I'll come. Just tell me where."

Where was all this motivation before? Erin held her breath. *What do I do?* An asinine part of her wanted him to clamber up the mountain and sweep her off her feet. Why shouldn't she get a happy ending after all he'd put her through? Weren't great love stories forged on second chances? Maybe he hadn't loved her like she'd loved him, but that could change. Right? She'd invested so much time in him. *But...*

What proof did she have? His word? Erin tried to remember all the points Mari had helped her realize. Points meant to strengthen her conviction and walk away. In the end, only one really mattered.

"I'm not happy," she admitted. "And if you really loved me, you'd respect me when I say, please don't call me. Don't call and don't text. Just...don't."

"Tell me where you are, damnit!"

Clamping her jaw, and squeezing her eyes shut, Erin shoved the phone at Mari. Only when his voice disappeared did she open her eyes. It might have been the cold, but an odd numbness settled over her skin.

Mari's grin split her face in two. "Girl, I am so proud of you!" Wrapping arms around her friend of twenty years, she added, "Don't worry, *chica*. There's something better for you out there. And when you find it, you won't even *want* that trash."

"Great," Erin drawled, her voice stoic. "I can't wait."

Chapter Five

Contradictions

Erin

"Rise and shine, *princesa!*" Mari shouted through the door.

Erin rubbed her face and squinted at the light streaming through the window. The night before, upon opening the second bottle of wine, Mari had promised no more crazy antics, and Erin grimaced at the dull ache in her tailbone.

She burrowed deeper under the duvet and groaned, "You said no hikes!" There came no reply.

With a huff, she pushed up to sitting, stretched her arms over her head, and yawned. Through the unobscured window, the snowy scene glowed happily back at her, and even as crummy as she felt, her lip tipped skyward. Staying up late and watching movies with her best friend had been exactly what she'd needed. Her numbness had given way to a tornado of emotions, and Mari just sat, listened, and laughed, topping off her wine glass as the Indiana Jones franchise played in the background.

Erin hadn't realized how the drama with Victor had smothered her. The anxiety. The sleeplessness. The low morale. Now, waking up with no expectations, no work, no plan, and no phone service, a serene peace surrounded her heartache.

Stepping back had been the right thing to do. As usual, Mari was right. *I shouldn't have kept sleeping with him.* She'd been hating herself for near on a year. Somehow in the muck of things, her moral compass had gone askew.

It amazed her how a solid night's sleep made for clearer thinking.

A familiar smell drifted under the door and her mouth watered in trained response. *Bacon.*

Erin inched off the bed, and shuffled, partially stooped, to her duffle, wondering how she could've been so oblivious to her own misery. Even when with him, she hadn't been happy, as if the time had been tainted with what inevitably came after. Loneliness. Self-loathing. Disappointment. She'd been wasting her time, doing things that didn't feel good, and always finding some justification.

Staying up late watching movies with Mari felt good. Waking up to the quiet and bright, white sunshine felt good. Heck, even hiking in the snow felt good until that last stretch when she'd misstepped.

Living as second best did not feel good. Constantly trying to prove herself grew exhausting. She didn't like pretending things were okay when they weren't. That was not the woman she wanted to be. She wanted to be strong and outspoken. Like Mari.

Set on doing things better, Erin rifled through her bag for an outfit. Dressed, she studied herself in a mirror that hung from the closet door, nodded to her reflection, then followed the smell of bacon. "Good morning!"

Turning from a sizzling skillet, Mari's eyes settled on the too-tight tank layered under the see-through white sweater. Her face lifted into a blinding smile. "¡Buenas días! Hot date?"

Erin batted her lashes, then grinned back. "Just you," she teased, approaching the coffee pot with optimism.

Having learned her lesson, she went heavy on the grounds and measured the water *before* pouring it in. As the coffee pot growled to life, she gazed out the window centered over the kitchen sink. The view boasted snowy trees with shafts of magical sunlight breaching through their branches.

"God, it's beautiful here," Erin exhaled as a few soft flakes drifted around on a playful breeze.

"If I didn't know better, I'd say you got laid last night." Mari moved over to the window and peered out. A line creased between her brow as if she'd been expecting to see something. Or perhaps, *someone.*

"No. Just a much needed dose of mountains and Mari. And a solid night's sleep."

"Stop it. It'll go to my head." Mari play-swatted the air between them with a pair of greasy tongs. "No nightmares, huh?" Erin's smile grew in response. "*Perfecto. Simplemente perfecto,*" she sang as she returned to the stove.

Mari hummed as she flipped the bacon and shoved slices of bread into a tiny, dented toaster. "So..." she started.

Erin lifted an eyebrow, the setup oddly familiar. Her eyes darted to the front window and the quiet cabin across the street. Feeling benevolent, she played along. "So?"

"How's your tailbone?"

"My tail—?" Erin drew her eyes back to her friend, processing. "Oh. It's sore."

"You should ice it, maybe."

"I think sliding down half a frozen mountainside on my ass covered that step." Erin cringed at the memory. She could still feel the rocks she'd discovered poking out of the trail on her rapid descent.

Mari shrugged, pushing the toast down. It popped right back up. She *tsked.* "It wasn't half the mountain."

"It felt like it."

"We should probably get you some better shoes. Boots!" She checked the power cord, then tried to send the bread down again. Nothing.

Erin agreed on the boots, though she wasn't sure the expense for just this trip was worth it. "I could just stop being such a wreck."

"You're not a wreck," Mari sighed, leaning back and eying the sad little piece of metal. "You just need to get your rhythm back." She stabbed her finger down on the little black, springy button several times in a row. "Ugh! You didn't want toast, did you?"

"No," Erin laughed. "It's fine."

"Good. Any-way," Mari drawled, her tone scheming, "I know the perfect way to get your rhythm back."

"I hope you mean curling up in front of the fire for a much-deserved rest and relaxation."

"Not exactly...*Mira,* let's start with a little walk."

Erin deadpanned her wordless response.

"*Chica*, it's gorgeous outside! Don't you want to be out in it?"

"Sore tailbone."

"Movement will help. You say all this stuff is making you feel better, right? Why fight it?"

Crossing her arms, Erin pointed out the obviuos. "Because it's warm in here and cold out there."

"You can use my coat." Mari pressed her hands together, fingers up. "Please?"

"How about we go to that ski shop we saw, instead? Maybe they're having a sale."

Dropping her head back, but only in momentary defeat, her friend persisted. "Or..." She straightened and pretended to check the bacon, but even from Erin's position, she could tell Mari was looking out the front window. "We go for a walk around the block, you borrow my coat, and *then* we go shopping." She switched off the burner and turned back to meet Erin's narrowed eyes.

Oh, what could it hurt? "Fine. But only if you won't need it."

"Nah."

Erin looked out the kitchen window again and raised a dubious brow to the white flakes dancing on the breeze. "Okay, if you say so."

"Three words, *chica*." Mari ticked three fingers as she spoke. "Pop. Up. Circuit."

Erin envied that kind of energy. "Don't you ever slow down?" It was a rhetorical question. Mari stuck out her lower lip and Erin shook her head, chuckling. "Just so we're clear, I am *not* doing squats."

Tossing golden curls over her shoulder, Mari smirked, then danced a cha-cha to the stove. "I wouldn't dare. Get me a plate and a paper towel?"

Bacon squared away, Erin selected a chunky, ceramic mug with a moose on it in the hopes that its mountain vibes could make her coffee taste better.

It didn't.

Mari insisted on leaving the breakfast clean-up for later. Erin agreed because the cast iron was too hot to hold anyway. She shoved her arms in the loaner red, down jacket. The sleeves hung past her fingertips and the hem—which had been designed to sit at the waist—fell at mid-hip. A gray beanie finished the look.

Erin adjusted the ponytail at the back of her neck as she stared at the sheer strip of fabric on Mari's leggings, the kind strategically placed along the thigh to make men think about sex. Despite best intentions, she felt like the kid in the Christmas story, the one with the puffy snowsuit.

"Ready?" Mari chirped.

She nodded, following her friend out to the deck like a grouchy, red Michelin Man. But as soon as the outside air hit her face, Erin concluded that the look was worth it. Turning back to latch the door behind her, she appreciated the cheery blue framing on the front of the cabin and how it played with the rustic planking and knotted wood door. The place felt quaint and otherworldly, almost as if they were in the Alps, or on some mountaintop in a fairytale. Piles of pristine, frozen fluff around them only added to the effect.

"You're sure you're not cold?" she asked, feeling guilty.

"I'm good!" Mari bounced from foot to foot as they moved across the deck. "If I get too far ahead, I'll come back around, okay?"

Erin was about to ask why she needed to be there at all, but her friend had already breezed down the steps, navigating the snow to the street, looking like a walking advertisement for cold-weather activewear. She followed more slowly, focusing on the path in front of her, without slipping, which felt like a win.

A creaking echoed through the street, bringing both women's eyes to Jude's cabin. Etta came barreling out like an awkwardly, oversized puppy. She hovered at the edge of his porch, tail beating side to side, and head cocked, watching Mari do a series of knee-to-elbow lifts. Jude came out then, his back to them, locking the door, from the looks of it. A brightly colored leash swung from his arm.

Erin trudged over to where Mari had stopped for her first "circuit."

Mari beamed as Erin came up beside her. "Perfect timing."

"You couldn't possibly have planned this."

"Maybe we should invite him to join us."

"Please don't," Erin shot back, but it was too late.

Mari threw her hand overhead in a wave. "Good morning, neighbor!"

Erin stared at her. "Really?"

Looking up, Jude paused, gave a vague nod, then took a minute to pull on his gloves. Etta whined and the next thing, she was bolting down the porch steps and across the street toward them.

"Etta!" Jude shouted, and with one glove on, one in hand, he jogged after her. She ignored him, approaching Erin first and sniffing her fingers under the overlong coat sleeves.

"Etta, come here." He approached the trio and caught hold of her collar.

Erin tried smothering a smile. "She probably smells the bacon," she explained.

"That would do it," he grumbled rather unenthusiastically.

Clicking the leash into place didn't seem to deter the curious canine. She strained forward with a whine as he forced them a step back. *Is he always such a downer?* Feeling cheeky, Erin extended a palm out so the dog could get to it.

With a sigh, Jude slacked the leash and Etta lurched forward, searching for every trace of bacon to be had. Erin twisted her hand around to offer a scratch behind the ear, but the dog kept rolling her head back to lick her fingers

"You're ridiculous," he chided, eyes to his dog.

Erin giggled. "She's sweet."

Mari came forward, greeting Etta with a rub on the back. "Hey, girl! Are you going for a walk?"

With a puppy-like attention space, the dog nosed a new set of hands, her tail thumping loudly against her owner's leg.

Mari looked up at Jude. "This road makes a circle, right?" Earnest as the question sounded, Erin suspected she was up to something.

His gaze dip down to the sheer strips of of fabric on her leggings. "It does," he affirmed, bringing his eyes back up. "But it's only about a mile."

"Perfect! I promised Erin an easy walk today." She leaned in as if she had a secret. "She broke her tailbone yesterday on a hike up the mountain."

Erin shrunk in her coat.

Jude's brow rose, and he reigned Etta back in on a tighter leash. "You broke your tailbone?" To his credit, he sounded genuinely alarmed.

"No," she rushed out, shooting a contemptuous look at Mari. "I just slipped. It's fine."

"On that mountain?" He tipped his head to the trailhead that started at the end of the street and she shrugged. "You hiked up *that* mountain?"

A satisfied smile curved Mari's lips. "We did. Five miles."

His gaze swung between the two of them, then lingered on Erin. She wasn't sure what he expected to find.

Then, his eyes dropped to her sneakers. "Those are terrible shoes for the snow."

Indignation roared in response. "They're all I have!" She shifted her weight between feet, wishing he'd take his dog and be on his way. He didn't. He just looked at her with an unreadable expression for an awkwardly long moment.

That is, until Mari broke the uncomfortable silence. "So...Are you walking the loop too?" The scheme-y grin was impossible to miss.

Erin's eyes grew wide, mouthing a silent threat, which her friend ignored.

He sighed. "Usually let Etta pick."

She suspected that sigh came from the knowledge that this had now become a group thing. Erin held back her own sigh. At least they had that in common.

Springing up from a squat, Mari announced, "Okay, I'm ready!" Then shuffled over to whisper, "You can thank me later."

Erin balked as she took off as a jog. The brightly colored leash threaded through Jude's loose grip and danced along the white road as Etta bolted after her.

"Jesus," he grunted.

Erin glanced between her new walking buddy and the two fleeting figures, feeling outright betrayed. "Shouldn't you...aren't you going to chase after her?"

His lack of response irked her. She started moving, slow and stiff, as she worked to avoid slippery spots. She could feel yesterday's escapades in her hips, knees, ankles and especially in her butt bone, but now that she had an audience, she felt driven to prove herself unhindered.

Heavy boots crunched in the snow a few steps behind her.

Etta came loping back to them, tail swinging vigorously, and tongue hanging out the side of her open mouth. It had to be the angle, but it looked like she had a big ol' grin on her hairy face. Erin smiled as she blew by and looped around Jude like a herding dog.

He bent down and muttered something as she came to heel. And when he took off the leash, Etta practically vibrated with excitement, her tail whipping a snow angle behind her. "Go on," he granted.

She thundered off again, up ahead to where Mari had stopped to do jumping jacks and standing crunches. The sheer exuberance made Erin laugh. *Maybe that's what I need. A dog.*

"Your friend is very...energetic." Jude's words took her by surprise, his sudden proximity more so.

She looked up to see him next to her, staring thoughtfully ahead. Oh, who was she kidding? He was checking out Mari.

"Yes, she is. She's a fitness trainer. She can't sit still. Ever."

"I see that."

Was that a smile tipping the corner of his mouth? Erin pushed down the envy. *He's not even my type.* Turning her head to hide a frown, she tried not to feel so average. It should've made it less awkward, knowing Jude wasn't paying her any attention.

"Jude!"

Erin turned to see a woman waving as she walked from a cabin to her car. Two boys trailed along behind her with their heads down in handheld gaming devices.

"Pauline," he greeted from Erin's side.

Pauline was very pretty. And when she looked up the street to where Mari threw a stick, her smile just amplified that beauty. "Etta has a new friend?" she asked.

Jude nodded. "Guess so."

One of the boys tried to open the car door. "Mom!" he called out rudely, "It's locked!"

Pauline turned to address her son with sharp eyes, but even as she did, she hit the key fob. "Gotta go! I'll call you later!" She gave another wave, then climbed into her outback.

Jude's gaze lingered on the car as it backed out of the driveway disappeared past the bend at the end of the street. Feeling very much an awkward third wheel again, Erin dug her hands deep in her coat pockets and started walking again, faster and less cautiously than before. Her muscles protested but the discomfort seemed to fit her mood. The rhythmic boot-falls crunched behind her again.

The traitorous two rounded to the left and disappeared behind the trees. Increasing her pace, Erin eased the zipper down, now too warm in the heavy jacket. She tried so hard not to care, not to jump to conclusions.

So what if Mari has a fling? I have to work anyway. It's better this way. She won't be around to give me a bad—

Foot met slick surface and she fell back, landing butt, then back and then head, all in rapid succession. The last gave an unnerving crack against the frozen asphalt. She lay there, blinking at the cloudless sky, dazed, winded and momentarily paralyzed.

Jude appeared over her seconds later. "Are you okay?"

His breath materialized in short bursts above her, quick and heavy. She blinked again, unsure how to answer. As the shock wore off, things started trickling into her brain, mostly mortification, but also sharp, physical pain. It made his face look wavy.

"Erin," Jude called, his tone more urgent. She forced her focus to his pinched brow and taut face.

"I'm...I'm okay."

"You sure? Does your back hurt?"

"Uh..."

"Can you move your fingers and toes?"

Erin didn't understand his question, but she held up her hands, wiggling fingers for him to see. It seemed to ease the tightness in his features.

"Come on, let's get you up."

He reached out and grabbed her upper arm with one hand, supporting her back as she sat. She felt puny as the world spun and tilted.

Jude squatted down to her level. "Headache?"

It took her a moment to process. She nodded.

"Pain anywhere?"

A solid yes, but she desperately tried to save face. She shrugged, the motion releasing a heavy throb across her entire skull. It made her more dizzy. What she wanted most was to go back to the cabin for a good cry, and then a nap. She leaned forward, tucking knees under herself to get up.

"Whoa, hold on. Give it a minute," he insisted, placing a gentle hand on her shoulder and pressing her back down. The nerves where he touched her seemed suddenly hyper-sensitive.

"I'm fine."

"Erin, sit down." Despite the pain, her name on his lips did something funny to her stomach. "Look at me."

Settling back onto the frozen ground, she looked up. So used to the hostility and irritation, his expression startled her. She wondered if maybe her head was bleeding or something because he looked genuinely worried.

He pulled off his glove and lifted his hand in front of her face. "Follow my hand with just your eyes, okay?"

"Are you an EMT?"

"No."

She followed his hand to the left. "Firefighter?"

"No." He brought his hand to the right and her eyes followed.

"Nurse?"

He moved his finger to his nose and she couldn't help looking at him instead. He didn't seem to notice, or if he did, he didn't react. Maybe rough and rugged was her type.

"Uncle's a retired firefighter." His lips pressed into a line. "Your pupils are dilated."

"What's that mean?"

"Could be a number of things. Could be a concussion."

"A concussion?" she uttered. "In that case, I'll just go back to the cabin." *Or home...*A frozen behind and cold, soggy sneakers were enough to cancel this trip. But a concussion?

As she pushed up from the ground, she noticed Jude's frown deepen.

"You sure you're ready to get up?"

"Mmmhmm," she lied, stifling a groan.

"Okay..."

He shoved his glove in a pocket, and moved in close, sliding hands below her underarms and lifting. The sudden closeness threw her. She lost her footing, arms flying out to grab something—anything. Strong hands tightened around her ribs, pulling her firmly against his body as her fingers gripped the breast of his jacket.

"Sorry," she blurted, trying to straighten, despite the spinning.

A whiff of campfire and soap hit her nose. Her chest stuttered and the dizziness grew more intense. "Sorry," she said again, taking an automatic step back.

He moved with her, his grip still firm. "You dizzy?"

"I'm okay. I'm fine." She squinted. The bright snow sent a sharp stab straight through the top of her skull.

"You don't look fine."

She couldn't think straight. His proximity wasn't helping. Needing space, she pushed gently at his solid chest. *Very solid.*

He didn't budge. "I think we should probably get you back to the cabin."

We?

Erin pushed again at his chest as a chill swept over her. She swore she heard him grunt in protest, but he moved back, his hands sliding out from under her. Then, she forgot how to breathe as his fingers found the zipper pull and closed up her jacket.

He met her eye. "Better?"

Heart racing, brain faltering, she took a tentative step forward.

Jude hovered in close, shifting to the side and pressing a palm to the small of her back. "More ice here," he indicated, navigating them around a perilous patch.

She could hardly hear over the thud of her heart and the thumping in her head. The gentle touch at her back over-rode the pain in a way she couldn't understand. Still, she took it slow and Jude followed Erin's pace. Up ahead, Mari and Etta had stopped for a circuit break.

Jude slowed. "Need to stop a minute?"

She shook her head. *Mistake.* "No."

"It's better not to push it."

"I'd rather just keep going," she replied tersely. He let it drop.

Pushing herself forward, Erin focused on the end goal. *Cabin, cry, nap.* She could tell herself it was because of the pain, but in reality, intimidating or not, Jude *was* hot, and at that moment he stood unforgivably close. And she was only human.

Mari had just tossed a branch out for Etta when she noticed their approach."What's wrong?" she asked, jogging over to meet them. Her eyes shifted between the pair, then rested on Erin. Etta came up from behind her with her stick.

"Your girl here took a fall. Says she's fine but..." he shrugged.

"Oh my God, *chica.* Should I take her to the ER?"

"I'm fine Mari. I just want to go back to the cabin."

"Okay." She nodded. "Yeah. Okay. Of course." She looked to Jude, no charm or flirt, just honest worry. "You mind walking the rest of the way with us?"

"Yeah. No problem."

They finished the loop together in silence except for the occasional, "good girl," when Etta returned a stick. Erin kept her gaze on the road in front of her, eyes heavy from the pressure in her head. A new mantra rolled in her mind, *Cabin, Motrin, Nap.*

Jude helped Erin to the deck of the rental. Etta loped over to her own porch and flopped lazily on the stoop to wait, tail less animated, but still thwacking against the snow dusted doorstep.

"Thanks for your help," Mari said, typing in the door code.

"You feeling sick?"

Erin looked up, realizing Jude's question was for her. "No."

He studied her face. "Dizzy? Uncoordinated?"

If she said yes, would he insist they take her to the hospital? The tears stung the backs of her eyes. She'd gotten to the point where it was either laugh or cry. "How bad is a concussion anyway? I mean, will I wake up forgetting who I am? Because that might be okay." Joking aside, forgetting Victor would't be the worst thing to happen. And maybe this whole charade. And Jude's hand at her back.

He stared, brow sinking. "That's not how it works."

She looked down, sullen. *Crying it is.*

His jaw ticked, then his gaze cut to Mari. "Keep an eye on her. If she seems off balance, has a seizure, or something, take her to the ER."

Mari nodded, her mouth tight and face grim.

Erin dislodged herself from Jude's arm and stepped past his reach. It brought his attention back to her. "I'm sure I'm fine," she insisted.

"Right. Well, you need anything..." he started to offer, then paused. Closing his eyes, with an almost imperceptible head shake, he finished, "...you know where I am."

Unsure how to take the reluctant offer, Erin stuck with a simple, "Thanks."

He nodded once, then pivoted sharply and strode back to his cabin where Etta waited. She popped up at his approach and squeezed herself through to door as soon as he'd gotten it open. Jude hesitated, but only a moment, before following her in and swinging the door shut behind him. Erin tried not to read into it, tried not to take it personally, but how else should she interpret his actions?

Mari called her back to reality. "You coming in?"

"Yeah."

Erin sighed, defeated, and vowed to make an extra effort to avoid him in the future.

Then she beelined it to the bathroom to find some Motrin.

Chapter Six

Best Laid Plans

Erin

"Don't hate me," Mari pleaded.

"I don't hate you. Things come up. I get it."

"You sure you're feeling okay?"

"Yes," Erin answered for the fifth time. "Stop asking that. I'm fine."

Mari eyed her *again*. "Okay. Get your stupid work stuff done before I come back, got it?"

"I'll try." Erin's eyes skimmed over the bags by the door. "You really want to drive all the way back?"

"Of course! It's only two days of PT sessions. The rest of the week is clear, like it was supposed to be," Mari scolded, raising a brow.

Erin brushed it off, looking around the cabin. It felt awfully big for just one person. Her eyes paused on the wine and bottle of tequila neatly lining the back counter. "I guess you better," she warned, tilting her head towards the kitchen. "I can't drink all of that by myself."

"Oh, I'm sure you'd manage." Mari winked. "You know I wouldn't ditch you if it wasn't important, right?"

Erin didn't feel like going home, but staying on her own left her uneasy too. "Maybe I should just go, too."

"No! ¡*Mamacita!*" Mari crowded her, putting hands on her shoulders. "*No.* You need this. Even if you are going to be lame and work." Erin opened her mouth to protest but Mari cut her off. "You told me yourself, you feel better here. Soak it up! Get some sleep! Enjoy the views!"

Erin huffed. "Why do you always have to be so..."

"Smart? Caring? Thoughtful?"

"Right," Erin inserted.

Mari grinned. "Close enough. *Mira,* you have my car. Go do something fun. Go skiing or something."

"Skiing?" Erin laughed. "Mari, I've fallen twice on my own feet in two days. I don't think strapping those feet into skis is a good idea." Erin paused then added, "I don't know, the more I think about it, the more I think I should just go back too. How are you so sure you'll have a ride back up?"

"Shauna will take any excuse for a trip," Mari assured her, and as if sensing her misgivings, pressed with, "You should stay. You look better than I've seen you in a long time."

Erin nodded but her heart wasn't in it. They'd already talked about it and slept on it. Mari had argued with her for over an hour to stay at the cabin and continue her vacation. And though she didn't voice this, having the car meant, if she wanted to, she could come home at any time.

Mari dropped her hands to check her phone.

Erin sauntered over to the couch, glanced out the window, then flopped down into the red cushions and stared at the ceiling. "When is Shauna coming?"

"Eleven," Mari replied, nose in her phone. "She says she left the Chalet on time."

Erin sat up. "Are you sure you're comfortable with me driving your car?"

Mari looked at her. "Yeah. Why?"

"It's just, I've never driven in snow before."

Her friend swatted a hand in the air as she strode to the kitchen. "You'll be fine. They plow. If it's really bad, just stay in the cabin."

She nodded again at Mari's sound advice. The woman had an answer for everything. But even with assurances, there was something eating at her. She'd felt it when she went to bed and it weighed heavier on her now.

"You know how back at the pub," Erin started as Mari filled a water bottle at the sink, "you said my dream was trying to tell me something? Like intuition?" Mari craned her head around to look at her. "I think I'm having that again."

"What? I thought you said you didn't have the dream last night." She turned off the tap.

"I didn't," Erin reassured her. "It's something else. I don't know. Something feels...off. I don't think I should stay."

Mari screwed the cap on her bottle, then, coming back into the living area, she cocked her head and smiled. "Are you afraid without me here you're going to lose all control and ravage the hot neighbor?"

"What? No!"

"Because that's okay, you know," Mari whispered with a wink, "Ravage away."

"No. Mari. No." Erin flopped back into the couch with a sigh. "Besides, I'm pretty certain he's into *you*."

"If you say so," she chuckled, shoving her bottle into an already stuffed tote.

At a few minutes past eleven, a shiny black Escalade pulled up in front of the rental. With a beep, and motor still running, the very definition of 'snow bunny' hopped out: white coat, white pants, white boots, platinum hair. And cute enough to pull all of it off.

"Shauna!" Mari squeaked, rushing out the front door.

Erin peeled herself off the couch and followed as far as the threshold.

They met at the street, giving air kisses, then small talked their way back to the cabin. The white pompoms on Shauna's fur lined boots bounced with her perky gait. Wrapping arms around herself, Erin ducked back inside to grab the throw from the couch. She draped it over her shoulders as they were coming in.

"And this is Erin," Mari introduced.

Erin smiled at the infamous Shauna. "Hello. It's nice to finally meet you." She held a hand out from under the blanket.

Scoffing, Shauna stepped forward and hugged her. "Mari has told me so much about you!"

Surprised, Erin placed an arm around a pristine, puffy parka, and gave it a pat, wishing she'd changed out of her pajamas. *Is she always this friendly or did I miss something?*

"One of these days, you'll have to come up to the Chalet!"

"Yay!" Mari squealed. "Girls weekend!"

"Oh. Okay. Thank you." Stepping back, Erin readjusted the blanket as Mari hefted bags over her shoulders. "Do you need help?" She rushed forward, pulling the door open wide and watching her friend navigate with the awkward load.

"Girl, you aren't even wearing shoes."

Erin looked down at her feet. "Oh."

Shauna grabbed the last bag and followed onto the deck.

Feeling useless, Erin called after them, "Just let me get some sh—"

"Stay!" Mari interrupted, clunking down the steps. "And Erin," she paused at the bottom and met her eye, "If you need anything…"

Her friend winked, then marched across the snow to the waiting Escalade. Erin sighed. That's what Jude had said. Mari's innuendos were in jest, but as she watched them load up, she couldn't help thinking, *I'm just a Plain Jane in a sea of Marilyns.*

Shauna shot her a departing smile and a wave as she rounded to the drivers side.

Erin waved back. "Bye."

"Oh! Heeey!" Mari shouted, her eyes directed across the street.

Shauna turned to look. "Hi neighbor!"

Erin's gut clenched, but she followed suit anyway. Jude stood on his porch with another, older guy. Both men seemed to have paused their conversation to stare at the farewell party. Jude nodded at the car, but, Erin noted, he didn't look over at her. At all. *Plain Jane.* She wrapped the blanket tighter around herself to cover her pajamas—not that it mattered—and focused her attention on the Escalade.

"I'll call you, *chica*," Mari hollered over her shoulder as she climbed in the passenger seat.

"You better," Erin returned, trying for a convincing smile.

Mari gave her a thumbs up, blew her a kiss, then swung her door shut. Shauna pulled out onto the road. And like a glutton for punishment, Erin's eyes meandered back across the street. She watched Jude's gaze follow the SUV until it disappeared around the bend.

The older man caught her staring and said something. That was when Jude finally looked over. She stiffened, gave a non-committal wave, then turned and disappeared into the cabin, feeling like idiot.

It was Monday. Erin had to find internet connection. The library was closed, as was the little mom and pop café by the overpriced grocery mart, so she trucked it to a Starbucks in a busy shopping area downtown. The drive over nearly gave her a panic attack, but she made it without skidding off the road.

She picked a table tucked in the back corner, then, because of the noise, covered one ear to hear her boss as she phoned in. "Hi Paul, it's Erin."

"Guess you're having fun up there," came his brusque greeting.

"Sorry, I know I was supposed to check in sooner. The cabin I'm staying at doesn't have any internet or cell service," she explained. "It look me a while to hunt down a place with free WIFI."

"Are you in one of those Deliverance cabins?" Concern pushed past his discontent.

"No. It's in a neighborhood. A pretty nice one, actually. It's just, the owners haven't gotten everything set up."

"Ah. Well, lucky for both of us, there isn't much for you today. Bryce is still finishing his account. I gave him until end-of-day today. Any chance you can give me a few extra early hours tomorrow? I want you to check it over before we send it off to the client."

Erin took a deep breath. It wasn't her job to check her co-workers accounts. That duty fell under management. Yet it had become a regular thing over the past year.

"Are you going to promote me and give me a pay raise?" she snarked, then stilled, horrified that she'd let that comment slip.

Never, not ever, had she spoken like that to Paul before. *What is wrong with me?* It was one thing to draw the line with Victor. But this was her boss! An agonizing minute of silence stretched between the lines. "I'm sorry Paul. That was out of line. I'd be happy to—"

"You want a promotion, huh?"

Flustered, she tried again. "What I meant was—"

"Didn't think you were interested. In management. But if you are..." he seemed to be thinking out loud.

"I didn't mean to put you on the spot. I just meant, with all this accounts checking, it's falling outside my job description. That's all. But I'll do whatever you need. Sorry. This mountain air must be getting to me or something," she finished lamely.

"Or something," he repeated, his tone amused. Erin felt only slight relief. "Listen, can you take a look at *BrandBar* and check in with Bryce and Donna today. Then, be available first thing tomorrow morning."

"Sure. I can do that." Her voice sounded perky but she frowned. How could she make those few tasks last until five-o-clock? With Mari gone, Erin wasn't looking for a day off. If fact, she'd counted on being busy.

"Great. And when you get back in town, maybe we can talk about a promotion."

"Oh. Okay. Thanks Paul. But really—"

"Enjoy the snow."

He hung up first and Erin sat, staring unseeing at her laptop screen. Had she heard him right? A promotion? With a pay raise? Did she actually want the extra responsibility? *Some extra income would be nice.* Erin shook it off and tucked her phone away. No reason to go through "what-ifs" for now.

Scanning emails, she sipped at her latte—a double shot —so much better than the muck she'd been making at the cabin. A real cup of coffee would have been her first pick, but this was the next best thing.

People in partial ski gear came through to order hot drinks. A group of what looked like ski instructors sat at a large table trying to outdo one another with the most extreme slope story. Their laughter echoed in the cavernous cafe and mixed with with hiss of the milk steamer. It took a lot of bring her focus back to her laptop screen.

Erin pulled up the *BrandBar* report for review—a smaller account which she completed quickly. She checked in with the her team, answered a few questions, and responded to emails. Then she reviewed a side account as a favor.

She checked the clock in the corner of her screen. All that had only taken her an hour and a half. *Darn-it.* Letting out a deflated hiss, she frowned. *What to do now?*

Staring out the floor to ceiling windows at the front of the cafe, she decided to just pack up and head back to the rental. On her way out, she held the door for a guy in a ski bib and a bushy beard, who juggled six beverages in one of those cardboard trays. *What am I even doing here? I don't ski.*

"Thanks," he muttered as he passed.

She wrestled with just going home, but on the arctic walk back to the car, Erin decided she'd just make the most of it.

Starting with a nice, long, hot bath back at the cabin. Firing up the engine, a real smile snuck in. She turned the heat up to full blast and pointed all the vents in her direction.

"Live a little."

"That was fast," Mari teased. Erin adjusted her cell, tucking it under her beanie so her ears would stay covered. "It's been what, two hours since we left? You miss me already?"

"Well, yes. Always. But that's not why I'm calling," Erin replied. A shiver traveled from head to foot.

"What's up?"

"The water isn't getting hot."

"What water?"

"Any water. All the water." She shuffled side to side, then marched around in the snow, trying to stay warm.

"Did you check the pilot light?"

Erin didn't reply. She knew *of* pilot lights, but she didn't know what one looked like, let alone what to do with it. A benefit and the curse of renting apartments.

Mari chuckled. "Hold on." She had a quick, muffled conversation on the other end. "Okay, back. Shauna says don't worry about it, she'll call her guy."

"I c-can probably figure it out," Erin chattered. "Maybe someone can walk me through it?" She hadn't meant to make a big deal of this. The last thing she wanted was to be a nuisance.

"Don't worry about it," Mari repeated. "Shauna says the water heater is older than dirt. She's got a guy on call for cabin stuff. She's on the phone with him now."

Erin sighed, drawing an arch in the snow with her toe. "Okay, tell her I say thanks."

"Sure. Hey *chica*, what are you wearing?"

Erin paused at the weird question. "The only thing you packed. A dinky tank, leggings, and my fleece. Why? Can you hear me freezing through the phone?"

"No reason. Love you! Call me later!"

"Back at you."

Erin hung up, shoved her hand—phone and all—into her pocket and high-tailed it back down the icy street to the cabin. She'd trekked a good few blocks down to get a decent signal. Thankfully the furnace had been running all morning so when she got inside, a welcoming blaze of heat melted her frozen limbs.

Hot bath...hot bath, she reminded herself. That's what she had to look forward to.

Erin left her shoes by the door and beelined it to the kitchen to start some tea. While waiting for it to boil, she sifted fingers through her messy hair then wandered to the bathroom to find a hair tie.

She thought she heard a knock and stuck her head out the bathroom door. *Already?* She listened. When she heard it again, she snagged her ponytail, then hustled to the front to answer it. *Shauna must pay really well.* Elastic tie between her teeth and hair held back in a fist, she yanked the door open.

"Sorry I—Oh." Her tie fell to the ground. She stooped to pick it up. "What are you...uh. Sorry, I was expecting someone else."

Jude stood at the door, tall and silent. And too darn sexy, in her humble opinion. As she rose, Erin noticed he held a small, red tool box.

"Oh...you're the...you're here about the—"

"Water heater," he finished.

She nodded. "Right. Of course you are."

Avoiding his eye, Erin stepped back, using the elastic tie around her fistful of hair. This all felt oddly like the setup for a porn film. Only, he wouldn't be staring at her with cold, grey eyes. No, he'd have her pushed up against the wall, in the throes of ecstasy, moaning his name, as the pull of raw, sexual desire encased them both. Key word, *both*. Unfortunately, this porn was missing its star female. Worse, now that image had burned into her brain.

She cleared her throat. "Sorry, come in."

He kicked the snow off his boots on the door frame before he entered. When he did, he walked straight to the back, no hello, no smile, no nothing. Gritting her teeth, Erin closed the door.

He stopped just past the kitchen, in the little hallway that led to her bedroom. She wandered over to watch, but *only* because she was determine to learn what to do next time.

He opened a narrow door on the wall.

"That's the water heater?" she asked.

"Yup."

Jude squatted, craning his head to the side to look under a metal shield near the bottom. He 'tsked,' then pressed a red button to the right of the shield and held it. It click several times, then Erin heard a *whoosh*. Jude stood and stepped back.

She stared at him. "That's it?" He nodded but he didn't look at her. "That's the pilot light? All I had to do was press a button?"

"Yup."

Now she felt really stupid. "Someone could have walked me through that," she grumbled under her breath.

Jude looked at her then, his eyes narrow.

"Sorry, nothing. Just...I didn't realize it was that easy to fix." A part of her wondered if Mari'd shut the thing off before leaving for this very set-up. "Do I have to do anything to *keep* it on?"

"Nope. Should stay lit."

"And the water will be hot?"

"Give the tank time to heat up. Then test it."

The tea kettle whistled. Erin rushed over and turned it off. "How long does it take to heat the tank?"

Jude glanced at her, then studied the tank. "This size? About thirty minutes."

"And if it goes out again, I can just keep using the button, right?"

He looked back at her a long moment before answering. "I'll stay a minute, make sure the pilot stays lit."

"Oh. Okay. Do you want some tea?"

"No."

She tried to ignore the stiff line in his body and how his mouth tipped down in the corners. Whatever kindness he'd shown the day before had clearly been a fluke and very likely for Mari's benefit.

Erin pulled a mug down for herself. She avoided his gaze by staying busy, making each step a laborious task. But the air grew unbearably thick and in uncomfortable situations, she tended to ramble. "Can I ask you something?"

He grunted, and she glanced at him. Hands on hips, his laser focus could have burned a hole straight through the water heater.

Just when I thought it couldn't get more awkward. She cleared her throat. "I've only ever rented an apartment. So I've never had to...uh, do any kind of house maintenance...stuff.

Are all pilot lights like this? I mean, just a button? Because I always thought there was more to it and my mom had this story once about my dad's eyebrows and—" He looked over at her and she bit her lower lip to stop talking.

"No."

Erin nodded. "Oh." *That's all? No?* Tipping eyes down to her mug, she sipped at her tea, deciding maybe no talking was better.

"This is an electric start," he added after a minute of awkward silence. "You just press and hold till it lights. But a gas valve, you have to do manually."

"Ah," Erin responded, pretending to know what that meant.

"Gotta twist the valve to turn the gas on. Then light it with a match or a lighter."

"Mm." *Am I that transparent?* She looked down past her tea to her chunky, wool socks. A strand of hair slipped out of her ponytail and floated down next to her face.

"Sometimes the safety doesn't work and you have to shut off the gas first—let it air out—otherwise you get a big flame. Probably what happened with your dad."

"Oh. Well, now I know," she muttered, tucking the strand behind her ear. "I won't have to call you next time."

"It's no problem."

Erin looked up. His arms were crossed now and his stance wide. She wondered how long he planned to stand there.

As if sensing her impatience, Jude turned back to the water heater and stooped to check the pilot. "Still going strong." When he stood again, with toolbox in hand, he didn't motor to the door like she expected. "How's your head?"

"What?" The shift from impatient to social caught her off guard. "My head? Oh. It's fine."

"That's what you said yesterday."

"It's much better. Thank you," she amended. He nodded but kept eyes on her as if conducting a lying test. She forced a smile. "Nothing left but a sore spot. And that doesn't hurt unless I touch it." To prove her point, she touched it, then grimaced.

His expression relaxed for a moment and maybe she'd just imagined the corner of his mouth tip up, but even so, Erin forgot all about her list of flaws. Her breath got stuck somewhere on the way past her chest.

"Give it another twenty to twenty-five minutes then try it out," he uttered, turning and closing the water heater cabinet. "If you don't get hot water, come get me." Jude then made his way unceremoniously back to the front door, like she'd expected him to do before.

Erin following a few steps behind. "Um, Jude?"

He paused in the entryway, turning. She tucked the loose strand behind her ear again, eyes fixed straight ahead which was approximately his chest level. She hesitated and he waited without a word.

"Can you give me the invoice?"

His brow furrowed. "Invoice?"

"Yes. I'd like to pay whatever the fee was for you to come over, especially because it was such a stupidly simple fix and its just me which hardly seems worth all the trouble. Shauna seems nice but I don't want to be a nuisance." It all came out in one long rapid succession of words.

Jude stared at her for a moment, then his gaze moved over her head and around the cabin. "Your friend left?"

"Mari?" Erin's heart sank a little, just like her shoulders. "She, um, she had to get back to the city for work." Instead of seeing what would undoubtably be disappointment on his face, Erin worked at picking pieces of non-existent fuzz off her sleeve. "She has a bunch of rehabilitation patients. Timing is everything with some of that," she explained, only adding to Mari's glowing reputation.

She crossed her arms to stop fidgeting but the aimless movement just traveled down her body and into her feet. She stepped back and tried leaning her butt into the edge of the dining table but the pain in her tailbone had her squirming even more. She leaned back to support herself on her hands, shoving work papers everywhere. And Jude saw all of it. She hadn't felt so awkward in her own skin since middle school.

He took a step back into the cabin and a sudden, somewhat unwelcome image overtook her—her legs wrapped around his hips as he pressed her into the table. Papers flying everywhere. The thumping of wood against wood as the table and chairs collided with their rhythm. She forced a swallow and shamefully let her eyes drop just enough to glimpse below his waistband. Maybe she should have just stuck with a cold shower.

"How much for starting the pilot?" she asked, her voice a little rough. She turned to rearrange her work stuffs and hide her flaming cheeks.

"Don't worry about it."

"Look, I'm sure you have some kind of deal worked out with Shauna," she set her neat stack back on the table, "but I'd really like to settle this here for today." She forced herself to turn back, looking him right in the eye.

"No charge."

"I mean it," she insisted.

"No charge. Like you said, 'stupid simple.'"

Erin opened her mouth, then shut it. Did he think she was stupid? Or simple? "Fine," she forced out. "But your time...you had to come over here and—"

"Erin." The way her name rolled off his tongue...it wasn't fair. "No charge."

While she stood there, heart racing, he opened the door and let himself out. "If the water doesn't get hot, come get me."

She should have uttered a "thank you," but her mouth just wouldn't cooperate. Hot water, cold water, it didn't matter. She needed to stay away from him.

Chapter Seven

Distractions

Jude

As soon as the door clicked shut behind him, he breathed easier. Had he imagined it? Because the way she looked at him felt almost carnal. It should have offended him, or reminded him he needed to keep his distance, but it didn't. Seeing her like that, up against the table...well, he could think of a few things that didn't involve eating food. What the hell was his problem? Who was this girl?

He couldn't. He shouldn't. But it'd been a while since he'd been with anyone. All the pent up frustration conveniently clouded his memory and the bullshit he'd been dealt. He knew there were reasons there somewhere. He knew he shouldn't make an exception, especially this time. Because Erin...well, she was just the type to get under his skin.

Problem was, he wanted to get under her skin too—like an itch he couldn't shake off.

And damnit, he actually liked her—cute and funny, even when she didn't mean to be. She seemed like the kind who cared about other people. And she had no idea how it chipped away at his resolve. He needed it to stop, and keeping his distance was the only way he knew how.

Easy enough, he figured, as long as nothing else came up at the cabin.

Jude frowned at the street. She'd been uneasy around him. Perhaps she hadn't wanted him there. And maybe that was the draw—a refreshing change from flirting. Except, when she'd bitten her lip...

Damn. He shook his head. *I bet she tastes good.* He clenched his jaw, pushing the thought away. *Get it together.*

He could feel something in him ticking, something almost foreign, that sense of purpose he'd lost years ago. It felt stronger when with her, and fuck him, he liked it. And now that it had subsided, he wanted it back.

He strode back to his cabin, torn between hoping he wouldn't see her again and wishing for one more excuse to get close to her. That strand of loose hair had just about driven him crazy. He wanted to touch it, brush it back, twist it around his finger.

He was too idle. He needed to be busy.

Jude had slated thirty minutes for the water heater and it took five. He'd figured on the pilot light—that unit was older than dirt—assuming it wasn't just a ploy to get him in the cabin, which he'd also suspected. Hence why he'd acted like a dick.

He rubbed a hand over his face. He fully expected the pilot to go out again but she wouldn't call him for it. She wasn't stupid. But he was. Stupid and masochistic.

He shouldn't have asked about her head. He should have just left. When she said it still felt sore, he'd wanted to see it, check her, touch her.

She kept brushing him off, acting tough. Same as the day before. Almost to the point of overcompensating. *Why? Does it have to do with the person she'd hoped to forget? A man?* He stormed across the street, fists clenched. Then grumbled his way up the steps to his cabin. *Shut it down and get busy.* He had twenty five minutes to kill.

Opening the door, he urged Etta back into the house with a knee. Without realizing it, his eyes stole a quick glance back. Something had made her blush and he wanted to know what. Worse, he wanted to make her do it again.

Jude grabbed a quick lunch before heading over to Pauline's place, his next job. He topped off Etta's water before he left.

"Be back, girl," he called as he headed out.

He shoved his hands in his pockets as he strode down to the street. Pauline's husband had a good set of tools so he didn't bother bringing his own. If he needed anything, they'd make it available.

The lights were on in Erin's cabin but he didn't see her in the front as he walked by. He figured she'd have her hot water by now. Was she taking a shower? The thought of her naked, wet body made him falter. Clearing his throat, he picked up his pace, and adjusted himself. *What shitty timing.*

He gave himself a moment before wrapping on the door.

Pauline greeted him with a smile. "Hi Jude." She opened the door wide and beckoned him in.

She was a good looking woman in her forties with smooth skin and straight, shiny black hair. Jude liked the smile lines by her eyes and the fact that her place always smelled like baked goods.

Her family came up to their second home several times a year. Her boys were always wreaking havoc and she'd come to rely on Jude when things got out of hand. From holes in the wall to electrical shorts...she'd called him. Today it was a broken window.

"Hi Pauline." He followed her in through the kitchen. The house seemed oddly quiet and he commented on that.

"Oh, Craig took the boys snowboarding."

Jude smiled. As she'd told him before, she liked the snow but preferred to wait at the bottom of the slopes and watch. Or stay home and bake.

As they moved through the living room. Jude saw the open romance novel on the sofa table. *Baking or reading*, he amended, fingers sliding over the dust jacket. Pauline's self proclaimed guilty pleasure was romance books.

"You still into this crap?" He picked it up and inspected the cover. It looked like a cowboy romance. Shaking his head, he set it back down next to the a half empty cup of tea.

"And loving it! What's your deal with those anyways? It's just a book."

"Says you. Tell other women that," he grumbled, regretful for having started the conversation.

She'd stopped and studied him.

"You gonna show me the window?" He didn't mean for it to come out so brusque.

"From what I recall," she started in her mom tone, crossing her arms, "you had no qualms inviting all those women over. And you seemed pretty contented in playing out all those fantasies."

Jude straightened. He hand't realized Pauline paid any attention to that. They hadn't officially met until a year after he'd moved in. She raised her brow as if daring him to challenge her. Next came the knowing head tilt-total mom move.

"Yeah, well, turns out there's a lot of different ways to be used," he muttered.

"You saying you had a change of heart? Because those women didn't seem to mind."

"I wasn't talking about the women. You gonna show me the window?"

"You should get that worked out, you know." Her voice came at him softly but the words bit. Jude stared down at the reading material with disdain. "It's just a book."

"Window?"

"Okay, have it your way."

Pauline led him back to a large, rectangular window that looked out to the rear of the property. Jude saw that they had taped cardboard over the golf-ball-sized hole, amazed the glass panel sat still intact. The projectile must have been flying pretty fast. He didn't ask.

It was an old window—one of the original aluminum single paned ones, and one of only a few left in the cabin. Good news for Pauline and her husband. He figured they'd want to replace it eventually anyway. Jude noticed a tape measure on the sill for him. He picked it up and took measurements.

He pulled a small notepad from his back pocket. "What kind of replacement do you want?" he asked, scribbling down the numbers.

"Double pane. Nothing fancy. If you could match the color to other, newer windows that would be great."

"Yeah. I can do that," he told her as he noted down her preferences. "I'll see if there's anything in stock. If not, may take a few weeks to get it. Can't do it when a storm's coming anyway."

"Oh yes, I saw the weather forecast!" she exclaimed. "Do you think this cardboard will be good enough until the window gets fixed?"

Jude looked at the patch on the window. "I'll swing by and cover it over with some plastic sheeting from the outside."

Pauline smiled. "Thanks, Jude. I appreciate it."

"Probably call in a buddy to help," he thought out loud. "It's a big window." He looked up and Pauline nodded but her eyes were studying him. "Once it's in, going to need to paint a new frame on the outside. You got any of the house color left anywhere?"

"I should still have some in the garage. I'll leave it out for you before we head back home. You just let me know the damage."

"You got it. Anything else while I'm here?" Jude asked like he always did. Pauline kept looking at him, so he waited.

"Is everything okay?" she asked finally, crossing her arms and settling into a stance that told Jude he wasn't going to get past until he gave her something satisfactory. Still, he tried evasion.

"It's all good," he gave a tip of his lip.

"You seem...distracted."

Shit, she came right out with it. "Distracted?" He felt his body tense.

"Not in a way I'm not pleased in how you do your job," she rushed to clarify. "Just...distracted."

"Maybe," he gave to her with a shrug and a frown.

Then she frowned. "You know, it's okay to have fun once in a while."

"Pauline, you're such a mother hen."

When she smiled he felt some of the tension ease. "Why, thank you Jude!" He smiled despite himself. "What's her name?"

Jude looked down to his open pad. "Who?"

"The one you were walking with yesterday."

He clipped out a sharp laugh as he flipped the pad closed and tucked it and the stubby golf pencil back into his rear pocket. Leave it to Pauline to call him out at his weakest point. *Mother Hen.* Good thing she wasn't back there in the rental or he really wouldn't hear the end of it.

"You know the boys adore you," Pauline reminded Jude, something he already knew. "And if I wasn't very happily married..." Pauline laughed.

Jude shook his head with his own short chuckle. She said things like this but he knew how devoted she was to her family.

"What I'm saying is, you're a good guy, Jude."

"Thanks." *Moving on.* "How long you here for this time?"

"We're not sure. We may head back mid-week. We should probably go before the storm hits though. Maybe sooner. It all depends on Craig's caseload. He just took on a new client."

Jude nodded. He had keys to the place so he could do the work anytime. He actually preferred the flexibility. Then he could squeeze it in between other jobs, or start it up when he needed the distraction.

Too bad this window will probably have to be special order, he thought. He could really use the distraction now.

"I'll let you know about the window," he told her. "Gonna head to the store right after this."

Pauline smiled and led him back through the house, stopping in the kitchen. "You want a muffin for the road?"

Jude eyed the cooling rack overfilled with perfectly shaped, perfectly browned muffins. "Apple cinnamon?" She nodded with a huge, knowing smile. Those were his favorite. "Yeah, I'll take one."

She ripped a paper towel and used it to collect three muffins. Jude didn't say anything. He just smiled as she set the bundle in his open palm.

"Thanks."

"Anytime, Jude."

As he headed back toward his place, he finished off the first muffin. He started on the second while hiking the steps to his front door. He didn't look at Erin's cabin as he passed this time.

He took Etta out back to do her business and ate the third muffin. Once Etta came back in, he grabbed his wallet and keys. "Need anything?"

She cocked an ear up at him.

He laughed but it was self-deprecating. "You think I need a life?" Etta just stared at him, those eyes boring straight into his soul. "Yeah. You're right. Don't answer that."

He opened the door. "I'll be back," he called, then headed out, hoping to keep himself distracted.

Chapter Eight

Smoke Signals

Erin

Erin heeled out of her cold sneakers and left them by the door, then hustled over to the thermostat. Since she'd gotten an early start, heading out in search of WIFI, she'd left it set at sixty-five from the night before. Paul had worried her into thinking she'd be scrambling to make ends meet, but without interruptions, she'd gotten through all her reviews and accounts in record time. Leaving her with another free afternoon.

She'd left the cute little mom-and-pop cafe just after lunch with a promise to the owner that she'd be back. They had good coffee, served hot, and what more could a girl ask for?

Erin's finger hovered over the temperature controls. With the rest of the day to herself, she could get a fire going and nestle in with a book. Smiling, she pulled her finger back, and sauntered to the kitchen to make some tea. *Maybe I'll read Mari's saucy paperback.* She selected a bright red mug from the cabinet and dug a Rooibos tea bag out of her stash of teas.

While she waited for the water to boil, she wandered over to the fireplace and peeked into the half barrel that held chopped wood. Pickings were pretty slim. The few small twigs and thin branches would be good for kindling and not much else. But Mari'd mentioned that Shauna had a huge pile of firewood stacked on the side of the cabin.

Erin dug out what remained in the barrel and carefully made a teepee with the sticks like she'd seen Mari do. She shoved the crumpled newspaper underneath then lit one of the long matches that sat in a canister on the mantle.

The kindling caught easily and Erin grinned triumphantly at her little flame. *My first fire.* She didn't let how pathetic that sounded spoil her moment. There was a first time for everything, even at the ripe ol' age of thirty-three.

The kettle started whistling so she stood, despite the stiff, sore joints, and shuffled to the kitchen to turn off the burner. *No more falling*, she grimaced, rubbing her lower back. Then, eager to keep her flame strong, she moved to the door, shoving feet back into sneakers.

Jacket zipped to her chin, hat over messy hair, she tossed one last backwards glance at her little flame, grinned, then set out to find some wood.

The sun hid behind voluminous, grey clouds and Erin could see her breath in front of her as she rounded the cabin. It felt ten degrees colder without the sunshine and already, the chill permeated through her fleece and stung her nose.

Just like Mari'd said there would be, Erin found the wall of cut logs stacked against the exterior side of the cabin. The top row loomed a good two feet over her head. A brown tarp meant to cover the large stack had flipped back and hung in shreds off to the side. Erin saw evidence of Bungee cords that had probably fastened the tarp to the stack at one point. Long since disintegrated, all that was left were the black plastic hooks and a spray of faded, frayed orange fibers.

Erin approached the stack, taking a tentative stretch to see how far she could reach. On her toes, she just brushed the top row with the tip of her middle finger. Stepping back on flat feet, she contemplated the pile. With the uneven ground and snow-pile, a stool wouldn't be stable, not that she'd trust herself on one anyway.

She turned, scanning the ground near the tree line at the edge of the property. Several small, wispy fronds and spindly sticks littered the untouched blanket of white. She kept looking until she found something sturdier—a thicker, solid branch about two feet long. Stomping through the soft powder, she grabbed it and re-approached the stack.

Using the end of the branch, she shifted then dislodged a log from the top. She held her hand out ready for a catch as she worked her selection to the edge. It teetered then collided with her outstretched palm, plunging straight past and into the snow.

"Ouch!" Erin shook it off and flexed her fingers, cursing herself for underestimating how heavy wood could be.

She repeated the process, this time letting the logs just fall to the ground, until she had enough pieces to more than fill the barrel inside. Picking out two medium-sized cuts, she carried them into the house and tossed them onto her steady flame. It wavered and she panicked, shoving a bunch of extra newspaper and stray sticks under the stack to give it a little more 'oomph,' just in case.

Then she went back outside to collect the rest of her bounty. It took several trips, and left her winded, but with barrel overflowing, her chest puffed with satisfaction. She'd been able to do some of this rugged mountain stuff all on her own. *Now, time for some tea.*

Smoke billowed out of the door as Erin staggered from the cabin. Her eyes stung and watered as she coughed.

"Shit," she gasped, looking back.

She took a deep breath, held it, and plunged back into the cabin to open the front windows. Grabbing her phone from the dinning table, she made it back outside just in time for another coughing fit. Feet wheeled down the steps of the deck and she jogged out to the street, eyes to her cell, preparing to call 911. Just as soon as she had a signal. And was able to breathe without coughing.

"What happened? Are you okay?"

Jude materialized beside her, still shoving his arms in his coat, his gaze volleying between her and the rental.

"I...I was just trying..." She stopped to cough. "Trying to warm up the cabin," Erin finished, panicked. She leaned forward with hands on her knees, fighting to catch her breath.

"The furnace is smoking?" he asked, sounding alarmed.

"No. No, no, no. The furnace isn't even on," she rushed out before coughing some more. "I had a fire going." She tried for a slow, deep breath but the cold air stung her raw throat, making it worse. She looked up, eyes pleading. He'd have to call 9-1-1.

For a beat, Jude stared at her in total disbelief or horror or something. Whatever his expression, it made her feel small and utterly lacking. Her stomach plummeted. She just couldn't get a win.

"Is the fire contained?" His tone felt a little patronizing and Erin balked.

She might not have been a fire expert, but she wasn't *that* stupid. It wasn't like she tired to build a fire in the middle of the living room!

"It's in the fireplace, if that's what you mean," she bit out. "At least, what's left of it."

His features relaxed, though only infinitesimally, and his gaze shifted again between her and the rental. That's when Erin realized that maybe he wasn't asking to be patronizing. He might have asked out of concern for the safety of the neighborhood. That made her feel even lower. She could've put the whole street at risk, pretending to be some kind of savvy mountain woman.

Erin looked back at the open door and watched the gray haze creep out. Jude released a heavy exhale then pushed past her. Taking the steps two at a time, he disappeared into the cabin. Erin followed and poked her head in the doorway. The smoke had dissipated some but the air still looked and felt thick.

The fire itself had gone out. Her happy little flame was dead, as was her confidence. Inching inside the doorway, she scrunched her nose at the sting and stink. Jude squatted at the fireplace, muttering an exasperated string of impolite words. He ran his hands down his face then turned and noticed her in the door way. She winced as his expression hardened.

He held up a blackened log. "Where the hell did you get this wood?"

"Out-outside," she replied. "There's a whole pile stacked against the house. I thought that was all supposed to be firewood." She shivered, a whole body quake. She hadn't thought to grab her jacket on the way out.

"It's wet. You can't burn wet wood," he said with exaggerated clarity as if he were talking to a child.

"That's all there was. How was I supposed to kn..know that?" As she said it, Erin realized how stupid that sounded. Thinking of it *now*, of course wet wood wouldn't burn.

This whole thing was a disaster. She'd be lucky if Shauna let her finish out the stay once she heard about this. Forget about ever coming back. Erin stormed over to the hook by the door and grabbed her jacket. It stank but she shoved her arms in and zipped it to her chin. Jude dropped the wet log back in the hearth and stood, shaking his head. Then he turned and seemed to survey the room. His eyes stopped on Erin.

"Open up all the windows, get a cross breeze," he told her, his voice low.

She got into motion right away, pulling open all the windows in the main living space. The cold breeze blew right through the room and through Erin's layers. She felt like a popsicle.

Jude stood at the thermostat, arms crossed and mouth in a thin line. "Something wrong with the furnace?"

"N-no."

He stared at her like he wasn't sure what to do with her.

"I just wanted to have a fire." She looked at her feet. "It's a cabin in the mountains and I...I don't have a fireplace at home." He probably didn't care. He lived here. Fires and snow where his daily grind. When he didn't say anything, she glance up to meet his penetrating stare.

"You're killing me," he breathed, looking away.

"I'm sorry," she mumbled, tucking a stray hair behind her ear. She ducked her head again. "Thanks for your help."

"Didn't do much." Jude crossed to the fireplace again, peering into the half-barrel. He dug around, shaking his head. "This is all wet."

"Yeah. Well, thank you for rushing out and for being here...."

"It's my job," he said, looking up, his eyes cool and serious. "Shauna pays me to keep an eye on her cabin."

"Right. Of course."

Somewhere under all her panic and insecurities, a small part of Erin had wondered if he'd rushed over to check on her. *So stupid*, she knew, but that's where her brain went.

"Well," she started, trying to recover some dignity, "You don't have to worry, I won't try it again."

Chances were, Jude would be escorting her off the property anyway, once Shauna caught wind of this fiasco. Hadn't Erin told Mari she'd had a bad vibe? She watched Jude nudge the wood in the hearth with the toe of his boot.

"Look, if you t-talk to Shauna...tell her I'm really sorry and I'll j-just—"

"I'm not gonna call Shauna."

"You...you're not?"

"No. This'll clear out." He shoved his hands in his pockets. His face looked pained as he let out a sharp hiss. "I'm probably going to regret this." His eyes shifted to hers. Erin furrowed her brow ready to reject whatever followed. "Got a bunch of dry wood across the street. You clean up in here and I'll chop some up for you."

"Oh." For a moment, Erin was stunned silent. "No, it's okay. You don't have t-to, I'm not—" He turned his back to her, bent and grabbed the wet logs from the hearth, and tossed them on top of the half-barrel. Then he moved to the door.

"Jude, you d-don't have to—"

"Open the rest of the windows—bedrooms, bathrooms, even upstairs," he clipped and she bit her tongue. "I'll bring the wood over in a bit."

He paused in the doorway, looking around—hesitating. She stared, shivering.

"Jesus..." he muttered. "Where's your other jacket?" Coming back into the cabin, he looked around by the door.

"W-what other jacket?"

"The one from the other day. The red one."

"Oh," Erin frowned. "That's n-not mine. That's Mari's. She took it with her."

"You don't have a warmer jacket?"

"N-no."

He exhaled, making an exasperated sound, and grabbed the back of his neck. Erin watched the muscles in his jaw flex. Then, he shrugged out of his fleece-lined flannel and held it out and open for her.

"Oh, nonono. It's okay. I'll just crank up the heater."

"Not going to work too well with all the windows open," he pointed out.

He glowered at her and judging from the harsh lines on his face, the subject was not up for debate. Erin bit her lip, then turned to thread her arms into the sleeves. His body heat lingering in the fabric and a wave of campfire and soap swarmed around her, covering the stink of smoke. She felt lightheaded and lovesick.

"Thanks."

"Be back. Open the upstairs windows," he called from halfway across the deck.

Erin closed the door.

It should have been a nice gesture—the jacket. But the offer felt begrudging. He'd clearly acted out of duty, not affection or kindness. Erin stood there wondering how he could have seemed so concerned the day she fell but so put-out now.

She tried to be grateful for his cold demeanor. The last thing she needed was a crush. It wasn't his fault. He had a job to do. She hadn't meant to make things so difficult for him. Nor did she want him feeling he had to go out of his way to cater to a renter.

Erin hiked up the stairs, going from room to room, opening what windows she could. By the time she'd finished, she'd decided to go over to Jude's and tell him not to bother with the wood. Nicely, of course. It had always been her prerogative to *kill 'em with kindness*. Then, she'd pack up and return to the city where she belonged. Mari would understand.

Chapter Nine

Saying and Doing

Jude

She'd scared the crap out of him. He didn't like that feeling.

Jude dug gloves out of the top of his tool chest and grabbed an axe from the inside of the shed before stalking back out to his chopping block. He swiped an arm over the block to clear the snow. Then he leaned the axe next to it and trudged around the left side of the house to collect some dry logs from the back.

Letting Erin into his house that night had been a mistake. Seeing her in that cute little sweater under her big honking, red jacket had been a bigger mistake. She'd just smacked her head and all he could think about were those breast pressed against him. That too, would have been a mistake.

He couldn't do nice and keep himself distant. It was either be a dick, or get caught up. So he'd be a dick and she would stop being all cute around him because she wouldn't want to be around him at all. And he *would not* let her into his house again, not under any circumstance. If all this nonsense had taught him anything, he had much less of a handle on himself and his damn hormones than he thought.

Damn, he wished he could find some kind of balance. He didn't like being an asshole to people. But what other choice did he have? No one was going to take care of him. No one would put him first.

He didn't know her story, but he knew his role in it ended when she packed up and headed back to the city. He wasn't interested in casual flings. After he delivered the wood, bar any other accidents, which, actually were a legitimate worry with this woman, he'd keep to himself. *No more favors.*

Jude propped the back door open in case Etta wanted to come out and keep him company. Then he loaded up his arms with logs and trudged back around to the front of the cabin. He thought about her shivering in the rental with all the windows open. One of the logs teetered from his stack and fell. As he stooped and picked it up, he wondered if his jacket would smell like her when he got it back.

Jude growled. That kind of thinking reiterated his point exactly—keep it distant. *Just be a dick.*

So she seemed to care about other people? There were a hundred other reasons he had for not getting involved. Exceptions became habit. He didn't need that. Women made things complicated. He didn't need that either. He liked the simplicity in the routine he and Etta shared, his gigs, and coming home to a quiet house to do whatever the hell he wanted to. And he really, really didn't want to get caught off guard again.

Jude dropped the load of logs to the ground next to the chopping block. Picking one, he set it upright and centered on the platform. He gave his neck a stretch, then his arms, then picked up the axe.

The problem remained, the more he was around her, the more he wanted to be. "You're such a ponce," he muttered to himself.

Jude lifted his arms up overhead and swung down into the center of the log. It split clean down the center. Here he was, promising to be a dick, to keep his distance while chopping up wood for the woman. All so she could sit cozy in her little sweater and wooly socks in front of her fire.

Jude positioned the half log for another cut, lifted and swung another perfect split. He pushed the pieces off to the side and stabilized the second log half in the center of the block. He lifted for another swing.

Who comes to the snow without a decent jacket? She'd been drowning in his, and it couldn't have been sexier. Or maybe he just liked that she was in his jacket. *Jacket and nothing else might nice....*

The axe came down and imbedded solidly into the side of the log. Jude groaned with frustration so tangible that it hung in front of his face like a cloud. He held his foot on the log as he jerked the axe out. Distraction, that's what she was, but he missed the irony in that.

Erin

She crossed the icy street with caution. Both hands held steaming mugs filled to the brim, a bad habit of hers. She saw Jude to the left of the cabin, axe in hand. On one side of him was a big pile of split logs. On the other, a smaller stack of large rounded logs, presumably waiting to be cut.

As she approached she noticed his body stiffen. She could see this clearly because the green henley he wore left little to the imagination. Erin gaped how well it all fit over his muscular form as he swung the axe up and brought it back down onto the log in one fell swoop. The axe went clear through and one of the halves teetered and fell to its side. He brushed the hair back from his face as he repositioned the log for another cut. Mari'd been right again, he was everybody's type.

He didn't look up or acknowledge her.

Erin pasted a smile on her face, refusing to let him get to get her. "You make it look so easy." No response. *Kill 'em with kindness. Kill 'em with kindness.*

She didn't expect to make him smile but she did want to make a gesture that showed her appreciation. He'd probably gone above and beyond for Shauna in the few days they'd been there. Erin didn't want him to regret his deal with her. She also didn't want him to feel taken advantage of.

He'd told Erin he hadn't done much, but the fact that he'd showed up at all had helped her own panic subside. She hadn't really expressed herself well in all of the chaos and smoke. Plus, words weren't her strength, hence, the tea.

She inched nearer, paying close attention to the hot liquid that teased the rims of the mugs. She shouldn't have filled them so full but it was too late to turn back and if she dumped some out, she might lose the bag. He kept swinging and chopping as if he hadn't seen her.

Erin tried to let it go and carry on, but the closer she got, the more she doubted her tactics. His rigid posture felt like a warning. She remembered his hard 'no' when she'd offered tea before. *Maybe he doesn't like tea. This was a stupid idea.*

She wavered between continuing on and turning back. She'd surely done stupider things. So much for not letting him get to her. She took another tentative step forward. *It can't get any worse, right?*

Jude paused when she stopped about five feet away, letting the head of the axe rest on the chopping block. "I said I'd bring it to you."

She could see that he was sweating and his chest heaved slightly on each breath. Jude pushed his sleeves up his forearms and set hands to his hips.

Erin tried to hide her disappointment. "I know." *Kill 'em with kindness.* Why did she care so much what he thought of her? "I brought you some tea," she offered bravely, lifting the mug.

Hot water sloshed over the edge and cascaded down her hand. She hissed at the sting. Flustered, she didn't notice how quickly Jude moved, or how he let the axe drop, forgotten, in the snow. He confiscated the offending mug.

Erin shook out her hand, then wiped in on her pants. "Thanks." She avoided his eye. "You probably don't even drink tea."

An awkward silence followed. Erin had planned to tell him she didn't need the wood. But his pile was almost through and he seemed very hostile and it was easier to just let him do his thing. At least, that's what she told herself.

She held her hand out to take the cup again, intent on scuttling back across the street in shame.

"Sorry, I'll just..." she pivoted, nodding to her cabin, indicating her intent.

His eyes grew shrewd on hers. "Why are you doing this? What's your endgame here?"

"My what?" Her brow creased. "My endgame?"

"Yeah."

"I...I don't have an 'endgame.' I'm just trying to be nice. Which I'm kind of regretting now, actually."

He scoffed. "Nice? What do you get out of this?"

She pushed back a wave of heat. Clearly he didn't know how this worked and she wasn't going to explain it to him. "You know what? Never mind." She blinked back a frustrated tear, holding a hand out again to take the mug. "I...this was a mistake. I'll just take that back—"

He moved the mug out of her reach. "What kind is it?"

"What?"

Jude looked into the cup and sniffed.

The speed in which he switched gears threw her. Erin stared at him a moment, mouth slack. Who was the one playing games here? She found some words even if they weren't exactly the sentiments she'd intended. "Maybe you can just leave the mug on the deck."

She turned back to her cabin. Time to start cleaning and packing.

"Erin."

She stopped. "What?"

"What is this?"

"It's nothing, Jude," she snapped. "It's just tea."

"That's not what I meant."

She turned around. "Then tell me what you mean," she huffed, exasperated.

Instead of speaking, he brought the mug to his lips and took a sip. Then he took another. His tension seemed to melt and his face smoothed into something almost friendly.

"I do like tea," he told her. He took another sip. "I like this."

He lifted his eyes to hers and her heart stuttered. The intensity in his gaze seemed at odds with tea drinking.

"Rooibos." she answered finally. "One of my favorites." And after a pause, "It's also good with milk."

"It's good just like this." He held her gaze as he took another sip. "Thanks."

Erin couldn't decide between anger, desperation, frustration, or admiration. "You're welcome."

His eyes dipped to her torso and his lips twitched. She looked down to see what amused him, but all she saw was his blue fleece-lined flannel coat he'd lent her.

"Thanks for lending me the coat. I think it's actually colder in the cabin than it is outside."

She watched him take another sip and managed a careful one of her own. Then he turned and set his mug on the porch step.

"I'm almost done with this bundle," he explained, returning to the chopping block.

It wasn't a dismissal per se but she didn't know what he'd meant by it. Was he done with his tea? Should she take his cup? Did that mean he wanted her to go away? Erin wavered between staying and heading back to her own cabin. Now that he decided to be friendly, would it be rude if she left? How fragile was this new mood of his?

She took small sips from her mug, stalling, and using her it to hide her frown. Jude made short and sexy work of the next log but she needed less reasons to be attracted to him, not more.

"How did you learn to chop so well?" she asked as he placed another log on the block. "Is it just a mountain thing?"

He laughed.

Erin stared in awe and something bubbled low in her gut akin to arousal. His white teeth flashed against scratchy stubble and lightened his whole face, an expression that both looked and felt exotic.

"No," he answered, still chuckling. "No. When I first moved here I was pretty useless at it." His eyes danced as if he were reliving some humorous memory. "But with enough practice..." He brought the axe up overhead.

"Makes perfect?"

His arms came down in another perfect split. "I wouldn't say perfect."

Erin wanted to disagree, but she didn't. Instead, she took another sip of quickly cooling tea and admired his unassuming perfection—whether he believed it or not. Set, swing, chop. He had it down. She knew she just tortured herself, staying to watch him, but she couldn't retreat. And he didn't ask her to.

A car sped past, startling her out of her daydream. She checked herself for spills, then turned but the driver had already disappeared around the T at the end of the street. She thought it odd that a neighbor would plow through like that on such a short stretch with curves and ice. *Weird. Stupid.*

Jude stared off at the end of the street too, shaking his head and probably thinking the same as her. After a moment, he returned to his task.

Erin lifted her mug to her lips and took a larger gulp, in case there were any more surprises. No sooner had she swallowed, then Etta came bounding around the corner from behind Jude's cabin, mouth open wide in a doggie grin, tongue lolling to the side. Erin had little time to react before the dog pummeled right into her.

Erin fell back with an *oof*, butt first into the snow. Her tea went flying over her head and crashed on the pavement behind her while hair sniffs and sloppy kisses assaulted her.

Jude muttered a "Shit," dropping his axe, and hurrying over to rescue her *again*. "Etta," he growled, giving her collar a tug. She resisted. "Etta, back. Right now!"

The tone in his voice must have permeated through her excitement. She sat with a pout and a whine.

He extended a hand to Erin. "If I didn't know better, I'd say you like falling." She took it and he hauled her up. "You okay?"

"I'm fine. It's fine. Just surprised," she reassured him. Despite her words, Erin's heart sped. They hadn't been this close since he'd picked her up off the ice. She'd thought she'd imagined it all, but now...

Jude stooped to look at her straight on, his face not more than six inches away, his eyes boring right into hers.

"I'm okay," she repeated again, calmly even though her heart fluttered wildly.

Jude didn't back off. His forehead wrinkled and his brow dipped.

"What?"

"Your pupils just dilated again," he informed her. "And you've been falling a lot. Just want to make sure—"

"Really. I didn't even hit my head." Could her feel her heartbeat? She stepped back and out of his grasp. "I'm tougher than I look."

He followed her step and got in close again. Erin froze. Jude raised an arm by her head like he was going to caress her hair and she forgot how to breath.

"I'm...fine," she forced out.

He brought his hand down gently at the back of her head. *Oh my God, is he going to kiss me?*

"You have snow in your hair." His voice came low and unbelievably tender as he brushed the it off.

"Oh."

"And your back," he added, his hand sweeping over her shoulders and back.

Erin stilled, afraid to move and her heart went from thumping to hammering until finally Jude stepped back. He scanned the rest of her, all the way to her sneakers. She looked down and saw a solid coating of snow below her waist. Thinking he might try to help her with that, and knowing she'd never survive it, she rushed to brush off her legs and butt. Jude watched, a small smile playing on his lips, but she didn't catch it.

Erin straightened and Etta swung her head back and forth between the two of them, ears cocked at contrasting angles.

Jude still stared at her. "What? Did I miss a spot?" She did another scan, twisting to check her backside.

"No. You got it all," he assured her. "You sure you're okay?"

"Nothing a warm fire from some freshly chopped wood can't fix," she told him, then frowned, remembering she'd said she wouldn't try lighting another fire. Her frown deepened as she recalled she wasn't staying anyway.

"Then what's the frown for?"

Oh shit! The mug! Erin spun and stared at the mess of ceramic pieces strewn across the snowy pavement—so many pieces!

"Shoot!" She moved to the edge of the road and squatted, collecting larger shards. "Do you think I'll lose my security deposit?" She grimaced. They didn't leave a security de-posit, but she felt pretty confident Shauna would not be inviting her back. *Smoke damage...broken mugs.*

Behind her, Jude let out a full bodied laugh. Erin whipped her head around and stared. He absolutely glowed. He looked like something out a magazine, a candid shot just after a joke or a snowball fight. There was so much expression coming from him that she thought maybe she had actually hit her head again.

"You're funny," he mused as his laughter died to a deep chuckle, "I'll give you that."

Etta whined from her spot, vocalizing her displeasure that no one was paying her any attention. Jude gave Erin one more small smile, then stooped to look his shaggy com-panion in the eye.

"Etta," he started sternly. Etta dropped her nose and coifed it with her paw. Erin just about died. "Do we jump up on people?" Her nose stayed pointed to the ground. "I thought so."

She twisted her head to look up at him.

Jude gave her a scratch and stood. "Okay," he told her.

Etta stood too, then bumbled over to a still crouched Erin. The dog leaned into her and Erin had to throw a hand into the snow to keep from tipping.

"She's apologizing," Jude clarified.

"Oh." Erin smiled, putting the mug pieces down, and combed her fingertips along the top of Etta's head. "It's okay Etta. You're just a big girl, huh? A big girl, but a good girl."

Etta turned on the puppy-like charm again, planting wet kisses up Erin's face and across her ear.

"Okay. Okay," Erin laughed as she stood. Etta followed her and jumped up, trying to keep at it. "Hey," Erin said, bringing hands to the side of her scruffy face. "What did daddy say?"

Etta whined, but dropped back down to all four paws. Erin peeked at Jude who'd come over to them. His whole face lifted in a smile, all eyes on Etta. *What I'd do for someone to smile at me like that*, she marveled. He caught her staring.

Erin rubbed the side of Etta's face and neck. "How long have you had Etta?"

"About three years." He ran his hand down her furry back, ending with an affectionate rump pat. "Be good," he warned, then walked back over to the chopping block. He placed a log in the center.

"Did you get her from a breeder?"

"No. Nothing like that." He brought the axe up. "I uh, I adopted her." Jude grunted as he split a log. "Although, could say it was more the other way around," he added, looking over at Etta. "We crossed paths during my first snow season here. Rough winter, but we got through it."

"Must have been hard, without firewood," Erin jested, remembering his earlier comment. The joke sounded so much better in her head. But soon as it came out, she regretted it.

Jude's face tightened. "Something like that."

"Sorry. I didn't mean to—I'm horrible at jokes."

"Don't worry about it."

He gave his full focus to the logs. Erin stood, hands in her pockets with Etta practically sitting on top of her. They watched Jude finish chopping his pile. Erin didn't mind the wet dog smell because Etta put out a lot of heat.

When Jude set up the last log, Erin realized she hadn't cleaned her mess. She pulled her foot out from under Etta's behind and turned back to the road.

Figuring the smaller flecks would get crunched up and dispersed in snow and rain, she collected the pile she'd started, then hunched down to grab any piece large enough to see. Without gloves, her hands quickly went from cold to numb. Erin just envisioned that fire she decided she would have while she cleaned the cabin and packed. Jude *had* chopped all this wood for her, after all.

She inched father out into the street to grab a piece, scouring the road for any she'd missed. Without warning, the sound of an engine roared, practically on top of her. Erin sprang back, startled, as a car whizzed by and honked.

"Jeez!" she hissed.

Jude called out to her. "You okay?"

"Yeah. Just startled." She stared out at the road. *There was plenty of road for them to go around.*

"People should get off their damn phones," he grumbled from behind her.

Erin gave herself another moment while her heart slowed back down, then she checked the road before darting out to grab that last larger fragment.

That was when she noticed all the blood. The pieces in her cupped hand sat in a pool of it. A muted groan rattled from her throat. The good news was, her hands were too cold to really feel any pain. She snagged the piece in the street, then trekked over to Jude. Drops of blood sprinkled the snow as she walked.

"Hey, Jude," she called tentatively. "I don't mean to be more of a bother, but do you—"

She didn't get a chance to finish because as soon as he saw her hand, he dropped everything and corralled her into his cabin. "Etta, come!" He called before closing the door behind them.

Etta followed them to the kitchen sink, sticking close. Erin used both hands to cup her collection of bloodied, broken pieces.

"Just drop them in the sink," Jude ordered.

"But—"

"Drop them."

Erin laid them in the corner so none of it would go down the drain. Jude turned on the facet, grasped her by the wrist and held her hand under the running tap. She flinched as the water hit her palm.

"I could have cleaned that up," he said roughly.

"It doesn't feel as bad as it looks."

He brought her hand out of the water and inspected it. More blood pooled from a gash about an inch wide. It made Erin's stomach churn. He grabbed a clean dish rag from a drawer, wet it, and pressed it firmly into her palm. She flinched again.

He met her eyes. "Tougher than you look," he agreed. "Keep holding this here."

She nodded, applying pressure, and he disappeared into the bathroom at the back of the cabin. When he returned, he held a nearly empty emergency kit. Inside were a few small bandaids, the end of a roll of gauze, some packages of cotton pads, and a curled up tube of ointment. He must have noticed her staring at it.

"Like I said, rough first winter."

Erin started to get a clearer picture.

Jude squeezed the last bit of ointment from the tube directly onto her cut. He opened a cotton pad and set it gently on top. Then he wrapped what was left of the gauze around her hand to hold it all in place.

Now fully thawed, Erin's palm started to throb. She lifted her arm up and stared at Jude's handiwork. It looked well wrapped, like he'd done it before. She wondered if she needed to the store and pick up her own first aid kit, or if the rental had one.

She glanced at Jude. "Thanks."

"You're welcome."

Erin suddenly got very shy. Maybe it was because he'd just played hero, or perhaps because she'd done something dumb again. It could have been his proximity. Then she decided it was definitely the way his body tensed before he stepped back.

Jude put his hands to his hips and shook his head, chuckling to himself. Then he lifted his eyes to the ceiling, letting out an audible exhale. Erin stared at him, perplexed. She wanted to ask what was so funny.

"Look, I'm sorry if I acted like a dick earlier." He settled gleaming grey eyes on her. "Seeing a woman run out of a smoking building does something to a man," he explained. Erin bit her bottom lip. "Not my finest moment."

"Well, I have no business starting fires, apparently. I should have known better about the wood."

"Still. Not right, how I reacted."

"It's okay," she insisted. "Really," .

"Can you just let me apologize?"

"Okay. Sorry. Thank you." She pressed her lips together.

He nodded, eyes dropping to her bandaged hand. "I'll get the wood and walk it over to your place." He grabbed his gloves from the breakfast counter as he moved to the door. "Meet me over there. I'll show you how to start a fire. The right way." The corner of his lip quirked up. "Etta, stay," he added before going back outside.

Chapter Ten

Good, Bad, then Ugly

Jude

Stepped outside, he let the cold air hit him like a much needed punch in the face. What was it he'd just said about letting her in his house? *Not under any circumstances?*

Shaking his head, he trudged over to the shed to get the wheelbarrow and wheeled it back to his pile. He started tossing the logs in. Why'd she have to smell so good? A log missed its mark and lodged in the snow. Jude picked it up and dropped it in to join its buddies.

Underneath the layer of smoke, he'd caught something fresh and sweet. *I'm screwed. He* already couldn't get the scent out of his nose, her voice out of his head, nor the electricity from his fingers from when he'd touched her. And damn, it felt good to be needed.

Wheelbarrow full, Jude made his way over to the rental. He glanced back to see Erin come out behind him and collect his mug before crossing the street. She hustled past him at the steps, then punched in the door code while he muscled the wheelbarrow up to the deck. Swinging the door wide, she stepped out of the way. He maneuvered the load over the tiled entryway, careful not to let it roll onto the light carpet—a poor choice in his opinion.

She hadn't been exaggerating. It was freezing inside. But the cross breeze had managed to clear out most of the smoke.

Jude left the load at the door and moved to the front windows. "I'll help you close up these up."

Erin set the mug in the sink, then climbed with a knee on the counter to reach over and close the kitchen window. He smirked as she hopped down. *Cute.*

While Erin took care of the upstairs, Jude made quick work stacking the dry, cut wood along the wall next to the fireplace. Then he rolled the wheelbarrow out onto the porch and closed the front door.

Erin thumped back down the stairs with heavy footfalls. "Thanks again for doing all of this."

He squatted in front of the hearth. "No problem."

She came close and squatted down with him. "You said you would show me?"

He looked over and when she smiled, it chucked away another chip in his wall.

"Yeah."

He walked her through the steps which she seemed to already know. He handed her paper. She crumpled it and shoved it in at the bottom.

"Dry wood," he teased, holding up one of the logs he'd brought over. She shot him a scathing look and he expected a sarcastic quip but she didn't say anything. Jude set the dry log across the angled stack of kindling.

"Want to do the honors?" he asked, snagging the canister matches from the mantel.

Erin grinned. "You trust me with fire?"

It surprised him how relieved he felt that she wasn't actually incensed. And he liked when she teased. He wanted more. Cocking his head, he scrunched his face. "On second thought—"

"Oh, give it to me!"

She reached out to grab the matches. He yanked them back out of her reach.

"Don't be a jerk!" she laughed, leaning in and he wondered how close he could get her. He stretched his arm behind him and she lunged forward, just like he'd hoped.

"Ow!" Her arm flew to her chest as she fell into him. Jude dropped the canister and caught her, sliding hands around her ribs.

Eyes clouded with pain, she clutched her injured palm to her chest."Sorry, my hand."

He should have felt bad but her face was in his and her breath felt warm on his skin and her hair smelled fresh and sweet. His eyes dipped to her mouth.

Then he notice how pale and tense she was. "Are you going to be sick?"

"No...it just really hurts."

"Sorry. I didn't think—"

"It's okay," she breathed.

She shifted away and his hands involuntarily tightened. Chip...chip...chink. So much for his wall.

She took a few slow, steady breaths. "I swear, I can take care of myself."

"I don't mind helping," he replied before he could think better of it. "We all have our days."

Erin moved back and this time, he let her go. She sat on her butt, knees up and feet flat on the carpet in front of her. Wrapping both arms around her legs, she studied her bandaged hand. Jude noticed a small, dark spot forming under the wrap but he was fresh out of supplies.

She sighed. "Maybe you should just light it."

He felt like an asshole. "My fault," he apologized, offering her the canister. "If your hand doesn't hurt too much. No tricks this time."

She took it gingerly. After a few tries, she got the head to light and held it under the kindling. She focused on her task. He focused on her.

'...*have some fun*,' Pauline's motherly advice sounded in his head. *Fun. But what then?*

"I should go." He stood before she did anything else that might change his mind.

Erin regarded him from her spot on the floor but he'd already made it to the door. He paused. She looked so lost sitting there. He didn't want to leave.

"As always, you know where I'll be."

"Maybe I should get a frequent shopper card," she joked halfheartedly.

He laughed. "Yeah, maybe. Later." And he left her there, closing the door softly behind him.

A hike.

That's what he needed. A good, strenuous, heart pounding hike. That, or he'd march right back in there and finish what he'd wanted to start. Dammit, the girl was impossible. *Impossibly addictive.*

Jude glanced up at the sky. It would have to be a quick hike. The weather reports predicted a storm and from the looks of it, they were right. Jude took the porch steps two at a time up to his place but stopped cold when he saw his door ajar. He approached cautiously at first, then threw the door wide open and stared into the empty house. It all looked just as he'd left it. All but one thing.

"Etta?"

He moved quickly but quietly into cabin, hoping to catch a scratch of a paw or a whine from the other side of a closed door. It happened sometimes—she'd get stuck in one of the rooms. He moved through the downstairs, looking and listening.

"Etta! Come on, we're going for a walk," he shouted.

Nothing.

His gut tightened. Jogging up to the second story, he let out a whistle, his heart pounding so heavy it made him sick. "Etta, come!" Nothing but silence screamed back at him.

Jude thundered down the stairs and marched back out to the porch. He did a scan up and down the empty street. Grey clouds rolled in and a cold wind picked up, whipping his hair.

"Etta!" He called over a lump in his throat.

Silence. Silence and wind. His mind raced, moving backwards in time. What the hell happened? Where was she? Even with the opportunity, Etta wasn't one to just disappear. He looked down to the slew of human and canine tracks in the snow and the drops of dark blood. With all the antics earlier, he couldn't tell if the tracks were new or not. It all looked like it could have been from before.

He mentally ran through their steps. *We were outside. Erin was bleeding.* He'd brought her in to take care of her hand. But he'd been distracted. Did Etta come in too? He tried to remember—he'd thought she did. Then he'd gone out to get the wheelbarrow. *I closed the door, loaded up the wheelbarrow then wheeled it across the stree*t. That's when Erin came out.

Jude's mouth tightened into a thin line. Did she close the door when she left? Even if she hadn't, he would've expected Etta to come bark at them from the deck of the rental.

Maybe she'd caught the scent of something? Jude looked to the T at the end of the street. It could have been thirty minutes ago. She could be anywhere.

He ran a hand through his hair and stalked back into the cabin. Grabbing a coat off the hook, he swept his eyes once more through the interior. A lot of things welled up under his skin but none of it would help him find her.

Shoving his arms into his coat, he stormed back outside. The blood in the snow caught his eye. He hadn't met anyone so accident prone. He'd thought it endearing. He'd even liked his role in the heroics. But now he saw he'd made a grave error. She was just flakey and he'd let his guard down. He didn't need the extra drama. And he damn well knew better!

Etta was missing. Because someone couldn't close a damn door. *If something happens to her...* He didn't finish that thought. He just let the anger take over. This situation proved exactly why he kept his distance, why he acted like he did.

She'd stood there, shivering at his door like a goddamned popsicle, breaking his wall as if it were made from goddamn...snow! He kicked a boot into the accumulation of white powder, sending it flying.

And dammit, he'd let her.

His anger stewed and boiled as he rapped on the door to the renal. First, he'd find his dog. Then he'd set the record straight.

The door swung open.

"Fire's still going...strong." The big, warm smile Erin offered him faltered and then disappeared altogether.

"Did you let Etta out?" Honest to God, he tried to act and sound neutral. He didn't need her getting all defensive until he got his answers.

Her brows drew in."When?"

"When you left my cabin."

"No. She was in your cabin. You told her to stay. I assumed you wanted her there."

"Did she follow you out?" he pushed.

"No...I-I don't think so. No."

Jude ran a hand through his hair, his jaw ticking. "You don't *think* so? Did you close the door when you left?"

"What's going on? Is Etta okay?" She sounded almost panicked and it rubbed him the wrong way. It wasn't even her dog.

Landing his hands on his hips, he pressed. "Did you close the door behind you?"

"Yes. Of course I did!" she snapped, crossing her arms.

Jude scoffed. "Then you wanna explain to me why the door was wide open when I got back?"

Her eyes widened. "What?" She dropped her arms. "She isn't in the cabin? Are you sure?"

"No. She isn't. Because I sure as hell wouldn't be over here if she was. Do you need me to spell it out for you?"

He watched her mouth slack, then her whole damn expression sag but at least she finally stopped asking questions. Then she straightened and her face got tight and determined looking. He might have been impressed at any other time.

"If you're so worried," she started, "then stop wasting time arguing with me and let's go look for her." She bent down and shoved her feet into her sneakers.

"What are you doing?"

Erin straightening, twisting a foot down into the shoe. "I'm going to help you look for her."

He laughed a bitter laugh. "I don't need your help."

"I know you don't *need* it, but I want to," she told him though it sounded reluctant. "Surely two of us are better than one."

"That's debatable." He turned and looked down the street at a noise. He'd thought he heard a dog bark in the distance—didn't sound like Etta though. Maybe a dog had wandered onto her territory and she'd chased it away. The barking sounded far off, maybe on an adjacent street? His mind turned over possibilities.

"Jude."

She'd spoken again. His head jerked back to her.

"I can see you're upset. But you don't have to be so rude. I can help you."

"I'm not being rude," he stated. "I'm being honest. Look at you. You can't even take care of yourself." He flung an arm out and pointed at the sky. "There's a storm coming. I don't have time to be hunting after you *and* Etta. Or carrying you back to the cabin after you fall again."

His gut dropped when the wave of raw hurt transformed her face. Her eyes grew glossy and she took a step back like he'd actually hit her. He watched in silence, as she took a deep breath through her nose but still managed to shrink right in front of him.

"Well, for Etta's sake, I hope you find her."

The door swung shut. Jude didn't have time to sort out what when through his head so he pushed it away. It didn't matter anyway. He had to find Etta before the storm rolled in.

Chapter Eleven

Unexpected Visitor

Erin

She slammed the bathroom door, shaking with anger.

The nerve of him! Did he really think she be stupid enough to let his dog out? And all the questions! For what? He'd already decided who to point fingers at. But that last comment...

He didn't deserve her help anyway.

He didn't even know her! It had been a chaotic day, she hadn't been at her best, but she would never do that. Never! And Etta was huge! Not the kind of animal to sneak out unnoticed. He'd crossed the line. He'd hit on her worst insecurities, intentionally or not. Erin was starting to think he'd have said it all regardless.

Her first impressions of Jude had been hostile and cold. She should have stuck with those instead of opening up and giving him the benefit of the doubt. She'd wanted to slap him. Something she'd never done to anyone before.

Erin paced the small bathroom—the farthest point from his cabin. She'd finally decided to give it one more day, to stay and see what happened, and then this! *Figures*. She'd told Mari something didn't feel right. If she'd just gone home, none of this would have happened.

Etta was smart. And huge. She could have shoved the door open herself. She was certainly ornery enough, and if she'd felt left out...

Maybe Jude should've taken better care dog proofing his house! How could an animal that size go missing anyway? Wouldn't someone see her? Erin frowned. She hoped Etta was okay, not for Jude, but for Etta's sake.

I don't have time to be hunting after you...

She felt sick. He'd only seen her outside of her element, probably at her worst. But was it true? Had she really become that hopeless and helpless? Is that why she'd been so afraid to leave Victor—to move on? Because deep down, she knew she couldn't rough it alone?

Erin rubbed her face with her good hand and leaned her elbows into the vanity. She felt betrayed. He'd been so sweet and smelled so good. And for a second, she swore he'd wanted to kiss her. But what did she know? *Nothing, apparently. I should've just gone home with Mari.*

She could leave now. Nothing was stopping her. Except for the exhaustion that came in the wake of her anger. And her hand hurt. She didn't want to clean and pack. She wanted to curl up under a blanket and take a nap. But she felt too riled up to sleep.

Erin leaned over the edge of the bathtub and ran the tap. When the water had warmed, she pulled the shower toggle and started stripping. There was something about showers that encouraged emotional purging like the one she'd been holding back since Jude's tirade.

She never claimed to be perfect, but nobody enjoyed being wrongly accused. Still, he could made his accusation and left it at that. The rest was cruel and unnecessary. She wouldn't have followed...probably.

Erin held her injured hand out of the spray of the shower as she got in. The heat stung her skin at first and opened up her chest for the purge. Her tears mixed with the water as she sobbed silently. All the words, all the accusations, all her lowest thoughts tumbled around in her skull and left her small and broken. And finally, when she was all dried out, she shut off the water.

Hair still damp, Erin donned her coziest pajamas and wandered into the kitchen. The clock informed her it was almost dinnertime. She opened the door to the fridge and stared at its contents. Nothing looked good. She made a cup of tea, closed the interior wooden shutters in the front of the cabin, then curled into the striped armchair facing a large, black television.

She thought about starting a movie but she couldn't decide what she wanted to watch. So instead, she just stared at the blank screen. And her mind drifted back to Etta. *I hope she's okay.*

Had she closed the door all the way? Did she hear the latch click? She couldn't remember.

Erin looked over to the fire. The extra logs she'd added were burning down. The heat and flames set a cozy vibe to the room but she felt cold. If Jude hadn't brought over those logs, Etta wouldn't be missing.

Pulling back the shutter, she peeked across the street. Jude's cabin was dark—no lights, no movement, no smoke from the chimney. No Etta. Heavy grey clouds filled the sky and hung there, giving an eerie gloom to the outside world. The wind shook branches and sent little flurries dancing through the air. As she watched, a light snowfall started and quickly transformed into something ominous and thick.

A heavy gust rattled the windows and the lights flickered. Erin looked back into the cabin and furrowed her brow. *Great, just what I need,* she thought sourly, *a power outage.*

With a discontent sigh, she rose with her over-filled tea cup and, holding it away from her body, wandered back to the kitchen. If the power went out, dinner would be a no go. She should eat something now, even though doubt and guilt kept her appetite at bay.

What if Jude was right and it had been her fault? She'd never forgive herself if something happened to Etta.

Erin swung the fridge door shut, holding a loaf of bread, a stick of butter and a block of cheese. She unloaded her arms onto the counter then dug in an upper cabinet for the box of tomato soup she'd packed.

Dumping half the soup into a pot, she set it on a heated burner. While waiting for it to warm, she buttered bread and sliced some cheese, her mind wandering to Jude and Etta.

The pop of bubbles had her jumping back to the stove. "Shoot!" She turned down the heat, then grabbed a wooden spoon, shaking her head. "Useless."

After scraping the sides of the pot, she did her best to mix in the congealed bits. Then she stared at the lumpy soup. *You can't even take care of yourself.* Jude's words just wouldn't leave her alone. Technically, she could...*lumpy soup is perfectly edible!*

Erin had just pulled out a cast iron skillet for the grilled cheese when it happened.

A knock came from the door.

The cast iron clattered to a cold burner. *Did he find her?* That was her first thought. She moved warily to the front of the cabin. Did he come to apologize? Or maybe he intended to ream her out some more? Either way, she hesitated. But she had to know Etta was okay. Erin took a breath and schooled her features as she grasped the door handle.

Cold air whistled through the narrow opening. Erin stared and blinked. Then she opened the door a little wider.

Her brows drew together. "What...what are you doing here?" That uneasy feeling crept over her, the one she'd tried to tell Mari about.

Her best friend and maybe her boss were the only ones who knew her location, and yet somehow, Victor stood at her door, sporting his signature black leather jacket. With it, the burgundy shirt she'd bought for him, the one he never wore because 'it was too pink.'

He smiled and shook the fresh snow off his jacket, forming a mini flurry around him. It struck her as turbulent, like the outer edges of a vicious storm, or maybe it was just the one building in the sky above them. The lights flickered again.

Erin's eyes traveled from his shirt of choice to the upwards curl of his mouth and his sly, squinted eyes. She suspected he'd worn that shirt for a reason.

"*Cariña,* my God it's good to see you," he greeted, the wind whipping up and blowing his hair into a fray. It looked like Saturday morning bed head. Back when Saturdays where hers and his alone.

"Hi." She offered a small smile. Then she asked again, "Sorry, what are you doing here?"

He barked a quick laugh. She hadn't meant that as a joke.

"*Cariña,*" he started, placing a hand in the door frame. "I missed you." He leaned in as if he meant to kiss her.

She didn't like how sexy she thought he looked. She didn't like that, despite her unease, her first impulse was to let him in. But she also didn't like the thought of sending him away in the middle of a storm.

When she didn't lean in for his kiss, he dipped his chin and brushed the loose hair back into place with a fluid hand movement. Then he looked up at her from under his brow.

Wow. Erin crossed her arms. The move was neither charming nor suave. It felt childish. This wasn't some bar for picking up women. Erin raised a brow.

Victor straightened. "Don't look so angry. I was worried. You didn't answer any of my texts. Or my calls."

"You mean your booty calls?"

Victor smirked. "You know I enjoy more than your booty." She shot him a look and he threw his hands up, "I can see that maybe now is not the time for jokes."

"Victor. What are you doing?"

"I heard you were up here all alone, I had to come to you."

He heard? From whom? Something didn't sit right but the wind blew in at her, turning her damp hair to ice and she couldn't hear her own intuition over the questions rolling over in her mind.

She stepped to the side, a wordless admittance. Without hesitation, he passed through the doorway and into the cabin. Erin shut out the cold and the wind behind him.

Shedding his leather jacket, he took in the cabin. "Nice place."

He turned toward the door and found a hook for his coat. Outwardly, everything about his manner seemed sincere and left Erin wondering what had happened after she'd stormed out of the pub that Tuesday night. Driving up the mountain was no small feat. Had he been so certain she'd let him in? Was she really that predictable? And why wasn't she thrilled with the grand, romantic gesture?

He looked over his shoulder at her. "There someone else staying here?"

"No. Not until Mari comes back."

He pursed his lips as he nodded, then hung his jacket on the hook next to Jude's loaner. Erin cringed, realizing she still had to return it.

When he turned back to her, Victor gave her a sheepish smile and her heart hiccuped. It wasn't a mystery how she had gotten sucked in to his world. Even so, she caught herself comparing him to Jude. Victor wasn't nearly as handsome as she'd remembered.

"Are you going to give me a proper hello?" he purred, moving in and wrapping his arms around her.

Erin stiffened as he planted a sweet, chaste kiss on her cheek.

He straightened, studying her. "Are you okay?"

"Mhmm. Of course. Why wouldn't I be." He cocked his head to the side. "I mean, other than surprised to see you."

She extracted herself from his hold and hustled to the kitchen to finish her dinner. "Are you hungry?" she asked, turning up the burners and giving the soup a stir.

"Starving. It took forever to get here."

Belatedly, she realized her mistake. She'd as much as invited him to stay. She avoided his gaze, plopping a prepped grilled cheese sandwich in the middle of the heated skillet. It landed with a sizzle.

Victor sauntered over to the breakfast bar. "Look at you in the kitchen," he laughed. "You're going to cook me something?"

Erin bristled.

"*Cariña,* I'm teasing you. You can cook for me if you want to." Victor came around the counter and stood *right* behind her. "I can help," he murmured in her ear.

His hands slid around her waist as he positioned his hip against her. It took her a lot of effort not to react.

He looked over her shoulder. "What is this? Comfort food? Oh honey..."

Erin gritted her teeth. She'd been caught. She could feel the satisfaction rolling off of him. He assumed she was lost and wallowing for *him.*

Victor pressed a delicate kiss into her neck. "Let me help."

"I've got it." She shifted, pressing an elbow back but he didn't move. "Victor, give me some space. I'm cooking."

"Mmm, feisty," he teased, nipping her ear. "I think it's cute that you're trying, but you don't have to, I already came all the way here for you."

Erin had never liked it when he called her *cute.* Not when she saw him with other women that were too sexy to be 'cute.' It didn't feel like a compliment coming from him. It felt like being awarded a second place metal when runner ups didn't count.

"Victor," she asked again.

He rocked forward, pinning her between at the stove for moment, before finally stepping back and taking his hands with him. She heard him tinkering around in the cabinets behind her, then recognized the sound of an empty glass settling on the counter.

"Look at all these choices!"

She flipped her sandwich, frowning at the blanketed crust. When he came around to sit at the bar again, he had a glass of Tequila, two fingers high.

She frowned. It felt like she'd been doing that a lot lately. "I'm sorry, who told you I was here?"

"Isn't the mystery of it more..." Victor paused lifting his hand up and wafting the air as he sought the right word.

"Disrespectful?" Erin offered.

"Romantic."

Erin sighed. "Victor, I told you—"

"Okay. Okay," he conceded, holding up both his hands in surrender. "I will tell you. Marisol was gabbing about this place with one of her clients. And her friend Shauna has an account with our firm. What do they say? Small world?"

"And what makes you think it's okay to just show up here?" Erin asked, pressing a spatula into the sandwich. Cheese seeped out past the crusts and sizzled at it met the hot iron. She flipped it and did the same to the other side.

"You don't think it's romantic?"

Stalling, she turned to grab a plate from the cabinet and took the grilled cheese off the heat. Then she started assembling another one. Erin wondered at her reaction. She wanted to like it. She wanted to feel swept off her feet, but she just...didn't. The reality of it all seemed underwhelming now. Or maybe it was because she'd been hoping for some-one else?

"Well?" Victor prodded. She wasn't sure what to say, though her silence likely said enough. He moved on. "I want to make it up to you."

Erin blinked back her frustrations and looked out the kitchen window. The snow fell heavier now. The road would be a mess by the time they finished eating burnt grilled cheese and lumpy tomato soup. She couldn't kick him out in this weather.

Offering a non-committal shrug, Erin plopped the second sandwich on the skillet. Then she realized she'd forgotten to butter the pan. She could feel Victor watching her, as if everything she did fascinated him. Scrapping the sides of the soup pot. Pressing the spatula into the buttery bread. That's how it use to be, back before he broke it off with her, an attentiveness and contentedness in the simplicity of doing boring things. *Those were good times*, she thought, her mouth tipping up.

"There it is," Victor stated with a cocky grin.

"What?"

"That beautiful smile I've missed."

"Stop it," she pleaded, purposefully turning her mouth down.

Victor laughed. "You don't have to play hard to get. I came all the way up here just for you, remember?"

So he kept saying. How was she going to make it through a whole night of this? "Maybe you can open up bottle of wine?"

Jude

He slammed the front door in aggravation. It was too dark outside to see anything and the snowfall made his flashlight useless. To continue searching was pointless. The temperature had dropped. The storm blew strong. And no Etta.

Jude stalked around his cabin, flipping on lights. Then he stopped by the cold fireplace, wondering what to do next. Dropping into the armchair, he leaning his head against the backrest and rubbed his hands down his face. He didn't know what to do and he hated that. He hated that Etta was out there somewhere, probably freezing, and he sat in a nice warm cabin, waiting out the storm.

He'd tried to follow some prints that led away from the house, but the new snow covered over buried everything before he got very far. He'd only made it about a quarter mile down the street. Who knew how far she had gone beyond that, and why? It just didn't make sense.

He'd had called the local kennel but they'd claimed they hadn't gotten any new animals. Jude gave them Etta's description anyway, figuring a giant Irish Wolfhound would be hard to miss. Still, he wasn't convinced that the kid on the other end of the phone actually took his information down.

He planned to go down to the kennel in person first thing in the morning. Maybe he'd have better luck that way. Or maybe not. Not if she was stuck out in this weather all night.

He let out an angry growl that just made the cold, empty cabin feel emptier. He was worried, angry, and stuck.

How could she be so stupid?

The whole time he'd been out searching, this wracked his brain. That and how equally stupid he'd been for letting his guard down. If this whole experience didn't teach him a lesson...well, it would.

He wasn't ignorant to the fact that women found him appealing. In fact, that truth had become the bane of his existence for the past three years. And rejecting the un-wanted attention had become a practiced art. Until Erin.

She just...she seemed so honest to God wholesome. Kind, caring, and modest. She didn't flirt with him. In fact, he got the impression she'd tried to avoid him, which only made her harder to resist. So he didn't.

Stupid.

He didn't need distractions. Not anymore. He'd gotten over his past as much as he probably ever would. And if he decided to have a fling, it certainly wouldn't be with another city girl.

But that was the thing, wasn't it? Because he wasn't so stupid to deny that he'd actually liked her.

He'd done this to himself. Even if it hadn't happened, even if Etta were sleeping, sprawled out at his feet at that very moment, Erin would still be the kind of woman who'd leave the door open. He just wouldn't have known it yet. He had no room in his life for more mistakes.

Jude's throat felt thick as the weight of the day all came crashing down.

Damnit.

She'd made him tea. He blew up at her and she still offered to help him search. She'd put on those crappy ass sneakers like she'd planned to take on the storm. Was she that selfless or just plain clueless? He ran rough fingers through his hair.

Jude regretted what he'd said. It had been dick move. He didn't used to be like that—not to women, not to anyone.

He sat up and leaned into his knees, staring at the little rug between his feet where a heap of grey fur should have been. His feelings towards Erin didn't matter. Nothing would change. Etta was all he had to rely on. If something happened...no amount of sorry could undo what he feared.

Jude popped up and strode over to the front window. With a finger, he pulled the curtain back just enough to catch a snow-obscured glimpse of the rental. Light bled through the shutters and smoke puffed with from the chimney.

He'd almost kissed her, back there in front of the fireplace. "Get your head back on, Jude," he grumbled, but he couldn't pull his eyes away.

That's when he noticed the second car parked outside the cabin. Even dark and dusted with snow, he knew an expensive model when he saw one. How had he not noticed it when he'd stormed back into his own place.

"Who the f—"

The front door to the rental opened suddenly and a man ran out into the snow. Jude clenched his jaw, watching, as the guy jogged over to the expensive car and retrieved a bag from the trunk. He jogged back, waiting a brief moment at the door, before being readmitted.

Jude let the curtain fall back over the window. *Fine*, he thought sourly. *Good. Good riddance.*

"Fuck!" he ground out.

Of course she'd been avoiding him—not hitting on him like all the others! He was such an ass.

Jude rubbed his hands together to burn off the chill of the cabin. He could get a fire going to heat the place up. Or he could turn on the furnace. Or maybe he'd just take a shower and call it a night. The kennel opened early. He wanted to be there first thing.

Chapter Twelve

Finding Etta

Erin

Erin opened a groggy eye. Heat pressed against her back and a heavy, bare arm draped lazily across her chest. The body connected to it let off a low snore.

Oh Shit.

Then she realized, with relief, she still wore her pajamas. She hadn't had so much wine that she would've made *that* mistake. At least, she didn't think she had.

Erin held her breath as she pivoted and shimmied off the side of the bed. Victor's arm slid limply from her chest and rested, unmoving in the warm space she'd left behind. Grabbing the throw that had made its way from the red couch to her bedroom, she quietly padded into the kitchen to start some coffee. She pulled the throw tightly around her shoulders, then stopped abruptly.

Two empty wine bottles sat side by side on the counter. *Two?* She didn't remember opening a second bottle. The thought made her sick. What else didn't she remember? Anxiety roped around her chest. That explained how she woke up with Victor's arm around her. She sucked at this whole walking away business.

She pull the grounds out of the fridge and grabbed the scoop on the way to the coffee pot. *It doesn't matter.* If the deed had been done, sex didn't change anything. Victor wasn't in the clear. Being sweet and attentive for a few hours didn't erase the past year he'd led her on and then left her hanging.

She hadn't yet asked about Lisa or Candy-Lips. For all she knew, he was still with them and if he was, then he wasn't with her. After her scene in the bar he should at least know that much.

Lost in thought, Erin realized too late that she'd forgotten a filter. She groaned, dumped the grounds into a cup and started over.

The coffee had just finished when Victor emerged from the bedroom in boxer briefs and a dopey grin. His hair stood up in disarray just how Erin liked it.

"Good morning, *mi Cariña,*" he purred, coming straight at her.

Erin gave him a small smile and a nod, putting extra focus into the eggs she whisked for breakfast. Victor crowded in behind her, nuzzling his head into the crook of her neck, and kissed the soft spot where her pulse hammered.

She rolled her shoulders back and whisked with exaggerated movements, hoping he'd see that she was in the middle of something. Hoping he'd back off. He didn't.

"Victor, I'm cooking."

"I see that. It's kind of sexy," he crooned. He grasped her mixing arm and pulled it away from the bowl, dripping whisk and all.

"Victor!"

She yanked her arm back, sending raw egg all over the counter and God knows where else. He *tsked* playfully and she glowered, thinking about how she'd have to clean all that up.

"Mmm," he hummed. "I like it when you get worked up," one thing clearly on his mind.

"Can you just let me make breakfast? I'm starving," she lied.

"Starving? I can fix that."

He leaned in, turning her body to face him, then grabbed the back of her head and landed his mouth over hers. He pressed himself into her, demonstrating what he had in mind. She didn't need the clarification, nor did she want it. Erin made a sound in the back of her throat and shoved at him with her elbow.

"Okay, okay," he breathed into her mouth before backing off. He held his hands up and took a few steps back, still smiling, but not as warmly as before.

Erin set the bowl down and cleaned all the splatters of raw egg she could find. Then she went back to whisking what was left. Victor remained quiet but Erin felt his eyes on her as she bent to get a pan from the lower cabinets.

"Don't you have anything to do?" She asked irritably as she straightened.

"I do, but watching you be so domestic in the kitchen...it's much more fun."

"Well, I need some space right now." She turned to face him.

He took in her scowl. "*Cariña*, I'm teasing. Well, not about everything." He tipped his gaze down to his erection as if it needed to be stated again.

Erin crossed her arms. He took a step back, lifting his brow. As her scowl deepened, he took one more. "Better?"

Erin moved to the sink to grab a damp paper towel. She handed it to him. "You have egg on you," she told him and gestured to his chest. He grabbed her wrist and moved her hand, towel and all, down his bare skin.

"Stop it," she hissed, yanking her hand back.

He let her go, taking the towel and wiping his chest off himself. "Not much of a morning person anymore." His smile gone, he shook his head. "Just to show how caring I can be, I will give you space."

Victor moved to the bedroom, then crossed to the bathroom with his bag in hand. Erin heard the shower turn on. *Finally*, she sighed, going back to the eggs.

Fifteen minutes later, Victor came out, fully dressed in the clothes he'd worn the night before. He spotted her at the dining table eating breakfast. She gestured with her fork to his plate on the counter. Nodding, he moved to the coffee pot where she had left him a mug. He filled it, then grabbed his plate and came to sit across from her.

Erin kept her eyes down, not wanting to elicit more playfulness out of him. After pouring her crappy cup of coffee, her mind had fixated on the small harem of women Victor had been keeping. It had put her in a mood.

What exactly did he hope to achieve by coming up here? Did he really intend to get back together? Or just patch up their little side relationship? He must have been charming and she'd been a bottle down, or two, apparently, so he'd made it into her bed. But this morning, Erin found his attention tedious.

It surprised her, how quiet he was being. Finally, curiosity won over and she looked up.

He smiled but it didn't meet his eyes. "Are you upset with me, *Cariña*?"

"I'm not sure how to answer that," she admitted.

He took a sip of coffee and his face puckered. "What is this?" he asked, eying the dark liquid in his cup.

"It's coffee Victor," she bit out, taking a sip of her own and fighting back the urge to pucker as well. And t*oday has got to be the worst batch so far.*

He shook his head. "Oh honey," he said softly like she didn't know any better.

Her eyes dropped back to her plate. No longer curious, she finished her dry scrambled eggs in silence. When Victor was done, she took their dishes back into the kitchen to wash. She noted, irritably, that he made no move to help clean up.

Erin struggled to keep her bandage dry. Victor hadn't asked about her hand. She wasn't even sure he'd noticed. Had he always been so self-centric?

She heard him moving around behind her and then he finally broke the long silence. "I have some calls to make."

Over her shoulder, she saw him staring at his phone. She watched as he moved around the front room, looking for service. Erin was tempted to let him carry on.

"There's no signal in the cabin," she finally called over to him. He looked up at her, forehead lifted like he didn't believe her.

"None? What about upstairs?"

"Not unless you've switched to Sprint, in which case you can get three bars at the front of the deck.

"What? You're serious?" He sounded agitated.

She nodded, knowing very well it was a rhetorical question.

He seemed to get overly upset about it all. Muttering something to himself, he sat to put on his shoes, then turned abruptly and spit out a quick "I'll be back." The door swung shut behind him.

A second later there was a knock. Erin sighed and moved to the front. When she opened the door, Victor leaned in. "Jacket."

She waited until her back was turned before she rolled her eyes. Grabbing it from the hook, she handed it to him. He closed the door with not even a "thank you."

Erin pulled back the shutter and peered out the front window. The snow on the porch piled up to Victor's knee! He stomped through it, looking stiff and shaking his head the whole way to his car. Then he folded into the drivers seat, and slammed the door. The engine started and the wipers sprung to life, flinging snow off the sides. Luckily for him, the plow had come early.

The sun shone again in a blue sky as if there'd been no storm the night before. It was the kind of day that beckoned kids out to play. And the kid in her itched to go out, to ditch Victor and prove she could have fun on her own. *But you have work*, the adult reminded her.

Victor's car disappeared past the bend toward town. Knowing him, he'd probably end up at the Starbucks. It was a small victory, but it meant she could have the mom and pop place all to herself.

"Good riddance," she murmured, dumping Victor's coffee and returning to the dishes.

With two hours before her check in at the morning meeting, Erin glanced back out the window. *So much snow!* A walk might help her resolve what to do about her unexpected visitor. The child in her giggled gleefully. *Maybe just a short walk...*

As Erin tugged her shoes on, she thought about calling Mari. But she didn't want to make her friend feel bad. So far, Victor's presence just proved annoying more than anything else. And Mari had sessions that morning. After which, she'd probably call to plan her trip back up anyway. *She's going to kill me for letting him in.* Erin stood, glad her tailbone didn't pinch anymore at the sudden movement. *I'll call her later,* she decided.

The cold hit her, but not unpleasantly. She waited until the click and beep of the keypad locking behind her. Mind wandering to the previous day, the hustle between cabins, she pictured Jude's door. *It closed, right?* Her eyes drifted to the dark cabin across the street and its empty driveway.

Has he been out all night? Erin looked around at all the new snow and decided to think optimistically. *He's probably already left for work.*

There wasn't anything she could do, anyway. He'd been clear that he didn't want her help.

She stepped forward, her foot sinking deep down into the powder and encasing her leg past her knee. She couldn't help it. She giggled like a five year old, but only because no one was watching.

Maneuvering across the deck, she lifted each leg straight up out of the hole before proceeding forward, one ridiculous step after another. It looked like something out of the *Ministry of Silly Walks.* She laughed to herself, thinking, Victor wouldn't have understood the Monty Python reference.

She leaned forward, letting her fingertips drag in the powder soft snow. Her skin tingled at the cold but it felt feather light and so she dragged a path along her way to the street level. Glancing back at the tracks she'd carved out, Erin decided then, she really loved snow, she just needed better attire.

Traveling up the street toward the T, Erin imagined she look like a yeti, trekking awkwardly, using her whole body to keep her balance. The effort warmed her though, and after about fifteen minutes, she shedded her fleece and tied it around her waist.

The early morning felt peaceful. As she turned down an adjacent street, she noticed how the neighborhood shifted. Small, A-frames became multi-story cabins, the mountain jutting up behind them, thick with trees and rocky peaks, all covered in pristine, virgin snow. Every roof had thick white tops like frosting and she marveled at how magical it all seemed.

The deeper she got into the myriad of streets, the bigger and more posh looking the cabins became. Facades were all decorated in ornate stonework or fresh wood paneling, and every house had a three car garage. Passing by one such house, she heard barking, and her heart skipped a beat. In an instant, she forgot the scenery.

Could that be Etta? Erin picked up her pace, straining to hear which house it was coming from. *Maybe someone found her and took her in.*

She brushed into a bare, prickly bush to get off the road as a suburban drove by. Something tinkled and sunk into the snow. Pausing, she looked down at the imprint it left, then bent to reached for it. She rubbed her finger over the embossing on the circular dog tag, knowing what it would say even before she read it.

"Etta J."

A phone number was listed below. She should call him. At least to give him the direction of where Etta had gone. That is, if he didn't already know.

The nearby barking grew incessant. Erin looked around at the doors and windows for signs of life. Then her eyes lifted to the roof lines. Two cabins had smoke puffing from the chimneys. *That's a start.*

She'd never been a fan of knocking on stranger's doors, but something compelled her. Erin went to the first house but when she neared the entrance, the barking got softer. Pivoting back down the snowy walk, she approached the second house.

The dog started wailing from the other side of the door. She could tell right away that it wasn't Etta. Still, she rang the bell. First came the yelling, then the clicking of heels, and finally, the barking stopped.

When the door opened, Erin faced a middle aged woman with a tight, blond chignon and the refined look of impatience. She could have been from a high end women's outdoor catalog, sans a smile, all outfitted for the glamour of snow.

"Yes?"

Erin forced a smile. "Hello. Sorry to bother you. I'm looking for...uh," Erin held up the collar as she tried to find the right way to describe what she was doing.

The woman's lip curled. "Was that *your* dog?"

"I'm sorry?"

"That mangy gray one."

"You mean Etta?"

"That beast nearly killed my poor Ronnie," the woman scoffed. "Shame on you! Letting that thing run wild!"

"Oh my gosh, I'm so sorry. Is Ronnie okay?" Erin didn't know why she apologized other than that she wasn't sure what else to say.

The woman left her at the door, disappearing somewhere in the house. Erin tapped her foot, unsure if she was meant to follow. Just as she leaned to peer in, the home owner returned, cradling a fluffy black dog that looked *just* too big to be called a lapdog.

Erin's brow furrowed. "Is this Ronnie?"

The woman nodded, lips thin and eyes sharp. "Thanks to *your* dog, my poor Ronnie won't take one step outside!"

Erin tilted her head side to side, searching for some sign of injury. When she found none, she reminded herself, *this is not my problem.* Etta wasn't even her dog. She just wanted to find her.

"I'm so sorry to hear about Ronnie," she reiterated. "It's not actually *my* dog, but I'm sure Etta's owner will want to make things right," and even as she said it, she suspected it was a big fat lie, but this woman didn't need to know that. "It's just, right now we're still trying to find Etta. Do you know anything that might help us?"

Ronnie's owner scoffed then glared, and Erin wondered if the woman thought herself intimidating. "I'd hate for anything else to happen while she's on the loose," she reflected aloud. She let the home owner believe what she wanted from the statement.

"That dog should be put down, you know." The woman's eyes dropped to Erin's bandaged hand.

She instinctively tucked both hands behind her back.

The black dog wiggled, then whined in the woman's arms, bringing both sets of eyes down to him.

"My poor Ronnie."

Erin pressed her lips together, working to stay silent, though she had all kinds of things to say.

"I had to call emergency dispatch," Ronnie's owner continued. "Your dog was out in the yard, fighting with some other beast, all teeth and growling and poor Ronnie got caught in the fray!"

"Two dogs?"

The woman leveled her eyes as if she thought Erin dense. "Yes. The brown one got away. But my husband trapped yours in the back yard until a fire truck arrived."

Fire truck? "So, she's at the fire station?"

"No. Of course not! Animal services came."

Oh, good grief. "Okay...well, thank you for your time." Erin turned and walked back to the street.

"I filed a report!" The woman called behind her. "You'd better be prepared for my vet bills! Among other things!"

She didn't look back. She just kept walking, breathing easier when the door slam behind her. "What a witch."

She wound her way back to the rental, Etta's collar tightly in her grip. The deep prints she made in the snow had lost their luster, her playful inclination dissipated. *Another dog? Teeth and growling?*

At the rental door, she kicked off the snow from her sneakers, steeling a glance to Jude's place—still dark, still no smoke. She wondered if he'd found Etta yet.

Maybe he'd gone to work early that morning. Maybe Etta slept soundly inside, sprawled out on her cushy bed under the stairs. Erin studied the tags in her hand. Her legs were freezing, and her toes were numb. She had enough time for a quick, hot shower before work. Her thumb rubbed over the embossed letters on the tag. *But what if...*

Her gut told her to keep looking. And for once, she was going to listen to it. And if any new information came to light, she'd call Jude. The thought made her stomach twist. She really, really didn't want to talk to him. But for Etta, she would suck it up.

Chapter Thirteen

Reunited

Erin

She dumped her purse, computer, and work files onto the passenger seat of Mari's car, then did a fast and dirty job scraping snow from the windshield. The heater defrosted the rest as she inched down the road, eyes bouncing between phone and icy, foggy view. She felt time pressing down on her. Wherever Etta ended up, she might be injured, or worse. And Erin couldn't help feeling at fault.

As soon as the cell boasted three bars, she pulled to the side, and scrolled for a local Animal Services number. With the limited network, it took forever to load. *I'd be better off with a phone book.*

The line rang. Stomach in knots, she watched the remaining ice on the windshield turn shiny, then slide down in little tracks. Animal Control confirmed the late night call and pick up of a large canine, directing her to another number for the local kennel. She called but the kid on the phone wasn't much help.

"Well, I just talked to someone with Animal Services, and they said they sent the dog to you last night. An Irish Wolfhound."

"Yeah, sorry. I don't think anything came in last night," the kid replied.

Erin sighed audibly. "Is there a manager there, or someone who could check a log or something?"

"He's out on a call."

"Do you even know how big an Irish Wolfhound is?" she asked, disbelieving. It would be hard to miss her. The kennel couldn't be that big.

"Huh?"

"Never mind," Erin grumbled. "Look, she was probably hurt when she was picked up. It's urgent that I find her. Can you just go check and see if you have any dogs meeting her description? Help me out here."

"Can't leave the front. Call the animal clinic," the kid said with a hint of attitude.

Erin clenched her jaw. "Do you have a phone number for that?"

"No."

She hung up. *Useless.* A life was at stake and he couldn't be bothered to look up a number that was probably taped on the wall right in front of him!

She turned up the heat in the car, then searched her phone for animal clinics nearby. There were three and the map froze when she tried loading it. Sighing, she started at the top of the list.

It was the second clinic she tried.

"Yes, we had a large, gray Irish Wolfhound dropped off last night. No tags, no chip."

"That must be her! Is she okay?" Erin asked in a rush of relief and trepidation.

"Let's see...looks like she needed some stitches and anti-biotics. We gave her a Rabies shot be safe. It was all pretty minor. Poor thing was a sweetheart, though. I was hoping someone would claim her."

"Is she still there?"

"No. Since she was stable and she wasn't chipped we had to call the kennel. They sent a truck out to get her about an hour ago."

"Is there more than one kennel nearby?" Erin asked, her tone hopeful.

"Nope. Just the one. Do you need the number?"

Erin's shoulders slumped. "No, thank you. I have it."

She ended the call, leaned back in the driver's seat, and head tipping up, she stared at the roof. *Of all the...*She redialed the number for the kennel.

"Yello."

"Hi," Erin started without pacifying her tone. "I called a few minutes ago looking for an Irish Wolfhound. I just spoke with someone at the clinic and they said the dog was brought back to the kennel. Would you mind checking to see if she's there please?" The silence on the other end of the line was asinine. "She's a huge, shaggy, gray dog. You can't miss her." she added, annoyed.

"Oh! You mean like, the really big one that just came in?"

"Yes, she is really big."

"Hey Carl!" the kid shouted. Erin pulled the phone away from her ear. "Someone is calling about the horse!"

Erin hung up again. She looked up the address and mapped a route on her phone.

The kennel was much smaller than she'd expected. There were at least ten parking spots out front but you couldn't fit five people in the lobby. At least, not before you hit the long counter littered with flyers, one of which, Erin noted with irritation, was for the animal clinic she'd called.

Behind the counter sat a young kid with sloppy hair and sloppier posture. His foot rested on the desk and his head tilted down at his phone. He didn't bother to look up when she came in.

She drummed her fingers on the counter, then cleared her throat. "Excuse me."

"Yello!" he said, popping his head up, then looking back down to type out what appeared to be a text. He looked exactly how she'd pictured him. Hopefully that Carl person was better equipped at dealing with people.

"I'm here about the, uh, 'horse,'" she stated.

The boy looked up. This time with recognition. "Righto. You gotta talk to my manager." He took a minute to finish tapping out his message before getting up and disappearing into the back of the building.

Erin waited in the tiny room that had no chairs or benches. She fiddled with Etta's collar until she heard the heavy footsteps of someone larger and more mature walking towards the front.

"Hi there. I'm Carl. You here about the wolfhound?" A man with thinning, gray hair rested his forearms on the reception counter opposite her.

"Yes." Erin replied, then added, "I'm not the owner. I'm just trying to help him find her."

Carl nodded. "I see..." He rifled on the desk and picked up a pack of paper, studying the top sheet. "You know she wasn't chipped, right?" he asked the paper.

"I did not know that."

"You got any proof that it's your dog?" He brought lazy eyes up to hers.

Oh, for the love of... "She's not my dog."

"Huh." He seemed stumped. "What is it you wanna do then?"

Erin tried not to let her annoyance get the better of her. "I'm trying to help her owner get her back. And I wanted to make sure it was her before contacting him."

"Well, I—"

"Actually, you know what?" She slapped the collar onto the counter. "How about I leave you the dog tags and *you* can contact him." A perfect solution, since she'd been agonizing over calling Jude anyway.

"Suppose I can do that." Carl nodded, scribbling the phone number from the tags across the top sheet of the packet. "Tell yer friend to bring her credit card. Vet bill, emergency service charge, and she's gonna have to pay for the chipping before she can take her home."

That's a lot of fees. "Why don't you tell *him* that? When you call him."

She peeked down to the top sheet, at a black-and-white photo of a sad looking Irish Wolfhound, and a column of numbers listed below. It wasn't her dog and it wasn't her problem, not really. Etta should have been chipped anyway. Except, if this had been her fault... The doubt and guilt had been chewing on her for a while now. "What's the chipping fee?"

"Fifty dollars."

"And the vet bill?"

He looked at the sheet. "Nine hundred and fifty-eight dollars."

Erin nearly choked. "What? Are you kidding me?"

"Says here...stitches, anti-by-otic, rabies shot...it's all right here." He flipped the sheet over so Erin could see the vet invoice. She wondered if he should be showing her all this, but she didn't say anything.

Stretching out a hand, she asked, "May I?"

He handed off the packet and she looked through it carefully. The emergency service pick up charge added another one hundred and fifty dollars, then the kennel fee...It was extremely expensive losing a dog for one night.

She worried the inside of her lip, wanting to do the right thing. "Can I see her?"

Jude

His cell rang just as he walked back into his cabin. Jude dropped his work gear at the door and pulled the phone out of his back pocket. *Unknown number.* His chest tightened.

"This is Jude."

"Hi there. This is Carl down at the Loretta T. Walsh Animal Center. Are you the owner of an Irish Wolfhound named uh..." there was a jangle of metal on the other end, "Etta J?"

"Yes. Yes, I am." Jude tried not to get overly excited. Carl didn't speak with a lot of enthusiasm. It could be bad news. "Did you find her? Did someone turn her in?"

"Picked her up first thing this mornin' from Mountain Rock Animal Clinic. She's down here at the kennel."

"Clinic?" Jude's gut tightened.

"Says here on the report she had a little confrontation with another canine. She's fine though. You wanna come get her?"

"Yes. I'll be right down. I'm leaving right now."

"Yeah, okay. We're here till—"

Jude hung up and turned on his heels, back out the door and to his truck. This was the same kennel he'd visited twice since Etta went missing, the same kennel he'd called several times over the past two days. 'Morning' was hours ago. How is it they were just now getting around to contacting him? Anger warred with relief. He had a complaint or two for the manager about the idiot running the front desk.

And it was the same kid as the day before. Still with his head in the phone, still looking like he was doing them a favor by just being there. That morning, there'd been a sign on the door saying, 'be back soon.' No estimated return. No explanation. It all seemed pretty poorly run. If that translated into care for the animals, they were going to have a problem.

With a scowl, he approached the reception desk. "I'm here to pick up Etta," he told the kid without any preamble.

"Uh, Etta?"

"Oh, for fuck's sake..."

Before Jude could lose his temper, a man with a receding hairline came out from the back. This guy had more years on him but he didn't look any brighter.

"Bobby, go take yer break," he instructed the kid, looking at Jude with a wary eye. "You Jude?" The man had the same energy and enthusiasm as he'd given on the phone.

"I am. You Carl?"

"That's me." The lanyard around his neck named him the manager.

Great. "I'd like my dog, please."

"You got proof it's your dog?"

Jude about snapped. "Proof? You're the one that called me! What kind of proof do you want?"

"You got a picture or something?"

Shaking his head in disgust, he dug out his phone and scrolled through until he found a photo of Etta. He held it up for the man to see.

Carl nodded. "That'll do. Let me go get yer mutt. It's cramped back there. She don't fit so well in a cage," he joked.

Jude didn't spend much time at kennels, but he suspected Loretta T. Walsh was turning in her grave. Several minutes passed, then came the familiar click of nails on linoleum mixed with an unfamiliar pause. An excited whine sprang out before Etta came bounding around the corner into the office area.

"You said she was fine!"

The manager staggered in behind her, hand wrapped around a short leash. "She is."

"She's limping!"

Etta stretched up and planted her front paws on the reception desk. Her tongue lolled out from a happy grin, and her tail whipped side to side, sending papers flying to the floor.

"Well, yeah." Handing off the leash over the counter, the older man stooped to collect the fallen items. "That's where she had the stitches."

Jude had to quell his anger and exasperation. "Stitches?" Etta whined at his tone. He scratched her ear with his free hand.

"Oh, hold yer horses. It's all on the sheet," the man groaned as he stood. He maneuvered around Etta's backside, searching the papers on the desk, then slid a packet across the counter. "I figured your lady friend woulda told ya."

Jude snatched the paperwork, scanning. "My what?" he asked, not really listening. *Emergency service fee, veterinary charges...*"Chipping fee! What the hell is this?"

"All dogs are required to be chipped and registered," came the practiced response. "She already has the chip. We just need you ta fill out this form." A printout slid across the counter.

"This is bullshit."

"It's the law. I have to keep the dog if you don't comply," Carl warned, jabbing a finger into the blank registration card.

Jude glanced up to a bored expression. Based on the use of big words like 'comply,' he suspected this situation occurred often. And, as upset as he was, it wouldn't do him any good getting tossed out. Not yet, anyway. He rubbed a hand over his face, releasing a frustrated growl. Etta whined again, and tried to stretch farther across the counter toward him. More things fell off the desk.

"Etta, down," he muttered, disheartened. She hesitated, then shifted to the floor and sat, watching him and waiting.

With a frown, Jude turned his attention back to the form. They'd stuck her with metal. His girl. On a slow, measured breath, pen met paper and he scribbled out his info.

The older man stood after getting the items from the floor. "I'm supposed to tell ya," he set the pile on the desk, "We're allowed to release your information to the owner of the other dogs involved."

"What? What other dogs?"

"Yeah. 'Cause of the altercation. It's the law. Report from the emergency response is in there." He tilted his head to the packet, then leaned in, like he had a secret.

Jude looked up from the form. *Now what?*

"The lady who called it in, she hasn't filed charges or anything." His tone sounded conspiratorial. "She prolly won't. Wealthy type—they're usually all talk unless their dog dies or something."

Brow lifted, Jude stared, totally dumbfounded, then shoved the completed registration form back across the counter. He returned his focus to the packet outlining the incident. "Are you kidding me?! Twelve hundred bucks!?"

Carl leaned in farther and glanced down at the sheet. "One thousand, one hundred and ninety-eight, actually." Jude shot him an unfriendly look. "Yeah, well...better than the dog bleeding to death, right?"

The casual response chaffed his already poor opinion of the place.

"Besides, it's already paid."

"What?"

"Yeah, the lady paid it," Carl said impatiently, like they'd already gone over the fact.

"The lady?"

"Yeah, you know, your lady friend. That mousy one who brought in the collar."

Mousy? Jude knitted his brow. Who the hell was this guy talking about? "What was her name?"

"How the hell should I know? How many lady friends you got, anyway?"

Jude didn't answer.

Carl waved a hand out, "You dog." He winked then squeezed behind the wolfhound, lifting the latch to the saloon style half-door which led to the waiting area.

Etta bolted out, dragging the leash behind her. Planting front paws on his chest, she dolled out several sloppy, wet kisses to his face.

Jude wrapped his arms around her and gave her a hearty scratch. "It's good to see you too, girl," he murmured, "but we don't jump." Bringing her back down to the floor, he un-hooked the kennel leash and dropped it on the counter.

Carl nodded his thanks.

"You don't remember what she looked like? A first name?" Jude tried again. "Did she pay with a credit card?" Someone had forked out twelve hundred bucks for his dog. He wanted to know who.

Slow understanding spread over the manager's features. "I'm not supposed to share that kind of information."

"It's a first name, for crying-out-loud."

Carl crossed his arms.

Jude rubbed the back of his neck and stared up at the ceiling. This whole thing had become a nightmare. All he wanted to do was take his dog home. "I'm not asking you to break the rules. I just want a first name so I can thank her properly."

The argument worked. "Yeah. That's a good idea. A lot of money she forked out."

"Exactly."

The balding man sat down, rolling the chair closer to the desk, and retrieved a small cardboard box from the corner. He flipped through the stack of receipts inside, mumbling the total amounts at the bottom as he did. Watching Carl lick his finger to flip to the next slip, Jude marveled at the high-tech way in which he protected 'that kind of information.'

Drumming his fingers on the counter, his mind racing with questions. Why would some stranger pay his bill? Where was Mountain Rock Animal Clinic? Did he know someone there? Was it an employee that felt bad for Etta? Why hadn't she called him directly? His number was printed on the damn dog tag.

Carl's voice pulled him out of his thoughts. "Just the first name...Looks like 'Evan?'"

Jude looked up. "Erin?"

"Yeah. Could be. Yeah...Erin," he nodded, then filed the receipt back into the box. "Ring any bells?"

Erin? Erin found Etta's collar? Where? When? Where had he been? Did she go out after he told her not to? Images of her braving the storm in those stupid sneakers assaulted his brain.

"She's *not* mousy," Jude retorted under his breath.

"Huh?"

He shook his head. "Nothing. Etta, come on." He led his girl out of the kennel, praying he never had to go back there.

After boosting her into the cab, Jude marched around to the drivers side. He knifed into the front and shoved the key in the ignition. *What the hell?*

He didn't know what to think. Well, he knew why she hadn't called him. But why the hell had she paid the fees? Regret brewed in his gut. Had he misjudged her? It made him feel like an outright asshole. Was this her way of rubbing it in? *That's a hell of a sum for a guilt trip.*

The right thing to do would be to apologize, but she clearly didn't want to see him. Otherwise she would have called, right? He had to do something—he wasn't that much of an asshole.

As he drove back to his cabin he decided a thank-you letter and a check for twelve hundred bucks would be sufficient. Simple, unassuming, and effective. He could just leave it at the door. But it wouldn't answer the burning question still rolling around in his head.

Why?

"Who the hell does that?"

Etta stuck her nose into the side of his head.

"Not you." He sighed, and gave her a rub.

He only had room for one girl in his life and that was Etta.

Chapter Fourteen

Wake-up Call

Erin

When she returned to the cabin, Victor's car was parked out front. She knew it would be. He'd called her in a mood, a few hours earlier, to get the door code. She'd missed the call. Actually, she hadn't gotten the call at all because, she remembered belatedly, she'd blocked his number. But it didn't block the voicemail. She'd texted the code with a one word explanation. 'Working.'

The little mom and pop cafe she'd found offered 'free WIFI' and the owners greeted her with warm, familiar smiles as they had the day before. Erin had stayed well past lunch, reviewing files at her table in the corner.

The owners were a nice, older couple that had moved to the mountains permanently after spending every vacation for twenty years driving up for the ski season. It had been their dream, and now they were living it.

The walls of the cafe were decorated will all kinds of photos and medals from their trips and down hill races. And every time a new customer walked in, they shared the joy of a dream-come-true in the form of smiles, hot beverages and flakey, baked goods.

Erin had never given much thought to her dreams. It had always been about getting to the next step, working day to day, waiting for her diligence to pay off, and hoping one day she'd find herself exactly where she wanted to be with enough in the bank to stay there. But where was that? She didn't know yet.

She'd worked while regulars popped in and chatted with the owners. They gave her friendly waves or teased her for 'working on a day like this.' Erin just smiled back, shrugged, or made a joke about having to pay for the lift tickets some-how. That last one got a few laughs. The real joke was, no way would she be caught dead in skis!

After the lunch rush had quieted, she hunkered down to reply to some emails and to check in with Paul. Two days before the major deadline, she had plenty to do while she sipped her decadent cappuccino, splurging for a second coffee drink that she paired with an after lunch pastry.

The last work task for the day included walking a newer co-worker through the client data input process. In person, it would've been challenging, but over the phone, it felt outright counterproductive. She prayed it all worked out properly as she signed off, packed up, and waved good-bye to the owners.

The husband smiled so wide his eyes were lost in the crows-feet. "See you tomorrow?"

"I expect so," she smiled back.

Shouldering the door open, Erin stepped out onto the sidewalk. The snowy mountains crested high above shops, cabins, telephone poles and tree lines, dividing land and sky in a way that simply took her breath away.

Man, what a view. Some things lost their luster with familiarity, but if this became her everyday, she didn't think she'd ever get tired of staring out at those mountains. As she got in her car, she felt cheery and optimistic.

Erin shut off the engine and stared at the rental. *What am I going to do about Victor?* She frowned as a weight settled over her. She grabbed her stuff and trudged up to the deck in the lightly falling snow. The sky had turned gray again on the drive back and the street sat silent and eerie. A weird, prickly feeling crept up her spine.

She chanced a quick peek across the street. There were lights on. That made her feel a little better. By now, Jude had probably gotten Etta home.

The wind gusted through the icy street as she shifted her armload to punch in the door code. Once inside, she kicked it closed with her foot. Victor had made himself comfortable on the red couch. His computer balanced squarely on his lap and his long fingers wrapped around a short tumbler of generously poured amber liquid. He hadn't bothered taking off his shoes. Something about that irritated her.

He looked up. It felt physical, the way he raked his eyes along her body. His cheeks were flushed.

Erin crossed the entry to dump her stuff on the dining table. She noticed he'd build up a nice fire in the hearth. It popped and danced, heating the room and giving off a welcoming glow.

"Where have you been?" His voice made her stiffen. It wasn't a question as much as an accusation.

Erin turned to face him, exasperated. "I told you. I was working."

"I thought this was your vacation." Before she had a chance to responded, he'd returned his focus to the computer screen.

She crossed to the door and heeled out of her shoes. "It was supposed to be," she mumbled.

The air in the cabin was suffocating. She needed something to do. Moving to the kitchen, she assessed the choices for dinner. Cheese and crackers would have been fine for her, but since Victor would likely need something, and he'd been drinking, she felt compelled to cook.

Erin stared at the contents of the fridge, lacking inspiration and growing more irritated. He was brooding about something and she didn't feel like defending herself. She'd been soaring on mountain vibes and fresh air until pulling up to the cabin and she resented him for raining on her parade.

Victor's moods were the one part of him she did not miss.

This was good, in a weird way, because it had been too easy falling into step with him the other night. No more sharing a bed. Mari'd be up the following day and she might quite literally shit a brick if she saw them together like that. Speaking of...Mari hadn't called yet.

Erin eyed Victor, wondering if he'd make a stink should she duck out to make a call. *After dinner,* she decided. She'd probably need a break from his brooding anyway.

"Are you hungry?" she called to the couch.

"No. I had something while you were *working.*"

"I was working."

"So you say."

Erin scoffed. "Whatever. It doesn't matter if you believe me."

Realizing she still wore her coat, she shrugged it off and went to hang it on the free hook next to Jude's jacket. She could feel Victor watching her. "Thanks for building a fire," she said, trying to appease him.

He rose, setting his laptop and glass down on the coffee table. "I was waiting for you." Right behind her, his tone laid on the guilt.

"Victor, I told you. I had work. And I'll have work tomorrow." *And hopefully Mari will be back,* she didn't say.

He sighed as if forlorn. "I guess you'll just have to make it up to me later." The sour of alcohol on his breath made her nose twitch.

It was fortunate Victor couldn't see her face. The notation that sex be owed for inconvenience was one of her biggest pet peeves, even in jest. She felt cramped. A weird, wiry energy danced off of him, which, mixed with his comment, put her on edge.

"How about I make some dinner?" she suggested, moving out of his space and towards the kitchen.

"I told you, I'm not hungry." The fact that he didn't comment at her domesticity proved his mind lingered on something else.

Victor sauntered back to the couch and kicked his shoes up on the coffee table, repositioning his laptop on outstretched legs. He eyed her as he reached forward to reclaim his drink and Erin wondered how many he'd had.

She moved into the kitchen like she intended to start cooking and discretely tucked the half empty tequila bottle in a cabinet behind a bag of chips. *Out of sight, out of mind,* she hoped. Drunk Victor was horny and persistent. Her best bet, feed him, then put on a movie or two and hope he'd fall asleep.

Erin pulled out ingredients for dinner and starting chopping vegetables. She decided to go all out. Not because she wanted to impress Victor, or because she felt particularly hungry, but to stay busy and keep him off of her. She paused to flex her bandaged hand. It had been throbbing most of the day.

Staring at the cutting board, she realized her reactions toward Victor painted a pretty clear picture as to where she stood with her conundrum. She wasn't swooning from his undivided attention, nor bending over backwards to ease his mood. How had she managed the sudden shift? After all this time? She was afraid she knew. Her eyes tilted up to the front window. It didn't matter. She'd accomplished her goal, which was to be over with Victor. Now if she could just get him out of her cabin...

Erin set a pot on the burner with some oil to heat. She tossed in chopped garlic and onion—the only thing she really know about cooking from scratch.

Her mind kept jumping around like the garlic that sizzled in the oil. Victor's mood. Client data input. The sudden and sickening feeling of buyers remorse. She'd spent nearly twelve hundred dollars on a stranger's dog! Why had she done that?

"Oh, shit!" Distracted, she'd poured a whole jar of marinara sauce into an overly hot pot. It sputtered and hissed and spewed burning, red sauce bombs at her.

She lurched back as the sting hit her skin. Then reaching out, she turned down the heat and gave the pot a quick stir. She grabbed a towel and wiped tomato spots from her arms, neck and as best she could from her shirt. She frowned at the red smeared on the fabric.

Sighing, she tossed the towel on the counter and went to the bedroom to change. She pulled the stained shirt carefully over her head to avoid sauce in her hair. Then, squatting down to her duffle. There were spots on her black pants as well. *Damn.* Not as bad, but still...

She wiggled out of those too, then dug around for a cleanish shirt. She'd just yanked a tank over her head when she heard a desperate wail from the front of the cabin. Panicked, she ran out into the living room without even thinking.

Victor sat frozen on the couch with arms up and away from his body. His face and brow were twisted and fraught with fury.

Erin approached cautiously. "Are you okay?"

He leaned forward and set his empty glass on the coffee table. She saw it then. He'd spilled his drink on his lap, the couch, and if she hazarded a guess, his laptop.

"Help me, dammit!" he barked.

She held her tongue and walked over to the kitchen to retrieve a clean towel, which she offered to him politely. He snatched it.

"You should probably turn it off," she suggested, looking at his computer. He wasn't listening.

"*¡Chingada!*" he cursed, dabbing the keyboard with the towel. "*¡Pinche!*"

She sighed and left him to it. *Drama queen*, she thought to herself, returning to her bedroom. She checked the stove as she passed, putting a lid on the pot before meandering to the back. Erin didn't realize her mistake until his empty glass slammed into the counter behind her. She jumped just as he curled an arm around her waist, dragging her back into the kitchen—into his body.

"Where are you gong?"

"I have to change," she uttered.

"No, you don't. I like you just like this," he insisted in her ear, his hand sliding over hips and down bare thigh. It felt dirty and he was drunk.

Erin cringed. "Can I get you some water?"

She waited for him to release her but he didn't. Instead, he teetered them over to his empty tumbler, reaching around her to grab it, and held it right in her face. She accepted the glass, expecting him to move them to the sink in a similar fashion but he remained by the display of wines.

His arm tightening around her waist."I'll take another drink."

"You'll have to let me go, or I might spill all over us."

"That could be fun." His words came low and eager.

Erin gritted her teeth. Something was...wrong. He wasn't just drunk and horny. "Let's start with water," she suggested. "Don't want you to check out too early." If she played his game, maybe he'd back-off and she'd figure the rest out later.

His grip loosened.

With relief, Erin wriggled out of his hold and made for the sink. She ran the tap, then handed him a full glass from arms length away. He watched her while he drank it.

"I'll be right back," she told him softly, like she'd address a spooked animal, and hoping he didn't notice how her voice shook.

As she turned to the hall, she tried to remember if he'd ever been drunk like this back when they were dating. What had she done then? *I probably thought it was cute,* she cringed. It wasn't cute now. Erin glanced over her shoulder, reassured to see Victor had stayed put. But when she turned back, with only a few steps to her bedroom, he moved like lightning.

She gasped in surprise as her back hit the wall, and too late she realized she'd been pinned. She stared, wide-eyed.

He smirked. "Too slow." His smile dropped. "You hid my booze?"

"S...sorry. I thought you were done. I was just cleaning up."

"Liar," he crooned. It gave her chills.

She looked away. She shouldn't have played his game, but she didn't know what else to do.

He pressed his palms into the wall on either side of her head. "What's wrong, *Mi Cariña*? You're suddenly so shy."

"You're acting strange. It's making me nervous."

"I could say the same."

Her heart thumped in her chest and her legs itched to run. If she got an opening, she'd make straight for the car, half naked, barefoot, and all.

He leaned his face into hers. "What are you thinking?"

"I, um...I—"

"'I, um, I,'" he chuckled. "You're cute when you're like this." Erin flinched back as he brushed his lips against her cheek.

"V-Victor..."

"I'm Victor, now?" His eyes raked down her body, resting at the hem of her tank and the skin below.

"Look, I'm not really up for this. I'm just tired. Okay?"

"Come here, M*i Cariña*."

"Victor—Vic, I'm right here."

"I said, come here!" His hand cupped the back of her head and he brought her to his mouth and kissed her hard. She shoved against his chest. His breath smelled sharp and his lips were rough and unrelenting. When he paused, she tried to push him away.

His hand tightened around the back of her head. "You like him better? Is that it?"

"What?"

"I take care of you when you come to me, horny and needy. But when I am needing you, what do you do? You find another cock to suck? You selfish little bitch."

Erins mouth dropped and her eyes grew wider. "I...I don't know what you're talking about." He'd never spoken to her like that before.

"Make it up to me," he demanded. "...*Mi Cariña*." His words felt hot and sticky and it made her stomach roil. He buried his face in her neck and trailed his tongue up to her jaw.

"Vic," she whimpered.

It wasn't obedience, it was a plea, but he groaned contentedly in her ear. Her mind raced. She couldn't do it. She couldn't give him what he wanted. Neither she couldn't fight him. She had to prove that he didn't need her, that she was just the older, plainer version of the women he could have. "What about Lisa? Or the girl from the bar or...Vic, you could have whomever you want." The desperation in her voice scared her. "You don't need me."

"But I want you."

It could have been the perfect line, but the timing was wrong.

"You could have younger, hotter...someone who can cook. Victor, I am nothing!" she tried again.

"I have nobody. And you made it that way," he slurred. "You owe me."

Erin's breath stuck. *What have I done?*

Mari'd been right. So right. The mountains had given her perspective, though not in a way she'd ever expected. But Victor was the one confirming it now.

"You're not kissing me," he growled. He stepped back and paced the kitchen.

Erin inched sideways along the wall towards the front door.

He shook his head and *tsked.* "Oh, *Cariña.*"

Snagging the empty tumbler, he threw it to the floor. Glass shattered, skating out everywhere. He stalked back to her, designer shoes crunching through crystal mines, and slithered a hand up her chest. It stopped at her throat and wrapped around her neck, pressing her back into the wall. She gasped and he squeezed until she could hear her own heartbeat in her head. Flashes of her dream swirled around reality and she couldn't tell them apart, fear shattering her coherence.

"Vic-tor, please let go," she whimpered. "You're scaring me."

"You're *mine.*" He came in close. "Not his. *Mine.*" He dug his hips against her.

Erin fought back as his hold tightened, fingers wrapping around his wrist, uselessly pulling and prying at his grip.

Her hand and head throbbed. Her throat ached. "Victor, you're hurting me."

"Say it then," he prompted. Hard eyes bore into hers, like he thought he could claim her by sheer force.

"P...please," she gasped out over a sob.

His fingers flexed and his grip eased, but not enough. "Try again," he breathed in her face, eyes dropping to her mouth. "*Mine.* Say it."

His other hand slid down Erin's front with rough, grotesque movements. She cried out, but it only made the collar at her neck tighter. Worse, she realized, he didn't even notice.

Pushing desperately against his chest, arms, and shoulders to no avail, she knew this was her fault. She'd let him into the cabin. She'd carried on with him well past the point it should have been over.

Shame swarmed her. "Victor....s...stop," she gasped.

Stupid, stupid, stupid. And trapped. She couldn't run. She couldn't move. Her chest burned and her head spun. She bucked her body, the only action she had left. Another mistake. He moaned into her hair, grinding himself against her. Her short, shallow breathes were not enough. She felt her body began to cramp, starting with the legs. She wasn't sure how long she could keep standing.

"Vic...too...tight," she rasped in final protest, but she wasn't sure any sound came out.

Terror. Regret.

"You've always been mine," he told her but she could barely hear it over the pounding and swishing of her own pulse. Spots moved into her vision.

His head tipped down. His hand worked at his pants. The grip at her throat was all that held her up. Erin squeezed her eyes shut, wishing like hell it could all disappear. Wishing she could just disappear. Knowing she just might.

Chapter Fifteen

The Bridge

Jude

Splinters flew from the frame as the door burst open with a loud crack. He stormed into the cabin, crossed the room in four long strides, and had the guy by the back of the collar before anyone could even react.

"Get. Off. Of. Her."

He ripped the man away, flinging him back several feet, and crunching over broken glass. Jude forced his eyes to follow. But in his peripheral, he caught the image of a ghost. *Pale. Too pale.*

The guy pushed himself off from the counter, squared his shoulders and puffed up his chest. It might have been humorous, how this piss-ant could think himself even remotely imposing, if Jude wasn't so damn furious.

Words slurred together when he spoke. "Who the hell're you?"

Jude offered no reply, other than to stalk closer. He pushed down the fire and waited for the cocky idiot to make a move.

It didn't take long. "I knew it. I fucking knew't," he seethed, closing the space between them.

Jude accepted the challenge, welcomed it even, glaring the several inches down at the drunken disaster who thought it a good idea to keep speaking.

"You don't get to touch her—"

He pulled his arm back and socked the bastard in the face.

His drunk ass staggered into the counter again, and he had the good sense to hang back. "What the fuck? I'm calling the fucking cops!"

"You do that," Jude replied evenly. "Saves me the trouble."

They stared each other down, and he tried to get a handle on his anger, but it faltered every time Erin wheezed behind him. That's when he processed all the broken glass. Fuck him, he should have been there sooner.

Clenching fists, he waited. Would the creep call his bluff? Jude wanted to beat the man to a pulp. Begged for an excuse. But if the cops came...He took a breath, then another. And one more because the breathing thing wasn't working for him.

The guy smoothed his hair back with a practiced swoop of his hand. "You fuck her?" When Jude didn't answer, his mouth tipped into a sick looking smile. He shook his head. "Figures."

Jude widened his stance. "You should probably leave."

Narrowed eyes evaluated his flexed muscles, hopefully saw the fury radiating from his skin. Only one of them had any business here, and it sure as hell wasn't this scum.

The guy teetered back and threw his hands up in surrender.

"Good choice," Jude clipped.

Jude shot the miscreant a warning look, then, keeping the stranger in his peripheral he turned to Erin.

Jesus. She sat against the wall, knees drawn into her chest. Every tremble was punctuated with a short, raspy gasp. She looked small and terrified—not at all like the woman who'd hand delivered him a hot cup of tea the day before. *I should have been here sooner.*

He scanned the floor around her. No blood, no glass. It was something. "Erin."

She didn't respond.

Movement caught his eye. He glanced back. The guy had scuttled down along the counter into the corner.

"You gonna let yourself out or do you need an escort?" Jude clipped.

With a sullen glare, he started collecting things that went into pockets. Keys, loose change...a wallet. Satisfied, Jude squatted in front of Erin.

Angry red and purpling prints marred her neck. His gut tightened and he held his breath until the urge to kill had passed. Eyes point to the space between them, he contemplated how to handle this. Logically, he knew to leave emotions out of it, to stay calm, and focus on her wellbeing and safety.

But she wouldn't look at him. And that bothered him more than he'd expected. He got it, he'd acted like a dick earlier. But how the hell was he going to get her out of there when she didn't trust him? Because she sure as hell wasn't staying here.

His thoughts distracted him more than he'd realized and he missed the soft hiss of a knife sliding from the wooden block behind him. Erin's erratic breathing and hitches masked the soft footsteps Victor took across the linoleum floor. The tip of a kitchen knife pressed into the back of his jacket.

Fuck.

Jude listed his head in resigned aggravation. He'd underestimated the guy. How had the idiot managed to navigate the glass in his drunken state? Or had emotions clouded his senses? Lifting his hands up to the sides of his head in asinine submission, Jude warred with the anger of his own fucking stupidity.

No more underestimating. No more stupid mistakes. He turned, stealing a sideways glance at his aggressor, and waited for an ultimatum—something stupid like, "get out of here." He didn't know if the man had it in him to follow through, but the knife was sharp and accidents happened. And Erin was prone to accidents. Not a good combination and not worth the risk.

As if she could hear his thoughts, Erin's head lifted suddenly, like she'd just come out of a fog. A glance was all he needed. Wide, glassy eyes relayed shame and fear above a trembling lip. It twisted his gut. He wanted to wipe the look off her face, give her something comforting, but that's when the ultimatum came.

"Get up."

Jude rose slowly, very aware of the sharp point slicing through that first layer of fabric. When the knife jerked, he couldn't hold back the grunt of pain. His gaze dropped to a thousand apologies in Erin's pale face, like this was her damn fault.

"Consider this *your* escort, my friend," the man bragged in triumph.

Jude flinched, grounding his jaw as the knife's point dug in deeper. *Don't be stupid,* he told himself. He let the creep walk him to the door. He could have fought back, but he had something else in mind.

"You should know," the guy breathed on his neck, "she only fucked you to get back at me. She always comes back to *me*." He gave Jude a shove past the threshold and into the falling snow. Jude let him.

This guy is a new kind of stupid.

He left the asshole with his kitchen knife in the open threshold of the cabin with a broken door, forcing himself to move slowly like a man defeated. And the guy was probably just stupid enough to believe it. Unfortunately, that meant he was also stupid enough to hurt someone.

Erin

Jude's departure, although understandable, made Erin's chest ache with loss so deep it almost burned out the pain in her throat. He'd literally been her only hope against Victor in this waking nightmare. A hope she didn't even have until he'd come storming in. And then, just as quickly, he was gone.

Shame, Fear and regret choked the fight out of her.

Victor kicked the door into the threshold where it hung off kilter, blocking the draft, and the view. A chill shook her from the inside. It was just the two of them again, her and a man she hardly recognized. Had she been so blind? How could the person stalking towards her now be the man she'd loved? How had she never seen this side of him before?

Her dream came in flashes as she watched his approach. It shook her like an omen. This was her doing. She *had* seen it. And ignored it. She'd known it all along and she'd done nothing to stop it. Even now, why wasn't she running? In her dream, she'd run.

Erin pushed against the ground and rose to her feet, the room swaying. Pins pricked the inside of her skull. Victor stopped in front of her. She felt weak. She couldn't fight him. When she met his gaze, his face softened and for a moment she hoped maybe he'd had a change of heart.

The corner of his mouth tipped up. "You always come back to me."

The moment fled and Erin cowered against the wall as his arm came up and held the knife point at her face.

"V-Victor," she pleaded hoarsely. He stepped in closer, the blade a whisper from her skin. "Vic...I'm not going to fight you. I'm all yours. Yours. Okay? Please. Please, put the knife down." She had no other cards. He'd won and she could do nothing. A tear slid down her cheek. "You got what you wanted."

A slow, smarmy smile spread over his flushed face. The knife dropped away, hanging loosely in his hand at his side. Her breathing came easier. As long as she didn't provoke him, it would be okay.

And she believed that until she read the intensity in his eyes.

Hungry, hot and lecherous, they burned into her. "Mine," he breathed.

He pressed in, even as her body recoiled, pinning her against the wall. The knife came up to her chin and she felt the blood drain from her face. With his free hand, Victor fisted Erin's shirt. She tensed, every muscles on alert, her adrenaline spiking and giving her the sudden strength to flee. But where could she go?

He leaned back and pulled the fabric away from her body. Then slowly, he brought the knife down and inserted the tip into the taut fabric above her breast. Her heart siezed, just centimeters beneath the cold steel. She couldn't breath, couldn't move, couldn't cry for fear it would be just enough movement to meet the blade with her skin.

"V...Vic," she uttered so softly she didn't know if he heard.

With eyes fixed to her breast, he applied pressure and the knife tore through the cotton with jerky pulls, all the way down to the hem. Erin tensed each time the knife reared back then dove forward again, coming within a breath of her skin.

"What I wanted..." he murmured.

He flipped the knife, sharpened side out, and nestling it between her breasts, then sawed at the fabric of her bra. She could feel the dulled side rub back and forth against her sternum. The blade cut through with one final snap.

"What I want..." he repeated, staring at her body and playfully caressing her exposed skin with the back and side of the blade.

Erin tried not to move under the cool metal but the harder she fought, the stronger the tremors shook her.

Victor chuckled. "I wouldn't hurt you. You are *Mi Cariña*." His breath fell hot and sticky on her. His face glistened with intoxication. His hooded eyes raked lustfully over her chest.

She closed her eyes and pushed back a wave of nausea. "You did hurt me Victor." Her voice was small and weak.

"*Cariña*, don't lie to me."

"When you held my throat."

His eyes met hers. "You needed a lesson. You hurt me. You broke my heart." The humor and playfulness dropped, leaving just the scorned, vengeful lover. "You cruel, heartless bitch! You didn't think what it did to me! You didn't think...you didn't care," he slurred.

Erin strained to piece together what he was saying as the back of the knife danced across her chest.

"I get no chance to win you back?"

"Not like this," she cried.

"You left me. Left me when I needed you. Erin. *Mi Cariña*...I needed you."

"Vic...I—I didn't..."

Her mind raced as the blade taunted her. What could he possibly see in a boring workaholic who avoided tight clothes, makeup and hair gel—a woman who fell over her own two feet. She couldn't cook, she couldn't ski, she couldn't even start a damn pilot light. How could that be what he wanted? How could anybody want that?

She whimpered as Victor pushed aside the cup of her bra and closed his hand over her breast. He groaned as he grounded his hips into her. "Tell me how much you want me," he challenged.

The knife pivoted off its flat surface and tilted onto the honed blade. Erin's voice stuck in her throat, though she couldn't think to speak anyway. His clouded eyes watched the metal play on her skin, dragging it lightly up her chest and toying and twisting dangerously around her collar bone.

"Tell me!"

Tears leaked down her cheeks. How had this happened? How had she gotten here? On a nothing Wednesday that started out like any other day? She should've gone back with Mari. She should've stayed home from the beginning. Never walked over to Victor's table and mouthed off. Never met Mari for drinks in the first place.

She wished she could go back. Back to when she was miserable but she didn't know it and she'd still had her stupid hope. Back when he was just Vic, the man who'd dumped her to be with another woman.

But she couldn't rewind and she couldn't forget.

Her tears fell steadily now. He leaned in and licked them. She thought she knew him. 'You broke my heart,' he'd told her.

This is my fault.

There was no warning. The slam of the front door hitting the wall came simultaneously with the recognizable cocking of a shotgun. Erin's eyes grew wide when Jude materialized in kitchen, barrel of the gun pointed at Victor's head. The knife jerked and she grunted as the hot sting of the blade sliced her skin.

"Drop the knife."

"You wouldn't," Victor challenged.

"You think?"

"You'd splatter my brains all over her face? You think that'll *impress* her?" Victor sneered.

Erin felt faint. She didn't want Victor's brains all over her face. But she didn't want him doing what he'd been doing either. In truth, she didn't want anything to do with either of them. She just wanted to disappear.

"I don't care how drunk you are..." Jude started.

"Who-the-fuck do you think you are?!" Victor interjected.

"...You are going to get in your car and drive away and you will not come back," he instructed, enunciating each word. His voice sounded strangely calm but when Erin stole a glance, Jude's face was tight and his mouth a hard, thin line.

"You won't shoot me."

"Be advised, this here, right now, this isn't about her. This is about you and me and my dog."

Victor seemed to think about this for a moment but still didn't move.

"Reason all you want," Jude told him, "I'm calling this self defense. You attacked me." He looked angry enough to kill. And she worried he might. "The evidence is on my jacke—"
A whine interrupted them. His eyes cut to the front of the cabin. "Dammit."

Erin shifted her gaze to see Etta just inside the threshold.

"Etta, home." The calm in his voice faltered. Instead of obeying, her ears tweaked back and her body went alert. "Etta!" Jude warned.

She took a step into the cabin and growled, showing her lower teeth.

"Found your bitch, I see," Victor spat.

What does that mean? Erin looked to him.

"I did. She's usually very friendly but she doesn't like you. Any idea why?"

Victor's grip on the knife tightened until his knuckles went white. Erin held her breath and watched his face. An unchecked storm brewed behind his eyes. He was drunk and angry and unpredictable.

"I'm not going to stand around forever," Jude pushed and Erin felt sick as the knife teetered on her skin.

Etta growled.

"What are you gonna do?" Jude asked. "What's it going to prove?"

Victor looked straight at Erin. "You stupid fucking—"

"How's this going to look when the cops get here?" Jude cut in and Erin wished he'd shut up.

Victor's face twisted in fury. Jude had just made it worse and the knife inched up to her throat. She shrunk into the wall in panic and for an agonizing moment, she could almost feel the blade slicing across her neck.

"You ready to go to jail?"

The pressure of the metal lifted from her skin. She took a jagged breath.

"Knife on the ground," Jude ordered.

The silence felt heavy as Victor rolled his head on his neck, his jaw tight, and Erin waited in terror for his next move. *Unpredictable.*

Finally, he opened his hand and let the knife clatter to the floor. Erin dared a sharp inhalation.

"Door," Jude instructed.

Victor stepped away and relief flooded her system. Without warning, his arm swung up and pulled back. Erin didn't have time to protect her face as his fist came racing towards her. She squeezed her eyes shut. The blow never came.

"Door."

Erin opened her eyes. Jude had him in a head lock with the barrel of the shotgun.

"Don't make me ask again."

"My shit's here," Victor garbled.

"Erin, get his *shit.*"

At first, she didn't realized he'd spoken to her. Then, it took her a second to get moving. She pushed off the wall and ran into the back to grab the bag he'd brought in. She gathered stuff from the bedroom and bathroom and tossed it loosely in his luggage.

Then she came out to get his laptop, making a wide berth around the men. She could feel eyes track her as she passed them. She shoved the computer and cables in his bag, then zipped it closed.

"Put it by the door," Jude ordered, his focus on the top of Victor's head. Erin did as he asked. "Now go in the back."

She stared at him, wide eyed, and afraid he was going to shoot her ex.

"In the back Erin!"

First palling at his intensity, she hurried to the back of the cabin and into her bedroom. There she sat, on the edge of her bed, on the verge of throwing up, and waiting for the sound of a gunshot.

Chapter Sixteen

Safe Haven

Jude

"Erin?" He entered the bedroom with Etta right behind him, though he probably should have waited. He was all keyed up.

She sat on the edge of the bed, white as a ghost. A trickle of blood started just below her neck and meandered south. Her clothes were cut down the center and splayed open, showing way more skin than Jude felt comfortable with in that moment. And she hadn't tried to cover up. Her eyes stared, miles away. He suspected she couldn't even see him.

"Erin," he called again, softly.

She didn't respond. *Shock?* A sharp, squeezing pain swamped into his chest cavity on top of all the anger threatening to boil over. The sensation felt foreign and Jude might've worried he was having a heart attack. But he knew better. He also knew that the longer she stayed there, motionless and exposed, the worse the pain would get.

Shit. The image of her like that would be burned in his brain forever.

"Be right back," he muttered, then strode back to the front to check the street one more time.

He should have trailed the guy out of town, made sure he didn't circle back. He hadn't been thinking straight.

Brushing the snow off his jacket, Jude came back in and scanned the interior of the cabin. He tried not to let his mind linger on Erin's empty eyes. There was shit to do, like put out the fire and deal with the pot still simmering on the stove.

He dumped the shotgun on the dining table then snagged a piece of firewood from the half barrel. With it, he pushed over the burning logs so they laid flat on the bottom of the fireplace. They'd burn out quickly now. Then he crossed to the stove, kicking the broken glass aside with his boot, and turned off the burner.

Next? he thought, trying to keep it together, but thoughts of that knife against her throat kept interrupting his focus. He moved into the living area and snatched a blanket off the floor. It was damp and smelled like alcohol but it was big enough to cover her yet small enough to manage.

He marched back into the bedroom and without pause, thrust the blanket out to her. "Here, take this."

She flinched. Etta's head lifted from her lap.

"Jesus...Erin. I'm not going to hurt you." His tone came out harsher then he'd intended. "Just take the blanket." She stared at it. "Take it."

Reaching out with shaky hands, she did as she was told. Jude noted the blood seeping through the bandage on her palm. Working his jaw, he tried to shut it down—the rage. Not the time to deal with that shit yet, not the time to get angry all over again. He had to get her out of the rental in case that asshole was stupid enough to come back.

Etta's head settled on the bed next to Erin and she let out a stringy whine. Erin's dull eyes just stared at the blanket in her hands. Instead of draping it around her body like Jude had expected her to, she just held it bunched up in front of her.

Fine, next? He forced an exhale out slowly as he surveyed the room. A large duffle sat in the corner. "This your stuff?"

Big green, eyes shot up to his. *Dammit, s*he looked scared. Of him?

"Your stuff?" he tried again, keeping his voice soft.

She nodded. "Y-yes."

He moved to the bag, digging around and finding all kinds of useless shit. Finally he came up with some pajama pants and a t-shirt, underwear and socks. He rolled it all up into a wad and tucked it under his arm as he stood.

Jude pointed at the blanket still clutched in a ball at her chest. "Wrap that around you. It's cold outside."

Her brow furrowed.

"You can't stay here," he explained, working to bury his exasperation. He didn't think it was that hard to follow. "You don't have a working door."

That's when she finally reacted. "Where...where am I s-supposed—" she stuttered out, her tone panicked as she straightened.

"I'm taking you over to my cabin."

She shook her head violently. "No."

"I'm not leaving you here by yourself with that...nut job on the loose."

'Nut job' wasn't his first choice, but a much more polite variation than what first came to mind. Still, she looked away. Just being in this place made him tick. It couldn't be much better for her. He wanted to go. What would it take to get her out of there?

"Look, I'm sorry for what I said earlier, okay? I was being a dick. But please don't let that get in the way of doing what's smart here."

That got her attention. She went rigid. The woman was killing him. For a brief moment, Jude wondered how poorly it would go if he just threw her over his shoulder.

No, he knew that wouldn't fly. He tipped his head back and stared at the ceiling, hoping for some inspiration or something. What if she remained unwilling? He couldn't leave her here.

Maybe he should just call the police. They knew how to deal with people in shock. But when he swung his eyes back to her he couldn't bring himself to do it. He couldn't put her through any more shit, not all in one night.

They'd bring her down to the station, and question her, and she'd have to relive it all over again. She'd have to get in the back of one of those police cruisers, like a criminal. They'd sit her in one of those sterile gray rooms, exposed and vulnerable and alone. It may have been a selfish call, but he just couldn't do it. He couldn't let her out of his sight. He'd figure out something.

Jude squatted in front of her, looking up and catching her eye. "Erin, I need you to move, honey." She looked at him with blank eyes. "I don't want to scare you, but this place isn't safe for you right now."

"Do you think he'll come back?" she whispered, the sound hoarse, and it nearly broke him.

"I don't know."

She nodded then and stood. And fuck him, she cradled that blanket like a baby, and moved to the door. Etta popped up and followed, tail drooping behind her. He rubbed a hand over his face, taking a breath, and pleaded with whatever powers out there for patience as he moved to block to doorway.

Dropping the wad of her clothes to the floor, he reached an arm out. "Give me the blanket."

She flinched. Her grip tightened around the wool.

"Erin, give me the blanket."

When she finally relinquished her hold, he shook it open and draped it around her back and over her shoulders, bringing the two sides together in front of her. Her nose flared and a strange look passed over her face. What little color she'd regained seemed to disappear.

Alcohol, he realized. That guy had reeked of it. *Shit.* "Take it," he told her.

Her hands slipped up from under the cover to hold the blanket in place.

Jude stooped to grab her clothes, then stepped out into the hallway and waited for her to follow.

"Come on," he urged. "I want you safe behind a locked door. We can worry about all the other stuff later, deal?"

She stared at him, expressionless.

"Jesus Erin, work with me here."

"Deal," she whispered, although it sounded reluctant.

He frowned. "Erin."

"What?" The word came out sharp and with more spite than he'd expected.

"Nothing. Never mind." W*orry about the other stuff later.*

She followed him out into the front. Jude grabbed the shotgun from the dining table as they passed. He saw her phone sitting there and picked it up as well, tucking it in her pile of clothes.

"You left the gun out here?"

He couldn't tell her it wasn't loaded, that he didn't even know if it worked. Instead, he left her inside to check the street again. "He's not out there." He came back in. "Time to go. Get your shoes."

She held the wall for balance as she stepped into her sneakers. He waited for her to readjusted the blanket. She was coming out of her stupor, even throwing attitude. Jude didn't know much about shock, but that all seemed like progress. Etta waited by her side through all of this, like Erin's sentry.

Once out in the snow, he positioned the door to look locked up. It would only take a finger to push it open but he'd deal with it later.

A flurry gusted through the deck and Erin shivered. "You okay?" he asked, eyes skimming her bare legs.

She nodded. White flakes settled on her head, eyelashes and shoulders.

If this were any other moment, he thought. "Okay, let's go."

He pressed his hand into her back just below her shoulder blades and urged her forward. The three of them cautiously made their way out onto the quiet, icy street and every noise had him checking the road.

He cast a glance to his truck as they passed it, half expecting to see broken windows, slashed tires, or at least a good keying. But from where he stood, it looked untouched. Still, Jude remained on edge. The guy didn't seem the kind of person to walk away with his tail between his legs, not without having the last word at least. And if the last word wasn't vandalism to his truck, then what was it?

As they climbed the steps to his place, Erin's body grew stiff and her step faltered. She resisted the gentle push at her back.

"I told you where we were going," he gritted out. "You wanna fight about it some more, out here in the snow?"

"No."

"Good. Can you get the door?"

"It isn't locked?"

"No. I was in a rush."

Erin hesitated and shivered beside him, otherwise un-moving. He took a breath but it didn't make him feel any better. Using the arm he'd had at her back, he reached around her to grasp the handle, and swung the door wide with exaggerated force. It slammed into the wall. She flinched and Jude cursed himself for not being able to keep it together.

Etta squeezed through into the cabin without pause—no hackles raised, no growls—and he relaxed.

"You going in?" He didn't push her this time. He didn't even touch her.

She entered the safety of his home in a few stiff steps in. Just far enough so that he could follow and close the door behind them.

"Why don't you sit down," he suggested and even though Etta seemed at ease, Jude did a cursory check around his place.

Satisfied, he came back to the front. Erin hadn't moved. She glanced around the room, then over at him. She looked tired, pale, and scared. Those big, round, green eyes made him want to do things he knew he shouldn't. That quivering mouth more so. He had to look away. He'd been pushing too much down and he could feel it all threatening to come up.

He needed to do something productive. He wandered to the armchair. "You can sit here," he patted the backrest. "I'll make a fire." Thankfully, she followed.

He replaced the dummy shotgun on the mantle, then kneeled down to build up the kindling, scooching Etta out of the way to do so. While the flame grew steady, he strode to the couch for a cleanish, dry blanket. As an afterthought, he sniffed it. At least it didn't smell like alcohol.

Erin studied the dancing flames so he draped the blanket on the arm of the chair and bent to give Etta a 'good girl' scratch. While down there, he tossed on another log. As he watched it catch, he wondered how to proceed.

Now that the situation was under control, now that Erin was safe in his cabin, reality trickled back in. Now that the adrenaline had worn off, anger trumped worry.

Standing, he checked the front door, ensuring the dead bolt was in place. It was over. He'd gotten her there like he'd wanted to. She was safe. And he'd been pretty calm through it all. Something had to give.

"Okay Erin, I've gotta ask," he stared, words bouncing back at him from the wood door. He turned, stalking to the armchair. "What the *hell* were you doing with that asshole!"

He raised his brow in challenge, daring those wide eyes open mouth to give him something. Anything. She looked ready to shout back at him. *Good.* He preferred it to this closed-off shit.

As if in slow motion, she reined it all back in and pursed her lips. "You don't have to yell," she uttered. "I can hear you just fine."

Jude inhaled sharply and tried again. "Who the hell was that guy? Is that your *boyfriend*?" The words tasted bitter. They sounded worse.

She turned away from him.

"Shit," he muttered.

Her boyfriend? That really messed with his head. He took a minute, pacing and running a hand through his hair. What was he supposed to do with that?

The silence stretched between them. He'd made it worse. She'd gone closed off again. Moving to the front of her chair, he squatted so he could catch her eyes. Etta sat up and started nosing his face. He pushed her gently back down with his hand and gave her a reassuring rub.

To Erin, he said, "Hey,"

She met his gaze with narrowed eyes.

"I'm sorry," he started again, resting elbows on bent knees. "I shouldn't have yelled at you. I'm not angry with you. This isn't your fault." Erin's breath hitched and he waited but she didn't say anything. "I won't yell anymore. Okay? At least, I'll try. I just..."

He just what? Let his anger get the best of him? Felt lost at what to do with this overpowering need to watch out for her? Agonized over blaming her for Etta? Hated how she looked at him just then?

"I'm sorry," he repeated.

"It's okay. You were just doing your job," she said cooly, her eyes blank.

"What?"

"Nothing. It doesn't matter."

Fuck.

He'd blown it. And he didn't know how to fix it. He held her eyes with his, hoping she'd see those things he was thinking so he didn't have to figure out how to explain them. He wanted this even though the thought of being that open around someone else made his skin crawl. If she saw anything, she gave no response.

He grabbed at the back of his neck with both hands. "Jesus, you're killing me here. Please say something. I don't care if you yell at me or call me names." Though he hoped she didn't, because stupid as it seemed, he did actually care what she thought of him.

"Thank you."

He waited for the, "but," or for her to lash out, but those two words were all she gave. A sheer glass coated her eyes and her jaw got tight. Lips twitching to the side, she sniffed. Jude realized she was trying not to cry in front of him.

He stood and grabbed the blanket off the arm of the chair. "This is for you."

She dipped her head and took the clean blanket. He turned to let her switch them out privately, but not before he caught a glimpse of blood smeared on her chest.

"Does your cut hurt?" he asked the fireplace. He heard her shift back into the chair.

"My cut?"

Turning back to face her, "Yeah, your...your cut," he reiterated, gesturing to his own chest, and wondering how she could have forgotten.

"Oh." Her face scrunched as she took a peek under the blanket. And damn him, it was adorable. "It's okay. Maybe..." she trailed off as she tipped her head down again, probing the area lightly with her finger. "Do you just have...a band-aid. Maybe two?" Her voice shook on the last part.

Tougher than you look. Admiration settled somewhere in his chest cavity. "Can I see it?"

Her eyes met his with a hint of dread.

"Fine," he backtracked. "How about your hand? That hurt?"

She shook her head.

Jude had a hard time believing her. He could just do it, dress the cuts anyway. But a strange wariness had settled over him, like he had something to lose in all of this. "Okay. I'll just leave the emergency kit in the bathroom for you. You'll want to replace the bandage on your hand too," he told her, feeling dejected. "It's bleeding again."

Jude did as he said he would, putting out things for her in the bathroom. When he came out, Erin hadn't moved. She stared blankly into the fire, a cheek on her hand on the arm of the chair. She looked tired and lost and lonely. He wanted to help, which felt at odds with his usual MO. He wanted to wipe the sadness off her face, but he didn't know his boundaries anymore.

Bullshit. He knew where *his* boundaries were. His wall was nothing but dust. Something about her had burrowed under his skin. And he wanted to see where it went. But her? What were her boundaries? Especially after what had just happened in the rental.

Jude wandered into the kitchen and leaned his palms into the counter. "You hungry?"

She looked over at him, her eyes dull. "No."

He supposed he could understand the loss of appetite. "Well, I'm going to make something. I'll make enough for two."

He watched her nod, eyes fixed back to the fire. Then he made minestrone soup from scratch. Well, except for the beans, which were canned. And every so often, he looked up to check on her. Etta'd put a paw up on her leg.

Dogs could get away with so many things humans couldn't, Jude reflected. He wanted to offer her comfort too, to touch her, to curl her into his lap and hold her there. He envied Etta in that moment.

While the soup cooked, Jude prepped Etta's chow and shook the bowl before settling it down on the floor in the kitchen. He heard the click of nails on the wood floor, then a few seconds later, Etta rounded the cabinets. She made short work of her dinner then, loyal to the core, returned to the arm chair and settled. This time, her big grey body sprawled out across her rug to soak up the heat from the fire.

Jude glanced at Erin. "Soup's on."

She didn't move. He wasn't sure she'd even heard him, but he didn't repeat himself and he didn't push it. He sat at the bar with his bowl and some bread. It turned out, he didn't have much of an appetite either, but he ate anyway, hoping she'd wander over and join him.

She didn't.

Standing with his empty bowl, she asked, "Last call. You want some soup?"

"No, thank you."

He tried not to be discouraged as he putzed in the kitchen, stealing glances. He filled the kettle and when the whistle pierced the silence, he pulled his favorite mug from the cabinet. Adding the water, he left a good inch of space at the top so she wouldn't spill it on herself. Then he brought it over and set it on the side table next to her chair.

"It's not Rooibos," he said apologetically, hoping he'd pronounced it right.

Her gaze moved over to the tea cup, then up at him. Something other than nothing shifted behind those glassy greens and it felt like a win.

"Anything else I can get you?"

She shook her head.

"Don't forget about that cut," he reminded her. She didn't look away like he'd expected her too.

Suddenly, Jude didn't know what to do with his hands. He started to shove them into his pockets but changed his mind at the last minute and stuck them at his hips. "Got a couple things to do," he told her. "You let me know if there is something you need."

"Okay."

She offered a weak smile. He nodded back, relieved. Then got busy doing stuff he didn't really need to be doing in the dark, like shoveling off the porch, fixing a part of the railing that had come loose, and then double checking his tool shed to make sure he'd locked up. He also went back to check over his truck, which looked fine.

He stomped the snow off his boots before coming back into the cabin. The heat hit his face like a tidal wave. He peeled out of his coat and hung it on a hook by the door. When he passed the armchair, he peeked into the mug. It was half empty, so he took it with him to the kitchen and topped it off with more hot water.

"Thanks," she murmured when he set it back down.

There wasn't much else he could do and he got the impression she wanted space. "I'm gonna turn in." Jude had no idea what time it was. "Your clothes are on the bar," he indicated to the breakfast bar. "Emergency kit is in the bathroom. I restocked it. You already know where the bathroom is." He paused and looked around. "Don't worry about the fire. It'll burn itself out. Though, if you think about it, maybe hit the lights." She nodded. "There's an extra blanket and a pillow on the couch for you."

What else? He didn't want to walk away but there wasn't really anything left to do or say.

"If you get hungry, help yourself to anything," he added. "Or just ask. You can come get me anytime." *Jesus, Jude, stop talking.*

He looked down to Etta, who turned a sleepy eye on him. Normally he'd send her to her bed under the stairs for the night, but he debated letting her stay at Erin's feet instead. The thing was, he knew first hand that exceptions became habits. He looked at Erin. He didn't feel right leaving her all alone. *Well, that's decided.*

Etta yawned and settled and Jude stood another moment trying to think of something reassuring to say. Nothing came to mind and the longer he lingered without purpose, the more he started feeling like an idiot.

"Right, well, good night," he said, pivoting and clearing out.

"Jude?"

He stopped and turned, hope flooding his chest.

"Thanks, again."

Her smile looked stronger, not quite to her eyes, but more than just the corners of her mouth. He smiled back, nodded, then disappeared into the back bedroom before he could do anything stupid, like kiss her.

Chapter Seventeen

Unrequited

Erin

She sat up, wondering if she could make it back over to the rental to grab her phone. The past—what felt like an hour—of solitude had slowly eaten a hole in her chest and she couldn't stand it anymore. But the thought of returning sent her heart racing and her stomach roiling.

Did Jude really think Victor might try to come back? She'd see his car...and if he hadn't come back yet, he probably wouldn't, right? *If I'm quick...* But first, pants.

She pushed herself to the edge of the chair. Etta stirred and lifted her large head.

"Shh, it's okay girl," she cooed, giving her a pet, and pointing her gaze to the pile of her clothes on the bar. Sitting on top was her phone. It gouged a chasm in her chest.

He'd thought of everything. *Too good to be true.* And in the morning, when she reassured him she was fine, he'd undoubtably send her back across the street to her own place.

She stood, careful not to step on Etta's outstretched legs, and retrieved her cell. It had full bars. All the times she'd wandered down the street, she could've just stood on Jude's porch. She wouldn't have, that would have been weird, but still.

Tugging the blanket around her, phone now in hand, she crept to the front, silently sliding the deadbolt out and slowly pulling the door open. It creaked and she froze, then turned to check the cabin.

Etta sat up and peered at her from around the chair, letting out a little whine.

"I'll be right back," she whispered, and as quietly as she could, clicked the door closed behind her.

Navigating to the top step of the porch, which had been cleared of snow, she sat, huddling under her fleecy cover. The chill stung through but her mind worried of other things. *Mari's going to freak out.* Her palm throbbed as the line rang.

"*Chica!*" Mari greeted.

Erin could hear the beat of music in the background. "Hey Mari."

"Oh no. You don't sound good. Give me one second." The noise in the background grew quieter. "What's up?"

"Please don't freak out."

"*Chica.*"

Now that she had to say it out loud, she wasn't sure she wanted to talk about it. Everything she'd managed to stuff down came back up and threatened to spill over again.

"Erin, what happened? Are you okay?"

She shivered under the blanket and watched her breath fog in front of her while she tried to pick the parts she could share without breaking. Tightness rose up her throat. "Victor came by the cabin."

"What!"

Erin pulled the phone away from her ear while her friend vocalized some high volume expletives in both English and Spanish.

"Yeah," she replied, once Mari had settled. "All those things."

"¡Dios mio! What the hell? How did he even know where you were? Is he still there?"

"No! God No. He isn't." Erin bit her lip. She had to tell her. And there was no way around it. "Victor said that he overheard you talking to a client at the gym." She held her breath. A long silence stretched on the other end.

Then Mari went at it again. "No! Oh, Erin! Soy tan estupida! Me olvidé que..."

Mari went on in Spanish but Erin lost her after "estupida." The cold sunk in past the gaps in the blanket, and she shifted to cover more of her legs.

"Erin, I'm so sorry. I can't believe how stupid I am!"

"I'm not mad. And I don't blame you. He's the one who came uninvited."

"Still, I can't believe I did that! I wasn't even thinking! I'm so sorry!"

"You already said that." She tucked her chin into the blanket and let the warm breath melt her frozen nose. "Mari, this isn't your fault. I'm the stupid one. I screwed up." Her voice wobbled. "You told me. You told me to ditch him."

"Oh, honey."

Those sympathetic words, the unrelenting support from her friend, it was what she'd needed. And hug, but she'd have to wait for that. Tears slipped down her cheeks like icy rivers. She sniffed.

"Are you crying?"

Then she sobbed.

"*Diga me*, what happened?"

Erin cleared her throat and wiped her cheek on the blanket. "He came to the c-cabin last night, but he left about an hour ago." Had it been an hour?

"He stayed *overnight*?"

"I didn't...we didn't. I didn't even want to." Erin assured her, though she wasn't positive.

"So he just left?"

"Sort of..."

"What does that mean?"

Erin couldn't bring herself to share the details as she looked down the dark, quiet street. He'd shaken her. He'd shown her a side of him she never knew existed. For a moment, she thought he was going to...She wouldn't...no, couldn't go there.

She heard someone talking to Mari on the other end of the phone. "Sorry, one minute *chica*."

A stead shiver traveled along her limbs. She should have changed into her clothes. Digging heels against her butt, she hugged her bent legs to her chest and rested her head on top of her knees. Campfire and soap wafted up from the borrowed blanket. Even though she knew she shouldn't, she let her mind wander into fantasy.

"Back," Mari said in her ear. "So...you were telling me--'"

"Are you still planning on coming tomorrow?"

"Oh. *Mira*, I should have called you earlier." Erin's heart sank in the pause. "I had to make another appointment for tomorrow. It's a mess over here. But I'll come up right after," Mari explained apologetically. "I should be there by 10."

"Do they need you?" The last thing Erin wanted was to make someone else's life more difficult. She wasn't a burden...at least, she tried not to be.

"I said I'd come back."

"Mari, do what you need to do." She secretly hoped this gave her the argument-free out to just come home. But she didn't want to get into that now. "I'm fine."

"You don't sound fine."

"I am. I will be." She stared at the tracks in the road that Victor's car left behind. Despite it all, she worried if he'd make it somewhere safely.

"I'm gonna come up."

"No. No—"

"I am. I don't think you should be alone." The beat in the background amped up as if Mari'd gone back inside a club. In reality, she was probably still at her gym.

"It's fine," Erin insisted.

"No. I'm coming up. Tomorrow. I'm gonna see if I can duck out earlier."

"Mari--"

"I don't want you by yourself. You get all up in your head and—"

"Mari! Mari, it's fine! I'm not alone!" she blurted.

The pause on the other side spoke volumes. Erin could guess what her friend deduced.

"Hold the phone...Jude?"

"What about him?" Erin deflected.

"You and Jude?"

"What? Why would you assume—"

"Oh *dios mio* Erin, I saw how he was looking at you! You seriously can't tell me he hasn't made a move!"

"A move?" *I wish.* "No, it's not like that," Erin replied.

"Is he the '*sort of?*'"

"What?"

"Oh! Did he kick Victor's ass?" Mari's enthusiasm was a little scary.

"Not technically. No."

"You're killing me! I need details!" her friend pleaded.

"It isn't...I'm not ready to talk about it yet," Erin admitted, her throat tightening all over again.

"But you're with Jude?" Mari pressed.

"Sort of...Yes. I'm mean, I'm staying at his cabin for tonight."

"His cabin?"

"It's not like that."

"How is it like?" Mari ask with a hint of accusation, the gossipy kind.

Erin groaned. She'd just dug herself into a hole. "I'll fill you in when you get here...or when I get home. Whichever comes first." No response. "I'm not going into it now," she warned.

"Okay...sheesh."

But she did need to pour her heart out at some point. Erin buried her face into the fabric at her knees and took in a deep, intoxicating breath. What was wrong with her? He wasn't even her type. She didn't go for tall, muscular...perfect men. Well, almost perfect. She wasn't a fan of his icy stares. But he hadn't given her any of that lately. Not that it would matter. She couldn't possibly be *his* type.

"What's his bedroom like?" Mari asked, thoughtfully.

"I wouldn't know."

"But his cabin? That just seems so...intimate."

"You just won't give up," Erin laughed half-heartedly.

"You could just tell me more. It'll get me off your back."

"I seriously doubt that." But her friend's eagerness and the conversation offered a welcomed distraction from the ickiness she felt inside. "Fine. But I'm only telling you this to prove you wrong, that there is nothing noteworthy going on. The short version is, Jude's dog went missing, I helped him find her, then, as a thank-you, he stepped in to help me get Victor off my back."

"Oh?" If they were having drinks, Mari would be leaning in conspiratorially. "And how do you know why he did it?"

"Why else would he?"

"I wonder."

Erin let out a bitter laugh. "Believe me, it was out of duty and nothing more."

"How can you be so sure? You know, you are constantly undervaluing yourself," Mari pointed out.

"I am *sure*."

"Did he say that's why he did it?"

Erin dropped her forehead to her knees. Sometimes Mari could be so persistent. "He didn't have to Mari! You weren't there."

"Then explain it to me."

"He said some things...They were true, but unkind. Then he made it pretty clear he wanted nothing to do with me. There. Are you happy?" A wave of regret washed over her.

"That doesn't make any sense. What did he say?"

"Look, I can't really talk about it right now," Erin pleaded, looking over her shoulder at the curtain covered window. She didn't know how well sound traveled through these cabins.

"Is he there with you?"

"No," she scoffed. "I'm out on the front porch. He went to hide in his bedroom just as soon as he could get away from me."

"*Mira chica*, I'm sure it isn't—"

"Oh it definitely is."

Mari sighed, but she stopped arguing. "I'm sorry, *chica*."

"It's fine," Erin sighed, tucking a strand of hair behind a frozen ear. "Things were going south before Victor showed up."

"If i'd have known..Maybe this trip was a bad idea."

"You had the best intentions. And it served its purpose. I am *definitely* over Victor."

Her friend didn't comment. They sat silently on the phone together. Her teeth started chattering, but even freezing under a blanket, Mari's silent companionship was better than the solitude in the cabin. Erin looked across the street at the dark, rental and the shadowed, broken, front door. What a mess. Hopefully Shauna planned on replacing it anyway. Still, until then, the place needed something that closed and locked.

She'd pay for it, of course, though she wondered how much it would rack up her already high credit on this trip. It wouldn't be a five minute job like the pilot light.

"Erin," Mari called in her ear. "Where's my girl at?"

"Huh? Oh...just thinking." She sunk her chin into her knees. "How close are you and Shauna?"

At that moment, the cabin door creaked open behind her. Erin jumped, nearly toppling off the top step. She whipped her head around and saw Jude filling the doorframe, silhouetted by the glow from inside.

He flicked on the porch light. The day's attire had been changed into flannel pajama bottoms and a long sleeve henley that fit him conservatively. She gulped, feeling heat rise into her face. Leaning a broad shoulder into the door frame, his eyes shifted to check the street.

They came back to her. "I don't want you sitting out here alone." Etta whined behind him.

"Hey Mari," she said softly, turning to face the street. "I've got to go."

"Mhmm. Don't do anything I wouldn't do."

"Yeah. No problem there."

She ended the call and stood, re-adjusting the blanket to hide her body. The cold crept in, sending her into a full body shiver. Jude blocked the door. She looked up. His expression was cold and distant, like that first night. Wasn't that just the perfect end to a shitty day?

He stared down at her a moment. Finally he stepped back into the cabin and let her pass. It all felt too familiar. She shuffled inside, passing Etta, and retreating to the chair by the fire. The heat worked immediately to shed the outer chill, but it did nothing for her insides. Even though they shared the space, she felt painfully alone.

The slide of the deadbolt echoed in the quiet cabin, and Jude didn't linger. "You done with this?" he asked, picking up the mug from the side table.

"Yes. Th-thanks."

He strode into the kitchen and she watched as he washed it by hand and put it on the drying rack. He seemed tense. Had she already overstayed her welcome?

"Sorry," she finally managed as he dried his hands on a towel.

"For what?"

"I thought you were asleep. I didn't want to disturb you...with the phone call."

"Not asleep." He tossed the towel down onto the counter.

Between his rigid posture, his short, abrupt responses, and his refusal to look at her, Erin easily put two together. He didn't want her there. "Maybe I should just go back to the rental—"

"Just stay in the cabin." His voice came at her harsh and nonyielding.

"Okay." Her eyes stung. "I'll stay in the cabin."

He finally glanced up at her. Silence stretched. He stared, arms crossed and mouth tight. "Don't forget to take care of that cut."

Erin pressed her lips together and nodded. *Don't cry. Don't cry.*

Cursing under his breath, he turned and walked out of the room. The sound of his door closing felt like a punch in the stomach. She had hoped, just for a second, that maybe he'd wanted to say something reassuring or that he'd offer to sit with her.

Stupid.

A little hole formed in her chest. She trudged to the couch and flopped down, curling her knees into herself, and pulled the blanket clear over her head. It smelled so damn good. Her body shook with held back sobs.

I'm such an idiot!

Etta's nails clicked across the wood floor, then stopped nearby. Her large body pulled the blanket taut as she settled next to the couch. It should have made Erin feel better, but it didn't.

How could one person be so bad at life? How had she wound up here, like this? She stared at the blurry fabric in front of her face until she couldn't keep her eyes open anymore.

Chapter Eighteen

Temptation

Erin

The smell of coffee woke her.

She sat up and a second blanket pooled in her lap. Staring down at it, she wondering briefly when it had showed up. But her attention drew to the kitchen. Jude bustled, and even with his back turned, he seemed refreshed, even peppy. His wet hair stuck up slightly on top of his head in a way Erin found sexy. All of his movements looked slow and deliberate like he was trying not to wake her.

She appreciated that. Her nightmare had come back, leaving her achy and groggy. Everything felt too real and too raw and she'd woken up panicked in an unfamiliar place. It'd been impossible to fall back asleep after that. Well, not *impossible,* because eventually it had happened. It must have, because she'd just woken up.

She watched as Jude dumped a dry oatmeal packet into a bowl then took a sip of his coffee. His ease made him look like a completely different man and left her wondering what kind of man she'd get when he noticed her.

On that thought, her eyes drifted to the stack of clothes still on the breakfast bar. She hated the idea of changing into something clean when she felt so dirty and stiff. However, parading back across the street in a blanket like a walk of shame didn't appeal to her either.

"You're up."

She startled, turning eyes in his direction.

He took her in with a cautious stare. She tensed, waiting for him to shift back into the Jude from last night, the one with the icy expression.

"How are you feeling?" he asked, bringing his cup to his lips.

"I, um...I'm okay, I guess." Her voice sounded so scratchy, she almost didn't recognize it. She cleared her throat. "Thanks for the extra blanket."

"You're welcome." Moving over to a cabinet, he pulled down a mug. "Coffee? Tea?"

Erin hugged the blanket tighter around her shoulders. She wanted a cup of coffee desperately, but she wanted a shower more. *Walk of shame or coffee?* While she weighed her options, her indecisive silence hung in the air.

"Or maybe you want to get cleaned up first?" he prompted.

"I can just head back to the rental." She gathered the blanket around her and stood.

His ease shifted to alert, that familiar hard edge forming in his jaw. He looked down into his own coffee and Erin half-expected to be kicked out on the spot. She braced for the cold and impatient Jude.

"I'd rather you stay here." He looked up and seemed to notice her surprise. "Door's not fixed yet," he explained.

Of course, she remembered.

"Also," he started but then stopped.

Shoving a hand in his jeans pocket, he glanced away. If Erin didn't know better, she'd have thought he looked unsure.

"Also, I'd feel better keeping an eye on you a little longer."

"You...what? Why?"

"Use my shower," he deflected. "I'd assumed you were going to do that last night." His gaze felt heavy on her like he could see the scabbed over cut through the blanket. "You should have cleaned up last night."

Looking down at her feet, she could hear his words echo in her head. *You can't even take care of yourself.* She'd managed to do a pretty good job of proving his point.

"There's a clean towel hanging next to the shower for you."

"Thanks." She chewed the inside of her lip, not seeing an easy way out of this one. With eyes trained to the floor, she found the bathroom and closed the door behind her.

Just as Jude said, a clean towel hung on the towel bar by the shower and the first aid kit sat next to an unopened toothbrush on the sink-top. Erin stared at it all, feeling shitty. He'd done all this for her and she'd just sulked and ignored him.

"Shower," she uttered, snapping herself out of her funk. She folded the blanket and balanced it on the free side of the sink.

Pushing back the clear plastic shower liner, she turned on the water. It heated quickly—much faster than the rental. When steam started to fill the small space, she stripped, throwing everything directly into the trash can. Seeing the shredded fabric gave her chills. She looked away.

The hot spray thawed her numbness as she stood, eyes closed, under the stream. *Shredded fabric. Blood. Soured breath.* Little by little, the water cracked her resolve, until finally the damn broke.

Her cut stung from the heat, but she refused to move —refused to diminish the reminders of her mistakes. Or maybe it was punishment. The water ran down her body, burning off the filth and violence. She turned up the heat to just bearable, and let it pelt over her some more. The bar of soap smelled like Jude as she scrubbed her skin once, and then again, the sensation oddly intimate despite the turmoil inside her.

Shattering glass. Choking. Mi cariña...

She braced herself against the wall as it came at her in shuddering waves.

Glinting steel. Stinging—pain. Desperation.

The water fell in rivulets down her face and shoulders and just when she thought she'd collapse from the pressure, *A gentle touch. Safety.*

She shut off the shower. A thick, heavy steam filled the bathroom. She toweled dry but the humidity turned her skin moist and sticky again, so she wrapped the towel around her body and tucked it in at her breast.

Standing in the small, warm space, Erin gave herself a moment to breathe through the lingering waves of desolation. That's when she saw her clothes in a neat stack on the closed toilet seat. Eyes widening, she glanced at the shower curtain. Even with the steam, it didn't leave a lot to the imagination.

Had Jude seen her naked?

She'd been nearly as such the night before, but in the shower it felt different...in the shower she'd washed.

It wasn't sexual, but it still seemed too sensual for an audience.

Maybe he kept his eyes averted, she hoped as she swiped away the condensation on the mirror with her good hand. The redness on her chest stood out, even in the quickly reforming fog.

Erin opened the medical kit and browsed its contents. There were a variety of new bandages, all different sizes and shapes. She picked a larger one and wiped the mirror again. Before she'd finished unwrapping the paper, her reflection had hazed over once more.

Adding ointment, she tucked her chin and tried to line up the pad with her cut but it wouldn't stick. Her skin was still too damp. Sighing, she tossed the bandaid and wrapper in the trash. If she couldn't get it to stick, there was no way she'd get her leggings up without a fight. Erin grabbed the new toothbrush.

Even after brushing her teeth, the room still hung thick with steam. She dug through the medical kit for cotton pads and stretchy wrap like Jude had used for her hand before. Once finished, she examined her work. It wasn't as nice a job as he'd done, but it was good enough and it stayed put.

Then she went back to the bandages, without any luck.

"Ugh," she grumbled, tossing another one in the trash.

She tried prying open the small window on the back wall but it didn't budge. And she couldn't find a switch for a fan either.

Finally, she turned to the bathroom door, contemplating her last resort. She could hear Jude clattering in the kitchen. *He probably won't come back here*, she reasoned as she cracked it open a few inches. She felt the cool air rush in.

Jude

He thought he heard the bathroom door creak open. Turning down the heat on the stove, he crossed back to the hall. *Maybe she didn't see her clothes?* Or was she done already? He caught a glimpse of her through the opened door and halted.

She wasn't done. Or even dressed. She was fussing with ointment and a bandaid that kept folding over on her. Scowling, she fought with the thing. Somewhere in the recess of his mind, he knew he should step away.

But he didn't.

He watched as she tucked her chin into her neck and tried to place the bandage over her cut. He couldn't see it with how she stood, but he could tell it hadn't worked when she growled in frustration and chucked the bandage in the trash. Forgetting himself, he laughed. Outright laughed.

Wide, green eyes whipped up to him, her cheeks blooming bright pink—a beautiful thing. Almost as beautiful as the glimpse he'd gotten of her in the shower. He knew what lay hidden under all that terry cloth she'd wrapped herself in.

Her skin glistened and she stood there, unmoving. *Screw breakfast, she looks good enough to eat.* But he couldn't. Shouldn't. He'd almost built up enough control to step away but then he caught sight of the angry, red cut across her collar bone.

"Jesus, Erin," he uttered, disheartened.

He hadn't realized how large it was—maybe three, almost four inches across. He'd handled the situation all wrong and now she might have a scar from it forever. She turned away, hiding the wound from view. Jude rolled his shoulders, thinking, the prick he'd gotten was nothing compared to that.

"It's not as bad as it looks," she told him but her voice shook.

Before he could think better of it, he pushed the door open fully and moved into the small bathroom with her. She stepped back but said nothing. He fingered through the medical kit, and finding the small brown bottle he'd been searching for, he brought his focus back to her. She just stared at him with those impossibly green eyes that shone like emeralds around the edges and faded in to new grass on a summer's day. *Beautiful.*

He handed Erin the bottle. "Hold this."

She took it without a word while wrapping an arm around herself. Back to the first aid kit, Jude pulled out a large roll of gauze and some tape, then washed his hands. When he turned back to her, palm out, she returned the bottle to him dutifully.

"This is probably going to sting," he said as he unscrewed the cap. "But it'll keep the cut from getting infected and seal it up."

She nodded.

Jude held the small brush from the bottle over her skin, eyes resting just below her neck. He didn't want to make it hurt, but it had to be done. He cut his eyes quickly to hers before sweeping the brush gently across the wound.

She hissed as she inhaled, her face scrunching in pain. He hesitated, pulling the brush away.

"Just finish," she said through clenched teeth.

Reluctantly, he dragged the brush across the cut with more antibacterial liquid. She grunted.

"Give it a minute," he told her. "It'll feel better when it dries." Then he blew lightly over the area while screwing the cap back on the bottle.

Her pulse jumped in her neck, gooseflesh rising across her skin on her shoulders and chest. He swallowed, trying to stay focused. Dropping the bottle into the kit, he picked up the gauze. Erin watched him as he cut it to size.

"Feel better?" he asked her. He caught her head bob up and down in his peripheral. "Good."

Gauze cut, he turned to her intending to keep his focus on his task but his eyes went to her lips instead, just barely parted. An impulse shot down his body. He swept the wet hair off her shoulder. The graze of his fingers on her skin almost made him forget what he was doing. As did the shiver that ran through her in response. Gently, his fingers smoothed the large strip flush to her chest.

He cleared his throat. "Hold this here."

Her fingers brushed over his to find the bandage before he pulled away. He cut the medical tape and laid it along the edges of the gauze. She smelled like his soap and her skin felt hot to the touch. His fingers lingered on the last strip of tape, already firmly in place. He could feel her heartbeat beneath his fingertips.

Did she want him, too? His eyes slid to her mouth again and her pulse quickened under his touch, offering just enough encouragement. He grazed the backs of his knuckles up along her neck and then down and out over her bare shoulder. Her skin reacted with more gooseflesh and he swore she let out a barely audible gasp. But she didn't back away.

Jude stepped in, his focus centered on the heat her body gave off and the softness of her skin. He forced his eyes up to hers, half-expecting her to shut it down and knowing deep down that it would be for the best if she did. He knew there must be some rule he was breaking here.

Her cheeks flushed and her gaze turned soft. Captivated by those eyes, he watched as her pupils dilated. Her reaction was not what he'd expected. Nothing about her was, including her next move, as she leaned into his touch.

Slow down, he told himself, but his pulse chose the rhythm without him. And she stood right there for him. Why shouldn't he kiss her?

He inhaled the familiar scent of his soap again and appreciated how it played differently on her skin. His fingertips forged a slow, meandering trail down her arm then tentatively slid around her waist.

He knew what hid underneath the towel. He shouldn't, but he did, and he wanted it. *So real, so soft, and so female.* She had no idea, and that made him want her more.

Her eyes dipped to his lips and his blood coursed south.

He'd tried—tried to hold back. *You gotta stop*, he thought with little conviction.

She'd had a rough night. He'd heard her cry out. He knew it kept her awake. The cabin walls were thin. He'd almost come out, but what would have happened? Something like this? Him acting like a damn teenager? What kind of man did that make him?

His fingers flexed at her side, digging into the terry cloth, and she let out a little mew.

He knew better. *Not the time, not the place.* But last night had been harrowing for him too, and it left him raw and unnerved. Even once he'd found Etta, he'd still felt ungrounded.

He'd acted rashly, barging into the rental with an un-loaded gun. He'd wanted to hurt the guy, really hurt him. And then Erin was in his house, an emotional mess, and he couldn't do anything to help. Not a damn thing.

The way she'd stared off into that fire like a shell of a woman, it tore him apart. It was the first time in a long time he'd felt utterly useless.

But here, now, her heat and her body made him feel rooted and solid. And he wanted to bury himself in the moment and stay that way.

Did she feel the same? He had to know.

He leaned his head in, his mouth just an inch away from her lips.

"Wait." Her voice came at him impossibly soft, yet shot him abruptly back to reality.

"Shit. Sorry. I'm sorry." He pulled back. *Idiot.*

She grasped the front of his shirt and he paused, looking up. What played on her face seemed a mess of so many things. Her grip tightened and she pulled him back towards her and he let her. Then he closed the gap, and found her mouth.

The kiss started urgent and heated when he'd meant it to be gentle. She surprised him, yet again, when her lips moved with equal intensity against his. Her arms wrapped around his neck and right then, he decided he liked surprises.

Her tongue breaching into his mouth, their kiss turning carnal. Jude pressed his body into hers, craving the contact, wanting to feel her against him. Her fingers dug into his hair, sending a message straight to his groin. Now he didn't just want her, he needed her. Now that he'd crossed that line, it all came in a rush and he wasn't sure, with all the momentum, he would ever be able to stop. He didn't care, not in the moment. It felt too good.

Jude's hands moved up over the towel and stopped near her breasts, fingers splayed, trying to feel her beneath the fabric. Then they curved around her sides and down, coming to the swell of her butt and he pulled her farther into him, wanting to tell her how she affected him. Her mouth moved primally over his, her taste addictive.

Fingertips drifted down, and he grazed the soft skin below her towel, curling the fabric up. He tugged it gently away from her body. It started to unwrap from itself. She didn't react. She didn't reach out to stop him or to slow him down.

His breath grew jagged. *Full of surprises.*

Suddenly the bathroom filled with shaggy, gray hair.

Heavy paw joined the embrace and the abrupt weight sent them teetering sideways into the sink. Erin shot back, away from his mouth with a startled "Oh!"

"Etta. Down!"

His loyal companion slid back to stand with all four paws on the floor but she didn't leave the now, very cramped bathroom. Erin hastily rewrapped her towel.

What crummy timing. "Come here, girl," Jude grumbled, stepping backwards and into the hallway. She followed him, tail wagging.

He looked over at Erin. She held her arms protectively in front of her body and her eyes wouldn't meet his. *Damnit.* He tried to let it go. She'd just had a traumatic night. She'd trusted him. And what did he do?

His fingertip tingled with the memory of her skin. *But...she kissed back.* His lips twitched up.

"I'm gonna get us some breakfast," he said, then closed the bathroom door for her.

He and Etta wandered back into the kitchen. "I don't know whether to thank you or scold you," he told her, reassuming his spot at the stove.

Etta stared back with those sweet brown eyes, tail swishing side to side.

"Yeah," he muttered, grabbing a slice of cheese and holding it out to her. "Thanks. You're a good girl."

Chapter Nineteen

Good Coffee

Erin

She stared at the back of the bathroom door for a long time. *That was...that...what was that?*

She shook her head, trying to breathe. *Breathe in, breathe out. In. Out.* Her skin tingled and even though the humidity has dissipated, the small bathroom felt unbearably hot. Erin sucked on her bottom lip, savoring the moment, remembering how his mouth moved over hers.

He was out there in the kitchen and she doubted, even with that small, parting smile, that he could feel even remotely like she did. If he had, dog or not, he wouldn't have stopped.

Was the pull between them that strong? Or had she just been trying to cover up her feelings with something stronger?

When her pulse mellowed and her breathing no longer left her light headed, she pulled on her leggings and yanked a T-shirt over wet hair. She had to pull her arms back out and twist the shirt around when she realized she'd put it on backwards.

She'd just thrown herself in without a thought. That wasn't like her. Normally, she was responsible and careful. *He just kissed me.*

Erin hung the wet towel on the towel bar and opened the door. She peered into the hall before creeping out and making her way to the kitchen.

Jude's back was to her but he must have sensed her because as soon as she stopped he turned. "Coffee or tea?" A small smile playing on his lips.

"Coffee," she answered without hesitation.

Jude's smile grew as he extended the spatula in his hand to the counter behind her. There, waiting for her, sat a nearly full coffee pot and an empty mug.

"Thanks," she muttered. She helped herself, pouring right to the rim.

"You want cream or anything?"

Breathing in the delicious aroma of a real cup of coffee, she answered, "Depends."

"On?"

She held the cup up to her face and enjoyed the experience. Tipping it lightly at her mouth, she sampled it black. "This is good," she told him, smiling into the cup.

She could feel Jude's eyes on her. She lifted her lashes to a huge grin. "What?"

"I just thought you were more of a tea person."

"Why can't I be both?"

"You can. But right now, you look more like a coffee person."

She liked how his smile warmed his whole face. "This is my first decent cup since I've been here," she explained. "Well, except for the cafe yesterday..."

"Glad I can be of service." His smile lingered as he turned back to the stove.

Erin eyed him. She hadn't seen him playful before. She liked it but at the same time it put her on edge. Had she sent him the wrong message? Was it the wrong message? She'd liked what they did. And she was an adult. She could have sex. But she worried if she gave in, she'd want more—a lot more. Maybe more than he'd want to give.

In a sudden moment of panic, she realized she'd made a terrible mistake. With only a few days left, if any, what could she possible gain in kissing him like that? Now, she knew exactly what she'd be missing.

"After breakfast I'll go have a look at the door," he told the skillet, butting into her thoughts.

"Oh. Okay." She took another sip of real coffee.

Did that mean he wanted her out of his place and back at the rental? She tried not to let it disappoint her. But her mouth could still feel his kiss, just like disembarking from a boat and still feeling the motion of the water. And she thanked her lucky stars a kiss was all they'd managed to accomplish.

"We'll get everything cleaned up," he continued, "then I need to get to work."

"Where do you work?" Guilt swamped her. Would he be late because of her drama?

"Today?" He picked up his phone and scrolled. "Got a couple appointments scattered around the lake."

"Oh. What do you do?"

"Handyman, mostly. Some plowing when it gets really bad, like the other night."

"Ah."

She moved with her mug to the breakfast counter opposite Jude and his cooking. "I don't want to hold you up," she told the counter as she hopped up onto a stool. "I can take care of the mess." She avoided his eye by taking a sip of coffee.

"Erin," he stated, and didn't go on until she looked up at him. Something in her face made him frown. "I've got time. And I still gotta fix the door."

"Okay," she whispered because what else could she say? She couldn't help feeling a little like a burden.

His eyes pierced into her and she swore he could tell exactly what she was thinking. A huge inconvenience, because she was thinking that she'd much rather hold him up doing what they'd been doing in the bathroom, not sitting around watching him fix a door. Her cheeks felt hot.

He smiled at her again, flashing white teeth, then directed his attention back to his skillet. Erin watched him move scrambled eggs around with the spatula wondering why she'd picked this spot right in front of him? She sipped her coffee and just when the silence became nearly unbearable, her cell phone rang.

Standing, she scanned the room. The screen flashed the caller ID from the side table next to the armchair. She half-groaned, half-sighed, and answered it.

"Hi mom." She did her best to sound cheery. "I'm surprised you're calling on a Thursday morning, aren't you at work?"

"Really, Erin?" her mother snapped. Erin stiffened. "That's how you want to start this conversation?"

"What conversation?"

"I spoke with Victor this morning."

Erin's stomach plummeted. "You've got to be kidding me," she muttered, turning her back to the kitchen. She did not want to have to explain things to her mother on the phone in Jude's cabin. She didn't want to explain things to her mother at all.

"Care to explain?" Helen clipped.

"I guess that depends on what he said," Erin replied tersely.

"He told me you kicked him out, in the snow, in the middle of a storm! In the middle of the night! Not to mention broke his heart."

Erin didn't even want to dignify that with an answer. And so what if she had? He certainly would've deserved it, not that Erin felt comfortable going into the details why. "He was not invited."

"I can't believe you! My daughter? He could have gotten into an accident!"

"Well, he's lucky he didn't," she ground back, hating that she felt somewhat relieved. "He came here completely unannounced!" Her mom of all people should understand the poor form in that.

"That is the point of a surprise, *dear*."

"Well, I hate surprises!" Why the hell had Victor called her mother? She took a breath and tried to even out her voice. "Mom, we've discussed this. I really don't like you two talking about me. What happens between him and I, that's none of your business. And why you'd take his word over mine is beyond me."

"I feel like I don't know you at all! What ever happened to graciousness and integrity?" Her mom scolded through the phone. "It's no wonder you are still single."

Erin bristled. She wished that hadn't bothered her so much. But her mother lived on the outskirts of her life and only got the highlights. "Have you ever considered," she started cooly, "that he isn't being honest with you?"

"So, you're telling me you are *not* up in the mountains with some other man, whilst blocking his calls and forcing him to drive the haul back home in a storm in the middle of the night."

She wished she hadn't answered the phone. "He is a grown man, mother."

"You don't deny it?" Her mother *tsked.* "I have no idea what you think you're pulling, but there are more honest ways to get a man, Erin. A relationship that starts with deceit and games does not withstand."

"It's not a game. There is no more relationship. It's done."

"So after a year of pining, you're suddenly over it? I hardly believe that," her mom accused like she was twelve years old again. "I've stayed out of your business in respect for your privacy, but I have to tell you, you are acting just like your father!"

Erin's jaw dropped.

"I had hopped you would have taken more after me, but clearly you inherited his selfishness and complete disregard for other people."

"I...I don't even know how to respond to that."

The phone suddenly lifted out of her hand. Erin whipped around to see Jude put her cell to his ear.

"This is Jude," he said somewhat impatiently into the phone. His eyes focused on her. "I live across the street from the rental your daughter has been staying at. Not sure why, but it sounds like she wasn't going to tell you this, so I'm just going to lay it out."

"Jude!" Erin hissed, clawing for the phone.

Her held he back with an extended arm. "I had to break into her cabin last night because that *uninvited guest* had his drunken hands clamped around neck. He nearly choked her to death."

Erin's throat felt tight and her eyes stung.

"Yeah, figured he didn't tell you that part," he went on. "He tell you he took a knife to her and tried to force himself on her?" Another pause. "You don't believe me I can send you a picture of his handy-work."

Erin could hear her mother's shrill voice on the other end but she couldn't make out the words.

"Yes. Last night. She's just been through a traumatic experience so it would be great if you could cut her a little slack. And maybe stop conspiring with that asshole."

Erin's eyes bugged. Her mother hated swearing. He stared levelly back.

"Yeah. She's okay," he murmured. "Yeah." He handed back the phone.

"Erin? Erin honey?" her mom called.

She shot Jude a contemptuous look as she brought the cell to her ear. "I'm here."

"Honey, my God! I'm so sorry. I had no idea! Truly, I feel terrible!" her mother gushed. Erin didn't say anything. "I want to see you, to make sure you're okay."

"I'll call you when I get back in town."

"Okay. You call me, please. As soon as you get home," her mom insisted. "You're sure you're okay?"

"Yeah," she sighed. "I gotta go, mom."

"Okay, honey. I'll talk to you soon. I'm so sorry."

"'Kay, bye."

She ended the call, eyes narrowed on Jude. He just stood there studying her. It felt like he was always doing that.

She drew her brow in. "What the hell?! You can't just—"

"He's the thing you were hoping to forget?" he interrupted.

"What?"

"When you hit your head, you asked if a concussion could make you forget things."

"I did?" She tried to keep her anger stoked. He'd just hijacked a private call! He didn't get out of it that easily.

"You loved that man?"

She didn't answer. It was none of his business.

Before she could get back to laying out her grievances, he moved in close and said, "So you know, I would never touch you like that. Never. A real man would never do that."

And just like that, her anger dissipated.

After eggs, they headed over to the rental. Jude insisted Erin use his coat.

She stared at the lone, maroon flannel on the hook. "I'm not taking your only coat."

"I'll get the other one from across the street," he replied. She'd forgotten about the loaner that still hung by the door in her cabin.

Reluctantly, she grabbed the coat in question. It fit even larger than his other blue one. But as soon as she stepped outside, she was glad he'd insisted. Erin wrapped her arms around her chest, her hands hidden deep inside the overlong sleeves.

Etta followed them across the street, chipper at her side, with tail swinging like a pendulum. Jude ducked in and grabbed his other jacket, slipping it on before setting to work. Standing on the deck with her new furry companion, she watched him evaluate the damage.

"Be right back," he said. "Etta, come on." They walked back across the street.

Already missing her furry buddy, Erin went inside to sweep up the broken glass. She tried repeatedly, to push up the sleeves of Jude's jacket but they kept falling so she finally shed it and hung it over a chair. Once the glass had been cleared, she cleaned up the rest of the kitchen and let the pot of congealed sauce soak in the sink.

The place felt heavier to her than she remembered. She went around opening all the wooden shutters to let the light in. It helped a little.

Jude returned with a tool box and no Etta. Tapping out the pins in the hinges, he removed the door and leaned it against the side of the cabin. Then started in on the door frame. When Erin ran out of things to do, she grabbed the maroon flannel and meandered outside.

She watched, thinking she'd probably never need to rehang a door, but it didn't hurt to see how one might go about doing it. Her keen interest only had a little to do with how sexy he looked while he worked.

He tapped short wooden dowels into the holes where the screws had been. Glue oozed out at the edges.

"Why are you doing that?" she asked.

"Making new holes. Old ones were stripped." He took a rag and wiped off the excess glue.

"Oh."

She had no idea what that meant, but he seemed to know what he was talking about. Watching him work, she wondered how he learned to do all this.

As if he could feel her gaze, he paused and looked over at her. "Yeah?" His breath materialized in front of the mouth that had kissed her senseless.

"Anything I can do to help?"

He chuckled, eyes smiling, and it stung. Erin remembered what he'd said the last time she'd offered to help.

She tensed and turned to hide back inside. "Never mind. I'll just be—"

"Actually, yeah," he rushed out, and she paused her retreat. "Can you take Etta on a walk or run her around for me? I'm not going to have a chance before heading over to the lake."

Erin noted his sincere expression. "Yeah, sure." The sting subsided a little.

Jude dropped the rag and crossed over to where she stood, nearly stepping on her toes, he was that close. Heat radiated off of him, even in the cold. His face looked serious as he stared at her intently. "Really appreciate it." His voice vibrated low and skimmed over her like a taunting summer breeze.

"O-okay."

Didn't she say she'd be better off not knowing what she was missing? For a tempting second, she indulged, silently begging him to kiss her. Then, on a sharp breath, she stepped back. Before he could counter, she crossed the deck and took the stairs to the street at a careless velocity. She focused on the task he'd given her rather than the way his body had leaned in or how his eyes looked as drunk as she felt when he stood that close.

He'd given her a task that she could actually do and she planned to do it well. Taking a peek over her shoulder, she saw him watching her. He smiled, nodded, then, after a beat, turned back to the door frame. Erin told herself that the warm feeling in her chest was just body heat thanks to Jude's big, lined jacket. She pulled the collar in closer around her neck and inhaled deeply, enjoying the traces of soap and campfire imbued in the fabric.

Approaching his place, she yanked the door open and barely remained standing as a blur of gray fur and excitement greeted her.

Chapter Twenty

Awkward Assumptions

Erin

She stripped out of the v-neck tee and put on a slouchy, wide-necked tunic. Stepping back, she scrutinized herself in the full length closet mirror, trying to imagine it with leggings and sneakers instead of jeans.

Erin frowned.

When she'd called Mari, her friend had begged her to wear this tunic. Then proceeded to apologize profusely because as it turned out, Shauna wasn't going back to the Chalet. And that meant Erin was on her own for the rest of the trip. The news hadn't surprised her. She'd expected as much, though it didn't seem as daunting now as it had when Mari'd first left. Was she getting ahead of herself?

Erin twisted, looking at the loose-fitting top from all angles. She'd never worn it before. Now she remembered why. It hung a tad too long, so while it probably looked great on long, lean Mari, it fit like a shapeless sack on her. Plus, how silly would it look with dirty sneakers? Erin glanced down at her bare feet. If she were staying in, it could have worked.

The tee just seemed too casual and it highlighted the big bandage across her chest—not that the tunic covered it all either. Neither outfit seemed fit for a first date. If that's even what this was.

Jude had invited her to a Mexican place down the road. But he'd said it offhand, like he went there every Thursday night. And he'd suggested it as he was taking off for work, with no real plan and no specific time. He'd simply mentioned he'd probably be back around five, but that wasn't even in the same part of the conversation. Would he even remember the dinner part?

Erin sighed at her reflection. She felt silly. A date would be nice. Mexican food sounded good. And if he did remember, she wasn't going to miss out because she didn't have anything to wear. But the problem remained—she had nothing to wear. Even after sneaking back to the rental to stick in a load of laundry once Jude had left for work.

Too bad my white sweater is still drying, she thought, adjusting the tunic so it slipped off one shoulder. It didn't help the shoe situation...or the fact that it made her look short and squat. She readjusted the top so it covered her shoulder and her bra strap again.

"It's just so...blah."

Tipping her head to the side, Erin squinted at her reflection, cinching her hands around her waist like a belt. *Nope.* She pulled the tunic up, and twisted some of the fabric, trying to make a knot. Nothing helped. It just didn't look good.

"He won't care what you're wearing," she scolded the mirror.

Erin mostly believed herself and only because she grew more convinced he hadn't intended for it to be a date. Plus, he'd already seen the bandage. Hell, he'd seen her mostly naked, so what did it matter what she wore? Her reflection stared back at her, unimpressed.

After a beat, she tugged off the tunic and retrieved the tee. At least it made her chest look good and it didn't clash as much with the jeans or the sneakers. She'd probably throw Jude's jacket over all of it anyway, if he didn't mind lending it again. And if he remembered about dinner.

Erin checked the time on her phone. *A few minutes before five.* He probably wasn't home yet. He could be running late or he might want to change and—

A loud knock came from the front of the cabin. Erin looked back at her phone. Her heart sped, suddenly nervous.

*Okay. Okay...*Pulling her hair back into a ponytail, she tugged and fussed until the strands at the top of her head puffed up in a voluminous, sultry kind of way.

Another, louder, harder knock echoed through the cabin.

"Yeah! Be right there!" she called from the bathroom and quickly dug a lip moisturizer out of her toiletries bag. It wasn't gloss or lipstick but it helped. And if he kissed her again...Her breath caught and a thrill raced up her spine then plunged low in her belly.

The front door creaked. "Erin?"

"Back here," she called, throwing everything from the sink-top into her bag and sticking it on a small shelf over the toilet.

Jude didn't say anything more and he didn't come into the back of the cabin so she took a last look at her reflection, then turned out the light and went to greet him.

He stood in the open doorway inspecting the hinges, pushing the door forward and back. It creaked as he swung it in and squeaked when he pulled it to the frame. Erin approached the entry and watched as his brow sunk. He cocked his head to one side, eyes scanning the hinges thoughtfully.

"Everything okay?" she asked, standing on one foot to tug a sneaker on the other.

He didn't look like he'd gone home to change. His pants were dusty and his hair disheveled. He read like a man who'd put in a day of hard work and it only added to the overall effect he had on her.

Erin wobbled but managed to get her foot in the shoe before dropping it to catch her balance.

Jude ran his fingers over the frame where he'd repaired the split wood. "Thought you were going to be across the street." His jaw ticked. He didn't look at her.

"Sorry. Paul didn't have much for me to do today—"

"Paul?"

"My boss," she explained. "And I—"

"You didn't take a personal day?"

"No. And I figured since you fixed the door I could just...come back..." she trailed off as his eyes honed in on hers.

"Maybe leave a note next time."

She shrank a little. Was he mad at her? Because she came back to the rental? "Okay. I'll uh, I'll be more considerate next time," she conceded. "But actually, I meant, is everything okay with the door?"

"Yeah, mostly," he muttered, back to scrutinizing his patch job. "It'll hold for now."

Erin tore her gaze away and pulled on the other sneaker, this time looking at what she was doing and finding that more successful. She felt his eyes fall on her like a wave of heat.

"You're ready." He stated, sounding disappointed.

She straightened, working hard not to react. Had he forgotten? Or changed his mind?

A strange moment fell between them where it seemed like someone had hit the pause button—he just froze. But it passed so quickly, Erin wondered if she'd imagined it.

He took her in, starting at her face, moving up to her hair, then sliding down to her lips. When his eyes dipped and lingered at the V in her shirt, Erin celebrated the small win, even if it amounted to nothing. Jude's eyes came back up, pausing at the bandage on her collarbone. She stiffened. *I should have gone with the tunic!*

"You changed," he observed. She didn't respond except to fidget with her shirt, tugging the hem down. The space between them went from casually awkward to painfully uncomfortable.

"I um..." she trailed off. "I spilled something on my other shirt," she lied. "And I didn't have anything clean to change into so I had to come back to do some laundry, and I was just thinking about taking Etta out for a walk," she rambled.

He looked at her funny. "Did you forget?"

"Forget?"

"About dinner."

"No! No. I just thought that maybe you changed your mind."

"Why would I do that?" He crossed his arms over his chest and blocked the entire door frame.

"I don't know...long day?" she hedged.

"Did you change *your* mind?"

Erin thought he sounded a little defensive. "No!"

"Good. Then if you're ready, let's go. I'm hungry."

"I just need to get a coat," she said, ducking her head and turning to the hooks where both her and Jude's jackets hung.

He reached in front of her and grabbed the maroon loaner then held it out for her. Erin hesitated before weaving her arms in the sleeves. When she turned back to him, his eyes focused on the bandage again. She pulled the jacket closed over her front.

Something in him finally cracked and he gave her a sly grin. Her breath hitched as he reached his arm out like he meant to embrace her.

He swatted at her ponytail. "I like your hair," he said close to her face.

"Th-thanks."

She tried to smile but it faltered. He couldn't stop looking at her bandage. Maybe the shirt had been a bad idea. Maybe *dinner* was a bad idea.

"Hey." His gentle voice drew her gaze from his chest to his face. "You look nice."

She opened her mouth to argue but he cut her off.

"Erin. You look..." He paused and seemed to be searching for the right word. "Nice," he finally finished but his voice dropped and his body shifted closer and she got the impression "nice" wasn't the word he really meant. Her smile held this time and his grew bigger.

They stood there as if stuck in the heat and tension of the moment. She felt so sure he wanted to kiss her again. She wanted it too, more than anything. Her lips tingled in anticipation as she inhaled a shaky breath. Then nervousness won over.

"So you *do* know the code," she blurted, breaking the moment.

"What?"

"That first night," she ducked her head down to zip up her borrowed coat. "You said you didn't know the code." Her fingers fumbled around all the excess fabric. She pushed the sleeves up but they slid right back down.

"I didn't say that. I just wasn't going to share it with strangers who had no proof of a rental agreement."

"I guess that's reasonable," she commented, reigning triumph over the zipper pull. She grabbed her purse off the bench.

Jude chuckled and ushered them both outside, shutting the cabin door firmly behind them. "Glad I have your approval."

"Look. About the door," Erin cut in. "I know I've said it already, but I'd like to pay for the work."

This was the third time she'd brought it up. He'd spent a good hour on it and before he'd left, she'd insisted on paying him directly. And now, hearing all the noise it made when it opened, she guessed he'd have to work on it some more.

"And I've said it already," he parroted, "we'll talk about it later."

She narrowed her eyes. Was that code for 'no charge?' She hoped not. He wouldn't have needed to do the work if it hadn't been for her and Victor. Still, arguing about it hadn't worked earlier. She'd figure out someway to pay him back, even if meant making up a number and shoving cash under his door.

"So, if you knew the code," she wondered aloud, then stopped.

He stared at her, waiting. "You gonna finish that thought?"

She sighed. "If you knew the code, why did you break the door?"

His chest seemed to expand and his forehead creased. "Is that a serious question?"

"Y-yes," she stammered.

"Erin, the man had you by your throat."

Watching his hardened face, she waited for him to elaborate. He didn't. Not for the first time, she wondered just how Jude had known she needed help, but the touchy vibe he put off made her reluctant to ask. Still, the question stuck there, begging to come out.

She cleared her throat. "Victor."

"Victor?"

"His name is Victor." She studied her snow dusted feet. "The man who...He was...still is my ex-boyfriend." Daring a glance up, she meet his eyes.

"Does he know that?"

She shrugged. She didn't really want to talk about Victor. She told him so.

"Yeah...neither do I," he muttered, still tense.

"Listen, if tonight isn't a good night to—"

"Come on. Let's get going." He started for the steps.

Erin shut her mouth and followed him to his rusted-out, yellow truck. If she hadn't put him off yet, she had no intention of pushing her luck. To keep herself from saying something stupid, she focused on his ride—a modest sized vehicle. Etta probably filled up the entire cab space. The fenders were rusted as were a number of scratches and dents on the body.

"Had this truck a while?" she teased.

"No, not really." He crossed in front of her to yank open the passenger door.

She palled, thinking she'd offended him, until she caught his lip turn up. She let out a short, anxious laugh. "You got me."

He grinned. "Sure did."

Erin slid onto the cold, leather bench seat, clenching as the chill bit through the seat of her jeans. Jude swung her door shut and rounded to his side, sliding into the drivers seat. For all the wear on the outside, the inside was immaculate. She hadn't thought about it before, but his tidiness seemed so unlike what she'd expect from a bachelor.

She snuck a peek over at him while he buckled his seat belt, noting again his disheveled hair and dusty clothes. How did he keep it so clean inside the truck with his kind of work? With not a wrapper or empty water bottle in sight. It made her realize just how little she knew about him.

Jude started up the engine and the cab filled with a metallic hum. Thighs clenched together to keep from shaking, Erin reached forward to turn on the heat. He caught her hand and brought it away from the dash, then looked over his shoulder as he reversed onto the street. Contrite, Erin tucked both her hands between her legs, eyed pointed to her lap.

"Just wait till the engine warms up," he explained. "We're not going far."

She kept quiet as Jude navigated down the windy street towards town. When they made it to the main drag, he turned up the heat. The vent on Erin's side pointed to the window but, reluctant to move it, she sat silently, shivering.

Certain she'd already started digging her own grave, she worried that the next thing out of her mouth would just seal her fate and he'd be driving her back to the rental. She'd been a little surprised he still insisted on going at all.

Stuck in her head, Erin missed the beauty of dusk falling, painting the sky like a watercolor and creating deep shadows which gave the snow covered pines a bolder, more majestic effect against the mountain range.

"You okay?" Jude asked, breaking the silence. He looked over at her before turning his eyes back to the road. "If you're not up for this, I can turn around."

Erin didn't want that, not even a little, even as unsure as she felt. This was the first date she'd been on in forever. If it was even a date...Is that what he wanted? Did he want to turn around? He cast another glance in her direction.

"I'm okay," she rushed out. He raised a brow and she panicked. "I'm just kind of a wreck sometimes...you've seen that already, actually, and I haven't had a first date in a while," she blabbered. It was about then she truly lamented the absence of her verbal filter in situations like these. So naturally, she kept going to try to fix it. "I mean, not that I...not that this is a first—what I mean is...I just haven't. Been. Out."

It wasn't a strong finish. But she managed to shut up. Erin braved a peek in her peripheral and saw Jude's upper body shaking. She met his eyes straight on before he trained them back to the road.

He shook his head, covering his mouth with a hand but Erin could tell he was smiling because it reached his eyes. "Yeah. Me too."

"Are you patronizing me?"

"No."

"Well, I'd hardly call you a wreck," she argued, looking out the front windshield.

"You've only known me a few days," he countered. "In a few more, you're going home. I only have to hold out 'till then." His tone was lightly, but the silence that followed didn't feel jovial.

She bit the inside of her lip. "Jude, if you don't want to do this, you don't have to, you know. It's okay." She tucked a stray wisp of hair behind her ear. "You can just take me back home, no harm done." She prided herself at how sincere she sounded.

The metallic hum of the engine and the fan pushing warm air into the cab were his only response and it spoke volumes. She'd said it was okay so now she had to pretend to be unbothered. It wasn't like he could actually see her chest deflate from disappointment.

She turned her head away, staring out her side window. "I'm sorry. I didn't mean to involve you in all my...chaos."

She caught his reflection staring at her before he said, "Erin, I would like to take you for dinner."

Chapter Twenty-One

Bad Aim

Erin

The truck pulled up to a restaurant called *Platos Santos*. It looked like a fashionable bistro, with its dark stained wood siding and painted black trim. Outside and to the right of the main entrance, string lights hung over a large, snow filled patio. Erin imagined how in the summer the place probably packed in hikers, bikers, and beach bums with a cold beer or a margarita at the fire pits.

It was hip—not what Erin expected. She stole a glance over as Jude let himself out of the cab, then back to the building, realizing she'd been making a lot of assumptions about him. She hopped out, swinging the stiff passenger door shut behind her, and met him around the hood. They walked side by side to the entrance.

From the front, the interior looked small but once inside, Erin saw it stretched back like an alley. All the empty tables led to her suspicion that the place was more of a summer spot. Still, the restaurant was warm, and the smell of fresh tortilla chips drifted at her like a beckoning finger. The ambiance helped to settle her nerves with intimate lighting and low key mariachi music which played softly in the background. A huge three-tiered fountain sat in the center of the narrow eating area, making a friendly and familiar trickling noise as the water dribbled over the edges.

The host led them to a small table next to the fountain. Erin took a peek before sitting. Coins of all denominations and origin littered the bottom two tiers. Taking off her jacket, she hung it on the back of her chair, then slid into the seat opposite Jude. She shifted, and tucked a stray hair back as she took a large, single sheet, card-stock menu from the host.

"Thank you," she said with a nervous smile.

"Thanks, David."

Erin looked up, surprised Jude knew the host, but then, he *had* told her this was one of his favorite restaurants. With an odd smile, the kind that tilts down suddenly at the ends to hide its true form, David tipped his head before heading back to the host's podium. Did David think her and Jude were sleeping together? *I wish...If only there weren't so many complications.* Was she the kind of person who could keep it casual?

"What are you in the mood for?"

Erin blinked, caught off guard, then realized, he meant the food. "Oh. I don't know yet. What do you recommend?"

The side of his mouth quirked up as he leaned his elbows into the table. "Honestly, it's all good. You can't go wrong."

"What are you getting?"

"Haven't decided yet." His eyes settled on her mouth and for a heart-stopping second, she wanted to tell him to have whatever he wanted.

Forcing her eyes back to the menu, she scanned the list. All the basics were present with trendy add-ons like mango mint salsa, créme fraiche and jalapeño glazes. Then her gaze drifted to the price column and she tried not to react. *He chose this place,* she reminded herself.

In her younger days, she would have selected something from a first date perspective. Dainty, moderately priced and easy to eat, like a salad. That way she wouldn't ruin her chances of a second one.

But as she stared at the menu, her stomach growled and she realized the chances of him asking her out again were already pretty slim, all things considered...If this even counted as a date to begin with.

With that thought in mind, she picked the 'dos tacos' plate, served with mango and pineapple salsa and the traditional rice and beans. Her twenty-something self would've crawled out of her skin, but with age comes wisdom. The benefit of good tacos outweighed the slim chance he'd take her out again before she had to return to the city.

The waiter came by their table and Erin gave him her order, handing off the menu. He and Jude gave each other greetings like old friends, the stranger patting her date on the back with a smile that reached his eyes. She felt too self-conscious to notice what Jude ordered. It wouldn't matter. Men didn't have the same stigma about date food as women did. And she couldn't think of anything he could eat that would turn her off.

The server came right back with chips and chunky salsa. Jude grabbed a triangular wedge from the basket and dunked it in the little black three legged bowl. They both spoke at the same time.

"Do you come here every Thursday?"

"What kind of work do you do?"

He smiled and leaned back, shoving the chip in his mouth before saying, "You go ahead."

"Oh. You seem to know everyone here. I wondered if this was your weekly haunt."

"My what?" he chuckled.

"Thursday nights at the Mexican place," she clarified, unrolling her silverware and smoothing her napkin on her lap.

"I'm not here every week," he defended, "but I do come here a lot. This is the best Mexican on the mountain," he reminded her with pride. Then he leaned in, "And, they have a Mariachi band tonight."

"They do?" she asked, looking around dubiously. "Where do they put it?"

Jude laughed. "It's a tight squeeze, I'll admit. But the band only has three guys."

"Ah." She nodded, grabbing a chip to recover from what she'd just witnessed. The man was already too sexy when he smiled, but laughing...

"Sometimes," he added, "if it gets really lively, they push the tables back to make a dance floor."

Erin tried to image Jude dancing to a mariachi band. The day kept proving how little she really knew about him. "But wouldn't that break some kind of fire code?" she thought out loud.

Her comment set him laughing again. "Maybe," he admitted, directing smiling eyes to her. "What do you say? You up for some cha-cha?"

Who was this man? Cha-cha? Chic Mexican? It didn't seem to jive with the emotionally distant, mountain persona he'd first shown her.

"Dancing, huh?" Erin asked, cringing while reaching for another chip.

"No pressure."

No pressure? All he had to do was smile at her. How could she say no? "I'll need a margarita for that. Maybe two," she half joked.

"That's doable." He lifted his arm to get the waiter's attention. "Hey Charlie, I'm gonna need two lime margaritas. On the rocks."

"You're the boss," Charlie chirped, before taking the order to the tiny bar by the host stand up front.

"Done," Jude announced, leaning back in his chair.

"Thanks. But, disclaimer—that doesn't guarantee dancing."

"Noted."

The conversation lulled. Scanning the empty restaurant, Erin relaxed a little. The place didn't seem to have a dance party vibe that particular night.

"You're turn," she prompted.

His brow furrowed. "Oh. Right. What do you do? That is, when you're not on vacation crashing some poor guys night?"

Flames licked the outside of her neck and face.

"I'm kidding," he laughed.

Charlie came by and left their margaritas on the table. Erin tested hers before answering Jude's question.

Her face puckered. "Wow, that's strong." She slid the glass back to the center of the tiled tabletop. "I track and document 401Ks and IRA's for small businesses."

"Wow. Really? You really are a numbers girl, huh?"

Cocking her head at his comment, she snuck another sip. "It's not really as interesting as it sounds."

"Don't sell yourself short. Those kinds of jobs can be really stressful." He spoke as if he knew.

"That's something I've got going for me at least."

"What does that mean?"

"Nothing. Anyway, yes, stressful—lots of numbers and reviewing and consolidating. Lots of uptight clients. You get that when it's their money on the line. But I don't do any of the trading," she rambled.

Erin dragged her cup back in front of her and took another several sips of her margarita then grabbed a chip and shoved it in her mouth. Any minute he'd realize just how boring she was.

"You work down in the city?"

"Mhmmm," she replied over her crunching. "So, tell me about how you found Etta."

He chuckled but dropped his line of questions. "Etta actually found me."

"Do tell."

He studied her a minute. Had she come across too eager? His focus drifted to just below her chin—on her bandage again. She bristled.

Why does he keep doing that? Fighting the urge to cover it with an arm, she grabbed another chip, this time taking salsa too. It dripped on the table en route to her mouth.

"Shoot," she murmured, grabbing her napkin and wiping up the drips so she didn't drag her arms or elbows in it later.

"It was my first winter here," Jude started, "and as I've said before, I lacked all general mountain survival skills."

Erin set her napkin on the side of her place setting. "Like chopping wood?"

"Yeah, like chopping wood."

She raised her eyes to see his attention fixed on her face.

"January rolls around," he continued, grabbing a chip, "and I'm chopping, or *trying* to chop wood during a snow storm and I'm struggling, as you can imagine. I got a little reckless." He crunches as he chews and in her mind, Erin runs through all kinds of meanings for the word 'reckless.' "Then I hear something behind me and I turn and there she is, just standing in my driveway, looking small and skinny, dirty and pathetic. I thought, 'poor thing's got it rougher than me. Probably a Christmas gift until someone realized her breed.'"

"What do you mean? You think someone dumped her because of her size?" Erin asked, appalled.

"Without a doubt. But her timing couldn't have been more perfect. I probably would have chopped my hand off if it hadn't been for her."

"Yikes," she responded, eyes drifting to his hands and feeling grateful to Etta. They'd helped her a lot in the past few days. She took a sip of her drink. "I'm glad she showed up, then."

"Yeah. You and me both." He flexed his left hand like shaking off a phantom pain.

"So Etta is kind of like your guardian angel."

"You could say that." He nodded, studying her. "She's certainly kept me out of trouble. For the most part." That last he added like an afterthought as his gaze skimmed the restaurant.

"The most part?"

"Well," he huffed, returning his attention to the table, "she seems to have taken a liking to you."

"I'm trouble? Never mind, don't answer that." She caught the corners of his mouth lift before looked to her lap. She couldn't deny what he insinuated. But why did it matter if Etta liked her?

"Chopping wood in a storm," she backtracked. "It must have been rough getting use to all the snow. I mean, I'm barely surviving the week."

"Nah, a good pair of boots and a decent jacket, and you'd be fine."

"I don't know. Even with the loaner, I feel like I'm permi-frozen."

"Permi-frozen?" He laughed.

She wished he'd quit doing that. At the rate he was going, she'd have a full blown high school style crush by the end of dinner. "Yeah...I just made that up."

"It sounds like a freezer setting."

"Maybe I missed my calling. Maybe I should have been a name giver...designator...person."

"Oh, is that the official job title?"

"Shut up! I don't know what they're called!" And despite herself, she laughed back. When he smiled at her, his whole face lit and a warmth settled over her skin, sinking bone deep. It definitely felt like a date.

The narrow interior filled up gradually as they waited for their dinner. At another lull in the conversation, Jude dug into his pocket, and pulled out a handful of coins. He slid them across the table to her.

She looked down at them. "What's this for?"

"The fountain. So you can make a wish."

A flutter lifted off in her chest. "Well, save some for yourself." She slid two back his way.

"No, I don't need to—"

"I insist."

"Alright, alright. Since you insist," he conceded, accepting offered coins.

Erin picked up her three and pivoted in her seat to face the fountain.

"Think you can make it in the top from where you're sitting?" he asked.

She tipped her head up. If she stood, she could almost *place* them in the upper tier. "Probably." Glancing back over at him, she caught his smile paired with a lifted brow. "You think I can't?"

"By all means, show me how it's done."

"You're messing with me."

"No, no. Go ahead," he pushed.

She twisted in her seat to face the fountain square on, and tossed her first penny overhand. It bounced off the side of the top tier and landed in the third with most of the other coins.

"Do I still get to make a wish?" she asked.

"Of course."

Erin took a moment, sending her secret desire silently out into the universe, before trying the nickel, underhand. It flew high but landed with a watery *plunk* in the second tier. She paused for her second wish.

"Last try," Jude jibed.

She turned to glare at him. "I can do it."

"Want to make a bet?"

"A bet? Like with money?"

"If you *can't* get it in the top, you come back to my place after dinner for a drink," Jude negotiated.

Erin stared at him. "I thought the point of betting was to coerce a person into doing something that they normally wouldn't do."

Jude smiled a very satisfied looking smile. "You saying you want to come over?"

"I'm not saying that. It's just that it isn't something I don't not want to do…" Erin frowned, unsure of what she'd just said.

"Just throw the coin," Jude laughed.

"Wait. What if I get it in?"

He flung a hand out in her direction, indicating for her to lay her stakes. Unfortunately, she lacked the courage to bet for another date.

"If I win," she thought out loud, "you have to… buy my dinner tonight."

He shook his head, smiling. "Fine. You're on."

Erin turned back to the fountain, feeling silly. The coin sat in her open palm. She felt its weight and size. *I can do this.* But did she want to? Losing didn't seem so bad.

She brought her hand down, and swung low to high again, sending the penny flying up and beyond the second tier. Its decent aligned perfectly over the center of the top level and a smug smile spread on her face.

The copper coin hit the mounded, stone center with a *chink* and ricocheted off, angling out and right into another patron's beer glass.

Erin's hands flew to her mouth as she let out a mortified "Oh!"

Jude's laugher brought everyone's eye to their table.

"I am sooo sorry!" Erin gushed to the man who peered into his glass across the fountain from them.

He looked up at her and cracked a swoon-worthy smile. "Nice aim."

"I wasn't trying for your drink. I swear."

"It's okay," he assured her. "You let me take you out and we'll call it even." The man winked.

Jude's chair scuffed against the wood planked floor. "Don't worry about it, man," he growled as he stood. "I'll get you another one." Erin's eyes followed him as he tromped down to the bar at the front of the restaurant.

"Guess he doesn't want competition," the guy joked from the other side of the fountain, and Erin turned back to look at him. He didn't seem offended, blue eyes light and playful, smooth face lifted in an easy grin. She gave a half smile and a shrug and then busied herself with chips until Jude sat down again.

"Sorry," she muttered across the table when he'd settled.

"No problem. I don't have to buy your dinner now."

Erin's mouth dropped open and she shot him a scathing look. It must have bounced right off him too, because he smiled back.

"It's fun teasing you," he confided. "But I won. You know what that means?"

"Yeah. Don't look so happy about it," she grumped, slouching back in her chair.

"Wow!" he exclaimed. "I never would have pegged you for a sore loser."

"I threw a penny into someones drink!"

"You sure did." His whole face lit up again and it cracked her sour mood. "Gotta tell you, that trick? The best thing I've seen all year."

"Well, it's only February," she grumbled.

"Still, that deserves at least one hundred wishes."

Erin stiffened, crossing her arms, unsure how to handle all the doting attention. It felt nice, but also embarrassing.

Jude's shoulders shook as he shifted in his chair to face to fountain. "My turn."

"No more bets."

"Yeah, probably a good idea. Now that I know how competitive you are," he jested again and gave her a wink. The gesture sent a new kind of flutter south of her rib cage.

She pursed her lips as he tossed overhand, the coin sailing easy and true right into the top tier with a light *thunk*. The second one followed in nearly the same trajectory.

"Show off," Erin muttered.

"I have to impress you somehow."

She snorted. "Oh don't worry..."

"Does that meant you're impressed?"

Hesitating, she tried to sense if his words were just more playful banter. "Yes."

"Good." His smile persisted.

Charlie brought out their dinner plates. Jude had ordered enchiladas swimming in a rich, creamy mole sauce. It looked messy. She watched him take that first, dripping bite and as she'd suspected, it didn't make him any less sexy or desirable. *Figures.* Though she wondered if that was just a side effect of the stupid crush she was forming.

A comfortable silence settled while they dug in. The restaurant lived up to Jude's rave review. The food tasted phenomenal. Part of it could have been Erin's own hunger since she'd skipped lunch. Leaning over her plate, she'd just stretched her mouth around the first bite of her second taco when Jude spoke up.

"So."

Her eyes lifted to his face as she closed her jaw around the taco with a crunch and tried her darnedest to chew politely. His expression had lost the humor from earlier.

When she'd swallowed most of the bite, she replied with a wary, "Yes?"

He rubbed his chin, then tilted his neck side to side. Her stomach tightened as she fretted, *Is he psyching himself up for something?*

"Victor," he finally stated. She stilled, nearly complete taco still hovering by her mouth. "What's going on there?"

She put her food down and it fell apart on her plate. Wiping her mouth and hands with her napkin, she bought herself some time. What could she say that wouldn't be incriminating?

"Victor is my ex," she explained and thought she heard Jude release a breath. But when she looked up, his expression hadn't changed. "We broke up a little over a year ago."

"A year? Then what was he doing in your cabin?"

"He had a change of heart...I guess."

"Right."

She didn't respond to his cynicism.

"And you?" he asked.

"Me what? Did I have a change of heart?" she asked, miffed. "I uh...no. I did not."

"Did you invite him?"

"No! Of course not!" she shot back. "I came here to...distance myself."

Jude picked at his plate some more and Erin returned to her mess of a taco. She tried re-stuffing it but eventually gave up and used her fork.

"He always been like that?" Jude's question broke another silent stretch, his voice sounding edgy.
"Like what?"

He stared at her.

"You mean...aggressive? No. No, never like that. Never with me."

He didn't speak but his doubt read clear in his expression. His eyebrows nearly disappeared in his hairline, and the downward curve of his mouth was anything but subtle. The head tilt felt like overkill.

"What?"

"If he's never been like that, why are you hiding up here?"

"I didn't say I was hiding. I'm not hiding," she argued. Then, in a more even tone she added, "I'm not here because of *his* actions. I'm here because of my own." She could feel the heat crawling up her neck and she prayed he didn't pry.

"Huh." He fidgeted with his fork then shifted his plate around which seemed odd. His words and actions always exuded so much confidence. Now, he seemed almost unsure. "He live near you?"

"He lives in the same general area. Why?"

Jude's jaw tightened then released. His head moved curtly to one side before he finally responded. "No reason."

"I'm not going to get back together with him."

He scoffed. "I would hope not."

His tone rose her defenses. "He isn't all bad. That wasn't *him* back at the cabin," she argued. "He isn't normally like that. He thinks...he said I broke his heart."

"Broke...his heat." Jude repeated. "After a year?"

He had no idea what a low blow he'd given. And if Victor was truly heartbroken, then she'd been just as cruel as he'd accused her of being, thoughtless and careless about his feelings, so caught up in her own.

"It's more complicated than that," she tried to explain. "There was this other woman...women, actually," she corrected. "I ended it officially, and a little tactlessly, last week."

Jude shook his head. "No. No. I don't get—"

"After he broke it off, we still sort of saw each other, just not...exclusively."

"Like an open relationship?"

"Not exactly." Erin looked down at her lap, smoothing the paper napkin.

"Friends with benefits?"

She didn't answer.

"Did you date anyone else?"

She stiffened. "No."

"Are you now?"

Erin shook her head, too ashamed for words.

"Okay. So, tell me if I got this right. He broke up with you, and you sat around hoping he'd change his mind while he jumped right back in the game?"

"I didn't just sit around!" she bristled. That absolutely described what she did.

"You know what I mean."

"Fine, but when you say it like that—" she started to argue.

"So now *he's* upset," Jude went on, "because you're not on call anymore?" Erin gasped at his insinuation but he didn't let her get a word in. "So tell me again why you think it's heartbreak?"

She opened her mouth, shut it, then opened it again. "You don't know him...or our history." Her reply sounded as pathetic as she felt.

"Clearly. Do you?" He held her stare.

When she didn't respond, he returned to his enchilada. Erin stared down at her own plate. She'd suddenly lost her appetite.

Across the table, Jude hissed on an exhale. "Hey." His voice sounded apologetic. She dragged her gaze up. "I didn't mean to ruin the mood. That guy just rubs me the wrong way."

She shook her head. "I get it. It's fine. To be honest, he kind of rubbed me the wrong way, too."

He nodded, eyes distant for a moment. Erin returned her gaze to her plate and pushed fallen taco guts around with her fork.

"I hope this doesn't make things worse," Jude warned, mouth pressing into a grim line, "but it's killing me and I gotta ask you something."

Erin sat back, very done with her dinner. She placed her cutlery on the plate, and pushed it away from her, bracing.

"You paid the kennel fee."

She tensed and waited for a question but he didn't go on. The topic was inevitable, but she hadn't thought ahead to what she'd say. She didn't want to admit to him that she felt responsible for Etta's escape. Not after the things he'd said.

Erin raised her eyebrows. "What did you want to ask me?"

"I want to pay you back."

"Okay, firstly, no. Secondly, that isn't even a question."

"Fine. How would you like me to pay you back?" he countered.

She glared at him.

"Cash it is."

"No, Jude. I—"

"Etta is *my* dog."

"I know that," she huffed. "But...I didn't do it expecting to get reimbursed."

"Yeah, I didn't figured you did," he grumbled, tossing his fork onto his plate. "Seeing as you weren't gonna tell me."

"Jude—"

"Fine. Here's my question." He leaned his elbows into the table on either side of his plate. "Why did you do it?" Grunting at her silence, he shoved back into his chair. "Then I'm paying you back."

"I won't accept it."

Erin knew it was stupid, but she had her pride to protect. There'd be consequences later, no doubt, but she couldn't budge. A trail of wreckage followed behind her wherever she went. The smoke from her damp logs. Etta's injuries. The splintered door frame. She had to do *something* to make it right.

Jude stared her down and she lifted her chin, holding her ground.

"Okay. Fine," he sighed, throwing up his hands.

Erin eyed him. "Fine?"

He flagged down the waiter and asked for the bill. Then he set his attention back across the table, his gray eyes piercing hers with a determination of their own. "I'm doing the door, no charge."

"No! That's absurd! And just bad business!" She'd already suspected he had no intention of charging for it, but that didn't make it right.

"And I'm buying you dinner tonight."

"Jude—"

"And tomorrow," he added.

He pulled his wallet out of his back pocket and slapped a card down on the tray before Charlie could even set it on the table.

"I'll be right back," Charlie muttered, and wisely whisked away.

"Figure, it's still not breaking even, but it's a start," Jude grumbled, looking at her as if daring her to argue.

She did. "You already did the water heater at 'no charge.'"

"Not even going to talk about that."

"The door is a much bigger project!" she went on. "Caused because of *my* drama. I'm paying for the work."

"No, you're not," He said with finality, raising his margarita glass and emptying the rest in a single gulp. "We should probably take this back to the cabin."

Erin looked around the restaurant, and noticed people seated close to them. The man with the coppery beer watched from under his brow with keen interest. The Mariachi trio had just come out to the floor, tuning their instruments, and their waiter, with uncanny expediency, came by with the charge slip. Jude signed the bill, then tucked his card back in his wallet.

"You gonna finish that?" he asked, gesturing to the dregs of her margarita. Erin hesitated, then chugged it back.

He stood so she did too. It wasn't how she envisioned the date ending, but what could she do? Maybe it wasn't actually a date, after all.

"We're not done talking about this," she said under her breath as she pulled her loaner jacket off the back of the chair.

Jude just smiled. He actually smiled.

Chapter Twenty-Two

Drinkable Cabs and Axe Murderers

Jude

He liked it when Erin dug her heels in. It should have been aggravating. It should have put him off. Maybe it would over time, but right then, he found it refreshing and intriguing. Women didn't usually argue with him.

But more importantly, he'd managed to resolve two concerns. She wasn't dating anyone, and he felt pretty certain she didn't have any ulterior motives. One issue remained, but he knew better than to bring it up when she was already so riled. And he didn't want to give her fodder to back out of the bet. He suspected she'd already considered it. The thing was, he really wanted her to come over.

He kicked himself for getting on her case about Victor. As ass like that would reveal his cards eventually. But it just pissed him off that she thought the guy had any integrity at all.

Jude shoved it all out of his mind as he led them towards the front of the restaurant, holding the door open for her, and following closely outside.

Pulling his borrowed coat tighter around her body, she paced to his truck. He hurried up ahead to unlock her side and yanked it open.

Delicate pink lips parted in surprise. He wanted those lips again.

"Thanks." She slid onto the bench.

He made sure she was all in before swinging the passenger door shut. When he rounded the hood, she'd leaned across the cab and unlocked his door.

Surprises all around. He smiled as he folded into the driver's seat. "You buttering me up so I cave?"

"What? Oh...yeah," she replied but he could spot the lie.

Knowing what he did about her, she'd probably done it just because, and he liked that—a lot. Jude started up the engine. Erin shoved her hands between her legs, still shivering in his big coat. His brain flashed on all the ways he could make that stop, several being inappropriate for the parking lot of his favorite joint.

"Car will heat up in a sec," he assured her while he backed out of the spot.

She didn't respond except to pivot towards her window. Little flurries of snow whipped around outside, looking warmer than the shoulder she was giving him. He figured he was in for the silent treatment the whole way home, but after a minute, she spoke up.

"I wish you'd just let me cover the kennel stuff."

His eyes cut to her. "Why? You looking to give away money? Why's this so important to you?"

She sighed, leaning her forehead into the window. "You were right." Her breath fogged up the glass. "It probably was my fault Etta got out." Her voice came out small.

"Dammit," he muttered under his breath, eyes back to the road.

If he'd just cooled his jets instead of looking for someone to blame this wouldn't have been an issue. But he'd gotten so use to people letting him down, that now he just expected it.

His fingers tightened around the steering wheel. "It wasn't you." Looking over at her, he paused, before laying it out and hoping like hell he didn't make it worse. "I think your man Victor did it."

Her head whipped to him, mouth open, and he felt it coming like a like a tidal wave.

"Don't take this on yourself," he rushed in. "That's all on him."

She shut her mouth, but her forehead creased, and he knew to her, those were just words. "You can't know that for sure," she argued.

"Neither can you." Still, he felt pretty sure. "He slipped when he admitted he knew of my dog."

"What? When?"

"You were a little...occupied." Jude stared out the windshield, haunted by the memory. Her pale face. Her trembling limbs. *How could someone do that to another person?* Though, as he thought that, he could see himself doing it to Victor.

Erin quieted, probably thinking it through, but thankfully she didn't argue this time. Jude had speculated plenty. Everything fit together, leaving no question that somehow that prick had interfered. When he'd stopped by the rental to leave a thank-you note for Erin, the creep had all but pissed on the front porch to mark his territory.

That got Jude thinking, and he realized, he'd recognized the fancy car from before, when he'd been chopping wood. Victor must have done a drive-by and seen them together out if front of his cabin.

He looked over to the passenger side. He wanted to tell her—make her see the kind of guy she was dealing with. But it didn't feel like the right move. She'd jumped in to defend him earlier. If anything, it would alienate her more.

Jude turned left off the main drag, and onto the winding road that led to the cabins. He needed to get them back on track. She'd made a deal with him—she'd promised drinks at his place—and he had no intention of letting her back out.

"I appreciate what you did," he eased in. "And I may even get why you did it. Admire it even. But I can't let you pay for Etta." He thought he'd picked the right thing to say, but Jude could actually feel the air in the cab shift.

"Why do you have to be so stubborn?"

He couldn't help it, he laughed. "*I'm* stubborn?"

"Are you really laughing right now?"

That made him laugh more, turning it into a whole body experience. It felt good, despite the angry fog-like tension in the cab. It had been a while since he'd laughed like that. "Ah, what am I supposed to do with you?" he asked the windshield, his chest still shaking and his heart feeling weightless.

"You could just say, 'thank-you,' and let it go," she grumbled from the opposite side of the bench. He worked to get his humor under control, and tossed her his best somber face. She spied him back from the corner of her eye.

"If I do all those things, will you come in for that drink you owe me?"

"I don't think that's a good—"

"A bet's a bet," he pushed, pulling the truck into his driveway.

He cut the engine, hoping to God his plan panned out. Taking a quick glance in the rear mirror to the dark rental, Jude knew there was no way he'd be able to sleep if she stayed there. Erin stared out the windshield.

He turned toward her. "Thank you." And he vowed to himself to do his best to let it go, for now, and see how things played out.

Her shoulders relaxed as she shrugged. "You're welcome." Then, after a silent moment, added, "Listen, I've already had a margarita. Anymore and I'll totally lose my filter."

"Good. You can tell me what you really think of me." He smiled wide and she rolled her eyes at him. "And I'm not a big wine drinker, but someone left a nice looking bottle at my place—"

"Oh my God!" she groaned, sinking her head into her hands and hiding her face. "I can't believe I did that."

"That was you?" he teased. "Don't be embarrassed. Just come in and have a drink with me. It's cold. I'll start a fire."

Erin lifted her head and he saw it then—the crack in her resolve. The woman loved a fire. Grinning to himself, he felt no qualms in exploiting that. Not if it got her safely in his place. He waited, at ease with the silence, because he knew deep down she wanted to come in.

"Okay," she sighed. "I'll have one drink."

Etta blocked the door when Jude tried to opened it.

"Move girl." He used his knee to urge her back but once they were inside, he let her do her thing, circling Erin with tail swinging, and nose digging into her hands solicitously.

Erin giggled and complied, scratching at any furry body part Etta provided. Jude ducked his head, seeking privacy in how pleased the exchange made him.

"I'll do the fire, you do the wine?" he prompted, heading to the hearth.

"Okay." Erin knelt down, giving Etta the double handed treatment behind both ears and down her neck. "Who's a good girl?"

Chin lifted, and still as a statue, with the exception of her tail, his furry housemate soaked it up like a queen. Jude caught it all in the corner of his eye, and his chest expanded from the inside out. Then, forcing his attention to logs and kindling like he said he would, he got to work. Behind him, the click of nails followed Erin into the kitchen.

"Wine's under the counter. Back wall, right corner," he called from across the cabin. He heard cabinet doors open and close. Then the heavy thunk of a bottle on the countertop.

"Cork screw?" she asked.

"Random crap drawer. All the way to the left."

"Random crap drawer?"

"Yeah. The one with all the random crap you don't know what to do with," he explained.

"I know what it is," she said, her voice bouncing with suppressed laughter. "I just didn't know anyone else called it that too."

Jude paused what he was doing, balancing back on his haunches, and looked over to her. She stared back at him and, *thank God*, she was smiling.

"Guess we have something in common," he commented, smiling back.

She straightened as if coming to awareness, then turned, giving him her back. "A cork screw isn't 'random crap,'" she scolded, digging through the drawer in question. "It goes with bottle openers and can openers and things like that."

"If I used it, which I don't."

She nodded. "I figured as much. I guess I should be lucky you have a wine bottle opener at all. I pegged you for more of a whiskey guy."

"Good guess." He turned back to his own job with an odd sense of satisfaction.

"Am I right, then, in guessing that you don't have wine glasses?"

He heard the cork squeak as she twisted the screw in. "Yes."

The kindling caught and Jude leaned back to watch it. He got lost marveling at how comfortable and easy this was, being with her. Except, nothing came easy. He knew that.

He stood as Erin came out of the kitchen with two glasses, one with dark red liquid, the other amber, two fingers high. *Oh, to hell with it,* he thought. *Why can't it be easy? Just this once?*

He accepted the offered glass and *clinked* it against hers, then took a sip, eyes zeroed on her face. She sipped her wine as Jude enjoyed the burn travel down into his chest. "Thanks."

"No sense in making you drink something you don't like."

He moved a step towards her, eyes dropping to her lips as she took another sip. "I don't dislike wine."

"Oh. Well," she cleared her throat, "then no sense missing out on what you do like."

"I'd like to kiss you."

She tucked her bottom lip into her mouth and it came out glistening. Jude decided right then that he'd probably prefer wine if it was served like that.

"I think I'd like that too," she admitted.

Her usual wisp of hair floated in her face again. Jude tucked it behind her ear, his touch lingering. He could see her pulse pick up in her neck as he sifted his fingers through her ponytail, the strands like silk. The subtle hints of his soap played in his nose. It was on her skin, and in her hair. A wave of possessiveness surged through him.

He pressed at the base of her neck and she teetered closer. His own body filled in the remaining gap. And he was right. He liked the taste of wine served on her lips, the flavor tangy and fruity like early grapes still warm from the sun, mixed with something strictly female.

The tentative kiss she offered back grew bolder. He responded, moving in deeper and crowding his body around hers like a barrier, like he was all that stood between her and the outside world.

His tongue snuck in and she gasped, then gave back in kind. And *damn*, but he really liked that. Jude let his hand slope down her back and curve around her butt. She pivoted into him and pressed her soft, rounded form against his body. Her hand fisted in the fabric of his shirt, preceding a small moan, and their breathing evolved into sharp, quick intakes and desperate exhalations.

She caught his bottom lip between her teeth and when she tugged, Jude couldn't help himself. "Is this you with no filter?"

"Not yet," she replied on a promise, releasing his lips for those two words before demanding them back like she couldn't help herself.

It pleased the hell out of him that the feeling was mutual. He found himself jumping ahead, wondering what her skin would feel like against his, how her body could move on him and just what she sounded like when she—

Sudden heat, weight, and fur pressed against Jude's leg, prying between them. Etta dug herself into their bodies, shoving her head up under his arm. Whiskey sloshed in his glass.

Erin released his shirt. He stifled a discontented groan. In a desperate attempt, he held his palm against Erin's head, maintaining the connection, and using his leg to urge Etta back. His canine companion persisted and he nearly lost his balance.

Erin tried to pull away again, but he kept her where his mouth could reach her. He refused to give her up. Not again. But when Etta shoved the rest of her large body into the embrace, he knew he'd lost.

On one final determined kiss, he growled his frustration into her mouth. Her lips curved up. With great effort, Jude released her head and stepped back. It took a second while his eyes refocused—he couldn't even think.

"Etta, bed." He loved his girl, but this was becoming a problem.

Etta didn't go to bed. She sat where she stood and whined by his side.

"Does she—" Erin started in a husky voice that caught in her throat. She cleared it and tried again. "Does she need dinner?"

"Right now, I don't really care," he admitted, greatly disappointed in the timing.

"It's okay. I promise not to go anywhere."

He took in her flushed complexion and heavy eyelids. She seemed just as disappointed as he felt. It gave him a little solace.

Erin took a step back, leaning into the breakfast bar. Holding his eyes over her glass, she took a sip of wine.

"You're not helping." He forced his gaze down to Etta. "And you. We need to work on your timing."

Nails clicked on the wood as she followed him into the kitchen. He felt Erin's eyes on him as he grabbed the dog bowl off the drying rack by the sink, and went through the motions for Etta's dinner. She didn't make small talk and he was too sexually frustrated to come up with his own.

When Etta finished eating, he tossed the empty bowl in the sink and stared at her furry back while she washed it all down at her water dish. "I should probably take her out to do her business." His tone sounded resigned because he knew the moment had dissipated.

Erin tucked her chin into her chest, but he caught the smile. At least his suffering was good for something. Jude grabbed his jacket from the hook, then took Etta out front. After an agonizing few minutes, Etta completed her business and he herded her back inside.

She sauntered over to her rug by the fire where Erin stood with a nearly empty glass in hand. He retrieved his whiskey from the kitchen and came to join them.

"All good now?" Erin asked, eyes leaving the mesmerizing flames to address him.

Jude tipped his head down to the furry mass at their feet. Etta returned his look with a questioning one of her own.

Sometimes her expressions were so human that he forgot she was a dog.

"Yup." He knocked back the rest of his whiskey. "Can I get you a refill?"

"Yeah, okay." She handed him her glass.

"You want anything else?" he called as he rounded into the kitchen.

"We just had a huge dinner."

"If I recall, you didn't eat all of yours."

She scoffed playfully. "Am I in trouble?"

Jude thought of a lot of responses to that. He settled on the safest one. "Only if you want to be," he baited.

She didn't respond verbally but when Jude looked over he caught her tucking her lips in, her eyes smiling. He poured healthy portions, and led her to the couch. Erin collected her glass from him as she sat.

He settled in next to her. "So," he started, wondering how to get them back to necking.

"So," she parroted, looking at him expectantly.

He decided on an easy topic. "What do you do for fun?"

She snickered.

"What?"

"Sorry, it's just the timing." Giggling, Erin looked away, getting herself under control. But as soon as she met his eye again, she lost it.

"Is this what happens with one margarita and a glass of wine?" he wondered aloud, letting his eyes browse to take her all in.

"No!" she rushed out quickly, then paused long enough for her cheeks to turn pink. Jude smiled. "I mean, usually not," she tried again.

"Yeah," he teased, "I like kissing too. Is that it?" he queired. She looked at him, head tilted slightly, brows dipping. "For fun?" He laughed. "You only like making out with outrageously handsome men?" She scrunched her face. "What? You don't think I'm handsome?"

"Well, you aren't modest," she mumbled.

"That's a 'yes,' then?"

Erin stared at him a while and in those first few seconds, he panicked. He knew other women found him good looking, but Erin wasn't really like other women. Then he noticed the pink in her cheeks had become more of a rosy red.

He tucked that stray hair back behind her ear again. "I won't think less of you if you call me handsome." He leaned in, eyes to her mouth. He could already taste the tangy flavor of the wine on her lips.

She straightened, pulling those lips away and smacked him on the arm.

"God, you're cute," he muttered, despite his disappointment.

She frowned.

"What now?"

"Puppies are cute. Chubby babies are cute."

Jude sensed she was trying to make a point. He took a guess at what that might be. "Allow me to rephrase. You're *acting* cute right now. *You* are sexy as hell." She rewarded him with a huge smile that lit up her whole damn face. "Besides, I like puppies and chubby babies," he added for good measure.

She burst out laughing. Jude grinned, enjoying how her chest pressed against her top and how her ponytail danced around her head.

"You don't have to answer my question," he informed her when her laugher died down. "We can just go back to doing what we were before."

"What was your question?"

Jude sighed. *Oh well, worth a shot.* "What do you like to do?"

"Well, I work a lot so I don't really have time for hobbies."

"Okay. I can understand that. But now you're on vacation, right? So what do you want to do with all that free time?"

She flashed him a look under her lashes, raking her eyes from his mouth down his body.

Jude's chest filled with satisfaction. "I told you, you don't have to answer questions. That's still on the table. Anytime."

"But now it's awkward and would feel totally forced."

"I'm okay with awkward," he offered.

Erin looked over at Etta who lazed by the fire. "Well, I'm not sure I'd survive another interruption," she confided.

"You got it that bad, huh?" Jude tried not to sound too cocky.

She didn't reply, just eyed him over another sip of wine. Settling deeper into the couch, he wondered if she always communicated like this or if the alcohol played a major role. He found it refreshing, being so up front. But he needed a subject change because he felt like a ticking bomb.

"Do you ski?" he asked, shifting to adjust himself. She snorted. "That's a 'no,' then?" He laughed.

"Have you seen me on my feet?"

"I have," he replied, looking at her intently and thinking he'd be happy to hang behind her the whole way down just so he could catch her.

"You? Do you ski?" she volleyed back.

"Sometimes. I'm not up the mountain all day, every day like some. But I get out."

"Snowboard?"

"Hell no! That's for kids," Jude admitted before taking a swig from his glass.

"Okay, old man," she said with a croaky man voice that nearly made him choke. "How old are you?"

"Thirty-seven. Am I allowed to ask you?"

"No. Besides, women don't share their real age." She leaned in, and brought a conspiratorial hand up beside her mouth. "Thirty-three," she whispered.

"Is that your real age?" he whispered back. She shook her head 'no,' then nodded 'yes' with a wink.

When she leaned back, she nestling into his shoulder. "I like to read," she mused, staring into her glass.

A red flag went up in the back of his mind. "Yeah? What kind of books?" he asked, aware of how his gut got tight.

"Mostly thrillers and crime novels," she replied, then snickered. Jude exhaled in relief. "That's why I thought you were an axe murderer."

"Excuse me?" His brow shot up.

She nodded like it was common place to make that kind of assumption about people. "Yup. That first night," she told him. "You were so serious, and it was dark, and late. And it took you *forever* to come to the door."

"I don't usually have visitors at eleven at night."

"And your face was so...frosty!" she exclaimed, sloshing her wine in her cup.

"I'm sorry I gave you that impression." And he meant it.

"Oh, it's okay. I figured out pretty quickly that you weren't. I mean, an axe murderer?" She laughed. "You wouldn't even let us in! Seems a little bad for business."

That didn't make him feel any better. "I have a hands off policy with renters," he explained. "Long story, but people get the wrong idea about me and—"

"Oh my God!" she blurted. Jude watched the color drain from her face. She turned her head away. "Oh my God...I'm so stupid."

She stood abruptly, too abruptly, tilting a little, then moved quickly and clumsily away from the couch. "You know...I...I just remembered. You know what? I have to go," she rushed out, sounding as surprised as he felt.

Jude jumped up, setting his glass on the table, and rounded to intercept her before she could make it to the door. He caught her by the arm, pivoting her to face him.

"Hey," he said softly. She wouldn't look at him. "Hey, what's going on?" he tried again, more firmly.

"I'm so sorry...I, I...you totally...Of course. I get it now. Icy face..."

"What? What are you talking about?"

"*I'm* a renter, Jude," she stated the obvious.

"Yeah. And?"

She stared at him, eyes wide. Then she threw her hand out, palm up as if to exaggerate the point she was making, a point that made no fucking sense. He crossed his arms over his chest and stared back. She shook her head, muttering again. "God, what an idiot I am. I'm just gonna go."

"Erin." For one syllable, he managed to pack a firm punch through her mutterings.

Her throat bobbed and when she looked up, her eyes had glassed over. "'Hands-off,' right Jude?" she said, her voice wobbling.

Jesus. "Have you been paying any attention tonight?" He didn't mean to sound angry, but it pissed him off that she would think he didn't want her there. She didn't respond. "Thought I made it pretty clear that my rule doesn't apply to you."

"I just...I—"

"You just?" he interrupted. "You just didn't pay attention?"

She seemed to shrink, looking contrite. "I just have a history of thinking something is more than it is," she mumbled, her words slow and so utterly deflated, it made him feel like an asshole.

Jude ran a hand roughly down his face, checking his anger. "I like you Erin. I want you here." He looked directly at her, no joking, no innuendos, just truth. Refreshing. "There. Is that straight forward enough?"

He waited for her to give him a smile, a sigh of relief, or something, but instead, her face turned green, a response Jude had never seen before. She rocked a little in place.

"Whoa." He threw his arms out, ready to catch her. "Are you okay?"

"I think I need some water."

"Are you going to throw up?" He looked around for some kind of receptacle.

"I hope not," she replied, closing her eyes for a second. "I ...can I sit down?"

He led her back to the couch. "I'll take this." Jude confiscated Erin's glass and headed to the kitchen. He checked over his shoulder to make sure she wasn't about to puke, then tossed the rest of her wine down the sink and filled her cup with water. He returned to the couch and handed it to her.

"Thanks," she uttered after a huge gulp.

"Maybe try little sips," he advised, eyeing her. Erin nodded and did as he suggested. "Feeling any better?"

"Maybe. A little."

"Still feel like throwing up?"

"Not as much," she said.

Jude waited for her to finish the water, then took her cup and refilled it again.

When he sat down next to her, she spoke. "Something's been bothering me."

He handed her the glass, noting she had some of her color back.

"Thanks." She paused, taking another small sip. "I'm really glad you showed up, but why...I mean, how did you know? The other night, you know, when Victor...when he—"

"When Victor had you by the throat?" Jude finished for her. "How did I know to come in?"

She nodded.

"Not sure I've ever been able to say this before, but I was just in the right place at the right time." Erin's forehead wrinkled. "I was out with Etta," he elaborated. "She heard something and got real edgy, ears pricked forward and hyper focused on your cabin. I came over to check and...well, I saw what I saw."

"Right place, right time," Erin repeated somberly.

"Yup."

"I can't remember if I've thanked you for that."

"You did," he told her, "But you're welcome."

"Thank you."

Jude got up again, and went to the kitchen. He pulled down a bottle with one of those obnoxious child proof caps and dumped a large, brown pill on the counter. Then he dug into a cabinet, grabbed a pack of popcorn and ripped the plastic off. He tossed it in the microwave and hit the auto setting button.

While the popcorn popped, Jude walked back over to the couch with the pill in hand, tagging a remote off of a floating shelf inside Etta's nook as he passed it. He handed both to Erin.

"What's this?" she asked, looking at the pill.

"A multivitamin. You think you can swallow it without it coming back up?"

"Probably."

She took it and chugged it back with the rest of her water. Jude waited. She looked fine so he turned back towards the kitchen. "Why don't you find something to watch."

"Watch? On wha—"

Before she could finish, Jude pulled a television out from under the stairs on a rotating arm. It hovered several feet over Etta's bed.

"Well, that's cool," Erin stated.

Jude smiled. "Pick something. I'll get the popcorn."

"I don't think I could eat anything," she admitted, her face looking a little droopy again.

"It's not for you," he teased.

The microwave beeped just as he made it to the kitchen. He upended the bag in a large metal bowl and walked it back over to the couch.

Erin studied his remote. "How do you work this thing?" She pressed buttons at random.

He chuckled. "Hand it over." He trading her the remote for the popcorn. She put it on the coffee table but Jude caught her sneak a kernel. "What do you like?" He brought up the streaming menu.

"Oh, anything," she said. Then stood.

He looked up at her. "Everything okay?"

She took a moment to find her balance. "Yeah. I just...um...I'm just going to...I need to pee." She wobbled around the coffee table and then teetered to the back of the cabin. Just as she made it out of sight, he heard a loud thump on the wall.

"You sure you're okay?" he called.

"Just pick something!" she hollered back.

The creak of the bathroom door told him she'd made it that far. Another 'thump,' then an "I'm okay!" sifted through the walls. He smiled as he turned his attention to the TV.

When she staggered back into the living area, he'd settled into the corner of the couch with a movie cued up.

"You look so serious," he commented at her approached.

"I'm trying really hard to walk straight so you don't think I'm a lightweight," she confided. "Is it working?"

"Nope."

"Damn."

"I promise I won't think any less of you," he reassured her. "Come sit."

She swayed over to the couch and *flumped* down beside him, almost on top of him.

"Whew! What are we watching?" She turned to him and caught him staring at her. "What?"

He didn't even know where to begin. "Nothing," he laughed and leaned forward to snag the popcorn bowl off the coffee table. "Walter Mitty."

"Huh?"

"The movie. 'The Secret Life of Walter Mitty.' Have you seen it?"

"No." She curled her head into his shoulder.

"Then you are in for a treat."

Erin made noises in her sleep. Quiet and cute ones, like little exclamations on puffs of air. Jude looked from the credits to the top of her head which now nuzzled into his stomach. He'd thrown a blanket over them about halfway through the movie when he'd felt her curling into herself. Now he was baking.

He reached carefully for the remote and turned off the TV. The fire had burned itself down, Etta slept in her nook, and the only lights on were the kitchen and the lamp behind him. He reached his arm back and clicked off the lamp.

Then carefully, he tugged at his long sleeve, inch by inch from under her head, until he was able to pull it off. Erin barely stirred.

He tossed the shirt to the table and it landed in the empty, metal bowl. Seeing it made him smile. For a girl who said she couldn't eat anything, she sure made short work of a bag of popcorn. But then, popcorn seemed to have that effect on people.

Jude straightened out his undershirt and settled back into the couch, letting his head tilt against the arm rest to look up at the ceiling. He was so content he didn't know what to do with himself.

It had been a long time since he'd felt like this. He didn't need anything fancy, didn't need to go out and spend a ton of money. He didn't even need to finish off the night with sex, although, admittedly, that would have been nice if she'd been feeling better. Still, he was perfectly happy crashing on his couch with Erin passed out on top of him.

If she spent the night, she'd be there in the morning, which meant he could probably wrangle in the whole day with her. He didn't work Friday. It was perfect.

Sleep eluding him, Jude thought over what activities she'd approve of, then tossed those aside and thought of something she'd balk at, but would love anyway. He smiled wider, then looked down to the spray of of silk hair sprawled across his chest.

Erin was not what he'd expected.

Now, he had a beautiful woman laying on top of him, one he'd been wanting since those green eyes had locked on his. How would he ever be able to fall asleep?

Chapter Twenty-Three

Salt and Satisfaction

Erin

She must have been asleep because something woke her. Erin's eyes popped open. The TV was black and the light from the kitchen gave the living room a dull glow. A half-groan, half-whine drew her attention to Etta's niche. The shadowy figure of Jude's furry companion *gruffed*, legs twitching, then she settled again, stretching out past the confines of her plush bed.

All through that, Erin grew alarmingly aware that she too lay sprawled out, *on top of Jude*. His legs stretched along the length of the couch, tangling with hers, his stomach her pillow. She fought not to wrench back the arm draped casually along his side. The position screamed lovers and in that moment, an overwhelming desire hit her like a snowball to the face. The lingering sleepiness vanished and in its place came wired alertness.

She held still, her body rigid as a board. Jude's chest rose and fell steadily under her and his heart thrummed a low, rhythmic beat in her ear. Should she move? Would it wake him? Her suddenly overactive nerve endings picked up every shift, flex, and breath underneath her in agonizing anticipation.

She couldn't think straight. The hard, flat planes of muscles and the heat radiating from his body overwhelmed her, sending thrills southward. Under the pretense of night and sleepiness, desire threatened her sense of caution.

Slowly and carefully, she shifted, peeling her body, then pelvis up and away from his. She nearly jumped out of her skin when a strong arm slid around her and pulled her back down.

"Whatcha doing?" came the sleepy voice above her head.

She looked up. Jude's eyes were closed and she couldn't tell if he was awake. "Sorry," she whispered, hoping like hell he was, even if she lacked the courage to make a move.

His hands slid along her sides, then gripped firmly under her arms. Before she could yelp or back away, he hauled her up his chest. Erin's legs naturally fell to the outsides of his hips and her weight sank down onto him. Her breath caught in her throat and her mind went haywire as heat bloomed from the inside out.

Sex.

Afraid of being too bold, she held her head up and away, watching him, waiting—unsure what to do next.

"What?" he asked, eyes still closed.

"Are you awake?"

A lazy smile curled his mouth up. "Do you want me to be?"

Tipping his chin down, he looked at her, eyes at half mast. His hands meandered from her underarms down her sides and sent another string of sensations south. When she squirmed in his lap, his hips flexed in response, rewarding her with the knowledge that they were on the same page.

"You ate all my popcorn," he stated, his voice low, rough, and teasing.

"You shouldn't have put it right in front of me."

"Oh?"

"I don't have a lot of willpower when things are right in my face," she admitted, feeling a little lightheaded.

He leaned his head in closer to hers. "Like this?"

"Yeah," she breathed.

His mouth was so close. A tilt, one inch, and she'd have it. She wanted it. She needed it. But she couldn't do it.

She didn't have to. Jude's muscled arm curled behind her head and brought her down on him. He kissed her with an urgency that sent her every nerve ending into overdrive. His lips took her mouth, firm and driven, with a possessiveness that evaporated her inhibitions.

Erin's hand slid up his chest, around his shoulders, and under his neck. She needed an anchor or she feared she'd sail away. Arching her back up, she pushed both her lips and hips deeper into him. He groaned down her throat and pressed himself into the hollow of her thighs. It would seem, for everything she'd done wrong, this she did right.

His mouth moved across her jaw and down her neck as his hands played over her shirt, hungry and seeking. Then they were gripping the tee and pulling it off. She lifted up as the fabric peeled away from her body and fell to the floor.

"I showed you mine," she uttered, fisting his tee in her hands. He crunched up and together they ripped it off over his head, revealing taut muscle, tats, and that intoxicating combination of woodsmoke and spicy fresh undertone that would forever make her think of him.

He didn't fall back to the couch. With fingers splayed over her hips, he drew her on his lap, into a deep straddle. Like heat seeking missiles, mouths connected again, and her lower half rocked against him without thought.

He grazed his fingers down her back, sending pleasant chills along her skin. Traveling farther south, he planted palms firmly against her butt. She ground herself deeper into him and he strained back against her. Desperate kisses turned to teeth. When he bit the thrumming and heated skin at her neck, her whole body shuddered.

A hands roved up her front and over her breast. More waves crashed southward, like a building tide. She strained against him, against the fabric still restricting their connection, as an uncensored moan escaped.

"Fuck," he uttered, wrapping hands around her back and releasing the clasp of her bra.

It fell to the floor with her shirt. Solid muscle met soft breasts, and it nearly drove her over the edge. She'd had enough foreplay. Her hands wedged between their bodies to find the fastener on his pants.

"You on the pill?" His mouth took hers again before she could answer, urgent and driven—mirroring her own lack of control. Making her wild.

"Uh huh," she moaned out.

"Thank God."

His hands shot to her pants, then she was standing and everything she still wore slid down her legs. Stepping out of her clothes, she stood naked in front of him. He rose, leaning down to catch her mouth while he undid his own button. His pants dropped to the floor in the pile with hers.

Jude snaked his arm around her waist and yanked her down with him, back on the couch. She caught herself, knees into the cushions, with him between her thighs. His hardness pressed against her naked flesh, sending her into another plane of existence. Thought evaporated. She could only respond instinctually, like a beast driven in heat. His hands cupped over her breasts, brushing the sensitive tips of her nipples and the fluttering between her bare legs nearly overwhelmed her. She needed him more than she needed air.

Rising up, she dropped her gaze, appreciating what waited for her as she positioned herself over him. His fingers dug into the skin at her waist while his other hand held himself steady for her. She hovered with the barley-there touch of his sex at her precipice. Her whole body writhed in anticipation. She felt a hunger she'd not known before.

Eyes meeting his, she descended, taking him completely. A groan reverberated from her chest and her head fell back. Pleasure wrapped around her and filled her from the inside out. She pushed up with her thighs and sank down again. Another wave swept through her.

She saw things in terms of skin and not skin, heat and not heat. The traces of light from the kitchen blurred into stars and streaks as her eyes glassed over from the intensity and satisfaction of long awaited sensations.

Jude's hips tilted to meet hers, burying himself deeper into her. He dropped his head, grasping her nipple between his teeth and she pressed her breast into his mouth. Her skin rippled under his touch. Strong hands cupped her butt and he lifted her, then let her sink on him again, guiding the pace. She followed, pressing her thighs up and down to his rhythm.

He trailed hot kisses along her chest, up her neck, then found a spot that made her gasp and shiver. Just when she thought she couldn't withstand any more sensations, he came back to her mouth. Their rhythm increased and sweat pricked her skin. She rose and fell, their mouths fighting for control, his teeth biting her bottom lip, her tongue plunging into his mouth, he dove his deeper and she moaned down his throat.

She could feel herself tightening—the rushes growing deeper and more urgent. Her body lost his rhythm, driving with abandon as her breath escalated into short quick gasps and she felt her insides reaching for it.

So close.

Every time he thrust deeper, every time she sank down, she shivered and fought to keep her body moving. She grew tighter and tighter until she could hardly breathe. Then she couldn't move. Jude kept it going, plowing up into her until finally, she exploded. Her mouth disconnected from his and her body wracked, heaved, arched, and shuddered as she rode wave after wave on top of him.

"Holy fuck," he gritted out, working to keep the pace.

Then, planted to the root, she felt it, his own culmination. It fueled her sensations, making them roll over again. Her hips undulated over him, taking it and stealing more. Never could she remember it being this good. Never had it carried on this long.

Her shoulders slumped in exhaustion and her head fell to Jude's shoulder as she worked to bring oxygen into her lungs. His own breathing came at her erratically, his heart a heavy hammer in her ear. One hand held her low, just above her butt, the other tangled in her hair, pressing her cheek into his chest. They stayed like that a while and her body melted into his with languid satisfaction. She sighed. Her eyes grew heavy.

"Let's go to bed," Jude murmured in her ear.

"Mhmm."

Reluctant, she straightened, ready to push off, but he leaned forward, tucking his hands under her, then stood, lifting them both. She wrapped arms around his neck, linking her ankles behind him, and he walked them to the back of the cabin.

"Get the light?" he asked as they passed through the kitchen.

She swatted at the switch and sudden darkness engulfed them. Something about the blackness heightened her physical awareness, highlighting how he felt inside her as he moved them down the hall and into his bedroom. He kicked the door closed behind them. Desire stirred again and a heady rush swept over her at the thought of being in his bed. A shiver crept over her.

"You cold?" he asked.

"No. Not even a little bit."

She locked her elbows at the back of his neck and pulled herself to his face. In the darkness, she found his lips. She kissed him with renewed urgency, expressing with her mouth how her body felt. Jude's arms flexed in response and then they were down to his bed, Erin on her back and him over her.

He moved himself inside of her, out and back in, stoking the heat into another fire. She moaned her appreciation and he smiled against her lips.

"You are something else," he uttered, laying kissed down her neck. He found that spot she liked and she bucked when he hit it. "Yeah," he mused, holding himself up and looking down at her.

In the shadows, his body was solid male sex. She stared at him through half opened eyes, searching for words to tell him to come back and kiss her. She writhed beneath him and saw the subtle movement on his mouth—a smile.

"Better give my girl what she wants." He settled back over her and he did not disappoint.

Jude

Soft, morning light filtered in through the curtain.
Damn.
Jude wasn't ready for the day—not ready to let go of the sexual delirium from the night before. He tightened an arm around Erin's naked torso. Before they'd drifted off, she'd snuggled up on her side into his chest. She hadn't peeped nor moved since.

He tipped his head down and buried his nose in her hair. *Something else.* The only thing better than waking up to her curled into his body was waking up to her practically grinding against him.

Yeah. Something else.

Jude grazed a finger down her bare side and watched her skin prick and shiver. He liked what he made her body do. He liked what her body made him do. He liked everything all around.

Kissing the top of her head, he settled back onto his pillow. She hummed a little note and nestled deeper. *Not fair. He* never stood a chance. His finger brushed up her back and her body did a kind of rolling wave in response, like a cat arching down when petted.

Jude smiled, continuing a trail across her ribs and down her belly. He watched her lips part as he skimmed her exposed, inner thigh, her eyes fluttering open, but only briefly. He drew a finger up and around, teasing the boundaries of her sensitive skin. Her breath hitched. Even in sleep, she responded to him.

He dragged the back of his knuckle up across her center and she shifted to her back with a satisfied mew. One of her knees fell to the side and pure, unadulterated contentment bubbled in his chest.

He pressed a finger into her, and watched her hips lift. His blood pulsed south. Yeah, he liked what he made her body do.

A hand ruffled his hair.

"Good morning," he murmured, looking up to the sexiest bedroom eyes he'd had the pleasure of satisfying.

She squirmed at his touch, offering a small smile and sliding her hand down his stomach. It wrapped it around his already half-established morning wood. "Morning."

Touching him like that, he'd never last.

He shifted out of her grasp, then maneuvered to kneel between her open legs. She tried to reach for him. Catching her wrist, he held it over her head. He wanted to play without distractions. She had the good sense not to try with her other hand.

She gasped, and arched her back as he plunged two fingers deep into her core. Ready as she seemed, he liked making her squirm, so he built her up and taunted her until she'd almost reached her peak. When her felt her tightening, he stopped.

"Jude! You're killing me!" she whined, looking down her body at him.

It was killing him too. He was harder than rebar.

He leaned down and planted a kiss just below her navel, feeling her pulse course under her skin. Withdrawing his fingers, he moved up her body, and positioned himself at her swollen center. Her body reached for him with a magnetism he couldn't begin to explain, but understood all too well. In that moment, they felt like two halves of a whole.

He pressed in just enough to make her gasp. As he drew back, he watched her mouth a silent plea.

"Okay," he murmured, eyes crinkling down at her. "No more games."

He pushed his way in, and reveled at how her silky flesh wrapped around him. Deeper. Her breath hitched in that way he loved. Deeper. She moaned. To the root. Her breasts rose and fell with each hot, heavy breath.

He fell forward, holding himself over her, kissing soft skin, tasting her mouth and moving inside of her. He took his time rebuilding her orgasm. He slowed to draw out his. He wanted her to come undone on him, like she had the night before. He wanted to finish as she shuddered and moaned with the pleasure he gave her. He wanted to touch her, taste her, see her, and feel her as they came unglued together.

Lifting her leg, he swung it up and around, moving her body onto its side. Without losing contact, he settled against her back, his hips just below hers, so he could thrust up and into her from behind as her body lay spread out for him to see. He curled an arm under her head, and reached for one, hardened nipple. She quivered. Everywhere.

Moving in and out at a steady rhythm, he raked his other hand down over her stomach to touch her. He liked this position. A lot. He could see her, feel her, and touch her everywhere. And based on her little sounds, she liked it too.

Jude dipped his head and kissed her creamy neck. When turned on, the woman was pure sex—pure sex in *his* bed. A heady combination. A secret he didn't want to share. A treasure he needed to hoard and protect. Fire ran through his veins as he fought to hold on. She was close.

Her upper body tightened first. Then, her breathing hitched over and over like a stuck record. She gasped a strangled cry and he could feel it, the tightness course down her spine and clamp around him.

"Ah! Don-don't stop. God, Jude don't--" She rocked and bucked in his hold as he dove harder and deeper, her contractions sending him past coherence. And she came *undone*.

Thrusting, slamming into her from behind, he let loose his control. His pace became hard, fast, and urgent. *Fuck*, he liked what her body did to him. Her arm reached back and fisted in his hair as he took her.

Buried deep, he let go, the relief so profound he almost couldn't breathe. When she tilted her hips forward and back on him, the sensation nearly tore him apart. He wrapped his arm around her and drew her tightly against his chest, his own body now shuddering with hers. Her hand released his hair and trailed ghost-light touches over his arm. She intertwined her fingers with his.

Jude inhaled the scent of his shampoo on her hair. *Perfection*. And kissing her shoulder, tasting the salt from the sweat they'd made the night before, he settled into her with complete satisfaction. *No regrets*.

The minutes passed as euphoria seeped into his limbs. Erin sighed and sank deeper into his body. Light came in from the window more intensely now but it didn't bother him. Who needed night? They could do this all day.

Then, he both heard and felt Erin's stomach rumble.

Lifting up on an elbow, he leaned over her. Her creamy skin glowed and her mussed-up hair fanned out on his pillow. *Freaking perfection.*

"Gonna make some coffee," he murmured at her ear. "Take your time getting up."

"Mmmhmm," came the sweet and sleepy reply.

He kissed her shoulder, then carefully dislodging himself and rolled off the bed. Pulling a loose pair of sweats up over his hips, Jude grabbed a long sleeve from his closet. As he moved out of the bedroom, he paused, glancing over his shoulder. Erin all tangled up in his sheets, he thought, *Damn, my bed looks good like that.*

Smiling, he shut the door quietly behind him. *Fuck, it's gonna be a good day.*

Chapter Twenty-Four

Two Steps Back

Erin

She sat at Jude's breakfast counter, smiling into her coffee. Jude had gone upstairs to do something after she'd strutted out to the living room to collect her clothes. Well, not right after...

She sighed, reminiscing how he'd caught her, then wrapped his arms around her and the sheet she'd donned. Every time she pulled away to grab her garments, he yanked her back to his chest like a yoyo, kissing her neck or her shoulder. Who'd have thought? *Playful Jude? I could get used to this.*

But then her smile waned. Two days and she had to go back to the city. A little voice warned her not to get too attached. Long distance wasn't good, especially at the start of a relationship. But her body sang—something it hadn't done in a very, very long time.

So instead of being cautious, as she normally strived to be, Erin mulled over when she could take her next vacation. *It doesn't have to be a full week*, she thought, wondering if he might come out her way. *Would Etta even fit in my apartment?* She'd have to find out if pets were allowed in her building.

As logistics bounced around in her head, Jude wandered down the stairs and into the kitchen with a stack of papers in hand. Erin flashed him a smile.

"You look happy," he teased.

"Can you blame me?" She liked that she could be herself around him.

He hunched over on his elbows at the counter across from her, the corners of his mouth working to push it down like he was holding back a wide grin. She didn't realize she'd leaned over her coffee cup until Jude stretched forward and planted a sweet kiss on her lips that was over too soon.

"I'd be disappointed if you weren't," he told her.

Yes, she needed to come back. Erin looked to the packet of papers in his hand. "Do you have work today?"

"No..." he said, sounding hesitant. He looked at her a moment and his smile faltered.

Sudden panic pricked the inside of her stomach. "What? What is that?" Her eyes zeroed in on the papers as his gaze fell to the top sheet but he didn't answer.

For a moment, she wondered if he wanted to rip them up, his hands curling around the edges of the packet. Then, it was as if watching a balloon deflate. His whole stature seemed to shrink. Shooting her a leveled stare, he slid the stack across the counter to her.

Erin looked down and read the heading. "What—what is this?" Had she missed something? She glanced up.

Jude looked tense as he watched her. "It's exactly what it looks like."

Shifting her eyes back down to the top sheet, she shook her head, trying to follow the sudden shift from post coital bliss to...this.

"A restraining order? For who?" But she knew. "Is this...is this for Victor?" He didn't answer. He didn't have to. "Why? Why would you print this?"

"Why?" He laughed. "Are you kidding me?"

She straightened, stiff and cautious.

"Look, you told me yourself, the guy—"

"No. I mean, why now? We've have sex twice. Really good sex...but still! We haven't even lost the...the *afterglow* and you think...what? 'Oh, I'll just print this out, what the heck?'"

"Erin," he started but she kept on.

"Is this some kind of game? What are you doing?"

"It's just a requests. It's the first step in a whole process."

"Oh great! It's a whole process!" she snarked.

"I think you're overreacting."

"I'm overreacting? This is," she floundered for the right words as she scanned the documents pages. "This could have drastic effects on him."

"Oh him?"

"Yes!"

She brought her eyes back to Jude, searching for understanding. He clearly had no qualms with what he asked her to do. And he didn't seem at all bothered by his timing. Except, he'd known it would piss her off. Is that what he wanted? Had sex been more casual to him than she'd realized? She couldn't tell because his face had grown hard again, like a glaring, stone gargoyle.

Erin pursed her lips and returned to studying the form. She didn't know much about this kind of stuff, but surely it would affect his job, his networking...everything! It would go on a permanent record. She didn't want to destroy Victor, she just wanted him to leave her alone.

She struggled separating her memory of him with what transpired at the rental. Her brain couldn't quite find the line, instead consolidating the two. The mixed feelings turned her brain mushy and indecisive. Could a broken heart explain his actions? Did he deserve this legal intervention? If he thought she'd been cruel before...

"Jude, this isn't right. I can't—"

"What about that?"

Erin lifted her eyes. His were focused on the bandage at her chest. She stiffened.

"You think *that* is right?" Now, he was an angry gargoyle.

"This," she tapped her fingers lightly near the bandage, "this is just a scratch. This will heal. But a legal restraining order?" She held up the packet and flapped it in Jude's face.

"Do you hear yourself?" Anger shook his tone. He pushed away from the counter and paced the kitchen.

"You're mad?"

"Damn right, I'm mad!"

"Seriously? This isn't even your business. Sex twice!" She held up two fingers to emphasize her point.

"How many times then?"

"What?"

"How many times," he repeated, "do we have to have sex before I get a say in your safety?"

Erin opened her mouth but nothing came out.

He wove his arms over his chest, bulging biceps reminding her he'd had no problem hefting her up and carrying her off to his bedroom the night before. But paired with the cold look on his face, she also remembered the welcome he'd given them their first night in the mountains.

She got a sinking feeling that she'd made a huge mistake. "You know Jude, I can't seem to figure you out." She slid off the stool, ready to stand her ground. "First you want to be left alone, then you don't want me to leave. Now we're finally getting along and you pull out this?"

She tossed the form onto the counter, the pages sliding across. Some separated from the stack and fell to the floor on the other side.

"I don't get it," she huffed. "What is it you want?"

"Shouldn't be that hard to figure out if you were paying attention."

"That's not an answer."

He scoffed. "Don't play games, Erin. You're smarter than that."

She jerked back, staring. He didn't elaborate. How could she make him see? "I just don't understand why you're getting so upset about this," she tried again, her voice a false calm.

"You don't, huh?" He exhaled on a hiss. "I don't understand why you're *not* taking this thing with Victor more seriously."

"You don't even know him. You hardly know me!"

"Yeah, I get it. Sex twice."

"Don't even—"

"Some actions speak for themselves," he interrupted with cocky confidence.

Erin wasn't sure what he meant by his comment, but the way he said it made her blood steam. "You aren't listening. The little you saw in that cabin was not the real Victor!"

"That's funny," Jude clipped, "he seemed pretty real to me. The broken glass all over the goddamn floor was pretty real. The knife against your neck, that cut, your blood—"

"Stop it!" she yelled, reeling from the emotions his words triggered.

He fidgeted, probably fighting to keep his mouth shut, but his eyes held what remained unsaid. Erin felt sick. It had happened just as he'd insinuated, but she couldn't believe that Victor would do it again—not *her* Victor. He wasn't some villain. Jude didn't know him so he wouldn't understand.

Silence stretched between them and Erin worked to find calm, taking deep, shaky breaths. She'd try one last time to make him see. If it didn't work, she'd cut her losses and walk away.

"Please, hear me out," she begged. "Victor has never raised a hand to me before. It was a rough day, he was under a lot of stress, and he'd had too much to drink. Anyone in those circumstances would have acted poorly."

"He was having a snit, Erin. A jealous snit."

She shot Jude a warning look, but it must have bounced off his male ego because he just shook his head and carried on.

"I should have seen this coming." It was a sad, resigned statement.

"We all make mistakes, Jude."

"Of course you'd defend him." He rubbed a hand over his face, his fingers making a scratchy sound over his stubble.

His statement made her prickle, like somehow he thought less of her because of it. "What is this really about? Are you trying to get back at him because of what you think he did to Etta?"

"What? No! This has nothing to do with me! Jesus! There is no downside to a restraining order, Erin. Did you block it out? Did you forget what *just* happened?" She flinched. He was yelling now. "How many scars does it take?" He stalked around the counter toward her. "How many?"

Jerking and stumbled back, Erin nearly tripping over the stool behind her. She threw her hands up in front of her at his approach. "Don't!"

He halted, right in front of her, his heavy breath hitting her face. The air between them felt tense and parlous, like an acid bubble on the verge of popping, only to wreck havoc on those stupid enough to linger by. Her stomach twisted. She certainly felt stupid. But not because of any restraining order.

"Please don't," she pleaded.

His hands went to his neck, then fell angrily at his sides. Then to his hips, then his sides, until they finally stayed planted at his waist, and he looked away. His uncertainty disarmed her, but only slightly.

She shouldn't have had sex with him. A part of her couldn't believe it but she worried it was all just a big pissing contest. He said it wasn't about getting back at Victor, but why else would he do this? He hardly knew her. What did he get out of it?

"Erin." He brought eyes back to her, brows low, sharp stoney edges gone. "If you could see this from my point of view—"

"You don't know our history," she interjected.

He held up his hand to silence her. "You said he's never done this before. But what if—"

"He hasn't. He wouldn't. He won't." Why did she have to sound so desperate?

"But what if he *does*? What then?"

"It's my fault Jude. I should't have dumped him then disappeared before giving him closure. I should have dealt with it like an adult. If I send this in," she reached over and held up one of the pages, "then I'm no better than him. This is just retaliation. He hurts me so I hurt him back? How does that make me the better person?"

He scoffed. "That isn't even remotely the same thing."

"He said he loved me, Jude, and I walked away. What would you have done if someone you loved left without any explanation?"

Something passed over his face, a sad, resigned look, and Erin got the feeling she'd made her point. "He's hurting."

"Doesn't give him permission to do what he did."

"No. But I can forgive him for it."

Jude shook his head. "You shouldn't."

With a sharp exhale, he stepped back, dragging a hand though his mussed up hair. He studied her a moment before speaking, and when he did, his voice came calm like the low rumble of waning thunder.

"I'm not trying to raise your hackles, Erin. I don't want to alienate you, either. I just want you to think about how you're going to protect yourself." He looked like he wanted to say more.

"But?"

"But what?" he asked.

"There's more you want to say."

He looked away.

"Just say it," she insisted. "Might as well get it all out there now." She crossed her arms over her chest as he brought his attention back to her.

"You may not see it," he started cautiously, "what he's doing. But I see it. I saw it all over his face. This isn't about love, Erin. This is about power."

Her face fell. At least he had the decency to look regretful. "Power?"

"You doing what you did, leaving him, it took away his power."

"Power."

"Yeah," Jude confirmed. "Don't give him that power back by underestimating him."

"Is *this* about power, too?" she asked, her hand moving back and forth between them. "What you're doing here. Sex. The restraining order...is this a power move, Jude?" She hated how her voice cracked.

He shook his head, staring at his feet. It took him a minute to respond and in that time, a tornado of regret and shame lashed at her insides. In that moment, she thought she might throw up. What had she been thinking?

"Believe what you need to about *this*," he mimicked her gesture between them. "He hurt you Erin."

"It wasn't that bad."

"He could have done worse."

"But he didn't*!*" she shouted. "He only broke my skin because—" she shut her mouth. She'd thrown a low blow and she knew it. It wasn't Jude's fault. Clearing her throat, she blinked back the sting. "Whatever. It doesn't matter. I'm fine now."

"I don't like fine. Fine isn't good," he grumbled back.

Hadn't she told herself she'd just walk away? Why wasn't she walking?

"Erin." Jude took a step toward her and when she didn't stagger back, he reached out to hold the sides of her neck.

His palms felt warm and calming, despite their conversation and she hated it. "It took a gun pointed at him," he reminded her unnecessarily.

"Yeah. Your gun," she choked out. "It scared the shit out of him. It scared the shit out of *me*." He'd done nothing but try to help her, even if she didn't understand why. She didn't even care about the damn cut, but she felt cornered.

He fell silent at her words. She could see a torrent of things pass through him: hurt, anger, regret...One thing she didn't see there was surprise. He frowned and it etched deep lines into his hardened face. She hand't meant to tear him down. This wasn't her.

"Jude...I—"

"That's exactly my point. I won't be there to stop him next time."

His frown deepened, like the words tasted as bad as they sounded. But he spoke the truth, right? He wouldn't be there. A hole deep opened in her chest and all those silly vacation plans of hers fell into it.

"It's just a cut, Jude," she reassured him and maybe also herself.

"Yeah. Sure."

He looked to the side, taking his hands back to hips and pivoting away from her. Erin had thought that he'd looked defeated before, but now...now he looked destroyed. And she'd done that. A life full of education, training, and working, and her greatest strength was wrecking things.

He walked back into the kitchen. "Not gonna make you do anything you don't want to do," he called over his shoulder. "You're right, it's not my business."

Jude

What the hell was he doing? He sure wished it wasn't his business. It certainly would have been easier not to whip out the forms and piss her off. He told himself he'd done what any normal human would do—that it wasn't personal.

He hadn't meant to get so involved. But then she brought him tea. Just because. The woman was guileless. She had to be with those kinds of moves.

And the worst of it? He actually wanted it. He wanted to be that involved because when it was good, it was so good. When they connected...*shit*.

But at what cost? Should he push through and hope like hell it was worth it? Or just cut his losses? She was just passing through, for God's sake. *Two days*. What could he gain? The smart choice would be to fade back, to let it go and end it there.

But even fading back, he didn't want her returning home with that guy on the loose. Not without a plan. She had it wrong. Jude didn't care about power. Nothing he could say would matter though. She felt attacked. That asshole had manipulated her for too long. It was too ingrained in her.

"Jude, I'm sorry."

He thought he'd imagined it, the quiet apology. He turned and she straightened, looking right at him, her scowl gone.

"Jesus," he muttered. "Now you're apologizing?" He shook his head. Is this how Victor had done it, tricking her into thinking she was the bad guy?

She swiped her hand under her eye. "I...I'm sorry I blew up at you. You were just trying to help."

"It's fine," he replied.

"Fine?"

"Yeah. Fine." He didn't give it any sugar coating. "You're a big girl. You can make your own decisions."

A silent moment stretched out between them and he locked down his own frustrations. *When it's good...*He figured he could do a whole lot of good in two days. "Apology accepted."

Erin nodded, looking relieved. "And I'll um...I'll think about it," she said, picking up the pages from the counter and stacking them neatly.

He stared at her, fascinated. *Just like that?* Stooping, he grabbed the few sheets that had fallen to the floor. He handed them to her.

"Thanks." She sorted the pages, folding the completed stack in half and looking around the room. Apparently she didn't find what she was looking for so she tapped the packet against the breakfast bar and set it down again. "I'll look it over and I'll think about it," she said again to the counter.

He didn't know what to make of it. Problem solved and fighting done? It seemed too easy but only a fool would ask for more. And he'd felt rotten when she'd been upset with him.

He tipped his chin to the breakfast bar. "Need a warm up?"

She looked up, brow creased. For a heart stammering second, he thought she planned to excuse herself back to the rental. And what could he do? Her eyes tilted down to her mug, then back to him.

"Sure. Half a cup?" she finally replied.

Jude smiled at his own relief, uncharacteristically glad that he knew how to make good coffee.

She slid the mug across the breakfast bar at the same time he reached out to take it. His fingers linger on her hand. It seemed absurd, how that little contact could rev him up. *Oh, what the hell?* he thought. He couldn't fade back now if he wanted to. With a secret smile, he went about getting her that half cup. She'd perched on the stool again so he set it on the bar in front of her.

"Thanks."

He watched her bring it to her mouth, close her eyes, inhale the steam, then smile when the coffee hit her lip.

Worth every penny for those fancy beans, he grinned. *Just for that smile.* "You got any plans today?"

She scoffed into her cup, making a choking sound. "Me? Plans? That's funny."

"Why's that funny?"

Her eyebrows sat flat over her eyes as she studied him. He shrugged.

"No, I don't have plans. I never have plans. Just work," she snickered into her coffee. "Always work."

"On vacation?"

"Yes. Even on vacation."

Tucking a hand into his pocket, he asked, "Do you have to work today?"

She scrunched her face up. "What's today?"

He laughed. "Friday."

"Yeah. I might. I'll have to call in."

"When you do, tell your boss you can't because you have plans," he told her, the corner of his mouth tipping up.

"Oh really?" She set her coffee down and eyed him. "With you?" He liked how her face flushed. "What are we doing?"

"It's a surprise." He tried to appear mischievous as she studied him.

"I don't ski," she reminded him firmly.

His grinned. "I know."

Chapter Twenty-Five

Falling

Jude

"Why won't you tell me where we're going?" Erin asked as she pulled on one of his fleece lined coats. He watched her fiddle with the zipper, her hands getting lost in the extra length of the sleeves.

"Because. You're squared away with work?"

"Yes. And *because* isn't an answer," she huffed. She finally got a grasp on the zipper pull but she couldn't get the bottom aligned.

"You don't like surprises?"

"Lately?" She left the question hanging and Jude remembered the phone conversation with her mom.

She'll like this one, he thought as she tried brute force on the poor metal fastener. "May I?" he interjected, moving into her space.

Lifting her hands out of the way and with chin into her chest, she watched him grasp the zipper pull. He Leaned in, bringing his face right in front of hers. When she looked up, she did that hitching-breath thing he loved, like the prospect of kissing him thrilled her. And he had no intention to disappoint.

Taking her mouth, he kissed her thoroughly while his fingers aligned the zipper and tugged it upwards. "You look really cute in my jacket," he told her lips.

She smiled. "I was wondering what that was for."

"Do I need a reason to kiss you?" He eased back.

"No." She smiled wider and her cheeks flushed.

Just for that, he did it again, this time quick and sweet. "Good." Then snuck one more in for good measure.

She giggled into his mouth and he almost canceled their plans. He could think of several things he'd be happy doing with her right there in his own cabin. He felt like a kid in the candy store, overwhelmed with choices. How could he possibly pick?

"Are we going or what?" she sassed, leaning back and giving him a coy smile.

"Are you in my brain?" he retorted.

She shook her head and pushed a palm into his chest. It sent him back a few inches but only because he let her. Sighing dramatically, he grabbed a jacket for himself, his keys, then pulled the door open for them.

"Etta, stay," he called to the lazing hill of wiry fur on rug by the dark fireplace. She didn't even bother lifting her head.

Jude drove the windy road to the main drag while Erin stared out her window with a buzzing, excited kind of energy. He glanced around at the scene, and it felt as if he were seeing it again for the first time. It made him want to show her all his favorite spots. Obviously, he couldn't. Not in two measly days. Some things were better in the summer anyway. He wondered if he could lure her back when the snow melted.

At the main drag he cranked up the heat. She rewarded him with an appreciative smile. He was just happy she hadn't burrowed into the passenger door where he couldn't reach her. Still...

At the next stop, he leaned over to her side, and hooking an arm around her waist, dragged her to the center of the bench. She yelped in surprise.

"Much better." He smiled, eyes back on the road.

"Jude, my seatbelt..." she laughed.

Digging a hand into the crease of the seat, he shook his head. "Always something with you." He found the center lap strap and pulled it out for her. "Here."

She switched belts, and scooted in closer. Jude lifted an arm, resting it over her shoulders, as a warm feeling buzzed around in his chest. Being around her made him feel young again. He remembered how he used to joke and play and make dumb movie references—how he actually enjoyed doing things. Before Kat.

If I'd never put on a suit...never stepped foot in the city, he often wondered. But then maybe he never would have ended up here, now, like this.

Erin nestled and twisted into his side, eyes fixed on the front window. He pointed out things as they passed and her body gradually straightened, until it perched on the edge of the bench like she could hardly sit still. Her energy was infectious.

Pressing lips together, he tried to keep a straight face as he pulled into the parking lot of a ski resort.

Her head flew in his direction, long, feathery hair whipping against his cheek, and her eyes narrowed on his face.

"Jude," she accused, her body tensing at his side, "this is a skiing place."

"Sure is." He pulled into a free spot.

"You promised."

"Did I?"

Cutting the engine, he swung his door open, and hopped out of the cab, boots crunching in the snow. When he didn't hear the other door open, he turned back to the driver's side of the truck and leaned in.

"I can't believe you," she muttered, arms crossed, shaking her head.

"I didn't promise anything."

"You did!" After she said it, her eyes drifted up like she was trying to recall the conversation. "You said...well, you implied—"

"You gonna sit in the truck the whole time? Come on. Let's go." He ticked his head towards the resort's main entrance. She didn't budge.

Glaring back at him, she told him in definitive terms, "I'm not going skiing."

"Fine, you got me. No skiing," he admitted, pressing palm into the bench. "Get out of the truck."

"If this is a trick—"

He reached in, released her buckle, grabbed her waist, and yanked her across the bench.

"Jude!"

The startled squeal of his name on her lips moved through him and settled in his groin. She pushed and fought against him, but if the giggles were anything to go by, she didn't mean it. And if she knew what those giggles were doing to him physically...

He caught her arms mid swing and pinned them at her back, pulling and pivoting her the rest of the way to his open door. She *whooped* and threw out her legs to catch herself, heels bracing on the running board.

Jude tucked his body in between her open thighs. "You trust me?" he asked, an inch from her face.

Her play scowl dropped. She hesitated, eyes scanning his, but not in the way people act before delivering bad news.

"No skiing," he murmured, eyes dropping to her lips. "Promise."

When his mouth met hers it was more desperate than he'd intended. Being around her threw him off, and he'd not known how satisfying it would feel to earn her trust.

Her arms strained against his grip so he let her go. She wrapped them around his neck, pulling herself into him.

Should've just stayed at the cabin. "Woman," he growled, reluctantly pulling his mouth away, "you have no idea what you're doing to me."

"You don't like it, then stop kissing me like that," she countered, working to catch her own breath.

"That's not gonna happen."

"Then stop complaining."

He wasn't complaining, but he thought better than to argue.

Erin suddenly stiffened and released her hold on him.

A couple stomped by the truck in full gear, carrying skis over their shoulders. They nodded their heads and called out an overly friendly greeting. Jude thought it cute the way Erin tucked her lips into her mouth, like kissing in public embarrassed her. He leaned in to do it again, but her palm slammed into his chest.

"Is this what you wanted to do?" she rushed out, eying the retreating couple as she spoke. "Make out in the parking lot of the ski resort?"

"No," he laughed, accepting defeat. "But I'm flexible."

"And you said no skiing," she clarified.

"No skiing."

"Okay. Let's go then."

"Okay." He must've stood there too long because she gave him another push.

Chuckling, he moved back, and let her hop down. After Swinging the door shut, he grabbed her hand under the pretense that he didn't want her to slip, but really, he just wanted to hold her hand. Something playful surfaced—something nostalgic—and it excited him. The world suddenly looked different. It wasn't just a backdrop for work and responsibilities.

They walked around the main entrance, and all the while, Erin's eyes scanned the buildings cautiously, her posture stiffer than a board.

"Thought you trusted me," he teased.

"It's not that...I don't trust myself."

"Relax," he urged, using his grip on her hand to shake out her arm. They rounded the corner of the main building. "There you go."

Her footing paused and her expression brightened. Jude would have described it as pure glee.

"Seriously?" she chirped.

"Yeah. Seriously." He chuckled.

She swung around and punched him in the arm.

"What was that for?"

Erin didn't answer. She just gave him a look, then drew her eyes back to the scene ahead of them. "Have you done this before?" she queried.

"Nope."

That was when her smile nearly split her face in two. "Me neither."

The crisp, icy wind whipped at their faces as they built up speed. Erin let out a scream and Jude wrapped his arms tighter around her. They spun and bumped and tore down the hill, tucked in the elongated snow tube. Erin's back pressed into Jude's front, her knuckles white from her grasp on the front handle.

He saw trees, then hill, then trees again as the tube spun and carried them down without a care to the bottom of the hill, across the leveled landing and into a wall built up from plowed snow. They hit the barrier with enough force to send soft while flakes crumbling down on them like confetti. As they skidded to a stop, Erin threw her head back into his chest and laughed up at him. White sprinkles scattered in her hair, face, and shoulders, but she didn't seem to notice. And it was hard not to love every minute of it.

"Again?" he asked.

"Yes!"

He smiled so wide it hurt. He felt like a high schooler again.

"Jude?" Erin craned her head sideways, looking up at him.

"Hm?"

"You have to let me go."

"Do I?" he challenged, but even as he spoke, he loosened his grip.

She rose, tripping, slipping, and pushing up from the tube. Once steady, she turned and offered him her hand.

He stared, and something strange stirred in his chest, both invigorating and terrifying. He found it strange how such a small gesture could feel so good.

Meeting her eyes with a sly smile, he grabbed her arm and yanked. She yelped, then fell, knees into the tube, before toppling onto him. He wrapped an arm around her back as she tried to right herself.

"Jude!"

He persisted, enjoying how she wiggled and grunted against his body. When she pressed up with her arms, she hovered right in his face. *Perfect.*

"What was that for? I was *trying* to be nice."

Cupping the back of her head, he pressed his mouth to hers. "Just wanted to kiss you."

He didn't think she'd actually been mad, and she confirmed it when she kissed back. More so when she leaned into it, drawing her knees up to either side of his body and pressing deeper into his mouth. He didn't want to do it, but he jerked his head back.

"You gotta stop or we're never gonna make it back up that hill."

She shot him a look. "You keep saying that but you're the one who's instigating it."

That disgruntled tick in her jaw made him smile. And the knowledge that she too struggled to keep her hands off him gave him relief like a breeze on a sunny day. But she had a point. He was learning that she responded to him like a lit firecracker. Knowing that, it wasn't right to leave her hanging. He planned to remedy that later.

He took his hands back. "Fair point. You should get up, there are a ton of kids here."

Erin lifted her head, looking around and seemed to realize they were being watched. Her cheeks, already pink from the cold, flamed a deeper shade. Narrowing eyes on him, she scoffed, then pursed her lips, like she wanted to smack him again.

He laughed. "Why do you get so embarrassed kissing me in public?" The question spurred purely from curiosity. It didn't bother him, he just wanted to know.

"What?"

"You get all flustered and your face gets red when you realize someone's watching us," he told her.

She stood, brushing the snow off her pants. "Oh. I don't know. I guess I'm just used to keeping things private."

His smile faltered. More likely she'd become accustom to being hidden away like a shamed skeleton in someone's closet. Any man worth his sweat should have been flaunting her on his arm, claiming bragging rights that she'd picked him. That's what Jude would have done.

He watched her intently so he saw when her face turned solemn. Her eyes locked with his and he braced, expecting the worst.

"I'm um...I'm sorry about what I said earlier," she started. Jude cocked his head, not following. "I don't blame you. You know that, right?"

"For what?"

"Well, for anything, but specifically for what Victor did."

"Oh." He felt some of the tension ease from his shoulders. That made one of them.

"I just wanted you to know that. I shouldn't have said what I said, and I'm sorry."

"Forgiven."

She gave him a small smile and held her hand out again. "Be good this time," she warned as he reached for it.

He smiled, wrapping fingers around her wrist.

She tugged without success. "Jeez, you're heavy!"

Jude laughed, then pressed a hand into the inflated rubber to assist her. Once standing, he intertwined his fingers with her small, frozen ones and grabbed their bright orange tube by one of the black, plastic handles. "Shall we?"

"We shall," she replied.

He led them back towards the stairway carved out of snow on the side of the sledding hill. Erin's hand tightened around his and he wanted to believe it wasn't just because she needed him for stability.

Chapter Twenty-Six

Wrong Turn

Erin

"Oh! Pull over!" she blurted.

Jude followed her gaze out the window. "The flea market? I thought you wanted coffee."

That was true, she did want a cup of coffee. They'd been on the sledding slope for hours and her face needed to defrost. She was also feeling the lack of sleep from the night before—not that she'd complain. But she hadn't seen a flea market so enticing in years. Mostly because she never went out or did anything anymore, other than work.

"Please? I haven't been to one in ages!" she begged.

Brightly colored textiles hung from white topped canopies, floating lightly in the breeze, and ornaments spun and sparkled in the sun. It wasn't a huge market, but impressive all the same, with over a dozen little booths packed tightly in a small parking lot. People milled around with smiles and steaming paper cups. Erin looked up at Jude hoping she managed something akin to puppy dog eyes.

He shook his head, shifting his gaze back to the road. "How can I say 'no' to that?" He pulled into the middle turn lane and waited for the stream of cars to pass. "Tell me if you see a parking spot."

"What about there?" she asked, pointing to an SUV inching out from a gravel lot. "You think they're leaving?"

"Maybe." He coasted forward and cranked the steering wheel all the way to the left. When traffic broke, he flipped them around, pulling in where the SUV had been.

Wearing a stupid, toothy grin, Erin stared out the windshield at all the booths. It was bigger than she'd thought, stretching back from the street in a long, narrow lot that served several small shops.

It had been a really nice day. Jude seemed different: funny, energetic, and sweet. When he smiled at her, his whole face lit up. She found the expression so addictive that she kept trying new ways to make him do it: a task, she discovered, that wasn't all that difficult.

Easygoing. Playful. Thoughtful. Being with him made her feel like she didn't have to guard herself. She couldn't stop smiling. And every time he leaned in and kissed her for no reason, her stomach filled with butterflies.

Jude found a spot and cut the engine. Erin slid back to her side of the bench, snagging her purse and hopped out. Tucking her arms in tightly to her body, she danced in the snow-mixed gravel next to the truck to keep warm as he locked it up.

"You going to be okay?" he asked.

"Yeah. Why?"

"You're not gonna turn into a popsicle on me, are you?"

She laughed and shook her head and when she met him around the hood, he wrapped an arm around her shoulders.

"I'm good now," she beamed. He gave her a squeeze and they moved into the throng of stalls and people.

"How much for this?" Erin asked the young girl standing behind the table. She envied the huge, faux-fur lined parka the girl wore—the unofficial uniform for vendors. *Smart move*, Erin thought, shivering.

She held up a twisted gold hair accessory for the girl to see.

"Twenty-five."

Erin looked down at it, then at the array of other hair ornaments on display. Mari would love the bigger one, but... "How about this one?" She held up a smaller one with a charm hanging off the bottom.

"Twenty," the girl replied.

"Hey." Jude's voice came from behind her, and as she turned, he held out a steaming paper cup.

"Ooh, Is that what I think it is?" she hoped aloud, eying the cup.

"Coffee?"

"Oh my gosh, you're amazing!" She lifted up to her toes and planted an unabashed kiss on his lips.

"Anytime." The word rumbled straight down her spine like a comforting caress. And in that moment, with that smile and those crinkled fixed on her, she forgot where she was and what she was doing. "You gonna take it?" he chuckled.

"Oh. Right. Thank you." She accepted the coffee, wrapping her hands around the hot cup. The heat permitting through the paper was a godsend to her frozen fingers. Holding it up, she let the steam defrost her face. "Ahh."

"Something else."

She looked up. "Huh?"

The tilt of his head, the quirk of his lip, and those soft eyes on her, gave way to butterflies that lifted out of her stomach and climbed into her chest. And he wasn't even kissing her. *Is this what being with someone is supposed to feel like?*

He looked down to the item in her hand. "That's pretty."

"I thought so, too. Mari would love this."

"You're not getting one for yourself?" He sounded surprised.

"No. This isn't really my thing," she explained. "I don't do the accessory, gussy-up stuff." She caught him staring again, his face thoughtful. "What?"

"Yeah, you don't really need anything."

She forgot how to breath. *He's got to stop doing that.* When biology kicked in, she inhaled sharply, turning to the girl behind the table, and blurted, "I'll take this one."

The coffee helped keep the chill off as they wandered around the booths. Erin stopped to pick up little things here and there, and shoved it all into her purse until it wouldn't close. Jude held her hand as they walked around, waiting patiently by her side as she browsed, smiling each time she insisted it was the last stop. He knew some of the vendors so she pretended to browse a little longer while they talked, sneaking peeks at him when he wasn't looking.

"Did you have any questions about the sizing?"

Erin looked up from the hand tooled leather belts and cuffs and realized the vendor was talking to her. "Oh, no. This is all beautiful work, though."

"Thank you," he smiled back brightly.

Behind them, someone called out and the vendor looked past them. His forehead wrinkled, he groaned, then he hollered back in another language. Erin glanced over her shoulder to see who he was talking to. Based on the tone, she'd put money on his wife, or maybe a business partner.

"Jude, my friend," the vendor implored, rubbing a hand over his bristly, close cropped hair. "Would you mind standing here at the table a moment? I need to see what she wants."

"Yeah. Go."

The man gave little bow of gratitude, then wove through the crowd to the other side of the aisle, where a woman was holding a large metal lawn ornament.

Jude laughed. "Another one? Poor Anton."

"Another one?" Erin asked.

"His wife is a bit of a...collector."

"I see." Erin eyed the couple. Anton didn't look pleased.

"You can go on ahead, if you want," Jude offered. "I'll catch up."

"It's okay. I can man the table with you." She flashed him a smile, then asked, "Is Anton an old friend?"

"I guess. Met him my first winter here."

"Yeah?"

Erin looked over to where Anton and his wife argued: softly spoken words paired with sharp hand gestures. The lawn ornament sat in the snow between them. *It is a nice piece*, Erin mused.

Anton threw his arms up, turned, then stomped back towards them, his brow scrunched in, making his whole head crease like one of those really wrinkly dog breeds.

"Everything okay?" Jude asked at his approach.

"She can give it fancy names, but the woman is a hoarder!" Anton shook his head. "Twenty-two years married and she still does this. She will be the end of me!" He moved past

Jude and back into his stall. "You are lucky you got out, my friend."

Erin had been watching Anton, but now her gaze flew up to Jude.

He glanced over at her, jaw tightening, then back to Anton. "Well, she has to put up with you, so I guess you're even."

Anton whistled through his teeth and flicked a hand out over his wares. "We can't all be so lucky," he grumbled back. "Go. I don't need you anymore."

"You're welcome," Jude laughed, stepping back.

When he turned, he caught Erin's eye and the humor from his expression dropped. Shoving hands in his pant pockets, he looked away, and started walking down the aisle toward the back of the market.

Erin frowned. He'd been happily holding her hand all day. Now he wasn't even waiting for her? "Bye Anton. Nice to meet you. And good luck," she rushed with a little grimace. Ducking around other shoppers, she tried to catch up with Jude. "Hey! Wait up!" she called as he continued to stroll several paces ahead.

He slowed but didn't stop, and as she neared, she noticed everything about him seemed stiff. His back, the angle of his arms, his neck. Even his step looked forced.

The day had been good—very good—so she swallowed her doubts and wove her arm in the crook of his, matching his stride.

"Trying to shake me?" she joked even as her stomach flip-flopped unpleasantly. When he didn't respond, her nervousness sent her into ramble mode. "I would never buy a collection of lawn ornaments, just so you know. Not that it would matter...And I don't have a lawn anyway, I have a tiny apartment...but if I did—"

"Anything else you want to see?"

Erin bit her tongue and pushed down the pang that threatened to make her eyes water. Did she do something wrong? Had she misinterpreted his intentions? Was she just lolloping around like an idiot, thinking this was more than just a tryst?

She tipped her coffee up and finished off the last of it, then reclaimed her arm, and walked the empty cup to the nearest trash can. She didn't look back to see if he'd stopped to wait for her. Mostly because she figured he wouldn't. When she turned, she smacked right into a solid wall of flannel covered muscle.

Jude caught her as she staggered back. "I'm sorry. I didn't mean to act like a dick."

His words surprised her as much as his proximity. "It's fine. We can go if you're ready. I've probably spent too much, anyway."

"No. Go look at your little shops. You were having fun."

"Jude, I—"

He cupped his palms around her neck, then slid them up her jaw, bringing her mouth to his. This time his lips moved with reverence and the simple sincerity of an apology.

Erin pulled away this time. "Forgiven," she murmured.

"Good. You gonna finish out the market?"

She shook her head. "I shouldn't spend any more money."

"Then just look around."

Her first instinct was to point out that he clearly didn't understand women. Instead, she asked, "You don't mind?"

"As long as I get to watch when you bend over to look at all those little trinkets."

Her jaw dropped and she smacked his arm.

Jude laughed. "What? You have a nice ass."

"Hey man!" The unfamiliar voice startled them.

Jude pulled his hands away from her face as they turned to the speaker, a middle aged man with graying hair and a bright, crooked smile. He wore the mountain region handyman uniform of flannel and roughed-up khakis with boots.

"Hey, Jimmy," Jude greeted.

"Hey yourself! What the hell are you doing here?"

Jude ducked his face and Erin thought he looked like a kid whose hand had just been caught in the cookie jar. "Same as everyone else. What about you?"

"The wife wanted some of that bread," Jimmy grumbled. He jerked his head back and Erin noticed the vendor behind him with baked goods laid out on her table. "The stuff is like crack," he confided. She smiled back politely. "We haven't met. James Rienhart, " he stuck out a stained, calloused hand. "But everyone calls me Jimmy. I taught Jude everything he knows."

"That's a big claim," she retorted, accepting the handshake. "It's nice to meet you. I'm Erin."

He gripped her palm and gave it a good shake. "Erin," he beamed, looking at her with bright eyes like his prayers had finally been answered. When Jude cleared his throat, Jimmy winked, then let her hand go. Turning his attention to the soured expression on his friend's face, he went on, "Sorry I didn't call you back, man. Been pretty busy. But I can talk now if you've got a minute."

"Yeah. Sure." Jude looked to Erin. "You go on, I'll be right behind you."

He seemed annoyed so she didn't push it. "O-okay. Take your time."

She turned to head up the aisle just as Jude caught her by the arm and spun her back in close. Then, he planted a kiss right on her mouth in front of his friend. A surprised "oh" erupted from her chest and the vibrations from his laugh made her lips tingle.

"Thanks. You can go now." Smiling gray eyes stared down at her and for a second, she didn't have a single care.

Then Jimmy chuckled and reality swamped back in.

Erin stepped back. "Nice meeting you, Jimmy." Her voice cracked.

"Likewise."

Spinning to the direction she'd been going, she walked away, ever so grateful that they couldn't see the slap-happy grin on her face.

Erin passed a table which sat in a cloud of citrus and lavender, it's colorful array of soaps displayed in all shapes and sizes. She paused briefly, bringing one to her nose, deciding instantaneously that it was too strong. Smiling at the vendor, she moved on.

She skipped the glass-blown bong booth. Though beautifully made, she didn't have use for one other than as an overpriced flower vase. She walked past the next as well; she had a cabin full of snacks so she didn't need any seasoned nuts and dried fruit, although they did look good. And she wasn't much of a jewelry person, but something made her step falter at the next table. Her head swung around in a double-take.

"It's okay," the vendor called, coming up to the other side of the table, "I have that effect on people."

Erin stared at the vendor, noticing him for the first time. He reminded her of an aged surfer, with long hair and taut, tanned, skin. With mouth agape, she paused, not sure how to respond.

"Kidding!" He laughed.

"Oh." Erin fidgeted with her bag. "Sorry, I just saw this." Stepping up to the table, she extracted a half sheet flyer from the stand.

"That is the power-stone guide sheet," he explained, nodding.

"The what?"

She scanned down the column of images—all different colored natural looking stones that could have been cut from the mountain itself. And all she could think was, *this would be perfect for Jude.* She couldn't explain why. It was one of those phenomena where in finding the perfect gift, everything in the universe just came together.

"Do you have anything for men that has this in it?" she asked, pointing to the grey and white marbled stone on the guide sheet.

The vendor beamed. "Do I?"

Erin reigned in her glee as she watched her new surfer friend box up the bracelet she'd picked. She'd asked that he include the informational card about the product and the significance of the stones.

He kept pausing his task to look up at her and smile. "Who's this for?" he asked, shaking his long, loose hair behind his shoulders.

She dropped her eyes, tracing a line along the edge of his table with her finger, and fighting a shy grin. "A friend."

Giddiness built up inside her like microwave popcorn puffed up a bag, threatening to burst out. She'd found something he never would have purchased for himself which made it an awesome gift. The roughness of the filler beads made her think of the mountains and the jagged rocks she'd seen on the drive up. The colors reminded her of his tattoos mixed with snow. The combination of the power stones, filler beads and metal spacers all together, gave off an edgy Earthy vibe that seemed to compliment Jude's personality. And it didn't take a lot of imagination for Erin to picture how sexy the bracelet would look on his wrist.

"Do these power stones really do anything?" she wondered aloud, her eyes wandering back to the guide sheet.

"Depends."

"On what?"

"The intention of the giver," he replied. When she looked up, he winked. "Anything else?" he asked, handing Erin the package.

The small, white box was embellished with a shiny, silver stretchy bow. Jude would probably think it was too much, but she didn't care. Gifts were supposed to come in fancy packages.

"Nope. I'm all out of money," she replied, only half joking. He gave her a pity laugh and rattled off the total.

She rummaged around in her purse for her wallet, setting a few previous purchases on the table. "Do you have a pen?"

"You bet." He produced a sharpie like a magic trick.

"Perfect! Thanks!"

Trading him, she hunched down over the little white box, then straightened and handed it back. He passed her a stylus and her card, then flipped a tablet around to collect her signature. Signing a sloppy version of her name, she tucked her card into her wallet, and finagled her other items back into her purse. That was when she felt a large, familiar, male presence slide in next to her.

Jude stood with hands in his pockets, his lip curved and his eyebrows lifted. She snatched the small box from the table in front of her, covering the hand written label with her palm, and shoved it into the top of her bag.

"Thought you said you were done spending money," he teased.

"I can change my mind."

"Guess I should know better by now." Humor lit his tone.

"Actually, I am done. For real this time," she insisted. He eyed her. "Really. Unless there's anything else you wanted to see."

"I'm good." He nodded a greeting to the man behind the table. "Hey."

"How's it going?" the surfer replied with a big smile, eyes shifting briefly to Erin. She felt suddenly shy again.

"Not bad. You?"

"Can't complain. Business is good."

"She buy you out?" Jude teased. Erin scoffed.

"There's a lot of foot traffic today," the vendor observed, eyes skimming the shoppers milling around with arms full of handmade goods.

Tipping his head down at the table, Jude noted, "Yeah. Women love this stuff." He crossed his arms and shook his head like he just didn't get it.

"Men too," Erin's new buddy piped in.

Jude raised a brow. "Men, huh? Maybe boys and hippies."

Erin felt her face drop and she was pretty sure everyone caught it.

"No offense meant," Jude uttered across the table.

"None taken. It's not for everyone."

The friendly seller studied her, glanced at Jude, then looked back to her with a questioning brow lift. Erin bit the inside of her lower lip, trying not to frown.

With a hasty breath, she shot him a strained smile. "Thanks again."

"If you uh, change your mind, I accept returns," he offered, his voice meant only for her.

"It's fine, but thank you." Dropping eyes to her feet, she turned away from Jude and the stall, and started back to the parking lot at the other end of the market.

That last stop was starting to feel less like a happy accident and more like a wake-up call. What was she thinking? She didn't know anything about Jude, not really. Disappointment hit her harder than it should have, seeding her doubts. She was so out of her league. Only minutes ago he'd left her in the dust with a cold shoulder and no explanation. So what if he kissed her in front of his friend?

And what was a measly little bracelet to a man like Jude, anyway? What was she, for that matter? He probably treated all the women this sweetly, knowing full well he'd be off the hook when they left. How stupid would she have looked, grinning like an idiot, as he pulled off that stupid, silver bow? And why had she let herself get so wrapped up in this?

Finally, she'd let go of her inhibitions. Finally she'd stopped second guessing everything. Only to be shot down! She felt like a simple, silly girl with a school age crush. Except, even in school, she knew better than to reach so high. Men like Jude were off-limits.

Erin shook her head. *Casual sex.* Adults did that all the time. Why couldn't she manage to keep it superficial, too? She shouldn't have slept with him. *Stupid.* She felt small.

She wished she could take it all back, rewind and make different choices. Her only solace was that she hadn't given him the box yet. He never had to know just how deep her feelings ran.

"Erin!" Jude called, coming up from behind her. "What's the sudden rush?" His long strides matched her pace.

"No rush, just figured we're done, so we should go." She wove around shoppers, muttering polite "excuse me's."

"Are you mad? Because of what I said?"

She didn't answer.

"Come on, he didn't care," Jude argued. "He probably hears that every day."

"It's fine."

"Fine?" he parroted.

"Don't worry about it. It's not you, it's just me." She couldn't believe she'd actually said that. She picked up her pace.

"Wow. You really are angry," Jude laughed, but there was tension in the sound.

"No...Fine, yes. But I'm not angry with you."

"Then who are you angry at?"

Again, she didn't answer.

"Hey." He step a pace ahead of her. "Hey, Erin. Look at me."

She didn't look up, nor stop, just stared at his boots and pressed forward, forcing him to walk backwards.

He let out a frustrated sounding growl. "Look, it was a joke. I don't have a problem with men wearing jewelry. They can wear whatever the hell they want. It's none of my business."

"I can't believe I did it again," Erin muttered under her breath. What was it with her and men she couldn't have?

"What?"

"Nothing. Let's just go back to the cabins."

"Now, wait a second. A few minutes ago you were fine, all smiling to yourself and browsing stalls like you were in seventh heaven. Not a care in the world."

"Well, now I'm done," she bit out, her eyes roving over the snowy gravel at the edge of the parking lot.

"What the hell happened?"

His strides shortened. Erin slowed to avoid running into him, feeling his eyes bearing down on the top of her head. She couldn't answer because she didn't know what to say— certainly not the truth. Her pride couldn't take that kind of hit.

"What happened back at that booth?" he asked again.

"It doesn't matter," she said, disheartened and remembering something from earlier.

He'd told her that renters got the wrong idea about him. He'd never actually clarified what that idea was. The familiar pang of disappointment and longing jarred her. She was not doing this again. She'd barely gotten out of the last nowhere relationship.

"Erin, come on," he pushed. His boots stopped in front of her.

She halted and with a sigh, and lifted her head. "I just realized I was being thoughtless," she told him. "Here I am shopping for useless trinkets, taking up your whole day and you probably have tons of things to do."

"What?"

"Can you take me back to the rental?"

"You want to go back to your cabin?"

"Yes." Her voice came out thick. It was a wonder it came out at all with how tight her throat felt.

His eyes searched hers. Could he see? Could he tell that she was falling apart inside? Would he regret what they'd done?

She watched in defeat as his face iced over into the scowl she'd seen before, on that first day. Looking past the wall of untouchable masculinity that stood in front of her, she saw his truck up ahead. Staggering to the side, she moved around him, not stopping until she stood by the locked passenger door.

Jude

He didn't move at first, just stared at the spot she'd vacated, trying to decide if he was confused or pissed. Red flags shot up everywhere.

What the hell? They'd been having a nice day. Now, all the sudden, she wanted to go back to her place? Was there some kind of ulterior motive here? The thought angered him. Had he done it again—fallen into a honey trap?

That first winter he'd slated casual sex as the perfect diversion. Right up until he realized that his problems had just followed him—the city mentality. What do *I* need and how can *I* get it. It made sense. Most renters traveled up from the city. But Jude had mistakenly thought Erin wasn't like that. She didn't look like most city women. She didn't wear the mask of makeup and strategically styled hair—part of what drew him to her. She didn't come across as self-serving either. Not entitled or stupidly rich...she didn't even have a goddamn decent coat. So why get so indignant over a stupid comment, especially after he apologized? What had he missed?

Jude ran a hand though his hair, growling in defeat, and stalked over to his truck. He didn't want to take her back to her cabin. He still had a perfectly good day left before she went home.

She stood, eyes fixed to the hood of his truck as he approached. The sun was starting to go down behind her, putting her in silhouette. Next to his rusted out old hunk of metal, mountains stretching into an orange sky, she looked like the heroin in one of those goddamn romance novels. And in that moment, he got the allure of those things, or at least, the captivating images they slapped on the covers.

Fuck.

He brushed by to get her door. She didn't move or turn toward him so he left it open and rounded the back of the truck. He watched her from the corner of his eye as he unlocked his own side and got in. Finally, she slid onto the bench, purse in her lap. Jude settled in at the steering wheel as she reached to swing her door shut. Grunting, she gave it a yank but the force sent the contents of her purse all over the bench and down into the footwell.

"Ugh!" she groaned, rushing to shove it all back in.

Something was up. Jude watched her for a moment, at a total loss. She seemed bristly and closed off. Hugging her purse to her belly, body tucked to the passenger door, she gave him her back as her eyes pointed out the side window. *Definitely missed something*, but hell if he knew what it was. He turned a disappointed frown to the windshield and started the truck.

The cab felt painfully quiet as he headed back to *her* cabin, even with the metal hum of the old engine. It killed him. He couldn't help take it personally—she'd been fine until he'd said something.

"What the hell, Erin?"

She didn't respond or even turn to acknowledge him which pissed him off more. He'd actually been having fun, a novel thing for him. He actually enjoyed trailing along behind her at the market, catching those cute little smiles and curious noises she made as she'd browsed. And it felt downright awesome, the times he'd caught her staring at him when she'd thought he wasn't paying attention.

Then suddenly, she turns a one-eighty, has a hissy fit, and refuses to share why? He had every right to be pissed! *Why do women always assume men can read their fucking minds?*

He shot a few glances in her direction over the course of the drive but she sat there like a statue, tense and completely ignoring him. He tried not to brood. He tried not to think anything at all, even as he pulled into his driveway and cut the engine.

The cab grew deathly silent. She didn't move right away. A stupid, small amount of hope flickered in his chest. Had she gotten over her little tantrum? Was she going to let him in on the big secret? Apologize maybe?

"Thanks for the ride." Her voice was quiet and she said it to her window. She started fumbling for the handle—not what he'd expected.

Disappointment made him do something really stupid. "Look Erin, I don't know what your deal is right now, but once you get over whatever fit you're in, my door's open."

He didn't think he could regret words spoken as much as he did when she paused, then spun to face him. Her glassy eyes pinned him with something so hopeless it made his chest twist.

Anger clouded over her expression. "Don't wait up," she bit out.

The passenger door squeaked open and she was out of the cab. And, in true Erin style, her purse dumped out again all over the driveway.

"Are you kidding me?" she growled thickly, stooping to the ground.

Jude would've laughed if the mood had been different. He should've gotten out to help her. He did neither. Instead, he stared at the steering wheel until he heard the distant slam of the cabin door across the street.

"Fuck."

What the hell was wrong with him? He ran his hands over his face, then grasped the wheel, fingers flexing around the worn grip.

Why had he acted like that? Why couldn't he have just asked her to come in? She probably would have dropped her snit if he'd just made her a fucking fire. Jimmy'd razzed him about her and Jude hadn't even cared. He liked her.

"Forget it. I don't need this." His voice fell flat in the empty cab, his tone unconvincing.

It was better this way. He didn't need the city drama ruining his quiet hideaway. He acted like an idiot, like keeping her was ever really an option.

Flinging the door open, he exited his truck, locked it, then stormed up the porch steps two at a time. He didn't slam his front door, but he wanted to.

Chapter Twenty-Seven

Concessions

Erin

The clock read *12:37*. She stared at the wood paneled ceiling. In the dark, the grooves between the boards appeared to grow larger like it was pressing down on her, like the crushing weight she felt in her chest.

Inside her rib cage, her heart lay splintered and raw. She couldn't even say it was about him or what he'd said. The rejection hurt, but more, she'd finally done what she'd wanted without any filters even when it pushed her outside of her comfort zone. For a fleeting moment, she'd felt understood. Valued. Whole.

But she'd miscalculated. How could she have thought a man like Jude would want a bracelet? And, if she'd been so far off the mark with that, there were bound to be other things: his feelings, his intentions...his integrity. Had she read too much into his actions? Maybe it was just a power play or a pissing contest. Or just sex—which seemed all anyone wanted out of her lately. Why had she assumed it would be different with him? She felt like a moron.

Notwithstanding, the events of the day brought to light how little she'd been living lately. She'd put herself in her own little box. Staring up at the looming ceiling, she remembered why. She didn't like feeling silly and small. She wasn't like Mari, who could brush it off and carry on.

So where did that leave her?

Then her mind went there. She tried not to let it, but she felt so low, so exhausted, that it sifted in under her defenses. *Was Victor really that bad?* Maybe she was the problem.

He'd cared enough to trek all the way up the mountain. Jude had called it a power play, but what did he know? He lived in a rustic cabin, looking like a mountain fantasy, enjoying what women willing gave to him—herself included.

Erin fingered the bandage on her collarbone, and her mind went to that horrible night. Why would Victor do that? She'd been trying to understand it. And why had Jude reacted the way he did? Her chest throbbed and her head felt muddy. This trip was meant to give her a break, offer some perspective, but she just felt more overwhelmed and confused.

The closure she'd hoped to get felt as far from her grasp as it had ever been. Add to that her feelings for Jude. She couldn't go back and she couldn't move forward. She felt stuck—utterly desolate, small and achingly lonely in the dark and quiet cabin.

The unbearable mess in her mind had her up in bed and throwing her legs over the side. Her feet brushed the cool carpet, and her eyes stared out the window, seeing only darkness and darker shadows. *Mari would never be so self-pitying.* But then, Mari was everything that Erin was not.

She reached over to the nightstand and disconnected her phone from the charger. The display blared bright in stark contrast to the night, sending a jab of pain through her eyes and straight to her head. She squinted at the single bar at the top corner of her screen. And like a moron, she tried the call even though she knew there was no service.

The call didn't connect. "Damnit."

Erin shut the cabin door behind her, bundled up in everything she could find. The lit porch aided her way down the steps to the street. By the time the light from the cabin faded, her eyes had adjusted enough to find the boulder where she'd gotten cell signal a few days before.

"Hello?" Mari croaked on the other end of the phone.

"Mari? Sorry, were you sleeping? I figured, since it was Friday..."

"Erin? It's like...after midnight. Are you okay? What's wrong?" Her voice shifted from groggy to alert.

"I can't sleep."

"Why?"

"I'm sorry, I didn't mean to wake you up." Erin kept her voice low, eyes darting around for signs of life or movement. "I figured you'd be out and—"

"Erin. *Digame.* What's wrong?"

She envisioned her friend sitting straight up in bed, forcing that sheer, Latina willpower through the phone lines. Erin sighed and her gaze stretched out to the feathery outlines of trees. She felt a lot like the shadows they made: easily swayed, barely seen, and surrounded by darkness.

"I'm sad," she whispered around a tight throat.

"What happened?"

"Nothing...It doesn't matter," Erin started, anguished. "I wish I was you. You've got those beautiful, bouncy, Shakira curls and you're fit, and coordinated, and energetic, and confident, and outgoing, and funny...and sexy."

"Whoa, slow down."

"I wish I were all those things. I'd take just some of those things...any of those things." She sniffled and squeezed her eyes shut.

"*Chica.*"

Erin appreciated that Mari didn't argue back or tell her she was wrong. True friends didn't lie and she could count on that. Still, she held back a sob, feeling utterly pathetic.

"It's funny that you say that." Mari paused. "Not funny like 'I'm laughing' funny." She hesitated again.

Erin waited. Could she take the truth on top of everything else? Or did she just want someone to reassure her that she was going to be okay? The night chill began to permeate through her thick layers as Erin waited for her best friend to speak.

"Do you know," Mari started again, "I kind of wish I was you."

Erin blinked at the shadows as a breeze picked up, lifting the dark branches like a wave. The cold wind hurt her ears and stung her nose. "What? Why?" She felt certain she'd heard wrong.

"You mean aside from your good job and the fact that you're classy? You're just...you. There's no bullshit. You're smart, you're funny, adorable, and you don't even have to try."

"Are you kidding? I try. I try way too hard. That's the problem. The harder I try, the worse it gets."

"But you don't have to try so hard," Mari insisted. "That's what I'm saying. Me? It's so much work to keep up with the hair. The fitness. I know you think I just get out of bed like this, but I don't. And it's exhausting."

Mari's words bounced around in Erin's head. "I appreciate that you say that. You always make it look so easy."

"Seriously, girl. You're a catch. Anyone with half a brain can see that."

"I'm a mess," Erin sniffed. "Maybe you need to get your eyes checked."

"And humble," Mari added with a chuckle. "You're doing it now, and you don't even realize it, do you? People respond to all that honesty stuff. I envy that."

"What people? No one responds to me like that. No one hits on me at the bars or chats me up at the gym."

"That's 'cause you don't go to the gym," she muttered back. "But *mira*, they're only responding to my ass. And my sass. They think it's funny and cute, but it's not the real me. It's me trying not to be rejected."

Erin scoffed. "No one would reject you."

"Jude did," Mari pointed out. Erin didn't respond, thinking Mari'd been lucky. "The thing is, I sass and I joke, but sometimes I have to *pretend* I'm confident. And none of that stuff makes the world a better place."

"That's not true. Mari, you—"

"What you give...it's all of you. You care and you give that without needing anything back. You have no idea how it feels to get all that. That, that is a gift. The world needs more people like you."

Erin's eyes watered. She'd never thought about it that way. "Well, *you* can have that, without restraint," she promised, suppressing a wave of chills. "But as for everyone else? I can't do it anymore."

The line was quiet a moment.

"*Chica*, tell me what happened. I thought things were going good."

Erin hesitated. She'd planned to tell her friend when she got home. And she'd decided while on her frozen trek to the bolder, to return to the city as soon as possible. As in, if she couldn't sleep, she'd just clean the cabin and leave at first light.

"I slept with Jude."

"What! When? Why didn't you tell me?"

"It just happened this morning," Erin argued, cupping her hand around the phone to keep her voice from traveling. Her eyes shifted down the street even though she knew his cabin was dark. "And we've been busy."

"No, I mean, we've been on the phone for like..." Mari paused, "...five minutes!"

"Oh, I'm sorry. Did you want me to start the conversation with that?"

"YES!"

"Okay, well, now you know," Erin grumbled. She was not nearly as happy about it as Mari seemed to be.

"So?" Mari sang. "How was it?"

"I'm standing outside, in the cold, in the middle of the night to call you," Erin pointed out.

"Oh. I'm sure it wasn't you, honey," Mari consoled. "Let me tell you, just because they're hunky and muscular doesn't mean anything when it comes to sex."

"I wish that were true...because it was *so* good," Erin whined, her voice regretful.

"Then, I'm confused. What's the problem?"

"The problem is, I like the sex," she exclaimed. "And the coffee. And the stupid smile he gives he when I get embarrassed! What was I thinking? I came here to uncomplicated things! But now I'm just more confused."

"I think you're overthinking it."

"I feel used, Mari. He used me. I let it happen, again."

"But, you liked the sex too, right?"

Too much. She liked it too much. And everything else for that matter. And that was why she had to get away.

Silence hung between them. Erin wedged the phone between her neck and shoulder, rubbing her hands together, then huffing warm air on her fingers. They felt numb and clumsy. Her whole body did. "It doesn't really matter. It's done now, whatever *it* was,"

"But why? You're allowed to have fun. And feel good. Having sex doesn't make you a hussy."

"It's not..." Erin scrunched her face. "I thought that maybe it was more than just a physical thing. I kind of wanted it to be...more. Ugh!"

"Wait, wait, wait. Back up. Didn't he like, bust up a door to save you?"

"Technically."

"And then take you on a date?"

She frowned. "I may have read too much into that."

"Too much?"

Erin couldn't tell her that Jude may have been flaunting his feathers in a power play. That would require explaining why he had to do that in the first place. "I'm just going to come home tomorrow."

"I love you *chica*. I do. And I don't want you to be sad. But I really think you should stick it out and see what happens."

"Mari, what am I going to do here?" she argued, raising her voice. Lucky for her, the snow dampened the sound.

"Seriously? I don't blame you for not making it back up, but I don't ski, I don't—"

"I just hate to see you leave on a down note. Stick it out. Maybe he'll surprise you."

"Who? Jude? I don't really care what he does," she lied.

"Shauna thinks pretty highly of him, you know."

"Good for her." *Another snow bunny for Jude to add to his repertoire.*

Erin looked back in the direction of the rental thinking that she should probably wrap it up. The chill had buried bone deep, her teeth knocking harshly together, and she didn't want get sick on top of everything else. She tried to focus back on Mari, who'd carried on in her ear.

"...maybe it won't come to anything, but you still have a beautiful cabin, and snow, and wine! And you're going to have the same feelings no matter where you sleep."

"But I won't have to be reminded every time I look at his cabin." Mari made some good points, but wine and snow couldn't build perfect fires or make her forget how to breath.

"You don't have to come home," her friend insisted.

"Yes, I do."

"You don't."

"I do."

"It sounds a lot like running away," Mari stated point blank.

Erin squeezed her eyes shut. "It's late and I'm freezing," she deflected. "I should get back to the cabin. If I'm lucky, I can be out of the rental by breakfast time."

"Whatever you say."

"I'll see you soon."

"Don't be sad, *chica*. He's just a dumb mountain man."

"Yeah..." Erin replied, knowing full well it wasn't true.
"Hasta pronto."

"Night, Mari."

Erin ended the call and hustled back to the cabin. She couldn't feel her feet or her nose. Letting herself in, she deposited her shoes by the door but kept her layers as she headed first to the bathroom to blow her nose, then the bedroom.

Groaning to the empty cabin, she collapsed onto the bed. She didn't bother plugging in her phone. She just tugged the heavy duvet up to her chin and lay staring at the ceiling. Even under all those layers and downy fluff, she shivered.

"I'm not adorable," she muttered to the grooves in between the planks, "I'm a mess. And he saw it all."

Shauna thinks pretty highly of him. The unwelcoming thought suddenly paralyzed her. Was Jude also sleeping with Shauna?...who else had he partnered up with? *We didn't use a...*

"Oh my God," Erin moaned. *Stupid, stupid, stupid!*

What had she been thinking! Nothing! And that was the problem. A new anxiety stirred under her skin. *Definitely leaving tomorrow*...she checked the clock on her phone. *Today,* she corrected. *Definitely leaving today.*

Jude

It was a cold morning, in a stinging kind of way. And a Saturday. Jude had woken up on the wrong side of bed and went about his routine with a scowl. Normally, he didn't work on Saturdays, but an urgent call came in. And he had nothing better to do.

Locking up the cabin and storming down to his driveway, he pulled a beanie from his coat pocket and yanked it over his head. That was when something shiny caught his eye and his scowl tipped down to a frown.

At the passenger side of his truck, he squatted over the small white box, nearly invisible against the snow. He never would have seen it without the ridiculous, silver bow. Bold, black letters spelled his name across the top.

He dropped his head to his chest. "Shit."

Snagging the trinket, he stood, and stomped around to the drivers side of the truck. Angling in, he slammed the door, and stared at the box. He didn't suppose she knew any other Judes. He ripped his gaze from the angled lettering, checking his rear view mirror. The rental sat dark and still, just like any old day.

She's probably still sleeping, he reasoned. But he had this sinking feeling, like the place was already empty.

His eyes drifted back to the box, and curiosity peaked.

"Can't do this right now."

He tossed the gift onto the passenger seat, and tried not to think too hard on it. Instead, he brought the engine to life, sending a smoggy plume of heat out into the icy air. With one last glance back at the dark cabin, he did what he had to do—he minded his own business and went to work.

"Window should be here by next Friday," Jude told his cell as he drove past all the new cars parked on his street—a new wave of renters. He nodded, remembering the forecast predicted lots of new snow.

Coming up to Erin's cabin he saw lights on. He chose to ignore the hiccup in his chest. He'd half expected her to take off.

"No problem, Pauline. I'll send you a bill when it's done." He pulled into his driveway, eyes shifting to the rear view mirror as he put the truck in park.

"Yeah, you too," he replied, ending the call, gaze still on the rental.

A funny feeling assaulted his chest but he chalked it up to convenience. Now he wouldn't have to mail her box back. He cut the engine and hopped out. After a brief moment of indecision, Jude leaned back in, grabbing the gift and leaving the array of plastic takeout bags on the passenger seat.

His feet took him across the street while his brain worked out what to say. As he passed the front window, he caught Erin scrubbing counters in the kitchen. He knocked. Then he waited.

And waited.

And waited.

What's taking her so long? He knocked again, more decisively this time.

"Who is it?" Erin called, her response immediate. And directly on the other side of the wood separating them.

"It's Jude."

He shifted back on the porch but the door didn't swing open like he'd expected it to. His stomach grumbled, and he shot a longing glance back to his truck. The urgent morning call had taken longer than planned. His head just wasn't in it. Now it was after one.

He turned his attention back to the cabin. "You gonna open the door?"

It swung in and the smell of bleach wafted out at him. Erin stood there in a skimpy tank that didn't hide much of anything. She had her hair braided in two parts on either side of her head and Jude itched to tug them.

"You have ventilation in there, right?" he asked, leaning in and taking a peek around the interior.

"What? Oh, yeah. I opened a window."

Her eyes wandered to the side and that bothered him. He watched her fidget, but lost track of his intent when she crossed her arms in front of her, pushing her breasts up, and giving him a shot of unobstructed cleavage. She had no idea.

A smile tugged at his mouth. He tried to get back on track. "You dropped this outside the truck yesterday." He held the trinket across the threshold to her.

Eyes wide, she snatched the box. "Thanks." It disappeared behind her back. She looked damn cute when she got all flushed and flustered. "Did...did you open it?"

"No." But he'd wanted to. She didn't offer the box back to him and Jude tried not to read into it. "You eat lunch yet?" he asked instead.

"No. What time—is it already..." she trailed off and looked over her shoulder to the clock. "Oh. I didn't realize it was so late."

"Are you hungry?"

She turned her head back to him. He thought she looked surprised and maybe a little terrified.

"Hungry?" she asked like it was a test. "I'm, uh...I'm actually just finishing, and then I need to pack."

"I think you have time for lunch. You get till end of Sunday."

"I know, but I'm leaving today."

Her news gave him pause. *Today?* A part of him suspected as much, but maybe he'd hoped she wouldn't. He looked around the cabin again and saw the bags staged on the dinning table.

Quirking his mouth to the side, he couldn't keep the question to himself. "Why?" Was she really that pissed at him?

"I just want to get back."

Her tone seemed indecisive. Jude crossed his arms. If he played this right, maybe he could sway her to stay. "In that case, how about I feed you so you don't have to mess up the kitchen?"

"It's okay. I'll just grab something on the road."

"Got some Chinese takeout in the truck. There's more than enough to share."

Erin stared up at him, her forehead wrinkled and her brow drawn in. "I appreciate the offer, but really, it's okay."

"Did I do something? Say something?" he asked, wishing like hell he knew what was going on in her head.

"No." She sighed, biting her lower lip. "No. You didn't do anything." A chill shook her body.

Jude realized that standing in the open door was letting all the cold air in. "Can I come in?"

She hesitated, before stepping aside. Jude moved in and straight to the couch, grabbing the throw which no longer smelled like alcohol. He walked back to her and draped it over her shoulders. Her small hands came out to grab the ends from him and a moment of deja vu washed over him. Heart pounding, adrenaline spiking, Jude was overwhelmed with the sudden instinct to protect. But there was no guy, no knife and no blood. Just the two of them and a cabin that smelled like bleach.

Forcing himself a step back, he waited for the adrenaline to pass. Erin stared up at him with those eyes—still greenish but with all kinds of other colors surging out from their centers, like those photos of nebulas he'd seen on wall calendars.

"Thanks," she uttered.

"You're welcome."

The urge to grab those braids and pull her in for a kiss grew harder to resist.

"Jude, listen, I..." She stopped and didn't go on.

"What?"

"Never mind. It-it doesn't matter."

Damnit. "Is it important to you?" he asked.

She shrugged.

"Then tell me."

At first he thought she'd be stubborn about it but then she inhaled sharply and a stream of words spilled out so fast he fought to keep track.

"The thing you said about the renters, I don't want to be just another one of them, the kind you have to be hands off with. And I'm sorry, but I think I just got a little too involved, maybe it was all the drama, and I am already dealing with some emotional struggles so I am more sensitive than usual and that's why I'm pulling back because it isn't fair to you and I'm trying really hard not to be like that so I think you should probably just go."

Jude stared at her, processing the pieces he'd caught. "What do you mean, 'like the renters?' What does that mean?'"

She exhaled sharply, her jaw tightening, and her eyes glassed over, suddenly a distinct and vibrant green. "I like you Jude," she uttered, then immediately tucked her lips in under her teeth.

He tried not to let his own, immense relief show. "Good. Ditto. So, what's the problem?"

"More than just in a casual sex...kind of...way," she forced out, her face flaming.

"That's a relief because sex with you is anything but casual," he replied very matter of factly, despite the drumline coursing up and down his chest.

She gave him a small smile.

"Can I feed you now?" he asked instead of kissing her. "If you want to leave when you're done eating, I won't stop you," he added for good measure, though she might make a liar out of him if she tried.

"Chinese food?" she mused. "What did you get?"

Jude smiled. "Mango chicken, Kung pow beef, Szechwan green beans and fried rice."

"Oh." Her eyes grew wide. "That's a lot of food."

It was. More than any one man could eat in a sitting.

"That actually sounds pretty good," she admitted.

"Good. My place in ten?"

She nodded absently.

He leaned in, and her breath hitched. "Is it okay if I kiss you now?"

She head moved up and down, this time with greater certainty. Before she could change her mind, Jude pressed his mouth into hers. His body followed, hands coming up, and fingers wrapping around those braids. It didn't take long before he felt his control start to slip away.

"Gotta get the food out of the truck," he murmured, pulling back.

"Okay," she said, a little breathless.

"Let's make it 5 minutes."

"5 minutes," she repeated, dazed.

He tugged at her braids. Her eyes cleared, focusing all their annoyance at him.

"Couldn't help it," he chuckled. "I'm going now. Five minutes. Don't forget." He walked out smiling. He'd been given a second chance. He wasn't going to screw it up.

Chapter Twenty-Eight

Kitchen Antics

Jude

He shot a smile across the breakfast bar, over the empty takeout boxes, to Erin's nearly empty plate. Etta had given up on hunting for fallen scraps. She'd wandered over to her niche and flopped down with a canine harumph, and probably fallen asleep.

Setting aside his hatred for the city, Jude shared some old stories from back in his suit and tie days. It made her laugh, so he didn't mind reminiscing, he just left out the reason he'd banned himself from ever going back.

"I can't believe you used to own a suit! An advertising consultant, huh?" she ruminated, catching a shred of beef with her chopsticks.

"More or less." With a sly smile, he added, "However, that isn't nearly as interesting as my stint as a cook."

She turned to face him full on, brow raised—the exact reaction he'd hoped for. He told her how he'd learned to cook by sitting up at the counter of an old diner near where he used to live.

"Your parents never wondered where you were?"

"Not really. They worked late. By the time they realized I'd been ditching the local library, I'd become the diner mascot. They practically offered me a job."

"Diner Mascot, huh? Was that an official position?" she teased.

Jude liked how she did that. It felt intimate. "I suppose it was more of an honorary title," he admitted, eyes on her smile.

She laughed again and honorarily designated herself a 'lousy cook.'

"It isn't that hard. All you have to do is follow the recipe."

"Yeah, well..." She grabbed the last morsel on her plate with her chopsticks and made it disappear.

"I guess you *do* like Chinese food," he razzed.

Erin squinted her eyes at him before lifting her glass and draining the rest of her wine, the last of the bottle from the other night. Jude grinned, following suit with his own beer.

"Are you making fun of me, Jude?"

"I wouldn't dare." He definitely was. "You should know, I like a girl with a good appetite. You don't know how pleased I was when you wrapped your mouth around that taco at the Mexican restaurant. Dainty eaters drive me nuts." She glared at him. "You want anything else?"

"Not after you just accused me of being a hog," she said hotly.

"I didn't say you were a hog."

"You implied. Are you laughing?"

"Honey," he chuckled, "you could eat an entire side of beef and you'd still be sexy as hell." She stared at him, her expression strange. Wonderment? Disbelief? "You don't believe me?"

"I couldn't eat that much," she muttered, picking up a napkin and wiping her mouth, even though there wasn't anything on it. Then she started stacking the empty cartons. He watched her, feeling the time slip away.

"You're really going to leave today?" he asked, not bothering to hide his disappointment.

She nodded, her attention on the empty food containers.

"There's nothing I can do to convince you to stay?" he pressed.

"I have to go home sometime."

"Why can't it be tomorrow?"

"I'll clean this up," she deflected, standing.

Jude watched her go into his kitchen. She seemed stiff. He got the feeling she didn't want to go, but he couldn't for the life of him figure out why she insisted on doing so.

Grabbing her empty glass and his empty bottle, he followed her. She stooped, dumping the cartons into the trash under the sink. When she rose, he moved in right behind her.

"I'll take that," she said, wrapping her fingers around the glass he held.

He let her have it, but he didn't back up. He liked how naturally she moved around his kitchen. "What if I told you I wanted you to stay?"

She ignored him, washing the glass more thoroughly than Jude ever would have, but then, he'd have used the dishwasher.

Stepping in closer, he slid his hands over her hips, locking his fingers together above her navel. "I want you to stay," he murmured at her ear. Her diligence to her task was commendable, but unnecessary. He reached his hand out to confiscate the soapy glass and carefully set it in the sink.

"Jude, I—"

"Please?"

He hadn't meant to beg. And despite his actions, it wasn't just about sex. But she smelled good and his hormones were out of control. And time kept ticking away. The fear of wasted moments ate at him. What was it with this woman?

"Jude..." she tried again.

"Do you want to stay?"

"I do, but I—"

"Then you should stay."

"Why?" she asked. "What good is one more day?"

He deflated a little. He had lots of reasons, but if she couldn't see the point, maybe he'd gotten ahead of himself. But she'd get it. He'd show her. "I want to see you cook." He pressed his lips into her neck.

"I'm a terrible cook."

"Prove it." He kissed her shoulder.

"You sure it has nothing to do with what you're doing right now?"

"Can't promise that," he admitted.

"You said you'd let me go after lunch."

His arms tightened around her waist. There was no doubt she felt the electricity between them, too.

"Jude?"

"I lied. I'm only human. Come on, Erin. Don't run away."

"I'm not running." Her voice took on a defensive edge.

He eased his hands off her belly and fit them in at the narrowing of her waist. "What are you doing then?" he asked.

"I'm protecting myself."

"From me?"

"From heartbreak." Her voice came so softly that at first, Jude thought he'd misheard her. But he could feel the tension in her body, the metaphorical wall she tried to create between them. He'd hadn't been on this end for a while.

"I don't want to break your heart," he told her truthfully.

"What do you want?"

"I want you in my bed, it's true." His gripped tightened as her soapy fingers tried to claw him off. "But I also want to taste your cooking."

Erin scoffed, digging nails into his skin. "Jude, let go."

"And I want to take you skiing so I can prove I'll catch you. I want to make you coffee in the mornings so I can watch you close your eyes and smile into your cup." She ceased her protests, and he wished like hell he could see her face. He hoped to God he wasn't making it worse. "It's more than just sex."

She may not understand the gravity of what he'd just admitted, but he hoped to get the chance to enlighten her, somehow. Or maybe he was just being foolish. But at this point, he couldn't take it back.

The silence that followed made his heart thump. He'd thrown it all out there. He'd taken the risk he promised himself he'd never do. And even though her body curved against his, her heat permeating through the layers of fabric between them, he felt encased in ice, frozen and alone on a mountaintop.

"I guess I can leave tomorrow," she conceded, sinking her body deeper into his. She turned her head to the side, and caught his eye as he funneled oxygen back into his system.

Definitely foolish. And the thing about it was, in that moment, he didn't even care. "Don't give me that look," he scolded playfully, nipping the tip of her ear.

She angled her head back, revealing her long, slender neck. "What look?"

All the uncertainty had taken its toll. His need to be with her, *in* her, reigned above all else. Dipping his chin, he kissed her jaw line, muscles flexing into a smile under his lips. He dove a hand down her stomach, dipping in under her waistband, eliciting that little sound of hers that made his blood heat—his favorite sound.

A hum resonated from her chest as she shifted, giving him more room to work his fingers deeper. He took a moment to unfasten the button and zipper, then resumed his exploration. He wanted to say something stupid like, "where have you been all my life," but managed something less incriminating.

"I was thinking about you this morning. It killed me, you didn't come over last night."

She leaned her head back, to rest on his shoulder. "I wasn't over my 'fit,' as you called it."

"Did I say that?" he breathed, his free hand wandering up under her top, to her soft, warm breast.

"You did." She gasped when his thumbs simultaneously grazed over her sensitive peaks.

"I shouldn't have said that."

"No," she moaned, when he did it again. "You shouldn't have."

"I want to make it up to you."

"Sex doesn't solve things," she rebuffed, but her words seemed oddly contradictory.

"Do you want me to stop?"

"I didn't say that," she breathed as he pressed a finger into the heat between her legs.

"Good."

Jude planted kisses down her neck and across her shoulder as he toyed with her nipple. Her back arched against him, forcing her butt into his groin. He pushed his lower hand in deeper and she shifted her stance with a breathy moan.

Correction. *That* was his favorite sound.

Her body clenched and he tightened his arms around her, holding her up as she squirmed against him, crowding over her small frame. His fingers drove deeper and with greater speed. He felt her quiver, wanting that friction for himself. She didn't need to tell him not to stop. He could feel how close she was.

The pressure built, her breathing grew jagged, and then, she exploded, crashing into his frame, rocking with each wave that took her. It was a beautiful thing, accompanied by her uncensored moans, gasps, and single-syllable exclamations. In all his years, all his experiences, this was the hottest thing he could recollect.

Erin relaxed into his arms, coming down from her build up, inhaling heavy and deep. He enjoyed how her breast strained against his palm with each inhale.

When she pivoted into him, he moved his hands to rest loosely at her waist, skimming her skin under the hem of her tank. She faced him with those heavy-lidded, sensuous green eyes that sucked him in.

He hardly noticed her arms slither up and loop around his neck. "You really want me to stay, huh?"

"More than you know," he replied, his voice hoarse.

She stretched on to her toes, leaning in until her mouth touched his. "Good," she whispered after a sweet, chaste kiss.

He smiled, then bit her bottom lip, and what came next felt canal and wild. Her mouth locked on his and he shifted forward, pinning her into the counter. Erin responded by sliding hands down his neck, chest, then his stomach, his core tightening at her touch.

She fisted her fingers in the fabric of his shirt and pulled up. He gripped the back of it and in seconds, the thing was gone. He'd grant her access to any part of him she wanted.

Erin's soft lips started trailing sweet, little kisses across his chest, then up his collarbone and into his neck as far as she could reach. His brain jumped between the eroticism and heat of her lips, and the sensation of her fingertips lightly traveling across tattoo and muscle. A fire spiked in his gut and shot across his skin like he'd never experienced.

"Top's cute, but it's gotta go," he rumbled in her hair. He lost her featherlight touches but the tank came off and landed on his kitchen floor. Her bra followed.

"Anything else?" she asked, a little breathless as she leaned in to kiss him some more.

Jude loved how she pressed her breasts into his chest to get her lips at his jaw again. He turned his head to catch her mouth while his hands pushed down at her jeans. She stooped with him, their mouths still engaged, as he shoved the rest of her clothes down her legs. She stepped out of pants and panties and kicked them off to lie forgotten with the rest of her stuff.

Naked, in my kitchen. The woman was driving him wild.

He cupped his hands on her butt, kneading fingers into soft flesh, then lifted and deposited her on the countertop next to the sink.

"Ah! Cold!" she yelped, but even as she spoke, her legs wound around his wasit and pulled him in.

This time it was his satisfied groan that rung out. He pressed himself into the space between her legs, letting the course material of his jeans rub against her.

Her arms snaked around his neck and pulled his face down to hers. "Jude." The vibrations from that single word nestled deep in his chest.

"Hm?"

"You're still wearing pants."

"I'm am. You wanna fix that?"

Erin found his waistband before he'd finished speaking. With small, adept fingers, she made quick work of the task, then pushed his jeans past his hips enough for him to spring free. Like a woman on a mission, she drew him close again, using her thighs to direct him into position.

That first casual graze of sexes had them both panting and Jude's pathetically weak grasp on his control finally snapped. Pressing a palm to her inner thigh, he spread her wide and in a single motion, surged between her legs, rooted deep into her core. She grunted. The warmth and wetness of her body swarmed over him, activating a primal instinct.

His mouth crushed into hers, driven and raw, their breathing harsh and heavy.

He grasped her ass and hauled her to the edge of the countertop, needing to bury deeper, needing her closer. She responded, tilting her hips down and Jude nearly lost it. If he didn't slow down, he'd be done for. Shifting back, and steadying his breath, he worked to eased himself into her, one achingly slow drive after the next. She groaned and took him with increasing enthusiasm.

"Jesus Erin," he gasped as she tightened around him.

"Fuck me, Jude," she begged, then bit his lower lip.

With no intention of making her ask twice, he pulled out, then thrust back in. A guttural sound echoed in the kitchen, but he couldn't discern its origin. He locked his mouth on her lips, gripping the edge of the counter for purchase. Increasing his speed, Jude pounded then pulled back, giving and taking, and feeling her body clamp around his.

Her mouth lost intention. He released her lips and watched her head tilt back, her eyes unfocused. The knowledge of what he could make her body do intoxicated him. He didn't ever want to stop.

Nestling a hand between them, his knuckle graze against her swollen center. Her breathing grew erratic, mixed with moans and gasps, mews and little whines.

She was almost there.

He held on, planting a palm to her ass as he tried to keep his rhythm. Erin's hands flew back to brace herself and her whole body seemed to tense all at once.

"Fuck, Erin," he gritted out, right there with her. Then it happened. She detonated, and so did he.

Jude drove in hard, burying deep inside her, and they pulsed together. He banded an arm around her back, clutching her tightly to his body, their hearts hammering like a single unit and their skin feverish and sticky.

She wound her arms around his neck and held herself there, catching her breath in short, hot heaves against his chest. Jude buried his face into her neck, closed his eyes, and savored the high.

Several minutes passed before either of them moved. He slid in and out of her like a caress and she nestled her face deeper into his chest, the heat and her softness arousing him all over again.

Then, she stiffened.

He stopped moving, afraid he'd hurt her. "What's wrong?"

"Shit."

Staring at the top of her head, he waited for her to elaborate but she didn't. "What? What is it?"

"I didn't mean to...I meant to ask. God. Now this is really awkward." She tipped her head farther down so he had no chance to see her face. "We should have used a condom."

It was his turn to tense. "You said you were on the pill."

"I am," she rushed to assure him. "It's just...the other stuff."

"Other...stuff?" He realized what she meant. "Are you telling me you have—"

"No!"

"Well, neither do I."

She looked up at him, her brow wrinkled in doubt.

"I'm not just saying that. You want a printout, or something?"

"You have one?"

She grimaced and he could tell she wished she hadn't said it. He wished she hadn't either. It killed the vibe.

"Never mind. That's stupid. I'm sorry. I've probably totally ruined the moment now."

Jude stared down at her and almost laughed, but something hit him—a realization he wasn't ready for.

Chapter Twenty-Nine

Validation

Erin

She was drowning in Jude's jacket again. Under the too-long sleeves, her fingers gripped tightly on Etta's leash. Jude had linked his arm in hers when she'd almost slipped on the icy road. He'd tried to reclaim the dog lead too, but even with all the tugging and eagerness on Etta's end, Erin enjoyed herself. Also, she needed the distraction.

The way he treated her, it was something she never thought she'd have and hadn't known she'd wanted. It would be easy to soak it up this last day, but she wasn't quite sure what to do with it afterwards.

What's worse, it terrified her that she felt this way after only a week. Logic and experience told her that nothing came wrapped up so nicely, that if it seemed too good to be true, it was. And yet, the temptation to ignore logic seduced her—the things he said were unbelievably perfect.

Too perfect.

She'd gladly drink his coffee if he contented in ogling over her technique. She even found herself open to the idea of skiing because sooner or later—probably sooner—she'd end up in his arms. But these feelings had come on so quickly, she worried if she could trust them.

"You okay?" Jude's voice jarred her out of her thoughts.

"Yeah. Why?"

"Because you're walking really slow."

"Oh."

Etta waited up front, with her head turned back and cocked to the side. Erin could practically hear her saying, "Seriously?"

"Thought maybe you were having second thoughts," Jude jibed.

"Second...huh?" They'd come to the end of the street.

He jerked his chin forward. "Second thoughts?" he repeated, the hint of a smile tugging at his mouth.

Erin stared ahead at the start of the mountain path Mari'd taken her on that fateful day she'd slid half-way down on her butt. "Wait. There? Really?" Her face drooped and her step faltered. "I thought you said you liked me."

He laughed. "I do."

"Then what's with the..." she jutted her chin out at the path in similar fashion.

"I'd catch you."

"Yeah? And who's going to catch you when I send us both flailing down the mountain?"

"Thought you said you trusted me."

"I do. But I think you underestimate just how clumsy I can be. I've won awards."

He tossed her a warm smile that crinkled his eyes and she wished she had a camera handy...or a free hand to snap the photo.

"I think you underestimate my motivation." He winked and her heart missed a beat.

As they approached the trail head, Erin's legs seized. "We're not really going up there, are we?"

"You gotta give me something. I gave up skiing." His eyes danced.

Before she could argue further, Etta veered onto a little side path, taking Erin with her.

"Guess you're in luck," he sighed dramatically.

He was lucky her hands were occupied or she'd have smacked him. Instead, she ignored him by watching Etta run around sniffing at everything sticking out of the snow. Erin understood her shaggy friend's excitement. Everything posed picturesquely around her. The thick clusters of trees branches splayed out like exotic frond fans, showing off their collections of needles and powder. The meandering path coursed like a white river in the middle of a forest. Bright warm sun streamed in between the trees in shafts that highlighted the sparkling landscape.

"Wow," she whispered, her breath hanging a moment on the air in front of her.

Jude unhooked Etta's leash and let her run free up ahead. It reminded Erin of something.

"Did you ever hear from Ronnie's owner?" she asked.

"Who?"

"The lady who called animal services. The one who wanted to sue for...doggie damages," she explained.

"Sue? I don't know who you're talking about. Someone wants to sue me?" Jude's feet stopped.

"I guess that answers my question then," she muttered, halting with him. "I doubt at this point she'll follow though."

"What did she say?"

Erin scrunched her face. This was one of those foot-in-mouth incidences she wished she'd grown out of. "Nothing. She was just upset because her dog was skittish."

"Was he injured?"

"No. As far as I could tell, he was totally fine." She felt herself getting irritated all over again. "She hadn't even taken him to a vet, so it couldn't have been that bad."

"Do you remember what house it was?"

She looked up at him, her lips pursed. *I shouldn't have said anything.* "Don't worry about it. She was just on a power trip. And even if her dog was injured, and I'm telling you, he wasn't, you can't know that Etta was responsible. It could have been this other, mysterious third dog!"

He frowned.

"I mean it, the dog was fine! The owner is just an entitled...witch. If you go over there, she'll make all kinds of claims, and try to get whatever she can out of you! Or worse, file an order against Etta!"

Jude's expression seemed suddenly pained and pinched and she couldn't figure it out.

"Seriously Jude! I'm not going to let you make it so easy on her! If she wants to take advantage of you, she'll have to go though the claims process!" One thing was for sure, Erin had no intention of revealing which house she'd gone to, for both Jude's and Etta's sake. Jude didn't owe that woman a thing!

"Are you done?" he asked. His shoulders shook as a smile broke.

She didn't feel done. In fact, she'd gotten herself so steamed up, she considered going back to that house with a few of her own words.

He held her shoulders. "Erin, honey, calm down."

Staring up at him, a part of that fury just melted. And if Jude did find the house, the woman would get one look at him and forget what she'd been so upset about. Erin had.

He gave her upper arms a light squeeze. "You calm?"

"Calm-ish..." she grumbled.

"Good."

He stepped in, dusting a kiss on her forehead. It sent a gushy feeling under her ribs and Erin momentarily forgot how to breath. Again. What was with her?

"Remind me never to get on your bad side," he muttered, turning back down the path and linking his arm with hers.

"Don't be an uppity witch."

"Noted." His arm slid down to weave fingers into hers. He studied their interlocked hands before speaking again. "You like your apartment in the city?"

His question seemed like an odd shift in subject. Erin took a minute to respond. "It's comfortable...A little dated and a bit of a trek to work, but affordable, clean, close to public transit," she listed, like a rental ad. "And I've been there a while so thank-you rent control."

"Do you have roommates?"

"No." Erin wondered at his sudden curiosity. "It's just a one-bedroom." Could Jude be thinking of visiting her? The thought made her heart race gleefully.

Etta came barreling back, eyes wide, with a huge stick hanging out the side of her mouth. She skidded to a halt in front of Jude, sending a spray of white powder at them. Erin brushed the snow off her chest with a laugh, and Jude took the stick.

"Did you find a new toy?" he asked her in an enthusiastic tone.

Etta's tail whipped back and forth, and she lifted up to her back legs as if planning to plant her front ones into his chest. Instead, she landed back into the snow, her tongue flopping out as if she were laughing. Jude threw the stick with ease, sending it far off ahead, and she bolted after it.

"So...what's with all the questions? You missing the city?" Erin fished.

"No," he said with finality. "No. You couldn't get me back there. Not if my life depended on it."

"Oh."

"Look, I get people like it. I'm not trying to be a jerk. You can like it. It's just not for me."

"No. It's...it's fine," she rushed out. "I just thought...I didn't mean to pry."

Erin studied her snow covered sneakers with intensity as she navigated the path, trying not to frown. Jude's boots fell in time beside hers with an easy gait. For as gushy as her chest had just been, it now felt hard and hollow with the distinct weight of disappointment creeping in. *Not if his life depended on it?* What was she supposed to do with that?

She felt stupid for letting herself get so swept up, knowing all along this was just a vacation. When she returned to the real world, there'd be no Jude. She'd just thought...it didn't matter what she thought. Now she debated, *Do I pull back? Or just enjoy the rest of the day since the damage has already been done.*

"It's a long story, the city and me," he said, butting into her thoughts.

She shook her head. "You don't have to explain."

"But the short of it is," he went on, "I never wanted to go to business school. That was all dad."

The very short version, she thought, unclear why that had anything to do with the city. "What *did* you want to do?"

"No idea. Still don't know."

"Is that why you don't want to go back? Because you and your dad are on the outs?"

"'On the outs.'" He chuckled. "That's a good way of putting it. No. It has nothing to do with him, and everything to do with my life in that suit and tie he gave me."

Erin wasn't sure what that meant. "I'm not close with my dad, either."

"He in the city, too?"

"No. Texas. With his second wife—Karen." She hadn't intended that last word to come out so bitter.

His fingers squeezed hers. "Not a fan of the stepmom, huh?"

Erin wondered if she should just drop it. What did he care, anyway? But the silence might be worse. She didn't need more opportunity to get stuck in her head.

"I'm an only child," she explained. "And Karen wanted all my dad's attention. You can see the inherent problem."

"He chose *her* over *you*?" The anger in his voice startled her.

"Well, I didn't really say anything to him about it. He was happy."

"That's messed up."

"But it isn't his fault. He didn't realize—"

"Bullshit. We all make choices." Jude shook his head, jaw tight. "Is that why you settled on that other guy? Because your dad set a shitty example?"

Erin's jaw dropped. "Excuse me?"

"See, that would be a deal breaker," he went on as if she hadn't spoken. "If someone hated Etta, that'd be that."

"Hold on, let's go back a minute." She scrambled to organize her thoughts. "What makes you think you know anything about my relationship with Victor? Or my dad."

Etta sauntered back to Jude, and dropped her stick at his feet. Retrieving it, he slung his arm back, and hefted it far out ahead of them.

"Just saying, it makes more sense now."

"Make sense?" she scoffed. "What? That I would chose to date a handsome, successful, bilingual man who showed interest in me? Gee...thanks."

Erin picked up her pace but Jude matched it easily, keeping his fingers wound tightly around hers, even when she tried to pull away.

"Why are you getting so defensive?"

"I'm not defensive," she huffed.

"Liar."

"You don't know anything about my relationships. You only saw the tail end of one," she argued.

Jude didn't seem affronted at all. "Maybe. Still think you could do a lot better."

She didn't have a retort for that. And what business did he have in it, anyway? He wasn't offering to be that something better. He clearly had no intention of coming to the city and that seemed like a pretty finite boundary, and a clear enough message. She wasn't interested in any more one sided relationships.

Etta loped back, this time skidding to a stop in front of Erin. Taking the opportunity, Erin yanked her hand out of Jude's grasp, and picked up the stick. "My turn?"

Etta's tail whipped faster. *Oh, to be a dog,* she thought, wishing for some of that carefree bliss. She gave it her best fling, but it landed a few, measly feet away. Etta didn't seem to care. She bounded after it anyway with the same intensity as she had all the other times.

Jude watched the exchange, hands in his coat pockets, and the corners of his mouth turned up.

"What?" It irritated Erin that he looked so content when she felt so unsure about everything. Instead of waiting for an answer, she pressed forward.

He caught up moments later, sliding a palm down into her hand and locking her fingers in his once more. She didn't fight it, even when she knew she should.

The next time Etta returned, the stick dropped in front of Jude. He threw it without breaking stride, and they walked with the crunch of snow under their shoes.

"You still hung up on him?" he asked.

Erin shot him a questioning glance but he was looking up ahead. "Who?"

"Victor."

A bitter laugh snuck out. "No. Not anymore. Not like I was." Although, she wasn't sure she'd ever truly clear out the place in her heart he'd occupied.

She wished it was more cut and dry. Any rational person would assume she'd been turned off after seeing Victor's true colors. But Erin knew her feelings had shifted before then, when Jude had given her that first smile and made her stomach flutter. She didn't plan to tell him that, though.

Jude nodded as if in slow motion, eyes off ahead in the distance.

Was her answer too vague? Did he doubt her? She hated that it mattered. She felt the need to make him understand, and her uncertainty made her nervous.

"It's been a long time coming. Apparently I've been having a reoccurring dream about him. Only, I didn't realize it was about him, not until...well, Mari and I planned this trip so that I could get some perspective, and some mountain air because she said that's what I needed. And that's what I got...and it did. It helped. And when he came unannounced, that only solidified things. Even before the...violence..." She pinched her lips shut to stop talking. Somehow, she didn't feel like she'd helped her case. And now Jude had stopped to study her.

"Stupid dream? Is that the same one you had at my place?"

"What?" she asked, alarmed.

"You cried out that night, on the couch. Figured you were having a nightmare."

"Oh." Her cheeks heated. "You heard that?" Great...now he really had seen all her worst moments.

"Are you still having it?"

"No." *Thank God.*

"What did he do? In your dream?" His tone sounded casual, but something about how his grip tightened around her hand, she felt like her answer mattered to him.

"I...it's stupid," she defended. *Stupid how long it took me to see the signs.* She should have listened to her intuition. She focused her eyes forward. Etta pounced on something up ahead—not her stick.

"You always cry out?" he asked.

"I don't know." Erin shrugged. He gave her hand a light squeeze.

"How long you been having it?"

"Three or four months? It's hard to know because at first it was sporadic."

He whistled. "That's a long time."

"Yeah. I think it's just...work's been stressful. And then I saw Victor at a bar last week with..." she couldn't finish, it was too pathetic. "Well, it pushed me to make a change." He looked down at her and it made her inexplicably defensive. "Like I said, I didn't realize it was Victor at first. Not until—"

"Last week?"

"Yeah."

"What'd he he do in your dream, Erin?" Jude pressed.

Her hand went idly to her neck. Sometimes, when she woke and it was still dark, she could feel the phantom fingers wrapped around her. It sent a chill up her spine. He stopped asking questions.

They came upon Etta's discarded stick. Jude picked it up, and carried it while they walked in silence. Erin tried to live in the moment and stop fretting over the inevitable future or the mistakes from her past. But her mind kept drifting. She thought of all the wasted time she'd given Victor that she'd thought would one day pay off. Would she reflect a year from now and feel the same way about Jude? Without all the history, surely this unrequited affection would be easier to get over.

And she wasn't the same person she'd been a week ago. Who could have guessed it'd be Jude who'd help her see that she'd been hiding in routine, familiarity, and excuses. Jude who'd show her the difference between heartfelt smiles and obligatory ones.

Tilting her head back, she scanned the sky and the snow dusted pines. The chill invigorated her. Up ahead, the trees thinned, and the side of the mountain came into view. To the left, the path gave way to a drop-off and what looked like a frozen creek.

"There's something about these mountains, isn't there?" Jude voiced. She looked over and realized he was watching her again.

"Yeah..." she agreed, the single syllable bittersweet. Her reality was in the city.

He stopped walking and swung her arm around like he was leading a dance, spinning her in close to face him. Startled, her eyes lifted to his face. He looked different. Younger. The once hard planes she'd grown accustomed to had relaxed. He didn't speak, but the expression he gave her...she'd seen it before, though never directed at her.

In that moment, her heart beat too fast to speak and the world melted away. She didn't feel the cold seeping in her sneakers, couldn't hear Etta's impatient barking, nor the creaking of the tall pines swaying in the wind. And all she could think was, *if it's too good to be true, it probably isn't.*

"What?" she gasped out. "Do I have something on my face?"

As the moment stretched, her mind played with her. Perhaps it was pity, not intent or devotion. Why wasn't he saying anything? She felt she couldn't trust herself, not when she'd been so wrong before. Her only true, reliable skills were misreading situations and making things worse.

Erin opened her mouth to prompt him again, when her eyes drifted past him, to something so oddly familiar that time and place all but faded away. She stood frozen, yet transported, and her heart sped so fast, it made her dizzy.

Jude followed her gaze over his shoulder. "Oh." He laughed. "Don't worry, it's safe." Turning back to face her, he added, "We take this trail all the time."

Etta whined. Jude hesitated a moment, his eyes lingering on Erin's face, then he pivoted to throw the stick. It landed on the other side of the creek bed that cut through the path they were on. A creek bed that wove right under a splintered, wooden bridge half buried in the mountain.

"Hey," he called, his voice soft and soothing near her ear. "Trust me. It's safe."

She nodded absently as the week rushed back at her under a whole new light.

Jude flexed his hand around hers, and pulled her with him toward the bridge.

How...? she thought, staring in disbelief. She ran her hand over the rough, weathered handrail, its solid surface surreal under her fingertips. *Same splintered edges, same wide gaps between the boards.* As if in trained response, her adrenaline started pumping, hope surged, and fear coursed through her veins all at the same time. Logically, she knew she was in no danger, but she hesitated, her toes digging into solid ground.

Jude continued on, their arms stretching across the space between them. Turning back, he noticed she'd stopped. "Erin?"

She looked up from the mouth of the bridge to see his eyes searching hers, his fingers tightening around her own as if he expected her to bolt.

He moved back to where she stood. "You okay?"

"No. I...I um," she stuttered. "It's just..."

"Look. Solid as a rock."

He let go of her hand and jumped. The wood creaked under his feet as he landed, but it held. This wasn't her dream. This was real life, with Jude, right smack in the middle of it.

Shaking her head, Erin fought back a giddy smile. She didn't know how it was all going to work out, but suddenly, she had faith that it would.

She scooted a foot onto the first, splintered plank.

Jude braced her arm. "Just be careful. It's slippery."

Her sneaker skated over a patch of ice, and she grasped onto him, a laugh bubbling up from her chest.

He chuckled. "I got you. I won't let you fall."

The smell of his soap wafted into her nose. *Too late...*

They made it halfway across the bridge. Halfway, then her arm locked around his, and she pulled him back.

Jude turned to face her, his mouth quirked up in half a smile. "Erin, honey..."

She couldn't fight it anymore. She didn't want to. And maybe, she didn't have to.

She grabbed the front of Jude's coat with both hands and pulled him down to her mouth. She poured everything into him. Her hope, her doubt, the newfound sense of wonderment. She kissed him with no reservations and no restraint and it felt like her heart had finally been set free.

Etta's forepaws landed on their shoulders, and Jude braced them as the skidded back into the railing. Warm dog breath wafting into their faces, Erin finally released his smiling mouth.

"What was that for?" he asked, eyes lit and breath uneven.

"I just wanted to kiss you."

Chapter Thirty

Cooking Lesson

Erin

She struggled with the jars, bags and containers, while simultaneously trying to avoid icy patches in the road. When she made it back to Jude's cabin, she had to kick at the front door with her foot. It swung open almost immediately.

Jude's eyes bulged. He leaned in, grabbing the heavy bag hanging from her fingertips and the stack of containers tilting precariously in the crook of her elbow. "If I'd known there was so much, I would have helped."

"I actually didn't realize—Oh!" A container of salsa teetered off the stack. Jude lunged forward and caught it. "Thanks. We don't have to use it all," she assured him as he stepped aside to let her in.

They moved into the kitchen and dumped the food on the counter.

"What do you normally cook?" he asked, poking around in the bag she'd stuffed with non-perishables.

"Do microwave frozen dinners count?"

He tilted his head to the side and raised an eyebrow.

"Okay, well, I'm a wiz at salads with store bought dressing. And I *can* chop veggies for stir-fry and pasta. Not saying it turns out all that good but..."

"How about," Jude thought out loud, evaluating her, then the ingredients spread out on the countertop. He made a clicking noise with his tongue, picking up a wrapped pack of chicken, "Let's try a chicken bake."

"Oh, no...I don't do fresh chicken. Or baking," Erin warned.

"It's easier than you think."

"You say that, but you've never had to eat dry, rubbery meat three nights in a row."

"Cooking is about patience and when you use a recipe, it's about following directions." He eyed her over a sly smile.

"I can follow directions," she murmured.

His chest shook and his eyes crinkled. "Sure you can." Giving her a quick kiss on the cheek, he instructed her to "stay put."

The light touch on the small of her back disappeared as he went into his bedroom. Erin wandered over to the fire, crouching down, and giving the lazing canine a good rub on the belly. Etta had the right idea. Napping in front of the fire seemed like a much better option than blundering in the kitchen.

Jude came back into the kitchen. "Where'd you go?"

Erin stood to see him flipping through a cook book. When she rejoined him in the kitchen, he shook his head, but a smile played on his lips.

"Trying to hide already? Guess I've got my work cut out for me," he teased. "This," he held up the book so she could see the cover, "is a great beginner book." He pressed a thumb into the already flattened crease between the pages.

"First we read the *whole* thing. Start to finish." He set the book down on the counter in front of them.

She crossed to the sink to wash her hands. "But it's in steps."

"Think of it like pieces to a jigsaw. Isn't it easier to build when you know what the end result is?"

"That's what the picture is for, silly!"

"Not every recipe has pictures, silly," he pointed out.

"They should," she grumbled, drying her hands on a dishtowel.

Looking down at the text, she started feeling a little overwhelmed. "Do you do a lot of puzzles?"

"Stop stalling. Start to finish," he redirected, then backed away.

Sighed, she leaned elbows into the counter, sticking her butt out behind her. Jude cleared his throat, and she smiled. Then she read the ingredients and steps the *whole* way through. When she finished, she looked over her shoulder at him, pleased to note that he was definitely staring at her assets.

"We don't have bread crumbs or chicken broth," she told him, pretending to ignoring the heat in his eyes. If he wanted to do this, then so be it. Two could play this game.

He nodded, then went to a cabinet and pulled down a box of Cheerios. She furrowed her brow.

"Bread crumbs," he explained, shaking the box, then reaching into another cabinet. He extracted a can of chicken broth, and brought both over to the counter where she stood.

"Excuse me," he said from right behind her, reaching between her body and the drawer she was blocking.

She pushed her hips back into him so he could open it. Jude pulled out a plastic ziplock, and lingered a moment, before moving out of her space.

He filled the bag with Cheerios. "This is the fun part." Grinning, he dropped the closed bag on the counter, then slammed a fist against it, creating a very satisfying *crunch*. "You want to try?" He slid the bag in front of her.

Erin spread her palm open, gently smushing the Cheerios into the counter.

"Like you mean it!" He grabbed her hand, balling it inside his, and led it down onto the soon-to-be bread crumbs with a heavy thud.

A smile bloomed across her face, the kind a kid reveals after getting away with something their parent specifically told them not to do. Jude left her to it, bashing the poor bag until its contents were nearly dust. She slid it back to him, shaking out the sting on the side of her hand.

"I'll give it a few more, just for good measure," he reasoned, laying several additional, hammering blows. Erin watched how the muscles in his forearms flexed and how his smile grew brighter. Next time she needed an outlet, she'd be making breadcrumbs.

"Ingredients, check," he stated. "Now what?"

Erin suspected he already knew, but she looked down at step one. "Preheat the oven. I can do that."

She pivoted toward the range, then halted. The one in her apartment had five simple knobs. Five. Jude's oven sported all kinds of buttons and a display screen *and* knobs. *Well, shoot.* She felt him come up behind her, and she stiffened. "My oven isn't nearly this complicated."

"Relax," he chuckled, leaning in from behind her. He tapped the bake button, then the up arrow until the display read "375." "And start," he finished as his finger pushed the 'start' button.

"Thanks," she mumbled, steering her eyes to her toes.

"What's next chef?"

She bumbled back to the counter and hunched over the book. "Spray the pan?"

"I prefer butter."

"What's the point of a recipe if you go and change everything?" she asked irritably. She sighed as he handed her a stick of butter, then set a glass baking dish in front of her. Then stared at it, too embarrassed to ask what she was supposed to do with it.

"You really don't cook," he noted, curving his front around her back.

Her shoulders jutted up in defense. "This was *your* idea. I warned you."

"And I'm thoroughly enjoying myself. This should be fun. Why are you so tense?"

He rubbed her arms, which would have been nice, if she wasn't so on edge. Around this time, Victor'd be laughing and calling for takeout.

Jude reached around her and took the butter from her, peeling away the wax paper. Handing it back, he told her, "Just rub it on."

"Oh. Just rub it on? That's it? Why didn't I think of that?" She took it and grazed the bottom of the dish with a smear from the stick. Jude sighed in her ear. "What? I'm rubbing it on!"

"Honey, I want to eat tonight."

A muscled arm crowded hers and he closed his hand over her greasy fingers. His other arm curled around her to hold the dish. Pressing both their hands and butter firmly into the glass, he made small circles, getting the bottom, the corners, and the sides greasy with a thick coating of fat.

"Maybe you should just do this and I'll watch," she suggested.

"But this is way more fun." He pressed a soft kiss on the side of her neck. "Next?"

Erin looked down at her empty plate. "You're going to make me say it, aren't you?"

She shot a glance over her left shoulder at Jude. He twisted his torso to face her, leaning his elbow into the breakfast bar, and gave her a toothy, satisfied smile. *God, that smile...*

"No. You don't have to say it. It's written all over your face."

She scowled which only made him smile brighter. She wanted to be mad that he was right and she was wrong, but his flexed bicep and easy manner evaporated her resolve. Instead, she fought her own smile.

"There it is," he said softly, eyes on her mouth. For a fleeting moment, she felt like nothing else in the world existed. And suddenly, she wanted more than just his eyes on her. *Is it normal to feel so frisky all the time*, she wondered.

"I gotta let Etta out," he stated, voice low, as he lifted up from his stool.

Upon hearing her name, Etta popped up behind them, her tags clinking.

"Just gonna have her run around out back." His eyes looked a shade darker, still focused at the lower half of her face.

"Okay. I'll start cleaning up."

It took him a beat, but he nodded, then headed to the back of the cabin. Etta's nails clicked on the wood as she followed him.

Erin cleared the dishes to the kitchen sink, and started rinsing off the plates.

"Just use the dishwasher," he said, suddenly next to her and taking a plate out of her hands. He pulled the door down and loaded the dirty dish.

"I'm just rising them first," she explained.

"Why? Just load them."

"But—"

"What's the point of a dishwasher if you have to wash them anyway?" he argued.

"But it doesn't clean the—"

"This one does," he said, grabbing another plate from her grasp and sticking it in, still coated with cheesy remnants.

"But it won't—"

"Trust me. I spent extra on this thing just so it would do what it's supposed to."

Erin huffed and leaned her palms into the counter, staring at the empty sink.

"What?" he asked, clearly suppressing his own hilarity.

"You just interrupted me, like, a hundred times," she told the sink, exasperated.

"A hundred?"

Erin twisted herself around in the little space she had, to look up at him. "Seriously?"

He schooled his expression. "I'm sorry. What was it you were going to say?"

"It doesn't matter," she clipped, grabbing mucky forks and knives from the counter and depositing them into the dishwasher 'as is.' If he had to clean them again in the morning, it served him right.

"I like you just as much when you're like this, you know," he said softly, moving in closer.

"Well, thank goodness for that."

He curled his arms around her and nipped her ear. "Are you going to pout all night?"

"Maybe..."

"Fine. Want to have a sleep over?"

She'd always thought that term silly. "Will there be any actual sleep involved?"

"Probably not," he admitted.

Jude's fingers trialed down her bare arms, making her stomach flip-flop. She liked how he couldn't keep his hands off her. And she loved his playful side.

"You need anything from your place?" he murmured below her ear before pressing his lips into her neck.

"M-my pajamas?"

"No, you don't need those," he said, sliding a tongue down to her shoulder

"Then why did you ask?" Her heart revved and sensations tingled Southward.

"I meant, like your pill." He grazed his teeth over her shoulder.

She gasped. "I take it after breakfast." Her mind focused on how his lower half pressed into hers, the firm ridge of his arousal obvious despite the layers of clothing that separated them.

"Want me to run over and grab them?"

"I'll just get them tomorrow," she huffed, a little breathless.

"What if you're still in bed?" His mischievous tone assured her she would be. And she liked that.

"Then you can get them for me in the morning."

"Who says *I'm* going to want to get up?"

She closed her eyes and tilted her head to the side. Erin didn't really care about the pills. She was pretty sure she wasn't in danger of getting pregnant that week. She did worry, however, that if they didn't do something soon, she might combust.

"Where do you keep them?" He pulled away, giving her little choice.

She heaved a sigh. "Toiletries bag. It's hanging on the towel bar in the downstairs bathroom. Little plastic sleeve. Kind of greenish."

"Be right back."

She turned to face him, showing off her best pout. "You better."

He snuck a kiss, then grabbed a jacket, before sliding through the front door. Etta sat up, sending a little whine to the front of the cabin.

"Don't worry girl," Erin called, her own voice a little whiney too. "He's coming right back."

The extra large canine hefted up, and lumbered over to the kitchen, sitting at Erin's feet. She stared up with those big, puppy-like eyes.

Erin chucked. "What?"

Her tail swished once against the planked floor.

With a fond smile, Erin dried her hands on a dish towel, then smoothed back the corse fur at Etta's face, pausing and digging fingers in to scratch at the back of her ears. The heavy, bristly head pushed into her palms.

"Your dad is kind of persistent," Erin confided.

Maybe he worried that Erin wouldn't remember her pills in the morning. She couldn't really blame him. It sounded like something she'd do. But that got her thinking, *Does Jude want children?* She'd hoped for some, one day. And she didn't want to jump ahead of herself, but what if he didn't? She frowned. Could the universe be that cruel?

Etta pushed her face forward so Erin's hand traveled over her head and down her neck. Tongue lolling out, she flopped down to the ground, stretching front paws forward and exposing her scruffy belly. Erin must have hesitated too long, her thoughts on deal breakers, because Etta put a paw on her leg and voiced a high-pitched whimper.

"Persistent," Erin mused, looking down at her. "Did he learn that from you?"

Giving in, she squatted down to rub the fluffy, white belly being offered. From the other side of the counter, the cabin door opened then swung shut and latched.

"Erin?"

"Down here," she called, looking up just in time to see Jude's head pop over the breakfast bar. His face lit into a smile.

"She got you hooked."

"Don't say it too loud," Erin fake-whispered. "It might go to her head."

Jude laughed, and came into the kitchen, tossing Erin's pills on the counter as he did.

He squatted down on the other side of his pushy companion. "She already has a big head," he pointed out, then leaning closer to Etta's face, "don't you girl? Big dog, big head." He rubbed her muzzle with his thumbs, then stroked down her neck and along her ribs. "That's okay. You're *my* big dog."

Etta turned her *big* head and looked at Jude like he was her whole world, her tail sounding a rapid beat against the floor. She snuck in a few sloppy kisses across his face before he shifted out of her reach. The scene filled Erin's heart to brimming. This was no man-eater and Jude was definitely not an axe-murderer.

Erin stood at the sink with toothbrush in hand, remembering that first night she'd left the wine in his bathroom. She smiled, thinking about her red nose and messy hair as she brushed her teeth. Her hair was mussed again, but she had to admit, it did look a little sexy.

She heard Jude come in the back door and stomp his feet on the mat. The clicks of Etta's nails traveled down the hall and around the front of the cabin.

A light *knock* resonated on the bathroom door.

"Hey, you in there?" he called.

"Yeah," which sounded more like "yeow" around a mouth full of toothpaste. She spit and tried again. "Yeah. I'm just brushing my teeth. Why?"

"Making sure you didn't run out on me."

There was a beat, and then the door opened.

She stepped out of the way. "Wh—What are you doing?"

"I need to brush my teeth too," he said, looking down at her with a goofy smile.

He positioned her back in front of the sink, then reached around her to grab his stuff out of the medicine cabinet. Suppressing a giggle, she watched his reflection smear toothpaste on the bristles, toss the tube on the sink top, then shove the toothbrush in his mouth. Through it all, one or more parts of him grazed or pressed against her.

He finally acknowledged her attention. "What?"

"You couldn't wait?"

"No."

He went about brushing his teeth but he did step back enough for Erin to bend over and spit. She rolled her eyes though she didn't really mean it: his smile was infectious and she liked the familiarity of it all.

In a bold act, she set her toothbrush inside the medicine cabinet, hoping it didn't seem too presumptuous. Either Jude didn't notice or he didn't care.

He spit in the sink as she inched around him to the door. "You know what would be the best thing?" he asked. She paused and waited for him to finish. "If you were naked in my bed when I got there."

Chapter Thirty-One

The Next Step

Jude

He emptied the dishwasher, doing his best to keep quiet. But the monotonous activity didn't quite meet his needs. When he woke up to Erin against his body, so many things ran through his mind, the least of which being, today was her last day.

The little growl she'd made in her sleep as she'd locked her arm around him was new. It made him want to throw away years of hard learned lessons and dive in recklessly. Though, he'd already done that, to an extent. Something about this just felt right. He'd had more fun these past few days than he could remember having since moving to the mountains. *Too bold to ask her when she's coming back?* he wondered.

Coffee brewing, Jude eased the cast iron out of the cabinet, and set it on the stove. He intended to give her every reason to want to, starting with breakfast and coffee when she woke up. The cold from the fridge hit his bare chest as he grabbed the eggs.

Etta wandered out of her niche and moseyed into the kitchen with an exaggerated yawn, and the equivalent of a deep, canine grumble.

"Hungry, girl?" he greeted quietly, offering good morning scratches with his free hand.

She breezed by him and Jude followed routinely to the back door to let her out. Then he returned to the kitchen to make his girls breakfast. By the time nails clicked into the kitchen again, he'd already set Etta's bowl out for her. She wolfed it all down in her usual way, and Jude watched, whisking the eggs and thinking about the night before. Erin liked her. She'd even gotten down on the floor and rubbed Etta's belly like they were old friends.

He turned down the heat, and poured egg into the buttered skillet, wondering if Erin knew how to make a scramble. He smiled. If she didn't, he planned to teach her that, too. How could he not after that face she'd made at dinner? *Priceless*—all surprise and triumph. He liked that he gave that to her.

A rustling behind him caught his attention, and he turned.

Erin leaned against the wood-paneled hallway in one of his shirts, staring unabashed, and looking hungry—but not for eggs. Jude tipped his head down, evaluating his bared chest and flannel pajama bottoms. He looked back to where his shirt clung to her upper thigh. The feeling was mutual.

"Morning," he greeted with a lazy smile, moving towards her.

"Good morning."

She tugged shyly at the bottom of the tee. He chuckled. If anything, it was too long. He wound an arms around her waist and pulled her into him, planting a soft, lingering kiss on her lips.

She hummed into his mouth. "Mmm, you always smell so good."

"I do?"

"Like campfires and soap."

"Do I now?" He pressed her into the wall with his body, taking her mouth more firmly this time.

"Campfires...are one of my favorite...smells," she snuck out around his lips. Her arms snaked through his, to his lower back.

Heat funneled through him, like a reflex, when she moaned down his throat. And that was it. He wasn't even sure how he got them there, but they were in his bedroom again, his shirt flying from Erin's body and landing somewhere behind him.

"You're insatiable." Her voice beckoned him like a siren's call, as she tugged on his lower lip with her teeth.

"Funny. I'd say the same thing about you."

He pushed his pants down, kicking them to the floor, then leaned into her. She fell back onto his bed, hair sprawled out around her head like some kind of sexy, fallen angel. Climbing over her, he planted kisses along her soft, creamy skin, her stomach quivering under his lips as they traveled north. He paused at her nipple, encouraged by the gasps and squirming beneath him.

Jude dove a hand between their bodies as his mouth switched sides. Her hips pushed up to meet his palm, in an undeniable magnetism. He teased her, keeping his fingers just centimeters away from where he knew she wanted them, her skin achingly soft and heated against his.

Closing his eyes, he savored the feel of her under him, wanting and frantic. The energy that sparked between them made him burn with a need to keep her. A need stronger than hunger, or thirst, or self preservation. And just when he thought it couldn't get better, her hands raked over his back and shoulders, tender caresses turning into desperate pawing and nail digging. She didn't hold back and he fucking loved it. He wanted to drive her as crazy as she made him. Not out of spite, but because it made the ending so much sweeter.

His fingers circled around the outside of her sex.

"Jude, stop messing around," she breathed.

He smirked. "What's your rush?"

"You're killing me." To accentuate her point, she quaked beneath him.

He caught her nipple between his teeth. "You like it."

"You're making me crazy," she corrected, her back arching.

"You make me crazy."

"Fine, then we're even."

He could feel her body tightening. Her hands scraped down his stomach, wrapping around his shaft. He wasn't a kid anymore, but it had him twitching and straining in her grasp.

"Erin," he growled.

She shifted, lining herself up for him. He wanted there too, but he was trying not to rush through it.

Oh, fuck it, he thought. They could always do it again. *And again, and again, and again.*

Shoving her legs apart, he dove in.

"Oh, God Jude!" she cried, her hands flying up to grip the wrought iron bars of his headboard.

His breathing grew rough as he moved inside her, enjoying the smooth curves of her body writhing under him. She took everything he gave her, even as he drove harder and faster and deeper. Her wantonness made him drunk with lust.

He planted deep, and lowered his body to hers, connecting with her mouth. She took it back like oxygen. Pressing deeper, he couldn't get close enough—far enough inside her. His hips flexed in short, hard jolts, taking her there along with him.

"Don't...stop," she gasped.

He didn't stop. He wasn't ever going to stop. He'd take her to the edge and then when she came, he'd do it again, and again, and again, forever. He didn't care if it was impossible. He'd do it anyway.

So tight.

Erin screamed out as her body rocked and raised into him, the sound morphing into moans, and her orgasm commanding her limbs without thought or consent. Each sultry sound and every clench and spasm drew him closer and deeper.

Without warning, her body straightened, then pushed against him. Jude found himself on his back, her mounted, pinning him in place with a molten look so hot his skin sizzled from the inside out. Hands planted on his chest, with her body on display, she rode him. Mesmerized, his senses flooded—the flex of her thighs, the bounce in her breast— every time she came up then sunk back down onto him.

Her rhythm started slow, then increased, but he didn't want it to end. Gripping her hips, he curbed her pace. Without losing a beat, her body followed his lead, her inner thighs squeezing against him. Hair fell wildly around her shoulders and in her face. How was it that this woman wasn't snatched up for good?

Moving slowly did no good when she looked like a sex goddess taking him to paradise. He released her hips and crunched up to capture her mouth, fingers tangling in her hair and locking her head to his. She kissed him back, fierce and urgent, her tempo accelerating again—wild and mindless. *Too hot. Too primal. Too tight.* Surging his hips up as she sank down, Jude let go.

A sound he didn't recognize echoed off the painted white walls. A coy, triumphant smile lifted those swollen lips that had just been kissing him. His mind reeled and his chest heaved and he felt so fucking good, he wasn't ever going to leave his bed. And neither was she.

Erin

Erin sighed into Jude's neck with complete satisfaction. She shifted to slide off but he tightened his iron hold around her ribs, drawing her further into his chest. Hips still connected, she could feel him, still hard, and still inside of her.

A machine! she thought, and it struck her that she was actually living out a fantasy. Only better, because it was real. He liked her. He had to, to give a performance like that —the way he'd looked at her, like she was his forever.

She felt empowered, sexy, and invigorated—a refreshing change from the blundering mess she usually portrayed. And, in the possessive way his arm clamped around her, she also felt cherished.

She sighed, her eyes skimming the ink across his shoulder and down his arm. She'd never really looked at the design before, but it stretched over his skin like a scene right from the mountain, all intertwined with a thorny vine that she traced with her fingertip. "I'm thinking about blocking out some vacation time in June," she tested.

Jude's fingers flexed over her ribs. It seemed like an affirmative response, but not wanting to break the moment, she settled into his chest, quite content to laze there all morning.

Closing her eyes, she listened to the rap of his heartbeat against her ear. It lulled her into a drifting sleep, her body relaxing into his. That was when her stomach grumbled. She ignored it.

The second time though, Jude chuckled into her hair. "What was that?"

"Oh, nothing," she sighed. "Just my stomach telling me—"

"Shit!" Jude bolted upright, dislodging her before she could react. "Sorry. Be right back."

He darted out of the room, buck naked. Erin smiled outright and admired the view until he'd rounded the corner out of sight. She took a luxurious stretch, but heavy clanking had her jumping up and running out behind him.

"Are you...okay?"

He stood at the kitchen sink, shaking his head. A haze of grey loomed over the cooking area, stinging her nose. She wafted the smoke away from her face with her hand. Jude turned to her, glancing up from under his brows, almost bashful.

Tucking her lips in, she hid a smirk. There was something so comforting in knowing she wasn't the only one who could wreck breakfast, even if she held some of the blame.

"Eggs are no longer on the menu," he grumbled, clearly discouraged.

"It's okay. It was worth it." She gave him a coy smile.

His furrow lightened and from what she could see, he was thinking about forgetting breakfast again. *Machine.*

He left the skillet in the sink, and stalked toward her, catching her between his body and the edge of counter. Erin tensed momentarily, as the cold laminate top pressed into her buttocks.

Steel, grey eyes drank her in as his fingers trailed along her naked shoulder and down her arm. The gentle touch, paired with the intensity of his stare made it feel as if the goosebumps where *under* her skin. Grinning, he took her hand and wrapped it around his back. Firm, gluteus muscles flexed under her touch.

They'd already done it in the kitchen. She was about to suggests a new location, like the armchair in front of the fireplace, but Erin's stomach chose that moment to growl again, louder this time. She dropped her head into his chest with an embarrassed groan.

He pulled back, his chest shaking. "Let me make you some toast." Then, almost as an afterthought, he added, "You should probably put on some clothes."

She frowned.

"Don't get me wrong," he amended quickly, grinning wide. "I'd love it if you stayed like this. But it's distracting, and I only have so much food to burn."

His reasoning sound, Erin sauntered to the bathroom. "You could stand a pair of pants yourself," she threw out over her shoulder.

Dressed in clothes from the day before, she came back into the kitchen. Jude wore jeans, and nothing more. When he looked up, she quirked her brow.

"You said pants," he argued with a shrug. He flashed her a bright white smile, and took a sip of his coffee, his ease infectious.

She leaned back into the counter, ogling his well formed backside as he rummaged through the fridge. He caught her staring and straightened. Mouth flat and eyes intense, he stormed over to her.

Her breath caught. "What?"

Before she knew it, Jude's mouth found hers. His body pinned her in place and a sting of heat plunged straight between her legs. His kiss felt carnal. *Screw breakfast*, she thought, and nearly uttered it out loud when something cold met the back of her neck.

Yelping, she shoved him away. "What the hell?"

He grinned, holding up a jar of preserves. "Just trying to cool you down."

"Well, then you shouldn't have prowled over here, and done...what you did."

He didn't bother to hold back his humor, and Erin lost the fight. Smiling, laughing Jude was her favorite version.

"Then stop staring at me like that," he shot back. "I'm only human."

"How was I staring?"

He cocked his head to the side.

"Well, I put my clothes on," she pointed out.

"Yeah...that didn't help as much as I thought it would." He scratched the back of his neck, seeming suddenly shy.

"Breakfast," she reminded him.

"Yes." He nodded. "Breakfast." Turning, with the preserves in hand, he addressed the toast that sat waiting in the toaster. "Coffee's ready."

Erin moved to the coffee pot and filled an empty mug that waited for her. She hopped up on the stool at the breakfast bar across from him. Her birth control pills sat there, reminding her to take them. She supposed it was good Jude had brought them over.

After popping a pill out of the foil sheet, and tossing it into her mouth, she settled in to enjoy coffee and the show. A satisfied hum resonated in her chest as she reveled in that first, hot sip.

Jude studied her with an odd look. She tilted her head in question. Then, another smile cracked and lit his whole face. He shook his head, returning to the toast.

As she watched him, a weight crept in on her, of time ticking away. She had to go back to the rental to clean and pack. She didn't know how long it would take. Or if he would follow her over. What if this was it?

How would she bring up her burning question—what next? She didn't want to come off too eager or presumptuous. Maybe he we waiting for her to say something? She tried not to let doubt sway her. She'd seen the bridge from her dream! How much reassurance did she need?

"You okay?"

"Huh?" Erin looked up from her coffee.

"You just look...sad."

"Oh, yeah. No, I'm fine. I'm just thinking about all the cleaning I still have to do across the street."

"If it's stressing you out," he said, sliding the plated toast in front of her, "I can help you."

Stepping into the rental, Erin looked around to evaluate what tasks she still had left to do.

Jude jumped in, a step ahead of her. "Why don't you finish up the kitchen? I'll clear out the ash in the fireplace."

"Okay." Rolling up her sleeves, she got back to scrubbing the kitchen counters.

Jude dug out an old, paper grocery bag from a coat closet she'd never noticed, and knelt by the hearth to scoop out all the soot. They moved through the various tasks with few words. The silence wasn't uncomfortable, but unresolved plans hovered in the space between them.

What next? It buzzed in her mind like a mosquito that wouldn't leave her be. She couldn't think of how to smoothly breach the topic. She was staring off, lost in thought, when Jude came into the bathroom where she'd been disinfecting.

"Done vacuuming," he announced.

She tossed the last soiled paper towel into the trash. His nose crinkled, likely from the harsh stink of bleach.

He scanned the space. "You done?"

"Yup." She nodded, taking a final sweep of the room for any forgotten items. Her eyes came back around to Jude.

He fingered a hand through his hair, his jaw shifting back and forth. He looked unsure.

"What's up?" she prompted, hope burning a hole straight through her chest.

"We...uh, we should probably exchange numbers."

The burning bloomed into something warm and fuzzy, and the weight she'd been feeling dissipated. "Definitely." She beamed and Jude visibly relaxed.

Going for her back pocket, Erin discovered no cell. She realized she didn't actually know where she'd put it. "I just need to find my phone."

Jude pulled his out of his pocket. "Give me your number. I can call it for you."

Rattling it off for him, she finished with, "But you won't be able to call me right now. I mean, you could, but I won't get it." He looked up. "No signal," she reminded him.

"Right."

"I'm sure I'll find it before I leave. It's probably some-where in the bedroom."

Jude stepped back so she could exit the bathroom. She moved to the bedroom and began sorting through her stuff.

"I'll be right back," he said from the door frame.

"Okay," she called, sighing because her phone wasn't in any of the normal places.

She started digging around in her duffle. The front door closed just as her fingers wrapped around something small and rectangular.

"Ah ha!"

It must have gotten swept up with the rest of her clothes when packing the day before—the day she thought she was leaving. Erin frowned at the flashing low battery signal.

"Darn it," she grumbled. "Now where did I put my charg-ing cable?"

Chapter Thirty-Two

Avalanche

Jude

He jogged back across the street, cookbook in hand. The door squeaked as he let himself in the rental, but it didn't bother him. Erin shuffled toward him from the kitchen, duffle in hand. She dumped it by a line-up of other bags at the front. A pang hit his chest at seeing it all staged to go.

"Hey," she huffed with a smile, wiping sweat from her forehead.

"I could have helped you with those," he commented.

She shrugged. "Nonsense! This is my only exercise." She held up an arm to show off her bicep, then laughed.

"Not your *only* exercise," he corrected with a wink. Her cheeks flushed and a silly smile spread on her face. *Damn.* He was going to miss her.

"You're right," she mused. "Mari would be so proud."

"Mari?"

"That I got some exercise," she rushed out. "Because she is always trying to get me to go to the gym."

Jude decided he didn't care if her friend knew they had sex. "Wanted to lend this to you." He held up the beginner's cookbook they'd used for the chicken bake. Her eyes lit, and her whole face brightened. If he'd had any doubts before, he didn't now.

"Really? I can take it? I mean, I'll return it, of course," she rattled on.

He smiled. "Whatever you want."

"Oh!" She practically jumped. "I have something for you. too!" Bouncing over to the dining table, she dug around in a mountain of stuff.

"You want me to put this book anywhere?" he asked, peeking around at the bags by his feet.

"Sure. Do you mind sticking it in that black fabric tote?"

Jude turned and found it behind him, chocked full of random crap. It reminded him of his kitchen drawer, wine bottle opener included. With a snicker, he squatted, setting the cookbook on the entry tile.

"Did you even use half this stuff?" he teased, shoving a hand in the side to make space for his parting gift

"Probably not."

He laughed.

Another book had been wedged between charging cables, scarves, and things. Curiosity got the better of him, and he wiggled the thick paperback out from the mess. When his eyes caught the cover, his chest seized, and he froze.

The mountain in the picture could have been *his* mountain. Smoke drifted out from the chimney of a wooded cabin...He didn't need to read the title. He knew exactly what kind of book it was. But why did she have it? He'd asked her. She'd told him she read thrillers and mysteries or some such thing. Jude flipped the book, scanning the back cover, and hoping it wasn't what he thought, thinking it didn't have to mean anything. Praying he was wrong.

"Jude?"

His eyes ran over the words like a masochist, the synopsis too familiar. He felt sick. *She played me?* Sensing her approach, he rose and faced her, fingers clenching the paperback.

Erin's smile faltered. "What's wrong?"

"This your book?"

She hesitated. *Red flag.* She knew she'd been caught. Her mouth, the one he just couldn't get enough of, formed a little 'O' before she spoke. "It came up with me, but—"

"Just answer the question, Erin." His insides iced over. *Fuck.*

"Is...is something wrong?"

Jude took a breath. Then another one. Then he had to look away, get himself sorted. All the pieces fell into a new shape, one he was too stupid to see all along. *Her refusal to get a restraining order,* he thought, shaking his head. *Shy and guarded, then flipping to a fucking sex kitten once she finally got what she wanted. Probably knows how to cook too. And that fucking pilot light...* Was he really that blind?

The thoughts all sunk like a lead weight in his gut. He'd been played. *Again.*

Nodding curtly, he brought his eyes back to her, a muscle jumping in his jaw. The harness crept in like an old, familiar friend, urging him to ignoring the pain that flickered across her face. *An act too, no doubt.*

"Of all the things..." he uttered. He couldn't even look at her.

He didn't know why he still stood there. He didn't want excuses. But somewhere, a pathetic part of him dared her to prove him wrong. Problem was, he'd be damned if he'd let her fool him again.

"Things? What things? Are you upset about the book?"

He didn't bother responding.

"Jude, lots of people read romance novels. Is that a deal breaker, or something?" She had the nerve to snicker and shoot him an awkward smile. "I mean, I haven't even re—"

"Yeah. That's a deal breaker," he replied, serious as a heart attack.

"Oh." The smile vanished and uncertainty washed over her features. "No. I didn't...it's not actually—"

"You put on a pretty good show."

"What?" Her whole body seemed to shrink. "What do you mean? I'm confused, is this really about a book?"

"This isn't about anything, because nothing is happening here," he bit out. "Because this, you and me, was nothing to begin with." He didn't care if it made her feel bad, seeing as how she had no qualms tearing a man down for her own selfish pleasure. She wouldn't get the satisfaction of seeing how much this tore him up.

"Nothing?" She gaped. "Are you serious?"

He moved his hand to the door handle but she followed, using her small body to try and block his exit. Like that could stop him.

"That's bullshit," she challenged, her eyes glassy. "One minute you're helping me clean the cabin, sharing your cookbook, and now? Now you're...you're," she hesitated.

If she was looking for a word, he could think of a few. "You want to tell me about *bullshit?* This," he spat, shoving the paperback right up in her face. She flinched. "This is bullshit." He threw the book to the floor. "Move. I'm leaving."

"What the hell is your problem? It's just a stupid book! If you'd let me explain..." she cried, grabbing what she could of his arm. He tensed at her touch, and flipped her hand off, the force sending her sideways.

With just enough space to get the hell out of there, he swung the door in. "That's the problem," he lit in, with a low menacing voice, "I don't need you to explain it to me." He threw his uncensored contempt directly at her. "My problem is, seems I've always got women like you, who can't seem to stay the hell out of my business."

"*You* said you wanted me to stay!" she tossed back at him, making it impossible to take a dignified exit.

"Yeah, I did," he replied, disgusted. "Won't be making that mistake again."

"Wait. This doesn't make sense. Are...are you mad because I'm leaving?"

"Just the opposite. Couldn't be happier." Every minute he stayed made him more stupid, and yet, his feet felt nailed to the floor. What did he hope she could prove? The damage was done.

"I *have* to go home, I have a job. An apartment," she pleaded, completely missing the point.

"Good for you."

Her voice trembled. "Why are you being like this?"

"Like what, Erin?"

"Mean. Cold."

"Am I?" He wasn't the bad guy here. "You ever think that maybe it isn't always about *you*?" He shook his head, hissing. "Shit. It's never worth it. *Never*. You're not worth it. Nothing special, just the same old shit."

Bile rose up his throat as she staggered back like he'd struck her. Turning, he stalked out the open door. It shouldn't have been a surprise that Erin had the nerve to follow him. It was a bold move. Not anything like the woman he'd met earlier that week. He kept on as if she wasn't there, his gaze focused above her head as she tried to face him off.

Trodding backwards, she shouted, "Can you please explain to me the reason you're suddenly being such an asshole?"

Anger burned sour in his chest. *Fine.* If she wasn't going to back off, then she as good as asked for it. "Isn't that the pot calling the kettle black?"

"So now I'm not just worthless, I'm a pot?"

Jude ran a hand over his face. He needed to punch something. "You act like a skittish wreck all goddamn week, and *now* you suddenly have the balls to get in my face? Pick a tactic, Erin. No, better yet, just go home!"

"You have a lot of nerve! If you think I'm coming back now—"

"Don't bother sweetheart," he cut in. "I've had my fill." He let that hang, trying to ignore the jagged hitch in her breath.

"You. Are. Unbelievable. You know that!" She shoved her hands into his chest but it didn't slow him. "You're just as bad as—"

"Don't you say it."

"Victor!"

Jude loomed in over her, like prey, and she shrunk back, teetering off the top step of the deck. He shot an arm out, grabbing her. She looked terrified. Was it him, or her almost-fall?

"Don't compare me to that asshole!" he warned, violent anger simmering just under his skin.

She quivered.

Yanking her in a half circle, he let her go, and she staggered back several paces. He wasn't anything like Victor. "You know *nothing* about me."

"Likewise."

"Jesus, I fucking knew better. What was I thinking?" he muttered, mostly to himself. "You, acting like a goddamn mess!" He laughed, but it chaffed with irony. "Did your friend tell you to do that? Mari? Huh?" He didn't give her a chance to respond. "Well, it was a damn good act."

Her face palled.

"Do me a favor, in case you prove to be more desperate than you look. Next time your asshole boyfriend pisses you off, or the two of you are role playing some sick, fucked-up sex game, don't come running up to my mountain."

Her arm reared back and she flung something at him. The small, white box hit his chest and tumbled to the snow at his feet.

Fuck.

Without looking at her face, he stormed off, leaving her and her drama on the deck. Down the steps. Across the street. He didn't look back, didn't acknowledge the muffled sob behind him. What she had to gain by keeping it up, he didn't know, and he didn't care.

Marching up his own steps, Jude slammed his door behind him. He'd fucked up. He'd had it all together, living just fine on his own—content—just him and Etta. And then he had to go and fuck it all up.

Erin

She threw the door closed with a shaking hand, and collapsed onto the tile in a sobbing heap. Her insides hurt like she'd just been beaten. Was that how he got women to leave him alone once he was done with them? To keep himself blame free? *Coward!*

Erin eyed the paperback on the floor by her feet, fighting the overwhelming urge to rip it apart. Instead, she sniffed, wiped her face, and picked it up. She didn't get it. What did this have to do with anything? A blurry mountain scene stared back at her. Did he think she was pretending? Because of a book? A rich assumption considering she'd been more honest with him than she'd been with herself for over a year!

Erin chucked the paperback across the room. No one could shift gears that quickly. There was only one explanation. He wasn't who she'd thought. She'd screwed up. She'd fallen for unavailable. Again. Hadn't she been telling herself all along that it was too good to be true? She felt small. She felt used. Lost. Her time in the mountains had definitely expired.

Erin lugged her bags to the car. She didn't look up at his cabin. She hardly looked up from her own feet as she trekked back and forth across the tamped snow. Before her last trip out, she ripped Jude's stupid jacket off, with its stupid campfire smell, and dumped it on the floor near the door. She wouldn't have worn it at all if she hadn't packed her other one by mistake. He'd have to come get it, because there was no way in hell she was walking across the street to return it.

Stepping over the cookbook, she swung the door shut, the squeak from the frame nearly breaking her composure. The cold stung through her long sleeve as she hustled across the deck, careful to avoid the white box with its ridiculous silver bow. She did't have the heart to take it. She didn't want it. Jude could give it to his next fling, for all she cared.

Throwing herself down into the drivers seat, Erin slammed the door shut just as a trembling sob escaped. How had this day gone so wrong so fast? How had she not seen this coming?

Her head dropped to the steering wheel, and her body shook. It shook from the cold, from tears, and from the void forming in her chest. Everything assaulted her at once. His words. His tone. His face. Her crushed ego. She felt sick. Lacking. Drained. She couldn't fathom doing anything, certainly not driving, and yet, she couldn't stay.

He'd lied. He'd said he liked her. But *she* was the one putting on a show? Hiccups jarred her as sobs settled into sad little whines, as she fought to breathe.

All because of a book? She rocked her forehead side to side against the steering wheel. Book, no book, it was all an excuse so he could walk away blameless. She wanted to be mad at him, but in truth, she was more mad at herself.

A loud rap at the window made her jump. In that first second, Erin's chest seized. Then her eyes focused on the slight, female figure standing outside the car.

It wasn't Jude. Thank God, it wasn't Jude. She took a shaky breath as she started the engine, then rolled down the window.

The stranger studied her. "Are you okay?"

Not trusting herself to speak, Erin nodded.

The woman checked the street, then drew her gaze back to the car, forehead scrunching as she leaned down so her head was level with the window. "Listen, I don't know that you should be driving like this." Her tone sounded motherly and it tore a fresh wound in Erin's chest.

Betraying herself, Erin wiped fingers across a stray tear, then sniffed. "I'm okay. I just...I just need to get home."

"Where's home? Is it far?" "

Erin shook her head, mouth twitching, unable to get the words out.

"You know, it's supposed to snow again," the woman told her.

"That's—" Her voice caught. "That's why I have to get going." She hadn't actually known that. She hadn't kept up on the weather. But it didn't matter. She couldn't stay a minute longer. Snow or no snow, it was time to go.

"You're better off waiting it out than trying to stay ahead of the storm."

Erin shook her head. *Not in this case.* This lady had no idea what she'd already weathered. Concern and caring notwithstanding, she wasn't in the mood to share her heartbreak with a stranger, especially one who might know Jude. As if on cue, the woman looked over her shoulder at Jude's cabin.

Erin's stomach pitched, and for a second, she feared she might be sick all over the car. "I, um, thanks for your concern," she gulped, "but I'll be okay." She pulled the seatbelt strap across her chest.

The woman nodded with sad looking frown. "Okay, honey. Please, just drive safely."

With another nod, Erin rolled up the window, wiping back more tears. She could only image how horrible it all looked. She'd probably be the butt of neighborhood jokes for a year. *Hey, remember that stupid tourist who took off in a storm?*

The stranger stood there, still watching her as Erin shifted into drive. Ensuring her path was clear, she inching out onto the icy road, while sending a promise out to the universe. If she made it back home safely, she'd never fall in love again. And she'd never come back to this mountain. Not again. Not ever.

Chapter Thirty-Three

Doubts

Jude

He ran out of things to do in the house to keep himself busy. And he needed to be busy. Everything felt fresh and raw, like all his years in the mountains had just melted away and he was back in that first, horrible winter. What he'd left behind in the city was bad enough. But this? This was whole new level of cruel.

That first winter had been all about rebound sex. A perfect combination of distraction and physical outlet for him, a fun fling for them. Everyone came out a winner. He had no cause for complaint. Until he found that huge library of 'mountain-man' romances in one of the cabins. He hadn't even known that was a thing until he got a call to do some work on the place.

The books were all the same. He'd opened a few and tried to read them. He'd gotten as far as the description of the unwitting hero. They'd all read like him. Even down to the tattoos and emotional detachment. At first, it amused him. But the more it webbed around his brain, the more he realized, the very reasons he'd escaped the city had followed him up the mountain.

He'd thought it was all just fun and games, only to find, he'd been playing a role for these women who hoped to relieve their dull realities with a good, boot knocking fantasy. Suddenly, sex wasn't just sex anymore, but his past come to haunt him.

He didn't ask for it. And he never would have sought them out for the sole purpose of getting his rocks off. They were the ones coming on to him. What was he supposed to do? He'd felt like a stud. Until one of them flat out told him her friend had recommended she come by. She hadn't even bothered to take off her wedding ring. That was when he started feeling like a piece of meat.

And he was fucking tired of being used.

Jude blinked, his task coming back into focus. Clearing his throat, he stuffed the paperwork from the animal shelter into a folder labeled 'Etta.' His eyes glazed over the details and rested on the 'amount due.'

Why would she do that? The question had been burning a hole in his skull for the last thirty minutes. Logic and anger grappled for control. The sudden rage and panic he'd felt when he'd first discovered the book had since simmered down, and now he regretted how he'd reacted. He'd said things that were unnecessary and cruel. And untrue. And what kind of man did that make him?

A small seed of doubt planted itself in his gut.

But he'd held that damn book not forty-five minutes ago, and she'd admitted it was hers. Right? She'd played the part. He was sure of it. Mostly sure...Even if it hadn't been an act, those books gave women unrealistic expectations. They skewed reality. No man could live up to that crap.

Erin had said sex didn't solve anything. She'd been right about that. He shouldn't have slept with her, shouldn't have broken his rule. Never get involved with renters. But he hadn't anticipated that sex with her would be far better than just an escape from his bland reality.

Liar.

He raked his fingers through his hair. *Fuck.* He'd known. He'd known from the time she stepped on his goddamn doorstep. He wanted to keep it, to keep her. Despite all he'd learned, all he'd experienced, he didn't care. And then that fucking book...

Tossing the file on his desk, Jude made his way down the stairs with a growl. Etta looked up from her pig's ear and whined.

"Not you girl," he assured her, dropping onto the couch near where she'd stretched out.

He sat in almost the exact spot he and Erin had first had sex. Gut tightening, he stared at Etta. She stared back, one ear perked, and her head tilted to one side. He would have found her, even without Erin's help. He knew that. Erin hadn't *saved* Etta, not technically. And she hadn't even bothered to call him and tell him. The shelter had to do it.

Why try to hide what she did? It didn't make sense. Women liked to gloat about things like that. If she'd been trying to 'conquer' him, it seemed like a bad move. Even if she'd thought it was her fault.

He rubbed his face with his hands, the rough stubble prickling his palms. The whole thing with her ex just didn't make sense in his scenario. The more he thought on it, the more he had to believe that part had been real. And that little seed of doubt from earlier peeked through the dirt. There'd still been no 'last word' or retaliation from the guy.

A knock at the door broke his pensive silence. Jude's back went ramrod, and something damn stupid in him filled with hope. The smarter part kept his ass on the couch, willing the intruder to go away. His head was a mess, not in a position to handle whoever stood on the other side of that door. He'd said enough things he regretted for one day.

The knock came again. "Jude! It's Pauline. I know you're in there!"

Pauline? Jude rose and went to the door. Before he could greet her, she slung accusations at him.

"What did you do to that poor girl?"

He stood straighter. "What're you doing here, Pauline? Thought you'd gone home."

"Andy left his school books at the cabin," she explained, wafting a hand as if to brush off the annoyance of the extra trip. "Don't avoid my question."

"Listen Pauline, now's not a good time. I don't want to get into anything with you."

"And normally I wouldn't say anything, except...I don't know Jude, I don't think she should be driving, what with the storm coming. And she was pretty upset."

Jude lifted his chin and glanced over her shoulder. A rectangle of concrete and ice sat where Erin's car use to be. *She's gone.*

"Maybe you can call her and convince her to wait it out?"

"What?"

"The storm!"

"What makes you think she'll listen to me?" he asked, bringing his eyes back to his not-usually-so-nosey neighbor.

"She likes you," Pauline answered simply.

"Yeah, well, probably not anymore."

That's when she pulled the mother-hen card, crossing her arms and shooting him a stern, disappointed kind of look. The wrinkles in her forehead and around her eyes showed signs of her age.

Jude turned his back to her and stalked towards the breakfast bar. He picked up the order invoice for the new window and walked back to the door. "Since your here—"

"This isn't like you," she interrupted, batting away the offered sales summary.

"What's not like me?"

"You're a good person, Jude. I've always known you to do the right thing."

A bitter laugh made its way up his throat. "Come on, Pauline. People come up here full of their own goddamn bullshit and baggage all the time. How is this *my* responsibility?"

She shook her head. "No. It's more than that."

"It isn't," he lied, running a hand through his hair.

"Then *they* aren't the only ones full of bullshit," Pauline snapped back. Jude stared. Pauline hardly ever cussed. "The woman that drove away, I've seen that look. It was like her heart had just been ripped out. She sure didn't look like that when she got here."

"Don't talk to me about ripping hearts out."

"I don't get it, from everything I saw, I thought you liked her."

He didn't want to have this conversation anymore, not with Pauline, not with anyone. He started to close the door on her. "I'll call you when the windo—"

"Why are you acting like you don't care?" She shoved her hand against the wood, pushing back.

"Why? Why should I care? Nobody cares about me!"

"That's not true," she chided.

"Look Pauline, I'll call you when the window's done. Thanks for stopping by." Before he could swing the door shut, Pauline slid her foot in the threshold. "Oh, for crying out—"

"I like you Jude. I do. I truly do, but I do not like *this*."

"'This'?" he clipped out, exasperated.

"You're being unkind. I'm not saying you have to marry her. Just don't send her off in tears!"

Seed, to sprout, to bud.

Goddammit. "I don't have to explain my actions to you."

"You're right. You don't. But you do have to answer to yourself." She spoke softly but he'd be damned if it didn't sound like a scolding.

Pauline tilted her head back and looked up. Jude followed her gaze. Dark clouds were quickly rolling in. The air had taken on a new chill.

She leveled her stare back on him and delivered her parting shot. "I just hope she makes it home safely."

"Good-bye Pauline."

She shook her head, frowning, and marched away.

Jude itched to slam the door, but something bothered him. He glanced back to the charged grey sky. "How upset?"

"Forget it, Jude. Not your problem, right?" she called, navigating down the steps.

"Pauline, how upset?"

She didn't answer.

As he watched her walk down the street to her car, a knot formed in his stomach. He might be mad, he could even hate her for what she did, but he didn't want Erin to get hurt.

Jude stood in the open doorway, staring at the empty cabin across the street, then to the rectangle of snowless road where her car had been all week.

But he *had* hurt her, and he'd done it on purpose. Deserved or not, he was a better man than that. At least, he used to be. He could've just walked away. He should've just walked away. She was right. He'd been no better than Victor.

Jude swung the door shut. "Damnit!"

One call—he'd make one call to ensure she got home. Then, with a clear conscience, he could go back to his rules and his solitude. No more making exceptions. No more falling for women who were destined to leave him, break his heart, or both.

The cabin was silent except for Etta's teeth grounding on the pig's ear by the couch. He stared down at her, unseeing. Erin's face...the hurt that bled from her eyes stuck in his head like that sticky gunk from a price sticker he couldn't get off his tools. He'd put that look there. What had he said? He couldn't remember now.

Jude's head swam. He couldn't do this. He was better off on his own, doing his thing. But even as he thought that, he found himself stalking out the door and trodding across the street to the rental. If she left it behind, he had to know what she put in that stupid box.

Don't be an idiot, he told himself. *Why would she leave it?* But even as he thought that, he stopped on the deck, staring down at the silver bow by his feet. It rested exactly as it had fallen when she'd thrown it at him.

Ignorance is bliss. Part of him never wanted to find out what all the drama had been about. But a larger part of him needed to know. Something about it felt significant.

He couldn't shake it. And he just couldn't shake her. Was he wrong?

Jude stooped to pick up the box. It rattled as he brushed the snow off the sides. Behind him, a car drove by and the thought that his own drama could unfold for just anyone passing by had him crossing the deck.

He tapped the code for the door, letting himself in. It clicked behind him and he stood, motionless in the dark, empty cabin. His book sat in the tiled entry just where he'd left it, his jacket on the floor, forgotten. The bags were all gone. The paperback was gone. The place didn't just feel empty, it felt desolate.

Who was he trying to fool? He stared down at his name scrawled in slanted, black letters on the simple, white box. Swiping his thumb across the top, the silver string slid off and fell to the floor. He lifted the lid, eyes settling on a bracelet neatly tucked inside.

Throat tight, his head fell in defeat. "Fuck."

It made sense now, her sudden hissy fit.

"Fuck!"

She'd bought him a gift and he'd all but told her he wouldn't like it. Jude stared at the bracelet with its earthy-looking stone beads and metal spacers. It didn't look girly or hippie. It reminded him of his mountain. Fuck him, he liked it.

He took the bracelet out of the box, uncovering a note card tucked in the bottom. His eyes skimmed the text. She'd bought him something called a 'guardian' bracelet, the stones supposedly protecting his physical and spiritual self.

Jaw clenching, he studied the bracelet again. Never in his life...He couldn't remember ever getting a gift like this. From a woman or from anyone. A gift without reciprocation. A gift just because. A gift so...alarmingly thoughtful. And she hadn't even known the half of it. His chest ached.

Stretching the bracelet over his hand, he watched it settle at the narrowest part of his wrist. If he'd been wrong, that made him the biggest asshole. But God, he hoped he'd been wrong.

Jude dug his phone out of his pocket. The call went straight to voicemail. Scanning the empty interior, he wondered if she'd lost her phone or if she was ignoring his call.

Why hadn't she said something? Jude didn't know what to think. It all fit. She played him. It explained everything. Everything except the bracelet. And the attack. And the kennel fees...

Jude surveyed the place again, hoping for some kind of clarity. As his eyes cut across the spotless kitchen, he noticed a sheet of paper sitting under an empty mug on the counter. His boots took him there. Lifting the mug, he read the scrawl of words that were *not* addressed to him.

> *Shauna,*
> *I'm so sorry about the front door! Below you will find my address. Please send me any bills or receipts for the damages. It was my fault and I'd like to cover the repairs. Don't let Jude tell you 'no charge.'*
>
> *Thanks,*
> *Erin Simms*

He read the address at the bottom. If she relied on rent control, then she wasn't going to comfortably cover the costs of a brand-new-fucking front door. He crumpled the paper in his hand.

Everything inside of him conflicted: anger and worry, defeat and hope, bitterness and doubt—a lot of doubt.

Not my problem. Not my goddamn problem.

He tried calling her number again. Straight to voicemail. He didn't leave a message. What would he even say? Opening up the note, he smoothed it out on the counter, and stared at the rushed and sloppy handwriting. The last line was blurred like it had gotten wet.

'*...just don't send her off in tears...*'

When did he become the man who made women cry? He didn't like that, especially in light of everything. The more he thought on it, the more shitty he felt. He'd seriously fucked up.

Jude dialed her number again. *Voicemail.* Why wasn't she picking up? *No service?*

Several other scenarios ran through his head and he folded up the wrinkled paper. What if she was stuck somewhere on the side of the road, or worse? If something happened to her, he'd never forgive himself.

He growled into the empty cabin and a whole new wave of anxiety rolled over him. Shoving the note in his pocket, he tagged his book and his coat, then stormed out the rental. Phone to his ear, he jogged over a new layer of freshly fallen snow, up his steps and into his own place. The line picked up on the second ring.

"Hey, it's Jude. I need a favor."

Chapter Thirty-Four

Smashed

Erin

She stood, frozen in the open doorway of her apartment. The heavy duffle slipped off her shoulder and fell to the carpet with a thud. Other bags slid from her grasp with equal neglect. The drive back had been agonizing and long: ice, then snow, then tears and meltdowns made worse by stress and exhaustion.

All she wanted was to crawl straight into bed. Instead, she stared at the inside of her apartment as Jude's words came back to haunt her. *I won't be there to stop him next time.* And with dour pessimism, she wondered, *Will this day ever end?*

Erin leaned back on one hand, taking another swig of Tequila straight from the bottle. Though not her preferred drink, it went down easily now. She sat on the counter in her dark kitchen, heels of her sneakers kicking the cabinets to the beat of a 90's song she had stuck in her head. *I could totally be a drummer,* she mused, bopping along to what only she could hear. The tingling from the alcohol, the familiar smells and sounds of her apartment, and the improvised percussion, it was almost enough to forget. Almost.

...skittish wreck...not worth it...more desperate than you look.

A loud noise broke into her daze.

What the hell was that? Erin's legs stilled. She straightened, listening. Her eyes darted around the darkness, scanning for an intruder as her heart slingshotted into her throat. And for a moment, she thought she might throw up. Was someone there?

The sound came again. Five decisive knocks. Her eyes zeroed on the front door. Could Mari be there already?

Sliding her butt off the counter, she landed in a pile of shattered dishes. "Shit!"

The shadows spun as she staggered, groping for the countertop. She set the liquor bottle down with a *thunk*, then shuffled toward the the noise. On the way, her foot caught on her duffle.

"Shit!" she gasped again, stumbling into the door.

The room tilted, and she fought to push back the rising nausea. With a steadying breath, she stretched on her toes, holding her eye to the peephole. She leaned back, blinked, then looked again. *I think I drank too much.* Knowing it couldn't be right, she opened the door anyway. But only a crack, to be safe.

"Erin?"

The single word sounded like pure, unfiltered relief. No, this was definitely a drunk fantasy. She stared, trying to process what she thought she saw. *Why is he leaning?* she wondered, then realized, *Oh, no. That's me.* She straightened but overcompensated and grasped onto the door frame to steady herself.

"Jesus, you're drunk?" Was that a rhetorical question? His face looked scary-angry and he suddenly seemed big— bigger than normal. "Too drunk to answer your goddamn phone!"

Her eyes widened, and her jaw dropped. It took her a beat to recover. "I'm not *too* drunk. If anything, I'm not drunk enough!"

"Oh, you're plenty drunk. Damnit, Erin. I've been trying to call you for hours!"

She should have been overjoyed at this impossible turn of circumstances. Jude was standing in her doorway! But why was he yelling at her?

"I can't believe this," he moaned irritably, rubbing his hands over his face.

"Well, believe it." Though unsure what they were actually talking about, she nodded as if to prove *it*, whatever *it* was. Then she frowned and blurted, "you look tired."

He stared at her, brow low, eyes unblinking, jaw tight.

"Wow. What? Why are you—" she paused to burp. "Sorry, excuse me. Why are you looking at me like that?"

He exhaled sharply, and cut his head to the side, looking down the hallway. Erin leaned out and looked too. There was nothing there.

"Do you have any idea how worried—" he cut himself off, inhaling, and pressing his lips together.

She waited, finding it very improbable that he 'worried.' Jude settled hands to his hips, tipping his head to his feet. When he looked back up, his face was all stoney again. She hated when he did that.

Erin glared back with renewed purpose. "Ooooh yeah," she remembered, not too drunk to recall all the things he'd said. "That reminds me. I hate you." It came out sounding very matter-of-fact. Whether or not this conversation was actually happening, she felt she'd made her point, just as he had earlier. At least *she* didn't have to be nasty about it.

"I just..." he rubbed the back of his neck, "I needed to know you got home safe."

With an exaggerated arm gesture, she gave herself the once over. Then she pointed her stare back to him. "As you can see, I did. So if that's all, you can go home now."

She didn't yell, though she may have slurred, and it may have sounded sarcastic, but overall, Erin felt she handled herself pretty well considering the kind of day she'd had.

She retreated, aiming to close the door, but his hand shot out, pushing it back open. Startled, she stared at his decorated wrist, mere inches from her face.

What? She blinked, as if the hallucination might go away. It didn't. Wanting to ask, she just couldn't come up with any words. She looked at him, not knowing what to think, let alone what to say. He stared back in silence. Something felt significant here, but her brain kept peddling around in circles.

"What?" she huffed instead, responding to his stoic ex-pression.

"How much have you had to drink?" He eyed her as everything tilted again.

"I dunno. But I fully 'tend to finish the bottle when you leave-me-the-heck-alone," she shot back, not so matter-of-factly.

He ruffled his hair with his hand, looking down the hall again, then back at her. What was so damn interesting down there?

"Don't do that," she groaned.

"Do what?"

"Sex up your hair!"

His eyebrows rose, and when they finally settled back to their normal spot, he took a step closer to her door. That's when she realized he wasn't holding it anymore. She should shut it.

He moved in close. "Can I come in, please?" The smell of campfire and soap wafted right into her face.

She shook her head rapidly side to side, then winced as the hallway spun. She didn't want him to see the mess.

Jude cocked his head, his eyes looking steely and dangerous. "Why not?"

"WHY NOT?" The yelling may have been overkill, but it just seemed like such a stupid question. "Why not?" She laughed.

"Just let me in, Erin. You're drunk."

"That's exactly why you shouldn't come in," she pointed out.

He gave the door a light push and she panicked, countering, and throwing her body weight into it. She didn't need to prove to him what a wreck she was. She didn't need him there, reminding her that apparently she couldn't take care of herself. The anxiety roiled her stomach.

"Come on, I can't leave you here in...this condition."

"Oh? Being drunk is a condition?" Erin could feel anger and hurt rising over the tilting of the hallway. "It wasn't a problem when you thought you were going to get laid! Is that the only way you want me? Drunk and easy? Well, it's toooooo bad I wasn't very good at it!" The words poured out of her with raw contempt.

"I never said that!"

"You did! You said, 'it wasn't worth it!'" Tears stung the backs of her eyes.

"That's not what I meant. Please let me in..."

"No. Get lost! I don't want you here." She tried to shove at the door again but now his whole body blocked it. "Damnit, Jude!"

"You got something to hide from me?"

She stilled. His eyes narrowed like a predator. Erin's grip tightened around the handle and she averted her gaze. Could he see into her brain? How was it that he always seemed to know what she was thinking yet be so stupid about it at the same time?

"Is *he* in there? Victor?"

Her head whipped up and she stared at both of him in disbelief.

"Are you kidding?" she exclaimed, incredulous. "You know what, it's none of your damn business! If I don't get to come to *your* mountain, you sure as hell can't come to *my* apartment!"

Her words seemed to have little effect on him. Now that he was in focus again, he looked about ready to plow her over.

"Is he in there?" Jude asked again, but he didn't wait for an answer.

He forced the door open and sent her tripping backwards over her duffle. Light spilled into the dark apartment from the hallway, casting odd shadows on everything. Erin pushed herself up onto her butt, and sat, watching the sad state of her home spin around like a carousel.

She let out a slow, defeated breath. "Please don't gloat." The words sounded as pathetic as she felt.

"Gloat? Wha—Erin, what the hell is this?"

He looked around, then flipped on a light, the sudden illumination revealing the harsh truth. Crossing to where she'd landed, he hauled her to her feet, and stepped back, leaving her to deal with the sickening uprising of her insides. It didn't last long. Having someone else see what she'd come home to was all too sobering.

Erin frowned. As she'd suspected, it looked worse in the light.

"What the—" He scanned her space, eyes stopping at the bottle of tequila on the counter. "Did...did you trash your place?"

"What? No!" she shot back, indignant. "Of course not! It was like this when I got home!"

He let out a heavy exhale, resting hands on his hips. "Shit."

At least on that, they could both agree.

His eyes settled on the pile of ripped couch cushions in the living area directly in front of him. They skated to the hateful graffiti on the hallway to his left, then the broken dishes in the kitchen behind him. Without a word, he stormed through the open floorplan and down the hall, into the rear of the apartment where the bathroom and bedroom were.

"What are you doing?" she yelled at his back. She made to follow, but he returned before she gotten very far. "Jude!" she shouted, the sound rattling her brain like a church bell. It made no difference. She was invisible.

"That son of a bitch," he hissed, a new tightness to his face, more forbidding than the hard stare she'd come to hate.

Finally, he pinned his attention on her. Instinct told her to shrink back, and shut up. The rigid lines of his body were a warning, his pacing reminding her of a caged lion. But all she'd wanted was to wallow in private, and finish off her tequila. To get her buzz back. To let oblivion blur reality. Pain, sadness, and frustration rose up and a single tear leaked down her face. He froze.

"Good. Now that I have your attention," she sniffed and wiped at her face. "What the...what the fuck?!"

His brows shot up and he stood there, silent as snowfall.

"Seriously? God, what?!" she snapped.

"I've never heard you swear like that before."

"Well, if you don't leave, you're gonna hear a lot more of it!" She used anger to cover up all the other emotions. "You just...you can't...just show up and..." *And what?* He was the enemy, yet her stupid heart sped anyway. He couldn't possibly want her, but she longed for his reassuring touch. "It's been a really, shitty day. No thanks to you. So, it would be really good if you could just go."

"I'm not gonna go."

"Seriously? Please!"

"No." He widened his stance and crossed his arms over his chest.

She couldn't think. Her head hurt, her stomach churned, the room wouldn't slow down to let her off, and Jude had planted himself square in her apartment and refused to leave.

As a loss, she backed up to the wall, and slid down until her butt hit the floor. Drawing her legs into her chest, she hid her face in her knees. It was too much to process, so instead everything just burst from her eyes. If he wouldn't go away, then she'd drown him out until he did.

Jude

He'd been afraid to touch her, afraid of what it might do to him. She had every right to be mad, but no way was he heading back home with his tail between his legs before saying what he'd come to say. And now, fury raged. He'd been waiting for Victor's retaliation. But this? What a cowardly move!

Jude watched Erin crumple to the floor and hide her face in her knees. He rubbed a hand across his jaw. *Shit.* He hadn't been expecting this. Explaining his actions, making apologies, sure. But this? His own defense would have to wait.

He moved to the wall, and squatted next to her. When he touched her arm, she flinched. He didn't take his hand away. Instead, he leaned in, circling his arms around her, and her jagged sob tore a hole through his chest.

"Hey," he cooed, resting his chin in her hair. "We'll fix this. We'll get it sorted out."

Her apartment was a mess. Things were broken, thrown off shelves, ripped, and inked with crude words. How long had she been home? Had she been sitting there in the dark, surrounded by this hatred the whole time?

"What did I do?" she cried into her knees.

That pain in his sternum dropped to his stomach. "You didn't do anything. This isn't your fault."

"It is. I'm always screwing things up. Wus wrong with me?"

"Nothing. Nothing's wrong with you." Smoothing a hand over her hair, he kissed the top of her head.

"'xcept for being too drunk." She lifted her face to look at him, her mouth in a quivering frown. "You were right," she squeaked, then looked away. "I should-should've filed the r'straining order." Her frame shook as more tears came out.

Even pale, with puffy red eyes red, she was beautiful. Jude sat, and pulled her onto his lap, pressing her head into his chest. He wrapped her tightly in his arms, like a cocoon, wishing he had more to offer. She cried harder.

"Shh, it's okay." He rubbed her back in slow, circular motions. After a few minutes, her body stilled, and he wondered if she'd cried herself to sleep.

But then she stiffened. "No." She sat up and pushed at his chest. "No."

He let her go, watching helplessly, as she scooted back into the wall.

She shook her finger, burning him with a scorching stare. "I'm not doing this again. No."

"Erin," he pleaded, his chest thumping. He'd made her like this, and he didn't know how to fix it.

"Don't 'Erin,' me with that face, and those muscles, and that...that smell!"

She came to her knees, then stood, swaying. Jude rose too, moving in to brace her but she threw her hands up to stop his approach. "Who smells like a campfire? I mean, seriously?" She paced, a hand to her forehead, looking a little pale.

"Erin, I know you're upset—"

"How'd you even know where I live?" she asked, turning to him.

With a sigh, he reached into his back pocket, and pulled out the folded note she'd left for Shauna. Erin stared at it, opened her mouth, then closed it again. He waited for more wrath but she just turned and went back to burning a path across her entryway.

"You're not going to yell at me for stealing your note?" he tested, folding it back up and returning it to his pocket.

"Do you want me to yell at-chou?"

Jude felt it better not to answer that.

"Why're you here?" He would have responded to her second question but she didn't give him a chance. "No, don't. Doesn't matter. Now's not a good time." She traipsed over to the kitchen

He tensed, following her as she maneuvered around all the debris. "Erin, be careful."

She scoffed, then threw open a drawer full of random items. Digging around, she pulled out a Post-It pad. "If you wanna check for the door, or something," she slapped the pad onto the counter, "jus leave the amount and I'll send it later."

He stared at her. "I'm not—we already talked about that."

"Yeah, well, things change. Ob-vi-ous-ly."

Jude's jaw tightened. Deserved or not, that stung. "I'm not here for business. Erin, I—"

"No! Stop! I can't take anymore today. I'm full up!"

She threw up her hands, teetering, then brought them to her head with a grimace.

He spied the liquor bottle sitting on the counter behind her. He had no way of knowing how full it was when she started, but regardless, she'd be feeling it in the morning. *Time for a new tactic.*

"Okay. Fine," he conceded. He moved around the counter into the kitchen, and started opening cabinet doors.

"What're you doing?"

"Looking for a glass." He tried the adjacent door.

"Jude...dude." She snorted which made him look over at her. Erin fanned an arm out over the mess on the floor.

"An intact glass," he clarified, moving to the other side of the sink.

He opened the next cabinet and his diligence paid off. A single glass sat, *intact*, tucked all the way in the back. He grabbed it, and filled it at the tap, then handed it to her. "Please drink *all* of that."

She stared at it solemnly, huffed, then took it. Some of the water sloshed over the side.

After several swallows, he moved on. "You call the police yet?"

Her eyes met his, wide and guilty. "No," she admitted, her voice barely audible. "But I called Mari."

He felt frustration rising. "Erin—"

"My battery died! What was I supposed ta do?"

"Charge it!" he quipped, exasperated.

"I am charging it!" She shot a thumb over her shoulder to an outlet in the kitchen.

Jude ran his hands down his face again. At least he knew why his calls went straight to voicemail. He reached across the counter, and grabbed it. "What's your password?"

She snatched the phone, hiding her screen as she entered it. After two tries, she handed it back, peering at the display, while he searched the browser. "What're you doing?"

"Drink your water," he muttered. She scowled, and he waited until she took another sip. "*You're* calling the police," he told her.

Finding the local non-emergency number, he engaged the call, and held the cell out to her. She shook her head, looking paler than before. Maybe even a little green. Shoulders slumping in defeat, Jude brought the phone to his ear. He pointed to the half-full glass still in her hand. "Keep drinking."

A dispatch officer answered the call. Jude kept his eyes on Erin as he spoke. "Hi, I need to report a break-in."

He retrieved the note from his pocket and rattled off Erin's address. "No one was here. Yeah. Came home to it. About an hour ago?" Erin verified his guess with a nod. "No, I checked. There's no one else here." His eyes scanned Erin from messy hair to worn sneakers. "No. No one's hurt."

Jude looked around the place as he continued speaking. "Stuff's thrown all over, ripped cushions, walls are marked up..." Turning to Erin, he asked her, "Was anything stolen?"

She stared back up at him with those impossibly large, green eyes, like the thought hadn't ever occurred to her.

"Not sure," he said into the phone, then grabbed Erin's empty glass from her grip and refilled it. He handed it back with a you-know-what-to-do look. "Great. Thank you. No, we'll just wait here. Yup, this number's good. Thanks." He ended the call and plugged the phone back into the charging cable. "They said it could take a few hours for someone to get here."

"Okay."

Jude shoved hands in his pockets and leaned against the counter next to Erin, taking in the mess. If Victor's name didn't come up when the police arrived, he'd say something. This had his name all over it.

Erin set the empty glass on the counter between them.

"Good girl," he murmured without thought.

"I have to pee," she stated, turning and zigzagging down the hall.

She kept her gaze down as she passed the graffitied slur on the wall, and leaned on the doorframe as she rounded into the bathroom. "Oh!"

"You okay?" he called, moving to the mouth of the hallway.

"F-fine," she answered, but her voice trembled.

She hadn't seen the bathroom yet, Jude realized.

He leaned back against the counter again, making a mental task list. As soon as the cops gave the go ahead, he'd clear the broken glass and dishes. *What a mess...*He'd been taken around the ringer before, but at least his ex had never broken all his shit.

While she was occupied, Jude pulled out his phone and booked a hotel room nearby. After several minutes, he wandered down the hall, and listened to make sure there were still signs of life in the bathroom.

He tapped a knuckle on the door. "You okay in there?"

That's when she started vomiting.

Chapter Thirty-Five

Second Chances

Jude

Balancing the coffee tray in one hand, he rapped his knuckles on the door with the other. The smell of his favorite brew filled the enclosed hallway. Not the same beans he had at the cabin, but this stuff was strong. It seemed right up Erin's alley. Especially after last night. That is, if Mari would let him in.

Jude knocked again, his foot tapping on the worn blue carpet that spanned the hallway.

He took a courteous step back when muffled sounds came through the door. The bolt turned and it swung open.

Mari scowled. "You're still here."

"Yup."

"Why?"

"That's something I'd rather discuss with Erin."

The feisty sentry crossed her arms, unperturbed. Jude was glad Erin had a friend like her, but he wasn't the enemy here. At least, he hoped he wasn't.

"Come on," he pushed, "I was a good sport last night. Left when you told me to. I'm not here to cause problems."

"They never are," she sighed, shaking her head.

"I mean it. I'm here to apologize."

"Good, you should."

He waited but she didn't move.

"She can hear you from there."

Jude exhaled a sharp hiss, thankful he had his hands full. Otherwise, he'd have been temped to barge his way in. That would probably not bode well for his case. Studying Mari's bored expression, he wondered what it would take to get back in Erin's apartment.

He glanced at the tray of coffees in hand. Bearing gifts, apparently, wasn't going to cut it. If they only knew the kind of gesture he'd made. He wasn't ready to talk about it, especially from the hallway. He'd never been a share-your-wounds kind of guy. But if it bought him a chance...

His stomach turned over as the words came out. "This coffee's from my favorite place in the Embarcadero," he started, resigned. "My ex-wife and I use to go there every morning, before work." He noticed Mari's eyes narrow. He met the glare straight on. "Refused to go back after she divorced me for everything I owned. But, this is good stuff. And I know how Erin likes her coffee."

He wasn't sure the full weight of that single act resonated with them. They had no idea the panic he'd experiences at the thought of running into his ex. They didn't know how tainted the place had become for him, a reminder of the life he'd thought he'd wanted. A time he *thought* he'd been happy.

Mari scowled at the tray in his hand. "You went all the way into the city for coffee?"

He opened his mouth, ready to explain that he hadn't been able to sleep anyway, when Erin's face appeared over Mari's shoulder.

Looking pale, and tired, but otherwise okay, her eyes dropped to the cardboard cups. "You brought coffee?"

He permitted himself a small, relieved smile. *That's my girl.*

The women exchanged glances. Mari stepped back with a huff and Erin opened the door fully. "You can come in."

"Thanks." He brushed by Mari who crowded the door-frame. When she caught his arm, he paused.

"You're on thin ice," she warned.

Jude nodded an acknowledgment. *Believe me, I know.* But if even half of Erin's actions had been sincere, he had no intention of giving up on her. That is, if she wanted him.

Mari released his arm and he veered left, into the kitchen area. Erin stood on the other side of the counter in an over-sized T-shirt and socks. She tugged at the bottom of her hem and he fought the urge to go right up to her. *Slow and steady*, he reminded himself.

Jude set the tray on the counter that divided the space, as Mari slammed the door shut. Ignoring the hissy fit, he introduced his bounty. "Wasn't sure what you were in the mood for." He tipped his head to the brown paper bag that sat on top of the coffees. "There's a blueberry muffin, an orange scone, and a zucchini bread. Creamers too."

Erin moved the bag aside, and wiggled a cardboard cup out of the tray. She discarded the lid and held it to her nose, closing her eyes as she did so. Jude got a lot of satisfaction out of the small tilt at the corners of her mouth.

She took a sip. "Mmm. That's really good."

"Glad you like it. Mari?"

Twisting a second cup free, he held it out. Erin's body-guard eyed him, then the cup, before taking it, and crossing to the paper bag. The three of them huddled around the end of the counter in awkward silence as Mari emptied four creamers into her coffee. After a few sips, she seemed pacified, so Jude turned back to Erin.

"How're you feeling?"

"Fine," she rushed out, peeking in at the pastries. "I did the vitamin trick you taught me." She pulled out the zucchini bread then paused, eyes to the counter. "Guess I owe you thanks for last night."

"Didn't do much."

She broke off a small corner of the bread and tucked it into her mouth. Then took another sip from her cup, this time, no smile. "I didn't realize you were still in town."

The awkward tension in the room escalated. Jude glanced to Mari, and if looks could kill...He suspected Erin had filled her friend in on what happened and all the stupid shit he'd said. But he wondered how much she remembered from the previous night, and if any of that had been passed along in her account.

"I thought...," Erin mumbled, then stopped.

Jude turned his attention back to her as she shook her head. She finally met his eye, but something about the way her face lacked any expression, it made him feel like a cliff-hanger with no rope.

"What are you doing here? I thought you said you'd never come back. To the city, I mean."

Jude ran a hand through his hair, a habit he'd formed as of late. It's true, he'd said that. But it hadn't crossed his mind as he'd raced down the mountain, eye's peeled on the side of the road, dreading he'd find her car flipped. "Guess that goes to show," he shrugged, "you should never say never."

"You just did."

He caught the corner of her mouth twitch and it gave him hope. *Hopefully* he wasn't there just to make an ass of himself.

She took a huge bite of her bread, her cheeks puffing up like a chipmunk. Jude helped himself to a cardboard coffee cup, withstanding Mari's silent scrutiny and the almost tangible heat from her laser focus.

Erin shoved the last of her breakfast in her mouth, then balled up the wax paper and tossed it in the trash bin full of broken glass and dishes. The thought of replacing all those things had Jude's mind wandering to the vet bill and the cabin door. He wondered if she still insisted on paying for it all. He wondered if she had renters insurance, though he knew she'd tell him it wasn't any of his business.

"You going in to work today?" he asked, instead.

"Mari made me call in."

Jude nodded his approval. "In that case," he started, waiting for Erin to bring her attention back around to him. She gave him those green eyes, now mixed with blues and browns and his gut dropped, thinking how he might have to live without them. "Can I talk to you a minute?"

She hesitated, looking to Mari, then nodded. Mari pursed her lips but didn't follow as Erin wandered around the counter and down the hall to her bedroom. He followed.

Her room looked very much like it had the night before, and Jude realized, she hadn't slept there. She fixed her eyes to her feet as he closed the door behind him. *Where to start?*

He decided to just go for it. "First off, I need to tell you, I told the cop from last night about the assault at the rental."

Her shoulders sank. "Oh. Okay."

"I wasn't trying to hide it from you, you were just so upset at the time...and you'd had a lot to drink." She just shrugged. Tightness formed in his chest. "It's for your protection. They need to know, especially since I think it's related to what happened here."

"No, I understand."

Jude stared at the top of her head, wanting to know what she was thinking. She twisted her fingers in the hem of her shirt and he saw the hint of very short shorts underneath.

"Was there anything else?" she mumbled.

He wished she'd look at him. It felt like he was driving blind. "I didn't mean to over step my boundaries," he hedged. She shook her head. "Or embarrass you."

"Oh, I'm not embarrassed," Erin scoffed, finally tipping her head up. "I'm mortified. I mean, you already think I'm a wreck, but this..." She threw her arm out and swept it across the general area of her bedroom.

Jude worked his jaw. Had he called her a wreck? He vaguely remembered the term leaving his mouth in anger. "I don't really think that," he told her.

"Well, you said it. And you're right. I'm useless." Her words were loaded with so much more than just the normal 'could have, should have, would haves,' and he hated that. He'd said so many things he'd never be able to take back.

"I don't think you're useless. And you're not a wreck. The situation got a little out of control and I overreacted."

Expecting forgiveness seemed a lofty goal, not when he couldn't forgive himself. But there had to be something he could do, some way to prove he wouldn't let her down again. He took a tentative step towards her and she stepped back.

"Erin, you're not useless. You've given me things I didn't think I'd ever get back. Hope. Fun..." *Love.* "You cared about me, and I blew it. And I'm sorry."

It suddenly felt warm in the small space. Jude pushed his long sleeves up, resting hands at his hips. He'd had so much more to say but he couldn't for the life of him remember what it was. And did it matter? She wouldn't even let him get near her. Staring out the window, he wracked his brain.

Light fingertips grazed his wrist. Jude whipped his head back to find she'd moved in closer, her eyes fixated on the bracelet he wore.

His heart stuttered at the chance. An opening. "Thank you for my bracelet."

Her fingers caressed the beads, spinning them in place around the cord. Still, she wouldn't look at him. He lifted his hands to the sides of her face, and hope rose when she didn't pull away.

"Erin," he whispered. She sniffed. "Hey." He crept in closer, stopping only when his body touched hers. "You're not useless. You're kind. You're thoughtful. Sometimes un-nervingly optimistic, but you are not useless."

Sniffing again, with a thick voice, she uttered, "I thought men didn't wear crap like that."

Jude slid his eyes to his bracelet. He thought about telling her he never planned to take it off. That if it made him less of a man, so be it. But it all sounded too corny. "We've already established that I say stupid shit."

That won him a small smile. He slid his hand down her jaw to rest at the base of her neck. Her pulse thrummed under the pad of his thumb as he swept it across her soft skin.

"You like it? The bracelet?"

"Yeah. I like it."

She nodded, and it felt like approval. Leaning in, he brought his mouth toward hers, but before he could kiss her, something in the air shifted. Erin stiffened and pushed back, creating a void between them. He furrowed his brow and studied her.

"I...I uh, appreciate you coming all the way down. Helping out last night."

He stared. "You appreciate?" *Now what?* The sleeplessness and stress from the night before crept in on his patience.

"And thank you for the coffee."

"Erin, what are you doing?"

"But I think you should probably get back home."

He didn't believe her, not for one second. "No. No. You're joking, right?"

"Why are you here, Jude?"

He scoffed, rubbing his face. "You're seriously asking me that? After everything in the last twelve hours?" He spun and paced. Of course it wouldn't be so easy. Doubt reared. Did she even want him?

"*Victor* did nice things too," and the way she emphasized that asshole's name flipped a switch in him. "So you'll have to excuse me. I have a history of misplaced trust!"

"Yeah? Well, so do I!"

"Clearly!"

A knock at the bedroom door interrupted them.

"Everything okay in there?" Mari called.

"Fine," Erin blurted and Jude inhaled sharply, holding his tongue. They waited until Mari's footsteps could be heard moving back down the hall. Erin spun on him, taking him by surprise.

"You want to earn my trust?" she challenged, her face flushing. "You can start with explaining what the hell your problem was with that book?" He could feel the tension rising in her. "You switched gears so fast, I don't even know what happened!"

"Fine. You wanna know?"

"Yes, I do!"

"My ex-wife married me solely so she could divorce me for my money," he spat out. "She used me. Welcome trust issues!" He inched closer.

"Jude, I didn't know..."

"Then, I try to find a little bit of peace, but no! I got renters claiming they're into me so I'll act out little scenes from books just like that one. And you know the really messed up part?" She shook her head, her eyes filling with tears. "There's a whole goddamn library of trash like that in one of the cabins for them to choose from. They're referring their fucking friends to me! Like I'm a goddamn piece of meat!"

He fisted and un-fisted his hands, tension coursing through his veins. Jude hadn't known how much he needed to get that out. He tried reining it back in. He didn't want to scare her away. Of everyone, she should understand.

"I wasn't trying to use you." Her voice shook and tears fell down her cheeks.

"Yeah, I realized—"

"I haven't even read that stupid book!" she shouted, throwing her arms out. "But just so you know, that's the shittiest deal breaker I've ever heard! I mean, what's wrong with you! I gave you honesty! I bared my soul! Showed you parts of me no one gets to see. You made me trust you! All for a quick lay?"

"No."

"Well, that's what it felt like." She swiped a hand across her wet cheek.

"I know," he sighed, gripping the back of his neck. "I mean, I didn't know. I'm sorry. I screwed up."

"I just wished I'd never..." she rubbed her eyes, making them more red and puffy. Instead of finishing her thought, she growled.

"Never what?"

His chest physically ached from anticipation. Was it a declaration on her lips? Or scorn? She didn't answer. Instead, her eyes drifted away and her mouth pursed. Jude dug his fingers in the back of his head, frustrated he'd let himself get all worked up.

"Never what, Erin?"

"Nothing. It doesn't matter." She sniffed. "You didn't answer my question."

"Which was?"

"What are you doing here?"

He almost laughed. Taking her in, her rigid posture and her closed off expression, it hit him. She meant it. She really doubted everything—all his actions, his words, his intentions. And could he blame her? Hadn't he done the same thing?

Jude uncrossed his arms and tried to relax his shoulders. "Will you look at me?"

"No." She stared out the window as if to prove her point.

"Why not?"

"Because."

"Because isn't an answer," he teased. She didn't react. "Are you running?" he asked.

"I'm not even moving, Jude."

"You know what I mean."

She looked down, around the room, anywhere but at him.

"Looks like we both made assumptions," he muttered, grabbing her hand. Her body tensed.

"What assumptions?" She tried pulling away but he laced his fingers with hers.

"You made me tea," he started.

"Tea?"

"You bought me a gift," he added.

"So?"

"You found my dog..."

"You would have found her eventually." She tried to take her hand back again but he pulled it to his chest and she tumbled a step into him.

"You made me dinner," he continued, his voice low.

"No. You made me make you dinner," she argued, "and you helped."

"Stubborn," he teased. "Like Etta."

That made her look up. He couldn't tell if the pink in her cheeks came from embarrassment, frustration, anger, or some combination of them all. But she was right there in front of him. Jude suddenly understood why she couldn't say *no* to things that were right in her face. It took him just about every ounce of self control not to kiss her.

"You like me," he told her. She tugged against his grip. "At least, I think you do...I hope you do."

"Jude, stop it."

"Not just the sex. Or the mountain fantasy. You actually like me."

The hope and optimism in his own voice startled him. He sounded young—naive, even foolish—but he didn't care. Not if she forgave him.

Her eyes dropped to his chest, still fighting to pull away, but without any real conviction. Jude glided a hand under her jaw and tilted her head to his.

"I like you too."

"Jude. I can't." Her voice cracked.

"Can't what? Can't go snow tubing? Can't take walks with Etta, trips to the market, and popcorn on the couch? Can't get drunk then pass out on my lap, or try to prove you can't cook? What exactly is it that you *can't* do?"

"You said some really mean things, Jude," she whispered.

"Erin—"

"Why would you say those things?" Her voice sounded so small. This time when she pulled away, he let her. He deserved it.

"I know I can't take them back. There's no excuse. But when I saw that book, I panicked. I thought you played me and it crushed me, so I lied."

"Jude, I...I have been nothing but honest with you."

Her words opened the guilt he'd been pushing down. He nodded. "I know."

"It really hurt," she told him. "It's like you found all my weaknesses and just tore them open.'" She wiped her hand across her face again but her cheeks were still splotchy and damp. And, God, she was beautiful.

"Then let me make it up to you. Let me fix it. I don't want to hurt you, Erin. I want to keep you."

The silence that stretched nearly killed him. Had he made his point? Had he proved his intentions? Or had he caused too much damage?

"You drove down to the city," she stated, her glassy emerald eyes shinning, but he couldn't read her mood. "I didn't think you would. I mean, what you said, not even if your life depended on it...'"

"I was worried about you."

"You could have just called."

Jude smothered an uncomfortable laugh, running a hand through his hair. That answered his question about what she remembered from the night before.

"I did. I tried," he explained. "It wouldn't go through. I thought you were blocking me. Then I thought maybe something had happened."

"Oh," she nodded. "My battery was dead."

"Yeah. I got that."

He waited for a signal that they were good, that she forgave him. She stood there, in her tiny shorts and oversized tee, chewing on the inside of her lip.

"Jesus, Erin. Can we skip to the part where you're happy to see me so I can kiss you?"

Epilogue

Erin

Heart pounding, she pulled into the snowy driveway next to Jude's old truck. It always did that. It didn't matter that this marked her ninth trip up within the year.

But today it pounded with a new kind of anticipation. She had news—good news. At least *she* thought it was good news. But would Jude agree? Things were going so well, even with the distance, that she worried about stirring the pot. What if Jude liked the status quo?

The mountains were beautiful in June, July, August, September...and every month thereafter. Spring and summer proved as breathtaking as the winer snow. Jude had taken her to the lake for picnics, they'd frequented his favorite Mexican restaurant, she'd practiced her culinary skills under his mentoring eye, and she'd even agreed to go skiing. And true to his word, he caught her every time.

Back at her place, Erin had practiced a few of the recipes from his beginner cook book. The look on his face when she'd surprised him with dinner, how he'd thanked her later that night, it felt too good to be true. And it hadn't been limited to just that night—the sex was always amazing. So with all that stacked in her favor, she knew she had no reason to be nervous. Still, staring at the cabin, lightly dusted in snow, Erin's stomach tightened.

It'll be fine. She turned off the ignition.

The front door swung open and Etta barreled out to Erin's car, leaving doggy tracks from the stoop to the driveway. Jude came out behind her but stopped in the open doorway, pressing a hip into the frame and crossing his arms loosely in front of him—casual and smiling. How had she gotten so lucky?

She shot him a wide grin through the windshield, then eased the car door open. Etta practically crawled in with her, laying wet kisses on clothing and skin alike.

"Etta!" Erin laughed, giving her some hello rubs and scratches while holding her head back. "You still won't fit."

The huge canine ignored her, as was her usual routine. Erin squeezed out of the car, leading the big grey dog with her.

"You gonna help?" she called up to the porch.

"Nah, I'm just enjoying the show," Jude replied. But with a chuckle, he straightened. "Etta, enough. Come here."

Furred excitement eased off only long enough for Erin to close the drivers side door. Then it was back to tongue baths, tail whips, and high pitched whines barely contained inside that scruffy yet lovable body.

"I know girl," Erin giggled, inching her way to the trunk. "I'm happy to see you too. Just let me get inside. Jude!" She shot him a look.

He shook his head, humor lifting his eyes in little half-crescents. "This never gets old." He sauntered down the steps as if he had all day. "Etta, come on! Inside," he called. "She's not going anywhere."

Something about the way he said it made Erin's heart flutter—still, after all these months.

Etta eyed her owner's approached over a tall, boney shoulder with what could only be described as complete and utter obstinance. Jude stared her down but she didn't budge as he crossed the driveway, except to look away.

He squatted in the snow in front of her. "Who's in charge here?"

Erin tried not to laugh so it came out as a snort. Sighing, Jude tipped his head up at her. "Not helping."

"I'm sorry," she chuckled, covering a hand over her mouth.

He turned his attention back to his ornery charge and cleared his throat. Etta swung her head back so they were nose to nose, her course, grey brow rising in the middle.

"House," he instructed.

He held those big brown eyes with his own, his face stern. If dogs could 'harumph,' that's how Erin would have described the reply. Etta's tail drooped, then she sulked back up the steps, across the porch, and to the open door. With one quick pitiful look back at them, she disappeared into the cabin.

"She was fine. You didn't have to put her on time-out," Erin confided, still staring at the open cabin door.

"She's not a lap dog," Jude countered, standing. "She's gotta learn to keep off of people. Though it wasn't a problem until she met you."

"Guess that makes me special."

"Sure does," he agreed, his voice low and sexy. "You made good time. Welcome."

He moved close, wrapping an arm around her waist and cinching her hips to his. Then he leaned in and gave her a long, heated, *very* welcoming kiss.

"Did you bring those tiny shorts?" he asked, giving her a chance to catch her breath.

Erin had discovered that Jude was a leg man and he really liked those short shorts she'd always worn as pajamas. "Maybe."

From this close up, she noticed his eyes darken and mentally added another pair to her shopping list. He kissed her again, his mouth moving possessively over hers, and heat stirred between her legs. *Every time*, she mused. She didn't think she'd ever get use to him kissing her like that. When he pulled away, she felt lightheaded.

"Whatcha got?" he asked, crossing to the trunk. He popped it open and laughed. "Enough wine?"

"It isn't just for this weekend. I was hoping I could leave a few bottles here." She watched him smile into the trunk. "Some are from my mom..."

"I told you, I'm happy to buy you whatever." He hefted up several bags, including the two with the wine. "You just gotta tell me what to get."

Erin came around and grabbed her overnight bag before closing up the car and following Jude into the cabin. When she walked in, a fire blazed in the hearth, the aroma of coffee drifted across the open space, and she couldn't be sure, but she thought she smelled fresh, baked bread. *Oh my God, I've walked into Heaven.*

She tilted her head to one side and slid her eyes to Jude. "Are you baking something?"

"Maybe."

She set her bag on the floor next to the dining table—the one Jude had acquired, refurbished, and stuck in the cabin last July.

"Wow. If I didn't know better, I'd think you were trying to woo me."

"What if I am?" he asked, coming in close again, and curling his fingers around her waist. Etta came to join the huddle too, rubbing her head on anything she could get.

"Not sure more wooing is necessary."

"You're complaining?" he asked with a snicker.

"No. Not at all. I just don't have anything to woo back with." She cringed. "Wow, that sounded better in my head."

Laughing, he touched his forehead to hers. "You don't need to woo me," he confided, kissing her before she could argue. Pulling her lower half to him, he proved his enthusiasm.

"You must really like those shorts," she joked, and nipped his bottom lip.

"It's more than the shorts." He moved his head in, and Erin inhaled that intoxicating combination he wore like a cologne, as he kissed her.

Whining, Etta jumped up. Two giant, wet paws nearly knocked them over.

"Etta, girl, you're killing me," Jude groaned, pulling back.

"I think she's feeling left out."

He waved it off, trying again, taking her mouth swiftly, this time with tongue. "Mmm." His pleasure rumbled all the way down her throat and into her chest.

Etta's breath on her ear notwithstanding, Erin felt warmth collect low in her belly. But before it could settled into something sultry, anxiety swarmed in and tarnished the smooth and happy sensation. She knew she wasn't going to be able to enjoy this trip until she got her news off her chest.

"Before we get too...caught up," she uttered around kisses, "I have to tell you something."

Jude let her bottom lip go with a light and playful bite of his own, then held her just as far as his bent arms would allow.

He looked at her expectantly. Nerves wracked her stomach all over again, and doubt sent her second-guessing. *What if he only wants weekends? What if I overstay my welcome? Maybe he likes having the place to himself when I leave.* She took a deep breath and almost decided not to tell him at all.

"I talked to my boss," she rushed out before she could change her mind. "About a more regular remote schedule."

Something crossed over Jude's face—an unease— definitely not the outward pleasure she'd hoped for and in that moment she panicked.

"And?" he prompted.

"And he...um, he said we could work on transitioning into a part-time remote position..."

She petered out, the nerves crawling up her chest and making everything tight. What had she been thinking? He had a life up here! He probably didn't want her underfoot all the time. But it was out now. She couldn't take it back, however much she wanted to.

"Part-time, huh?"

"You know what? We don't have to talk about it now." *Or ever.*

"Well, I want to talk about it now." He took a step back, letting his fingers drift from her back to her sides. "What kind of part-time we talking here?"

Erin pushed herself to go on, despite the overwhelming urge to shut up and hide. "We, uh, Paul and I talked about scheduling two or three days on the end of a week that would be 'in-office days.' The rest I would do from..." She had planned to say "here," but that didn't seem appropriate anymore. "From wherever," she finished, tucking a loose strand of hair behind her ear and dropping her gaze.

"From wherever."

"Mhmm." She waited a beat. "You don't seem very happy." She fought it. She tried not to jump to conclusions, but she was failing miserably.

"I am. Happy."

Erin looked up, hoping for some kind of proof that he meant it. He didn't give her much, just a little tick at the corner of his mouth.

"Look, I don't mean to presume that I'd be here the whole time. I know this place is your peace. And if you don't want me here—"

"Erin."

She stopped, tucking her lips between her teeth, thinking she'd really screwed this up. Jude seemed distracted...torn, maybe. She waited for him to tell her she was moving too fast, or that he needed his space. When he didn't speak, it nearly made her sick. *Oh God, he's going to break up with me.* She had to know and she had to get it over with.

"Is there something you want to tell me?" She held her breath.

"Yeah. Actually."

Jude slid his hands back to himself, leaving her skin cold, even in the warmth of the cabin. Without elaboration, he turned, and moved into the kitchen, rummaging around in his random crap drawer. Erin waited, disappointment gnawing at her insides as he came back to where she stood.

"When's your lease up?" he asked.

"My what? My lease?" She didn't follow. "It renews in March? Why?"

He stepped forward, took her hand, and folded her fingers over something small and metal. "You're my peace."

When he stepped back, she opened her palm and looked down at the little, silver key.

"I was wondering if you wanted to bring your stuff up here. Permanently."

Erin stared at her hand. "You want me to...to...move in?" Her voice trembled. That wasn't what she'd been expecting.

She felt him shift closer and gazed up with watery eyes.

He wiped her cheek with his knuckle. "I hope those are happy tears. I know it makes a long haul to work. Figure you'll still need a place down there, or something," he thought out loud. "And it would be a lot of changes. I get if you're not ready. This is good, what we're doing here. I'm not saying I need more—"

"Bread."

"Bread?" he asked.

"The bread, the fire, the coffee. You *were* wooing me. For this?" She asked and caught his guilty smile. "But you didn't know about *my* news."

"I was hoping, when you said you were going to talk to you boss," he explained, "that it might be about that. Figured it it wasn't, we'd work out something."

He stared at her while she processed it all. *He'd been hoping? They'd figure something out?* Erin had never been with someone who'd been willing to make so many sacrifices for her. She'd never been one to earn this kind of devotion. How could she possibly return it in kind?

Jude took his hands to his hips in that nervous habit of his. "You're killing me here. Is it a 'yes' or a 'no?'"

Blasting him a blinding, goofy smile, she jumped up, and threw her arms around his neck. He wrapped her in a firm hug, and held her so her feet dangled.

"Guess that's a 'yes,'" he muttered.

"Don't be a smart ass."

"Sometimes, I think you're more trouble than you're worth."

She squeezed her hand around the key, feeling the edges dig into her palm, as a few deliriously, happy tears escaped, and spilled down her cheek.

Arms squeezing her tighter, he asked, "You happy?"

"Very. You?"

"Like you wouldn't believe."

Erin pressed her wet face into his neck and gave him a muffled, "Love you, Jude."

"Love you too, honey."

She tilted her head up and gave him a salty kiss, her chest too full for silly things like words. He kissed her back and she felt pretty certain he understood.

"Hey, Jude?"

"Hmm?"

"Can we try that bread now?"

Lexie Sloane

Lexie Sloane lives and works in the diverse Bay Area, California. She writes her novels in between shuffling her two daughters from school to karate, and on those rare but golden weekends when she dashes off for her writer's retreats. A sucker for a good romance, she writes about the little things and how actions speak volumes over words. Her inspirations comes from her devoted husband, her keen sense of observation, and some of her favorite romance authors: Katherine Center, Lori Foster, Rachel Gibson, and Kristin Ashley.

When Lexie is not writing, or reading, she's capturing memories with her family and having adventures. One of her favorite treks is along the picturesque, but windy, Route 50 through South Lake Tahoe (even though she gets car sick).

Originally trained in Theatrical Design, she has a flair for world building and storytelling (and she knows her way around a tool shed!). To her, writing is art—the words her medium. And an artist at heart, you will find she always has something creative on the back burner, waiting to be polished and shared.

CPSIA information can be obtained
at www.ICGtesting.com
Printed in the USA
JSHW042147270222
23245JS00002B/10